Jenni'

*No n~~~~
impossi~~ see~
may ~~ Toe hope~.*

lighter

GIA RILEY

Gia Riley

Cover Design by
Sommer Stein, Perfect Pear Creative Covers

Interior Design and Formatting by
Christine Borgford, Perfectly Publishable

dedication

*To my son . . . my inspiration
to never stop dreaming.*

*To my husband . . . my
source of strength.*

*My world wouldn't be
complete without you both.*

Thank you for loving me unconditionally.

prologue

"SOPHIE, WAIT! I'M SORRY. I'M just worried about you," Megan yells from the double doors leading from the locker room into the hallway.

She saw the bruises on my body.

I knew better than to change in front of everyone after gym class, yet I did it anyway because I was running late to meet my boyfriend. Blaine doesn't like it when I keep him waiting. Tossing my book bag over my shoulder, I round the corner and smack right into him—and he doesn't look happy.

"What did you say to her?" He questions with a deadly stare.

"Nothing. I didn't say a word." I didn't but I still avert my eyes, choosing to stare at the tile on the floor instead of him. Without warning, he grabs my arm and pulls me into the bathroom. It's empty.

"Please, Blaine." I'm begging him to stop. He hears me, but he doesn't listen.

"I told you what I would do, didn't I?"

I swallow, my hands shaking. "Yes."

He pins my arms against the wall, hovering over me. "And yet you still couldn't keep your damn mouth shut."

I try to yank my arms from his grasp, but his grip is too tight. His fingertips dig painfully into my arms, his nails breaking through the skin. "I swear I didn't tell her anything."

He inches closer to my face, the warmth of his breath hits my cheek. "Don't fucking lie to me, Sophie. What happened the last time you lied to me?"

"I'm not lying. Please, Blaine. I wouldn't."

"What happened, Sophie?"

He's going to make me say it—as if I'd ever need a reminder. It's impossible to forget. "You had to teach me a lesson."

"But you never learn. No matter how hard I try to protect you."

"I'm sorry," I plead. Regardless of the fact that I'm innocent, he morphs my apology into an admission of guilt.

"Damn right you are," he spits through gritted teeth. His calmness now completely gone and replaced with anger. "Don't you ever lie to me again, you hear me?"

"Yes," I whisper.

He grabs my chin, roughly scraping his calloused thumb over my lips. His dilated pupils pierce straight through me sending chills down my spine. "Tell me you love me." My words get lodged in my throat and I make the mistake of pausing a second too long. "Say it!" he warns as his fist pounds against the wall next to my head.

"I love you, Blaine." And maybe there was a time I actually did. He wasn't always like this, but neither was I. If I could go back in time, I'd tell him no. I'd push him away from me and keep my distance. But I'm just like my mother—unable to get away and desperate enough to stay. "Please let go of me. You're hurting me."

Finally he releases me, replacing his harsh words with sweet promises—his rough touches with gentle caresses. With a flip of a switch, he's back to the Blaine I fell for, masking any signs of the evil he's become.

"You make me so crazy, Sophie." He runs his fingers through my long blond hair, leaving a trail of light kisses on my neck. "I only get mad because I love you so much."

"I know." Painfully well. My scattered bruises a daily reminder of his temper.

His hand falls from my hair as he latches onto my hip, pulling me flush against his body. "Baby, I need you. You're *everything* to me."

Everything I don't want to be. Not anymore.

Beneath the surface, I'm scarred and broken; a much darker version of the girl I once was. There was a time I believed I was worthy of true love. But now, living in a hell littered with reminders of broken promises, I know what we have is anything but love.

It's in this moment that I know I'm not strong enough to fight another day unless I *get away from him*. But I don't know how. I need a plan—something to get me away from this town and its memories.

Closing my eyes, I say a silent prayer that my luck will change—that someone will save me from the hell my life has become.

CHAPTER *one*

Sophie

"YOU'LL WANT TO CONNECT WITH the therapist on campus as soon as you're settled. I've spoken with her and she's looking forward to meeting you."

I reach for the card in her hands, accepting it yet wishing I didn't have to worry about a therapist at all. Most girls my age are settling into their third year of college without the hassle of mind games and nightmares. It's not the case for me, but I wasn't dealt a perfect hand in life either. "Thank you. I will."

"You can do this, Sophie. You're strong. Remember that. Let this change be positive—don't get caught up in old behaviors."

I hope she's right. Part of me believes I can overcome anything while the other is positive I'll fail if given the slightest chance. "I'll do my best." A new town, new school, new friends, but at least I'll have my roommate and the team. The comradery is the only thing that's ever grounded me and made me feel welcome—like I belonged.

Home life has always been toxic and filled with turmoil. I've never had two parents who gave a shit about me. Nix that, my mom cares when she doesn't have to worry about my dad screaming at her or screwing her over. When it's just her and me, we have a real relationship. But the second he comes home, that's thrown out the window. At least the divorce is almost final—driving the last nail in the proverbial coffin.

I may not have had much of a home the past twenty years, but I've always had gymnastics. The sport has been my salvation since I was old enough to understand the chaos going on around me was neither healthy nor normal. While most ten year old's homes are full of playful memories, mine was stocked with cases of beer and an overflowing recycling bin full of liquor bottles. Each night they clanked together as a new one was added to the top. The homes lining the streets of suburbia may have appeared average to the common passerby, but what lurked behind our front door was enough to haunt my dreams for years. Appearances can be very deceiving.

When week nights at home became unbearable, my mom enrolled me in my first Intro to Tumbling class. Although nervous, the surge of power I felt while flying through the air trumped listening to my dad punch holes in the wall or gripe about his hangover. My mom may have taken years of verbal abuse before kicking my dad's ass to the curb, but I'm thankful she was able to provide an outlet for my own frustrations and aggravations. Often feeling out of control at home, pushing my body to the limit in the gym has been the one constant I've been in control of. Although I've always overdone my training, each bead of sweat, each sore muscle was because of me—not them. Nobody can break me down when I'm in my element. Especially not when I'm in control.

The thought of what I might have become without gymnastics scares the shit out of me. In and out of therapy for years, it took a school guidance counselor to notice the hazy look in my eyes and depleted self-confidence. Simply put, my give a damn was broken.

Ever since I gave up on my family's happily ever after, I've been determined to rise to the top. From a very young age, I knew my talent would be my one and only ticket to escape the small town I've grown up in. Living in a place with little opportunity, it's up to me to create a future different than the status quo.

So while I continue to remain invisible in my everyday

life with only a handful of people breaking through my protective outer shell, I choose only to come alive in the gym. The chalky floors, exhausting routines, and the nagging aches and pains, are daily reminders of how invested I've become in the idea of *more*. Though many in Ashland, Tennessee have settled for a life of monotonous boredom, often selling themselves short, I'm determined to rise above the statistics. This girl is going places.

Having said that, I almost ate my words a month ago when the pressure of the upcoming All State meet was eating away at my confidence. One night as the hours ticked by on my bedside clock, I asked myself if this dream of gymnastics was worth it. I needed to figure out what I'd have to latch onto once my career was over. Would I crash and burn without a distraction, or would I rise to accept a new challenge?

Contemplating giving it up altogether to enjoy my college experience as a normal junior would, I couldn't walk away. The thought alone had me panicking. Sure I'd had enough of being told what to do and when to do it at twenty years old, but I need the boundaries. I thrive off the discipline my coaches drill into my skull each and every day. Without it, I'm left to my own devices and nothing is scarier than feeling alone. But that's not the only reason I decided to stick with it. Without gymnastics, there's no way I can pay for college unless I want to be up to my ears in debt for the rest of my life. I'd be stupid to throw away a free ride, so I tossed the idea of wild abandon out the window while holding tight to my meal ticket.

Thanks to my impressive showing at the All State meet, I got noticed by a division one team. I applied to many my freshman year, but was rejected. But even though it's taken longer than planned, I've finally outgrown my cozy and safe oasis here at the local community college. While the idea of bigger and better opportunities flood my mind, if my new team isn't a good fit, I risk losing scholarship money and my shot at a college degree.

Seeking refuge in my therapist's wisdom, she laid it out in front of me plain and simple. Do I want to stay where I'm secure, or do I want to take a chance to allow myself to be vulnerable? *The choice is mine.* It sounded simple enough, but after a week's worth of sleepless nights, I threw caution to the wind and accepted the offer to attend the school of my dreams. They finally wanted me.

Once my decision was made, I packed my entire life into the car I'd been given as a graduation present from my father two short years ago. Of course he didn't show up for the ceremony, but he sent the car along with a note in his secretary's hand-writing. The same secretary I found him screwing in his office the day I picked up the keys to my new ride. Making no apologies, he tossed the keys in my hands and I saw myself out. So much for him doing the right thing for once in his life.

Looking back on it, I should have thrown the keys in his disgusting face, but I accepted the gift knowing that if I refused, I'd be forced back onto the public transportation system thanks to my lack of funds. My gymnastics schedule leaves no time for a part-time job, let alone one that would give me enough extra cash to afford a car payment on a brand new car.

My mom provides for us the best she can with her job at the retirement home, never accepting the money my father tried to pacify her with in the divorce settlement. I'm not exactly sure why, but maybe she cares more about her own pride than her bank statement. In fact, she's always thrown all of her extra cash into my gymnastics career, reminding me how important it was not to let her down. Whether a threat or a promise, her words create an intense pressure to be the best. But with pressure comes opportunity. Nobody has ever achieved greatness by taking a back seat.

But now, after years of blood, sweat and tears, the real journey begins as I cruise down the interstate getting lost in my favorite country music playlist. I'm leaving behind the anger, pain, and frustration for my shot at *more.* As the miles slowly add up on the odometer, my head bobbing to the beat, body swaying to the rhythm, I know I can do this.

Almost a straight shot to the south, the five hour drive leaves plenty of time for self-reflection which is both a blessing and a curse. Constantly consumed by my own fears, my nerves usually hold the happiness of my accomplishments hostage. But this time, after reciting a silent prayer, I ask God to show me in whatever way he sees fit that I've made the right decision. I don't know if I'm expecting something to fall from the sky or divine intervention, but when the five hour drive ends and I'm not any closer to clarity, I assume my answer is yet to come. And as scary as that is, I can live with it.

After two wrong turns in town, I arrive on campus with my car stuffed to the gills. My body is screaming to get out and stretch and once out of the car, I take a deep breath, inhaling the sweet southern air. Okay, it smells a little like shit thanks to the surrounding farmland. Picking at the cotton of my tank, the heat is intense with the sun creating a blinding reflection off the windshield. I'm well-adjusted to the summer heat but the humidity already has my tank top sticking to my sweaty skin. If I want to get inside and cool off, I need to start unpacking.

The back seat looks like a game of Jenga. It's a toss-up which box will make the entire pile collapse once I yank it out. Closing my eyes, I tug on various items, only choosing the ones that easily slip out of their spot without a fight. A few times I have to use my foot to push something back inside the car, but I manage to slam the door shut once my arms are full.

I adjust my boxes, leaving a small space for my eyes to peer through the heavy load I'm carrying. With my room assignment in hand, I'm ready to discover what awaits me on the third floor of Johnson Hall. Unfortunately, the parking lot's located at the top of a hill. The stairs are clogged with luggage, so I decide to trek down the grassy knoll instead. I begin my decent, careful with my steps so I don't topple over. One sway in the wrong direction and I'm doomed.

"Lookout!" I hear in the distance.

Considering I can barely see an inch in front of myself, I'm unsure of what I'm supposed to be looking out for. I find out quickly when I tumble to the ground with my bags and boxes scattering on the grass around me. Shocked stupid, a box of clothing rolls to the bottom of the hill spilling hangers with each jostling tumble. Next to me I find the culprit—a crashed skateboard with a small TV lying next to it.

"Holy shit! I'm so sorry."

"It's okay," I say as I regain my footing and start picking up my things one by one. Thankfully this trip didn't include any of my bras and underwear.

"I really am sorry. I set the TV down for half a second." He scratches his head and laughs. "I was gonna let the skateboard do all the work, but it got away from me and before I knew it, you were on the ground." He reaches out his hand to help me stand up. "Are you hurt?"

"I've got it. I'm okay."

"You're sure?" he questions.

"I've taken much harder falls than this one. I'm used to it."

Concern etches his bronzed features as he blows a piece of sandy blond hair out of his eyes. "Why do you say that?"

I start walking towards the rest of my fallen items. It's entirely too hot out here to chit chat. "I'm a gymnast."

"No kidding. Impressive."

"Thanks. I should get my stuff inside. I'll see ya around."

"I'm positive you will." He winks at me, but there aren't any butterflies from his flirtation. I do catch myself watching the bare muscles of his back flex as he runs back to his TV. He's not bad looking. Clumsy, but hot nonetheless.

Seven painstaking trips later, all my belongings are safely inside. My roommate hasn't arrived yet, so I leave the furniture where it's at and pick a side of the room along with a desk. I already know Cara and I are going to have a lot of late nights. We've spoken on the phone and have texted back and forth several times since receiving each other's information in the mail. Originally I had intended to have one short talk to discuss who was bringing the big items, but Cara has so much spunk in her, we ended up talking for at least an hour. Surprisingly, the conversation flowed naturally and we've talked a couple times since. While our worlds may be vastly different, with her coming from a wealthy family here in Alabama, complete with a country club membership and designer labels I'll never be able to afford, we discovered we have several things in common—country music and chocolate peanut butter everything. Hopefully she's as awesome in person as she is on the phone.

Now that everything's inside, I don't know where to begin. I glance at each labeled box, deciding to go with the most important items first. Considering I'm lost without my electronics, I try setting up my computer. Part of me hoped my mom would be here to help me today, but she said she couldn't get the day off. I'm not sure how hard she tried, but I give her the benefit of the doubt as usual.

Since my parents' divorce, I've been dreading leaving her all alone. She's been low and agitated trying to piece back together the shambled mess that is her life. At least at my old school I was only a short fifteen minute drive away should she need me. The five hours that now separates us will take a while to get comfortable with. Guilt is the only word I can use to describe my new found freedom.

Dying of thirst, I realize I left my case of water in the car, but what's one more trip at this point. The elevators are all packed with students moving in, so I take the stairs. I round the first flight and stop dead in my tracks on the landing. A gorgeously tanned male body is stretched out on the concrete staircase sans shirt. Careful not to disturb the resting hunk, I scoot as far to the right as I can and tip-toe around him. Two steps down and his hand shoots out to grab my ankle. I scream and hold on tightly to the paint-chipped railing before I lose my balance.

"Shit! I'm sorry, Sophie. I thought you were someone else."

I release my death grip on the railing, restoring blood flow to my white knuckles. "You're making my day far too interesting, whoever you are."

"I swear I'm not usually this big of an ass."

"I'll take your word for it. The day's only half over though. For your safety and mine, can we not meet like this again?" I hop down two stairs and freeze. "How did you know my name?"

"It's on your door."

"What are you the welcoming committee?" I jokingly ask with my hands placed on my waist; my hip cocked to the side.

His smile lights up his face when he realizes I'm not upset with him. "I guess I *am* the welcoming committee. A hazard or perk depending how you look it."

"Definitely a hazard, so far. You don't strike me as the welcome wagon type though. Not with all of that going on." I gesture towards his sweat glistening torso and chiseled chest that's covered in a few intricate tattoos.

"Then you don't know me at all," he says as he crosses his arms over his chest making his biceps bulge even more. Jesus, someone find this kid a shirt so I don't drool. I don't do underclassmen *or* boyfriends.

Quickly diverting my eyes, I play it cool. "You're absolutely right. What do I know?"

He laughs and shakes his head, "You're different. I dig that."

"Not the first time I've heard that," I murmur, mostly to myself but don't care if he hears me either way.

"So what's your story, Sophie?"

"I don't have that kind of time." *And I never will.* I start down the rest of the steps and as I pull open the rec room door at the bottom, I hear his voice bounce around the small stairwell, echoing off the brick walls, "See you soon, Sophie."

I don't doubt that.

BY LATE AFTERNOON, I'M COMPLETELY exhausted. Between the long drive and unpacking, I'm in need of a shower and a nap. My roommate is still nowhere to be found so I grab my shower caddy, flip flops, and towel. I'm a little nervous about testing out the communal showers. It's always a toss-up about what you'll find on the other side of the plastic curtains. Considering it's the first day on campus, this is as good as it's going to get.

There's only one open, so I don't waste any time hopping inside. It feels incredible to wash the sweat off my warm skin. I'd stay in here longer if there weren't others lining up to do the same. As I come to terms with shorter showers, I wrap my hair and body in my fluffy pink towels and flip flop my way down the hall, leaving a puddle in my wake.

Just as I put my hand on the door knob to my room, it swings open sending a rush of chilly air with it. My face immediately heats, yet my body shivers. Standing in front of me is an absolutely mouth-watering specimen. I openly gawk, words failing me when I need them most. Guys don't come this built and sinfully sexy where I come from.

"Kippy, move! Let her in!"

He moves back, and watches me enter my room. This is my space, but it seems as if I'm the intruder.

"Cara, I'm going to get the last few boxes. You good?"

"Yeah, thanks. Scoot, she needs to change. Knock when you come back."

"I will." He looks down at me and I pull my towel tighter around my body. Suddenly it isn't enough of a barrier from his wandering eyes. "Lucky towel." He gives me a scorching smile and walks out of the room, closing the door behind him.

Cara runs over to me and throws her arms around my damp body, hugging me so tightly I can barely breathe. "It's so good to finally meet you, Sophie!"

She finally lets go and air begins to travel back to my lungs. "Who was that guy?"

"Don't mind him. He won't be here long." *I don't mind at all.*

"He's your boyfriend?" I ask, while hurrying to my closet to get dressed. I hop around on one foot, trying to get my leg into my underwear while still holding a towel around me. I'm not self-conscious of my body considering I'm usually in a leotard, but it's going to take some time to get adapted to this small space and its lack of privacy.

"No, that's my brother. He lives off campus. I'm *very* single and ready to mingle. You?"

Brother. No shit. At least I won't have to worry about running into that major distraction on a daily basis. I wonder if all the guys in Alabama are good-looking. The first two I cross paths with have me actually contemplating dating— and I don't date. Ever. "Single and *not* looking to mingle," I reply.

"Why the hell not? It's college, Sophie. You only get to do this once."

"My schedule doesn't leave time for dating. I have to stay focused, or I'll lose my spot on the team."

"When does practice start?" she asks.

"First thing in the morning, why?" I'm finally dressed and can hang up my towels to dry.

"Then tonight you're all mine! We're going out to find us some cowboys!" She's beaming with excitement and bouncing up and down. Her excitement is so contagious; I almost start jumping along with her.

"I'm not sure cowboys are my type, Cara." I laugh at the look of shock on her face. Apparently, I need to enroll in Cowboy 101 first thing in the morning.

"Sophie, this is Alabama. You aren't going to find much else, but tell me what you want and we can make it happen."

Even though I don't date, I'm not dead. There are a few qualities I'd want my man to have if I ever decide to have one again. "I still don't have time to date so it doesn't matter, but I guess a southern gentleman who enjoys physical things."

"What guy doesn't like sex?" She looks truly perplexed by my request.

"Not sex, Cara. Sports." She has a one track mind. Sex and boys.

"Oh. Well that can be arranged. So, a country jock then? It's totally doable. But no meatheads." She points to her temple. "There has to be something between the ears or you'll get bored."

"Okay. A jock with brains it is." See, I'm easy to live with. Already compromising with my new roommate on the first day of living together.

"I knew you had it in you, Sophie."

Now that we have my man preference squared away, we start rearranging the furniture into the perfect formation that has Cara as far away from the window as possible so she can sleep in. Since I'm up for practice before the birds and exhausted at the end of the night, I'm fine sleeping wherever my body falls.

The loud bang against our door has both Cara and I jumping in surprise. I forgot to open it back up when I finished getting changed. Rushing over, I pull the door open for Cara's brother. "Sorry, here let me help you with some of that." I take a few shopping bags dangling from his index finger. When I pull them off, I can't help but notice his strong forearms straining under the weight of the boxes he's carrying.

"Can I come in? This is heavy," he asks, while I continue ogling his arms.

"Sorry." I quickly step aside and let him in the room. He drops the boxes in the middle of the room with a thud. Before I can guide him to his sister's side of the room, he flops down on my bed of all places. He's exhausted, so I keep my mouth shut.

"Is that the last of it, Kip?" Cara saunters over to the pile of boxes and starts pulling items out while I'm still stuck in my spot next to the door unsure of where I should look let alone sit. With him sprawled out on my mattress my thoughts are quickly headed to dirty places.

"Yeah. That's it. It's too damn hot for this shit," he grumbles.

Shyly, I open our mini-fridge and take out a cold bottle of water. "Um, here." I push the bottle out in front of me, waiting for him to take it. He's seen me in a towel and I don't even know his real name. Cara has called him both Kippy and Kip, but they're obviously nicknames.

He lazily opens his eyes and accepts the water with a smile. "Thanks."

I turn away from him quickly. It makes me too nervous to look directly into his eyes. "You're welcome." I start busying myself re-organizing the books, folders and office products on my desk shelf to avoid any awkward conversation. When I can't fake unpacking any longer, I sit down on my desk chair, glancing at him quickly before turning my attention back to Cara. Watching her unpack, I pray she starts rambling as she does best. The silence is stifling.

From my peripheral vision, I notice him shifting his head on my pillow. His eyes are burning a hole into the side of my head as the seconds tick by. Not able to remain silent anymore, I open my mouth. "What?" I question.

"Nothing. I'm wondering what your name is though," he says with a cocky grin on his face. He's enjoying my uneasiness.

"Oh. It's Sophie."

He smiles, giving nothing away in return. "I knew it'd be something sweet."

"It's on the door." *It's on the door?* How lame can I possibly be? The welcome signs on the doors are cute, but feel more like a nametag you'd see on your desk in elementary school.

"I saw it, but I wanted to hear you say it."

Oh. "What's yours?" Could this be any more embarrassing of a conversation?

Cara drops her pile of clothes. "I'm so sorry. I totally dropped the ball on the introductions, didn't I? Sophie this is my brother, Kipton. Kipton, my awesome roomie, Sophie."

"Better late than never, Cara," Kipton jokes. "We were getting there on our own though."

I blush at his words. Yeah, it's a damn good thing he lives off campus. I can usually hold my own with guys, having had to protect myself for years while my mom was working all kinds of crazy hours. Despite that, the unfamiliar tickles in my stomach combined with the sudden inability to process a rational thought is foreign to me. If it was socially acceptable to climb inside my closet right now I would.

"What's your major, Sophie?" Kipton asks. He crosses his arms underneath his head and the movement causes his shirt to ride up the slightest bit. It's far enough to showcase some seriously toned abs. One peek wasn't enough, so I chance another glance. He catches me.

"Um. Kinesiology. I want to be a coach and an athletic trainer eventually." I fiddle with the frayed edge of my denim shorts, again not looking at him while I'm speaking. His eyes are on me, though. My pulse is well aware.

"No shit. A chick into sports instead of shopping. It's about damn time."

"Kippy, play nice. There's nothing wrong with shopping. I'm very good at it," Cara says sarcastically. From the piles of clothing she's putting away, I'd say she's an expert. With my limited budget, I typically buy a few pieces and then mix and match to make as many outfits as possible. I'd like to consider myself a fashion chameleon, camouflaging my wardrobe to fit my mood.

"You're a pro, Cara. I've seen you in action."

I laugh at his honesty. They have a dynamic I'd love to have with a sibling. Being an only child can be very lonely. While my friends always complained about their brothers picking on them, I'd always wished I had someone to connect with besides my mom.

"So what do you want to coach?" he asks.

He's staring at me again and it's hard to focus with his gorgeous body on display. When I wrap my blankets around me tonight, it'll be hard not to picture him exactly as he is right now. "Huh?"

"Coach. You said a trainer and a coach."

"I want to run my own gym someday. I'm a gymnast."

Kipton closes his eyes and moans, "Jesus. You're getting hotter and hotter. Keep talking."

I laugh and see him smiling. He's looking up at the ceiling with his hands behind his head, waiting for me to continue explaining. But I want to be lying next to him—my bed never looked as inviting as it does in this moment.

"Sophie, he's a wrestler. You're speaking his language right now. He spends a lot of time working out too," Cara chimes in.

"A real wrestler or a fake one?" I scrunch my nose at the thought of him standing in a ring pretending to be a testosterone fueled maniac. I understand it's a production and its purpose is for entertainment and shock value, but it's not the same.

Kipton sits up quickly; resting his weight on his forearms and asks, "What do you mean a fake one?"

"On TV. The guys who dress up in crazy costumes and fly around the ring." I definitely have his attention now.

"You don't enjoy that?" he questions.

I'm afraid of offending him, but it's too late to cover my tracks. Instead, I answer honestly. "Not so much. It's not what collegiate wrestling's all about, so I can't really compare the two."

"That's for damn sure." He shakes his head back and forth with a dazed expression on his face. "Where the hell did you come from, Sophie?"

"Um. Ashland?"

Before Kipton can respond, Cara chimes in again. "Sophie, he's just happy you're on the same page as he is as far as the sport goes. He hates that shit on TV. Plus, you're into sports. Looks like I've hit the roommate jackpot."

Kipton sits up slowly, his eyes never leaving mine each inch he moves. Although it makes me self-conscious and nervous, a part of me likes it. His love of wrestling explains why his body is absolute perfection. Between his muscular shoulders and stocky build, my eyes have trouble deciding where they want to look first. And his eyes, the most crystal clear blue I've ever seen—the perfect complement to his brown hair and exactly what I was referring to in my earlier description of my dream guy. Not to mention wrestlers are tough and sexy as hell. That's reason enough for the attraction.

"I gotta get going, Cara, but call me if you need anything, okay? I'm not far." He turns his head in my direction. "That goes for you too, okay?"

I'm too surprised to say anything so I nod my head in agreement. I want to tell him I'm not usually this tongue-tied, but of course those words won't come out of my mouth either.

"Thanks, Kippy. We'll be good. Promise."

"You better be." He turns to leave but stops. "I almost forgot, the wrestling house is having a party tomorrow night. You both should come."

Before I have a chance to process the invitation, Cara starts jumping up and down. "I'm allowed to come? Sophie you're already my good luck charm. He wouldn't let me within a mile of the wrestling house last year!"

Kipton rolls his eyes, feigning annoyance. "Cara, you're being dramatic. But there wasn't a chance in hell I was letting my little sister near the house. You're too innocent for that fresh meat shit they pull."

Cara shoots him the evil eye and I have no choice but to laugh. She stands up taller and raises her chin as she makes her point. "I'm a mature woman, Kippy. I've had sex." It's probably not the best point to make with your older brother.

"Cara, really? I don't want to hear about my baby sister doing that shit." He runs his hands over his face in frustration, most likely trying to erase the toxic words from his memory. I can't say I blame him. Some things are better left unsaid.

But Cara shrugs her shoulders and continues to fold her clothing as if it's common knowledge. "I'm being honest. I've *done* it. It is what it is, Kippy. In fact, I plan to do it again in the near future." She sticks her head out of the closet and giggles while she watches her brother cringe.

Growling, Kipton looks like he's two seconds away from passing out or going postal. My vote is for the latter. "Don't make me regret this, Cara. I know you want to go out so I'd rather you do it somewhere I'll be. At least that way I can keep an eye on you and make sure no assholes try to pull anything."

"Please don't tell all the guys I'm your sister and ruin it for me," she begs.

"Ruin what?"

"Nobody will want me if you threaten them all."

"Cara," he warns.

"Please, Kipton," Cara begs again.

"She's breaking out my full name, Sophie. She means business."

I smile when he includes me in the conversation, but don't dare put my two cents in. He plays the protector well and I'm not about to start off on the wrong foot with either of them. She doesn't know how lucky she is to have someone watching out for her all the time. I've always been on my own in that department. Unless you count Mr. Owens, my pseudo grandpa, who lives next door to my mom. He once caught a boy trying to climb into my window and pelted him in the ass with a rock from the driveway.

Kipton turns to me and asks, "You'll come to the party too?"

"I have practice early in the morning. It's probably not a good idea." Despite what I tell him, this is the first time I actually *want* to go to a party even though I've never had anything to drink before. I've spent too much time watching my dad get drunk and ruin his relationship with my mom to know the stuff isn't anything to play around with. In fact, I'm probably the only twenty-year-old on campus who hasn't experimented with alcohol.

Nothing good ever comes from whiskey and beer.

Whiskey and beer.

Hovering in a corner next to the bannister, dad throws an empty bottle of whiskey against the living room wall. He's cussing mom out for forgetting to buy him a pack of cigarettes on her way home from work. I sit in the corner chilled to the bone not wanting to watch the scene unfold, but too scared to make a run for it to my room. If he spots me, he'll only get angrier. I've learned to stay out of his way, especially when he's been drinking.

Not backing down from his harsh words, mom goes toe to toe with him, firing back a slew of bitter comments of her own. The shouting continues to escalate until it comes to a crescendo—his fist making contact with the drywall. Little pieces of chalky powder fall onto the beige carpet below. The gaping hole left in the middle of the living room wall is evidence of his uncontrollable anger.

Mom's half in shock yet not entirely fazed by his predictable tantrum. "What the fuck is wrong with you, Dean? Who's going to pay for that?"

A hallow laugh erupts from his intoxicated mouth. "Don't I make sure the bills are covered every damn month? Yes, I do. Because your worthless ass can only manage a part time job." He absentmindedly massages his hand, wiping the blood leaking from his cracked knuckles onto his jeans. Another fight will follow when she can't get the blood stains out of his pants.

Mom throws her hands in the air, rage winning over level-headedness. "I'm busy taking care of our daughter which is a lot more than you can say for yourself. When's the last time you did anything for either of us without being asked?"

"You're the one who got pregnant, Victoria. I told you kids weren't for me. And, don't get me started about her. I don't think

that's a conversation you want to have with me right now." He grabs a handful of tissues out of the box and wraps them around his hand.

Please stop pushing him, mom. Please.

"Don't you dare make her out to be a mistake, Dean. So help me, God. She's eleven years old. She needs two parents who love her. Not one responsible parent and a drunk. I've missed out on a lot over the years. You haven't made any sacrifices when it comes to her, that's for damn sure. Because you're too busy with your pants around your ankles in the ally next to the goddamn bar."

Dad roughly grabs onto her upper arms, jerking her back and forth like a rag doll. He is so close to her face, she's forced to turn her head sideways. "What I do is my business. Maybe if you were a better wife and not focused on her bullshit I wouldn't have to find it elsewhere."

"None of your poor decisions are my fault, Dean. I've never told you no—ever."

Releasing her from his hold, she stumbles backwards before regaining her balance. "I know your poor decisions all too well, Victoria." His evil eyes pierce her before he continues. "I don't have time for this shit. I'm going out." He grabs his hat off the coat rack and slams the door behind him. The force sends a few more pieces of powdery drywall trickling to the carpet.

Mom collapses to the floor, sobbing into her hands. It's no secret he doesn't want me, but the reminder always stings more than the last. With no sign of him coming back, I run over to her, rubbing her back as she continues to let years of pent up frustration, anger, and sadness pool in a puddle of wet tears. "Don't cry, Momma. I love you."

"S-Sophie," she sobs.

I lay down next to her, holding her shaking body—comforting her any way I can. I'm responsible for his hatred and I'll do anything to take her pain away. "Don't cry, Momma. Please."

"Sophie? Hey."

"Sorry, what?" I look between Kipton and Cara. They both glance at me curiously, but don't ask any questions. Even if they did, I'm not sure I'd have the guts to tell them about the darkness that haunts my past. It's safer to push it away.

"What if I have you home early?" Kipton asks.

I shrug my shoulders, unsure with my decision at this point. The angel on my right shoulder is telling me to go to bed early and focus on my training. Of course the devil on the left has me picturing every inch of him naked. *I have to stop this.* My hormones have been in overdrive since he caught me in my towel. "I'll think about it." It's a smart answer. This way, I leave my options open but don't have to commit yet.

"I'm definitely in," Cara adds with a clap of her hands and a shake of her ass. "And if I have any say in it, so are you, Sophie."

Kipton rolls his eyes but waits until Cara turns around to hang more clothes in the closet. When she's out of view, he mouths the word *come* and immediately I'm covered in goose bumps. I nod my head, accepting the invitation. My body answering before my brain has a chance to catch up. *What did I agree too?*

"Have a good night, ladies." Before he closes the door completely, I let out the breath I've been holding. I throw myself onto my bed, realizing the earthy scent of his cologne has seeped into my bedding. If I close my eyes, it's as if he's still laying here with me. Inhaling deeply, I cuddle my pillow against my chest. Mid sniff, the door to our room swings open. Kipton grabs his keys off the top of the TV stand and winks at me. "Won't get too far without these. See-ya tomorrow."

"Bye, Kippy." Cara practically sings from her closet. She's on cloud nine about this party. I, on the other hand, am in serious trouble. Mortified, I roll over to face the window, hearing Kipton chuckle as the door closes.

He caught me sniffing my pillow.

CHAPTER *two*

Sophie

CARA AND I ARE ON our way back from the dining hall, I'm lost in thought while she rambles on about the party to-morrow night. As she finishes telling me about all the hot guys that live with Kipton, I'm wondering how out of place I'll feel around all these people. While the guys all sound like a lot of fun, an introvert like me is just hoping to blend in to the crowd. "Do you think I'll fit in?"

"Anyone can fit in, Sophie. And you're new here. You can be anyone you want to be. Nobody knows a thing about you yet. That's the beauty of going away to college. Whatever stigma stuck to you in high school, you can shed it and break free. Believe it or not, I wasn't super popular. I mean sure, I had my group of friends that I went to the country club with, but I was never in the clique. Those girls were too much like the plastics.

"The Plastics from *Mean Girls?*" My school had a few of those too. No matter what they did, they were worshipped by many and feared by most.

"Completely. Look, Sophie. We have our first love note of the semester." Cara rips a taped memo off our door and we scan it together in the hallway. Our resident advisor isn't wasting any time jumping into things. I know this is college life, but I was hoping to be asleep early tonight. Between driving and unpacking, I'm beat.

"A meeting already? I'm going to talk to the RA. Late night meetings aren't going to work for my schedule." All I want to do is crawl into my bed and get some rest before hell week begins in the gym tomorrow. Coaches love to start training camp off with a bang that will set the tone for the entire season. It's never easy and fun wouldn't be a word I'd use to describe it.

"If he's hot tell him I'm single."

"I will." Laughing at her expression, I jog down the rest of the hallway to find Room 315. Walking by it the first time, I turn around and knock twice on the closed door. I hear laughter on the other side, but nobody answers. I knock again, a little louder this time.

The door finally swings open to reveal the only other familiar face I've seen on campus thus far. The guy who almost killed me with his skateboard. "Sophie! What's up?"

"You get around, don't you? I'm looking for Drew. Is he in there?" I try to peek around his shoulder, but can't see anyone else inside the room.

"You're looking at him," he announces proudly.

This has to be a joke. "Say what?"

Chuckling, he opens the door wider. "Come on in. Make yourself at home. To the right we have the bed and to the left the couch. Don't go getting lost."

He's humoring me, but I can't get over him being the RA of the floor. I saw him moving in just this morning. "You're serious?"

"Yes. I told you I was part of the welcoming committee."

He did say that. "That explains how you knew my name. I thought you were a stalker with a door fetish."

"Yeah. I usually don't make it a point to assault my residents with skateboards or nearly knock them down the stairs. I apologize for the rocky start."

"Apology accepted, but do you always act like a ten-year-old boy?" I pull my hair back into a ponytail and secure it with the tie I always keep around my wrist.

"Only on Mondays," he says while cleaning the junk off his coffee table. He doesn't need to clean on my account.

"Good to know."

"So what's up?" he asks. "Or did you just want to make nice with the RA?"

"Funny, but no. I can't make it to your meeting tonight."

Drew crosses his arms, taking on a defensive stance. This must be his *I'm the boss* pose. "Why not? It's mandatory."

"Because I have to be at the gym by six tomorrow morning. My bedtime is crazy early compared to most college students, but I have no choice. I'm not a morning person as it is. Plus, it's been a long day. I drove all the way from Tennessee."

"That's right. You're the gymnast. Well, maybe I can make an exception since you have special circumstances. Have a seat and I'll go over the info with you."

I walk over to the small black sofa lining the far wall. He's lucky he has a room twice the size of mine. I'd love to have some extra space for furniture besides the beds. "Thanks. What year are you?"

"Junior."

I laugh and he raises his eyebrows at me. "I thought you were a freshman."

"Ouch!"

"Sorry."

"It's cool. I was only having fun today. I've been here for three days sitting through boring meetings and it's been eerily quiet. I try to be approachable and meet the residents as they come inside. That wasn't even my TV that took flight."

"It's okay. You were just doing your job." He hands me a folder full of papers and goes over all the do's and don'ts of the dorm. Some are comical and make me wonder what happened in the past to need a rule in the first place. When there can't possibly be anything else to cover, he hands me one last piece of paper.

"This one usually gets the most grief," he says.

The paper goes into detail about how we aren't allowed to have guests of the opposite sex stay in our room during the week and if we have guests on the weekends, they have to be signed in and approved. It makes sense with the strict fire codes, but how they plan to keep guys out of girls rooms is beyond me. It's a co-ed dorm. "Well this shouldn't be a problem with me." I sign it right away and hand it back to him without a second glance.

"Okay. Either you're single or you don't enjoy sharing a twin bed with a dude. I can't say I blame you on that one. Or a girl, I'm not judging."

"Well, yes to both. Possibly."

"Still deciding?"

I snort. "No, there's no boyfriend and definitely no girlfriend. But you're right. Someone would definitely end up on the floor." I know I'm all of five feet tall, but I like my space when I sleep. I've never shared a room with a guy on a regular basis to know the difference anyway.

"You'd be surprised how creative you can get with the lack of space."

Cara would be all over that response, but I keep my comments to myself. "I'll have to take your word for it."

After a few more questions, we finish up the meeting. Drew actually turns out to be a pretty cool guy and not the total clown I pegged him for. He definitely has a fun side, but takes his job seriously too. I'm comfortable around him—the exact opposite of the way I feel around Kipton.

"How'd it go?" Cara asks from the comfort of her bed. She definitely has the right idea. I'm excited to relax in mine the rest of the night. I haven't sat down for more than a few minutes at a time today and my body is aching from all the heavy lifting.

"Drew seems cool. I'm excused from the meeting and can go to bed anytime I want."

"Is he hot?" She questions hopefully.

"He isn't bad to look at, no. Not my type, but he has a nice body."

"Since we're staying in, maybe I'll go say hello before the meeting. Or would that be too forward of me?"

Cara forward? Never. "You do whatever your little heart desires. I plan on watching a movie and falling asleep. The drive caught up with me."

She contemplates her decision for a few short seconds. "Well, you only live once right? Wish me luck." She scurries out of bed, gives herself a quick once over in the mirror and checks her own ass out. Literally. "It'll have to do. Good-night," she whispers before leaving the room. Something tells me Drew will be intrigued by her. He's just the right kind of crazy to handle her too.

Hoping to fall asleep in a reasonable amount of time despite the ruckus in the hallway, I turn on *Pretty Woman* and watch the classiest hooker I've ever seen get swept off her feet. A timeless treasure from the nineties I can watch over and over again.

The credits are rolling and I'm still awake when Cara returns. "Night, guys. Bye, Drew."

I smile; not at all annoyed I'm still up. "Mission accomplished, Cara?"

She squeals and jumps on my bed so hard she almost launches me right off. "Whoa, shit. Sorry."

"It's okay," I laugh. "I take it you kinda like him."

"He's freakin gorgeous, Sophie. And he's funny. I swear he could have told us we could only shower once a week in cold water and I would have agreed. For all I know he did because I couldn't stop staring at his lips." She tips her head back and groans. "*So* hot. Mark my words, Soph. This mission has only just begun! Now get some sleep so you don't hate me in the morning."

"Okay. Night, Cara."

"Night!"

SIX O'CLOCK SEEMS TO COME faster than usual and I'm filled with butterflies from the moment I wake up. Thankfully, I was exhausted and was able to get several solid hours of sleep despite Cara's late night excitement. Dressing quickly, I pack up my things as quietly as possible so I don't wake her. Slinking out of the room while being extra careful not to let any light in from the hallway, I close the door with a click.

I stand up a little straighter once I can make noise again. The halls of the dorm are silent, and campus is deserted at this early hour of the morning. Watching a random paper plate left behind by the retreating garbage truck take flight is distracting enough to refocus my nerves. My heart's been pumping powerfully since I woke up much like it would after I get done with an exhausting floor routine. I'm so hopped up on adrenaline; I know I need to rein it in so I don't hurt myself on the equipment. As the most recent recruit and reigning new girl, there's so much for me to prove today. I deserve this opportunity and by the end of practice today, I want everyone else to believe it too.

Inside the gym, I notice I'm not the only one eager to begin. There are already a handful of other girls warming up so I join them on the floor and begin stretching. A few smile at me, while another eyes me up and down, sensing competition. Averting my eyes, I focus on each championship banner hanging from the rafters. I'm reminded of the time my mom brought me here to watch the team take home the title. It was Coach Evans first year with the team, and as an eager thirteen year old gymnast, I wanted to meet him so bad. Mom said we had to beat the traffic and didn't have time to stick around. Of course I pouted, but instead of getting angry, I got determined. Determined to perform here myself one day. Maybe that's why this is all so surreal. Finally a dream come true—one that I never saw coming to a lonely girl from Ashland.

"Everyone, let's welcome Sophie to the team. She's our newest addition and I have high hopes she'll fit seamlessly into the lineup." A few hi's and hello's come from the circle of girls and my spirits lift when they aren't staring holes through my skull anymore.

"You're starting over here, Sophie. Follow me." Coach puts me to work right away. His presence dominates the room, making me want to disappear into the wall when I mess up. Considering how nervous I am, I'm fairly pleased with the way my vaults go. My landings were slightly off the mark, but my body was solid in the air. After a critique of my form, I'm sent to try again. Each vault I do is slightly better than the last, but they still aren't acceptable enough for Coach. Worried he's going to stick to me like glue the entire day, I'm relieved when he focuses on a teammate long enough for me to get my act together. I'm panting and struggling to catch my breath from the exertion, but once it's my turn again, he's right by my side critiquing each move I make whether good or bad.

"Faster, push harder with your leading arm! And for the love of God get your legs straight, Sophie. If I'd wanted mediocre, I wouldn't have spent so much time recruiting you," Coach Evans yells. He's known for his hard-ass-demeanor in the gym, and my future on the team depends on meshing well with his style.

I take note of the adjustments he wants me to make, but on the next vault, I miss the landing entirely, ending up on my ass. Peeling my already tired body off the mat, I get back up to fight through the next landing. Over and over, I'm corrected and challenged.

"That last one was completely *worthless,* Sophie."

It only takes one word linked in a sentence to set me off. Worthless.

"You spend so much damn money on her shit, Victoria. And for what? So she can get a meaningless medal around her neck and feel like she's somebody for ten minutes? That's not how the real world works. They don't give awards for not falling on your ass."

"Dean, it's not about medals. It's the life lessons the sport offers. That's what matters. It's both a mental game and a physical."

"Life lessons," he barks out with a laugh. "Did gymnastics teach you how to be worthless because you're damn good at that? Who knows, Vic, maybe she'll follow in your footsteps."

"Dean. That's not what I mean and you know it. If you weren't drunk ninety percent of the time you might be able to tell the difference." But he's always drinking.

He gets up in mom's face and challenges her—his authority towering over her small frame. She takes a few steps back and the fear in her eyes is unmistakable. "You're both worthless," he grumbles before stalking out of the room and planting himself in front of the TV.

"Don't let him see you cry, Sophie. Men never deserve our tears. We're stronger than words—you remember that always."

I nod my head. "I will, Momma."

"You'll never be worthless, Sophie. I may be too far gone to turn

it around, but you're bound to be a star."

I'm not anything close to being a star today. In fact, I'm no closer than I was the day he spit those hateful words at us. Maybe he was right. Maybe this *is* all a worthless dream. With my confidence taking a beating, I struggle through the next two exercises. When I'm certain I can't possibly do one more tumbling pass, we finally break for lunch. The other girls are running circles around me, making me stand out as the weakest link—a title I've never owned.

"Sophie, I need to see you in my office."

"Sure, Coach." I slip into my warm ups worrying he's changed his mind about having me here. "Have a seat, Sophie."

"Thank you." He hands me a bottle of Gatorade and I can't get the top off fast enough. Chugging the orange liquid, it's so cold I feel its entire journey to my stomach. When I finish my long drink, he's watching me intently. His look is one I have trouble describing—it's not angry or impatient, both being valid reasons for calling me in the office in the first place. Instead, he seems relaxed like he's getting a glimpse of me for the very first time. As afraid of him as I am, it's his authority I fear most—the way he holds my destiny in his hands. One word out of his mouth and it can all end. Right here, right now.

"I'm going to lay it out there for you. From the moment I saw you at Regionals last year, I knew you had something special. You still do. You've got everything going for you—elegance, grace and beautiful lines. But your conditioning needs improvement. It would make you that much more explosive off the block. It's all there, Sophie, but we have to fine tune your skill set to get the most out of you. I can get you there, but you have to work as hard outside of the gym as you do inside."

"Understood. I'll work harder on my cardio and weight training." *Hell, I'll do anything he asks.*

"I'm glad to hear that. Your body should be a tool, never a hindrance. We have some time to get you meet ready, but we'll need every second."

"Okay. I'll try harder."

"You'll get there; I can already tell you have the drive in you. That's one aspect of the sport I can't teach. So we'll focus on your conditioning and have you work with the team specialists. And please know you're not the only one on the team who is struggling. Remember, temptation is everywhere on this campus, Sophie, but you have to want to win more. You're only cheating yourself if you slack. I've seen the best of the best self-destruct so let me know if this environment is too much for you."

I nod my head in agreement. "I want this and I won't let you down. Thank you for this opportunity, Coach Evans. This is my dream."

"It's a pleasure, Sophie. You're in a whole new world, now. What was once good enough at your old school won't cut it here, okay? I brought you here to succeed because I saw it in your blood. You were born to do this."

"Thank you. I'm honored you chose me." *It's not over.*

"Don't let me down, Sophie. You're dismissed."

"I won't." My mind's a jumbled blur as I leave his office. The muscles in my thighs are already tightening up from the short time I was sitting in his chair. But it doesn't matter. *He wants me here. He actually believes in me.* I stretch for a few minutes soaking up the excitement of being a part of this team. I'm not in top form, I agree with him on that, but I can get there. I'll show him how regimented I can be when I put my mind to it.

I won't let my body fail me.

CHAPTER *three*

Sophie

CARA'S GOING TO BE DISAPPOINTED I'm not going to the party tonight, but there's no way I can risk it after the speech Coach gave me today. If I intend on stepping up my conditioning, the place for me is the gym, not a party.

As I'm finishing writing Cara a note, letting her know she can go ahead without me tonight, anxiety fills my body to the point the pen is shaking between my fingers. I hate letting people down, especially since we have to live together. I can't picture Cara acting spiteful or angry because of my decision, but we hardly know each other yet. *Anything's possible.* Then there's Kipton to consider. But gymnastics is why I transferred to this school—it has to come first.

Just as I'm finishing signing my name to the note, the room phone rings. Without the caller ID I'm used to on my cell phone, I'm nervous about who could be on the other end of the line. "Hello."

"Hey."

A warmth rushes through my body from head to toe from the sound of Kipton's voice. I'm racking my brain for something to say, but considering he called me, I'm at a loss. Instead of saying something flirty or settling for something interesting, I breathe into the receiver.

"You still there?" he questions.

"Yeah. I'm here." *Barely.*

"What are you wearing?" he whispers.

His voice is low and deep with his words morphing the original warmth I was experiencing into fire. My arms are tingling and my heart dips like I'm flying down the first drop of a roller coaster ride. "Um, what?" I look down to assess my outfit. "I'm wearing my team warm ups."

Playfully laughing, he says, "Relax, Sophie. I was kidding."

"Oh. Okay. Um. Cara isn't here. She's still at the library," I blurt out.

"My sister is in the *library?*" From his skeptical tone of voice, this must be a rare occurrence.

"That's what her note says."

"I'll have to find out which guy she followed in there. She never makes it easy for me. Anyway, I called to talk to you. You're still coming tonight, right?"

He called to talk to me? My mouth is suddenly so dry. I try to wet my lips with my tongue, but it's no use. I panic about what to tell him. "Actually, no. I can't make it. Something came up."

"Sophie." *My name sounds so sexy when he says it.*

"Yes?"

"I want you to come."

"You do?"

"Of course I do. I invited you, didn't I?"

Holy shit! I want to go so bad. If only it was that simple. Coach Evans would flip if he knew I went out partying. It's irresponsible yet exactly what I want to do after hearing from Kipton. But I can't let Coach down. I have to get into shape as quickly as possible or I'll get tossed off the team. Bummed, I tell him the truth. "I have to go to the gym. My conditioning is in need of some serious help."

"Is this because I saw you sniffing your pillow? Please don't be embarrassed, Sophie. I thought it was adorable."

I hadn't even thought of that until he brought it up. "Well, that wasn't my finest moment, but I have to get in shape. Coach gave me a warning today."

"On the first day?" he asks seeming genuinely interested. "What a hard ass," he adds.

"Yeah. A few form tips and that I need to condition harder. You know, work on the weights and cardio. I was sucking air big time today. It's my own fault for slacking over the summer."

"You lift? You're pint sized, Sophie."

"Very funny. You'd be surprised how strong I am."

"I'd love to find out," he mumbles. Although his words are jumbled and not meant for my ears, I hear them loud and clear. I can't tell if he's being sarcastic or flirtatious though. "What time will you be done at the gym?"

"Um. I'm not sure. I'll probably run for a half hour and then do a circuit on the weights."

"That still leaves plenty of time after you finish. Come by for a little. You know you want to," he whispers through the receiver.

I want to so bad, but I can't. "Kipton, that's not a good idea. I have to go."

He sighs in defeat, "All right, be careful."

"I will. Have fun tonight." I hang up the phone and want to kick myself. A large part of me didn't want to turn down the invite because guys like Kipton normally don't give me a second glance. I convince myself he's just being nice so Cara isn't alone tonight. It has nothing to do with wanting to see me for himself. Guys like him don't fall for girls like me—especially if he knew the truth. Nobody wants to deal with the ugly truth.

I'VE SPENT THE LAST HOUR and a half sweating my ass off. Of course I went overboard with my workout hoping I'll whip myself into shape that much faster. But now, the only thing I want to do is take a cold shower and crawl into my bed.

As my tired body inches closer to the dorm, the walk is the exact opposite from earlier today. While six in the morning is subdued, eight o'clock at night is rowdy. Everyone around me is getting ready to hit the town for a night of drunken debauchery. There's a couple walking hand in hand; kissing passionately every few steps. At the rate they're going, they won't make it off campus anytime soon. To my left a bunch of girls giggle as they stroll down the sidewalk in their tank tops and short skirts. A guy with the longest dreadlocks I've ever seen wizzes by me on his skateboard, forcing me off the path and into the grass. Everyone seems to have a place to be—except me. I wrap my arms around myself, suddenly missing the few close friendships I had to leave behind in Ashland. Instead, I'll have to settle for another movie and an early bedtime.

My stomach growls loudly at the thought of buttery popcorn, reminding me I skipped dinner. Although bummed, I suck it up. So what if I have to miss a few parties and go to bed early. There are much worse problems to have.

With everyone leaving the dorm, the elevator is waiting when I press the button. Inside I stare at the shiny metal wall, processing my defeated reflection. Today might not have gone as smoothly as I wanted in the gym, but tomorrow can only be better. I'm always stronger than I give myself credit for.

I'm surprised when I open the door to my room to find Cara still inside curling her hair. I figured she'd be long gone by now considering how excited she was about going to the party. "Sophie! Hurry and get a shower. I won't take no for an answer. You had your work-out. Now let's go find us some cowboys!"

I toss my gym bag on the floor and start chucking my sweaty clothes into the hamper. I'll have to check out the laundry room sometime tomorrow. "Did you wait here for me?"

"Don't make me beg, Sophie. I don't want to go alone and you need to have some fun. You worked your ass off today and deserve to let loose a little. I won't let you throw away the best years of your life. Now let's go drink cheap beer and make out with guys we won't remember in the morning."

I laugh at her and as tired as I am, I debate my options one last time. Kipton's voice replays in my mind, he looked so hopeful as he was asking me to come. The triumphant look when I agreed was exhilarating. I've wanted to be included for so long, I'm afraid if I blow this chance it won't return. *Just this once.* "I'll go, but I can't drink. And only for an hour. Then I have to get to bed."

"I'll take whatever I can get! It's been a long ass summer and my roommate last year was a gamer who never left her computer. I've finally landed a normal roomie and I intend to take full advantage. Go get ready!"

"Okay!" Rushing through my shower ritual, I realize how exciting it is to actually be doing something age appropriate with my night. I've always wanted to experience a real college party. It's taken me two years of college to get to one, but I'm finally going.

Knowing Kipton will be there has me wanting to look irresistible. Maybe if I look hot enough he will see me as more than his sister's roommate. The other rational part of my brain knows I don't do relationships and catching his attention for longer than a minute tonight probably isn't in the cards. With his sinfully delicious looks, I'm sure there'll be a flock of hungry vultures swarming him all night. For all I know, he has a girlfriend. Surely someone has claimed him for their own.

Staring at my half full closet trying to figure out what to put on, I choose my favorite pair of distressed jeans with a simple black V-neck shirt. Hoping to dress it up a little, I wear my favorite Alex and Ani bracelet. My lucky horseshoe necklace is also draped delicately around my neck. It was a present from my mom the day of my first gymnastics competition. I won my level that day and have worn it every day since.

"*That's* what you're wearing?" Cara questions. I didn't realize she was watching me, but she looks appalled by my choice. Sure it's simple, but I don't have any tiny skirts that show half of my ass. I'd rather keep Victoria's Secret a mystery.

"What's wrong with what I'm wearing?" Glancing down at my shirt, it looks nice enough.

She puts her hands on her hips and huffs. "How do you expect the guys to notice you if you're dressed the same way they are?"

"I'll have you know I bought both of these items in the juniors department, *not* the mens."

"I'm sure you did. Now let's sex you up a little. Here put this on." She tosses me an itty bitty jean skirt with a frayed hem. It looks more like a remnant of fabric than something meant to be worn on its own. Thankfully I'm extra short, so it ends up covering more of my ass to thigh ratio than the average girl.

"Here. Wear this tank." She hands me a pale pink camisole that looks simple. I slip it on right as she tosses a see through floral top at my head. "Add that over top of the tank. It's country chic. You'll fit right in, Sophie."

I inspect the shirt. It's forgiving compared to the skin tight tank top. "Can I wear my flip flops with this?"

She gasps at my request. "No! You can wear a pair of my boots. Guys love this look. Trust me. They'll be mentally undressing you the second they see you."

I try to stretch out the tank a little, feeling constricted by the spandex in the fabric, but it bounces right back. If I wanted to be uncomfortable I'd put a leotard on. "Don't all guys picture chicks naked, though? I don't think it matters what I have on."

Cara snorts. "It matters, trust me. But they'd rather see your clothes on the floor and *you* in their bed."

I pause and glare at her. "I'm not getting in anyone's bed tonight, Cara." I chance a peek at my reflection in the mirror and hardly recognize myself. I've never worn an outfit similar to this one. I'm so *girly*.

"Never say never. Let's go."

Dressed in Cara's clothing and wearing some of her makeup, I tug on my skirt making sure I'm covered up. This version of Sophie that's heading to her first party is the exact opposite of the one that walked into Johnson Hall a short forty five minutes ago. In true Sophie fashion, I start doubting my decision the closer we get to the party.

"Stop fidgeting, Sophie. You look seriously hot. I'd do you."

"I never know what's going to come out of your mouth

next, Cara, but thank you."

"I call 'em like I see 'em. Don't worry, I'm not into girls. I like the cock too much."

Shit. She's exhausting.

Cara walks inside without knocking, not that they'd hear it over the music anyway. I should follow her, but I'm still debating turning around and walking home.

"Get in here, Sophie."

"Okay. Jeez." *Here goes nothing.*

Shuffling into the small kitchen, I'm immediately caught off guard when there's a door being used as a table for beer pong. Being extra careful so we don't spill any drinks, we side step the small crowd. Cara grabs two cups next to the keg and hands them to the guy manning the tap.

"Two new faces. What's your name, beautiful?" he asks Cara.

"Cara," she says. She even giggles when he winks at her. He certainly didn't have to work too hard for that.

"Who's your friend?" he nods in my direction. I duck my head and suddenly take interest in the boots I'm wearing. They're too big and hard to walk in.

"This is my roommate, Sophie."

"Here you go, Sophie. Just for you."

Awkwardly, I stare at the cup of beer he's holding in his hand and debate the easiest way to say no without looking like a loser. "That's okay. I'm not thirsty."

"Oh, come on. It's just beer. Or do you like the harder stuff? I can get you some of that if you want."

Although I have no desire to drink, I succumb to peer pressure and accept the cup he offers. I'll dump it down the drain in the bathroom as soon as I find one. Coach would flip if he knew I had alcohol tonight. It's also louder than I expected in here and so damn hot. I'm starting to get claustrophobic as more and more people continue to pile into the small space.

"So, you're new here? I'd remember a gorgeous face like yours," he adds.

"Yeah, I transferred this year from Tennessee," I reply nervously. He's not my type at all. I could tell the second he opened his mouth to flirt with Cara.

Cara slings her arm around my shoulder. "Can you believe she's never been to a party before?"

I don't miss his shocked expression. "No shit. Then let me officially welcome you to the hottest spot on campus. I also insist on giving you the grand tour." He offers me his arm like we're at the prom or something. I look at him cautiously while he waits for me to latch on. "I don't bite, little lady. Unless you want me to."

"No, thanks. I'm good." I shift my cup to my left hand and accept his offered arm. It's a little sweaty but he still smells good, thankfully. Cara is walking beside me for all of thirty seconds before someone wraps her in a gigantic bear hug. She laughs in hysterics as he spins her around. I slow down to wait for her, but we get separated in the mass of bodies. I tug on my tour guide's arm, but he doesn't stop until we come to a tiki bar in the living room that's lined up with bottles of liquor for the choosing.

He leans down and asks, "what do you want to drink?"

I raise my red solo cup. "You gave me this beer a few minutes ago."

"Then you need to drink faster. Let's do a shot." He hands me a Dixie cup filled with red Jell-O. It smells like cherries, my favorite. "Down the hatch," he tells me. He's smirking while he watches me swallow.

Immediately I gag. "That's strong! Did you put the whole bottle in there?"

"It's a little Jell-O and a whole lot of vodka"

I chug the only thing I have to chase the alcohol, the beer. It's equally repulsive. "My mouth tastes like shit. Do you have some water?"

"No water here. Want some jungle juice?"

Juice sounds safe but I'm not stupid. I know this particular kind is laced with something strong. I set my beer down, knowing I won't be taking another sip. Now that I've tried it, I know I'll never be a beer girl. "Does the juice taste like ass too?" I gesture toward the cup of beer.

He laughs at me and shakes his head. "No. You'll love it. It's fruity." He lifts a trashcan lid, and I assume he's going to throw my cup away. Instead, he chugs the rest of the beer in my cup, grabs the ladle hanging from the side of the Rubbermaid bin and pours juice into my cup straight out of the trashcan.

"Don't worry, it's clean. I washed it with soap and water earlier today and we buy a new one for each party."

Cautiously, I take a small sip of the juice. All I taste is fruit punch and I sigh in relief. If there's any alcohol in it, it must be heavily diluted. This is a drink I can easily tolerate.

He fills up his own cup and asks, "better?"

"Much." It's strange not seeing any familiar faces as I look around the room. Sipping my drink, I sway back and forth to the music. Pitbull is yelling "Timber" and the crowd on the makeshift dance floor is going wild. We played this song at my old gym to pump ourselves up for competition. I stare off into space, reminiscing about my old teammates who I miss terribly. They'd never be out partying right now.

"You want to dance, Sophie?"

"I'm not ready for *that* yet." I appreciate the offer, so I try to make small talk instead to let him know I'm not a total bore. I nudge his arm to get his attention. He leans down to hear me. "You never told me your name."

"It's Caleb. Drink that up and I'll pour you some more. Then we can go get some air."

Air sounds perfect right about now. I chug the rest of my jungle juice and it goes down without a fight. It's delicious. Once I'm finished I hand my cup over to Caleb. He dumps a little clear liquid into it instead of juice.

"What's that?"

"The shot of the night. We call it a bender. Everyone has to try one."

I don't want any more shots, but he holds it in front of my face and waits for me to take it out of his hands. The quicker I get this over with the faster I can get some air. I toss it back and although it's strong, I kind of like it. Warming me from the inside out, I take another.

"Good girl." Caleb pulls me by the hand through the crowd to our next stop. There's still no sign of Cara. I would be worried if we weren't at her brother's house, but she probably knows a lot of people here. We walk up a flight of steep stairs. At the top, he opens the window and crawls through the small opening. He holds his hand out for me to grab onto. There's no lady-like way to get through in a skirt so I slide through the narrow space the best I can. Once through, I'm left standing on a small fire escape with a view of the entire main street. The breeze is refreshing, but with nobody else within earshot, I'm nervous about being out here all alone with him.

"So, you've really never been to a party before?" Caleb asks.

"No. I've never had time." It's the truth. Gymnastics keeps my schedule packed.

"You had time tonight?"

"Cara forced me to come. I was going to stay in."

Unexpectedly, he reaches out and cups my jaw in his hand, running his thumb over my bottom lip. "Your lips are bright red from your drink. I want to bite them."

I back away from his touch and he releases me. He's a little too forward for my taste, but I don't want to be rude. "You said you don't bite, Caleb."

He shrugs his shoulders. "Maybe I lied." He takes a step closer to me, eyeing my body up and down. It's sending up a bright red flag.

"Can we go find Cara?"

He takes another step closer, closing the distance between the two of us entirely. "You don't have to be nervous, Sophie." He reaches for my hand dangling at my side.

"I'm fine, but I came with Cara, so I should hang out with her too." My arms are starting to tingle and my lips are numb. "I need to sit down." I find a spot on the window ledge and set my cup down next to me. A bead of sweat runs down the center of my back and I fan my face trying to create an extra breeze. My long hair is sticking to the back of my neck. Lifting it up, I feel cooler instantly.

"You okay, gorgeous?" Caleb asks. He's leaning against the railing smirking at me.

"My face is tingling." I've never been drunk before but the longer I sit here, the more numb I become. My body becomes weightless and all I want to do is dance around and shake my ass. Caleb dumps some of his punch into my cup. "More?" I question.

He shakes his head yes. "If you drink that you won't be buzzed anymore."

"What will I be then?"

"Drunk. Isn't that why we're all here?" he says with a laugh.

I rest my head against the side of the house and close my eyes. When everything starts to tilt, I open my eyes back up and decide he's right. Now's my shot to live it up. Who knows when I'll get to another party or if I'll get to another at all.

Throwing twenty years of caution to the wind, I grab my cup and chug what Caleb poured in. Buzzed isn't going to cut it tonight. Tonight I want drunk—I want to be like everyone else. While the alcohol still makes me nervous, I'm smart enough to know I'm nothing like my father and I never will be. I raise my cup to Caleb. "You only live once right?"

"Atta girl." Caleb squeezes my thigh, inching his hand closer to the hem of my skirt.

We sit for a few more minutes and surprisingly, I could float right into the sky. Caleb was right, drunk *is* awesome. "Let's go dance, Caleb. I want you to dance with me."

"I thought you didn't dance?"

"I thought you didn't bite."

"I definitely bite, Sophie. We can go to my room if you want to find out where." He inches his hand even closer, his fingertips now under the hemline of my skirt.

"I want to dance, Caleb." He laughs at me and helps me climb back into the house as I struggle to find enough balance to crawl through the window. His hands are on my ass, pushing me through and I land inside with a small thump. Caleb climbs though, thankfully not stepping on me in the process. He holds out his hand and pulls me up off the floor. Holding my body tightly against his own, he pretends to bite the top of my head. It makes me giggle uncontrollably. "Let's go dance," he whispers.

"Okay."

I'm only two steps down the flight of stairs when my vision starts playing tricks on me. "Caleb, help me." He jogs back up the stairs and I climb onto his back, but he's tall and we misjudge the small doorway in this aging house, smacking my head on the top of the doorframe. "Shit!" My vision blurs even more, this time not from the alcohol, but the force of the impact on my skull.

He sets me down on the ground but my legs feel like rubber and I fall against the stairs, hitting my head again on the bottom step. "Holy hell." Caleb bends down and inspects the front of my head where I bounced off the door frame and step. "That's gonna leave a mark, Sophie."

"It doesn't even hurt. I *need* to dance!"

"Can you stand up?"

"Yeah, I'm good." I hold out my arms for him. "Up!"

Caleb spins me around and puts his front to my back, grinding into me from behind. His hands roam my body before resting on my hips, his thumbs tucked under my waistband. It's a heady mix of lust and danger—and I like it. I'm zoned out; enjoying the connection my body has with Caleb's when my phone vibrates in my back pocket. We jump apart from the unexpected sensation. I chase myself around in a circle like a dog trying to bite his own tail before Caleb pulls the phone out of my pocket for me. "Thanks, C. Hello?"

"Where the hell are you?"

"Right here!" I exclaim animatedly.

"Where is *here?*"

"At the party!"

"No, Sophie. Where are you standing?"

"In a house!" Caleb turns me around and nuzzles against my neck, kissing me softly. It feels strangely good. "Sorry, Caleb, they ask stupid questions."

"Sophie. What house and what room?" someone yells through the phone.

"The dancing room! Ouch! Caleb, don't bite me. Did you know Cara brought me here?"

"You're *talking* to Cara, Sophie. Are you wasted?"

"No. I'm Sophie, silly."

"Stay right where you are. I'll find you."

I hang up the phone and hand it to Caleb. I stick my ass out at him, waiting for him to put my phone back in. He smacks it hard before tucking the phone into my back pocket. I take another Jell-O shot from the bar we're dancing next to and although strong, it goes down like water. I could take on the entire world right now in my state of euphoria. I hold my arms out and spin in a circle with my head tipped back. I'm too hot and need relief, so I pull my shirt up over my head to free myself, leaving me in my tight cami. I tuck it under my bra and the air on my exposed stomach is cooling. After swinging my shirt in the air, I let the fabric fly, unsure of where it ends up landing.

"Jesus, Sophie. You're smokin hot," Caleb says in appreciation.

I smile and keep dancing, in my own world entirely. I hop up on top of a coffee table and continue shaking my ass. A small crowd forms around me and I become the most interesting person in the room. "Drink up bitches!" I yell to the mass of sweaty bodies. Everyone cheers in response, fist pumping the air to the beat of the music. This is the most alive I've ever been in my entire life. Why I've waited so long to experience all of this is beyond me. Alcohol is fun and powerful, not at all scary like I thought.

As I find my groove, I'm yanked off the table and thrown over a strong shoulder. The pressure on my full stomach makes me nauseous. There's a lot of shouting, jostling of my small body, and dizziness. The dizziness is unbearable. When I finally get put back down, I'm in a bedroom. But I'm not tired. I want to dance.

CHAPTER *four*

KIPTON

CARA'S WIPING TEARS FROM HER eyes and I'm angry. When I invited Sophie here tonight, I had intended on getting to know her better. After she told me she couldn't make it, I was bummed to say the least. Imagine my surprise when Cara told me she was here. Derailed by the jackass who took her to the library, she lost her roommate in the mass of bodies. I don't know who I want to kill more right now, Cara for losing Sophie or Caleb for getting her wasted.

To make matters worse, Sophie looks fucking sexy as hell in her boots and skirt. From the moment I saw her standing in front of me in her pink bath towel, she's been on my mind. She's also completely clueless about how gorgeous she is. In fact, I've never experienced a girl as hot as she is who doesn't act like a stuck up bitch. Instead, Sophie's insanely shy with me and I can tell I make her uncomfortable by the way she refuses to look at me when I'm talking to her. When I called her on the phone and her breathing noticeably increased, I wanted her in my bed.

Usually, chicks willingly sit on my lap, offering up favors while practically begging for a night with me. Hell, there's usually a girl waiting for me in my bed by the end of one of these parties. I should say no to them, but I want to feel as much as they want to please me. Knowing Sophie is the exact opposite of all of those qualities appeals to me entirely too much.

I've had my fair share of women, I won't pretend I haven't, but Sophie's an athlete too and we share a love of sports. As she was telling me about her major, I laid on her bed wondering how this insanely beautiful girl was still single. Then I'd caught her with her nose in her pillow, trying to get closer to the smell of my cologne, and knew I was in for it. It actually turned me on to know she wanted more of me. That was a definite first.

Inviting her here tonight was my attempt at knocking down one of her walls, hoping a more carefree Sophie emerged—one that wasn't too nervous to speak to me. But we didn't have a chance to get any closer thanks to Caleb getting her drunk off her ass before I even got to say hello. This wasn't what I had in mind when I wanted to see her break out of her shell.

"Where's Caleb? He makes me drunk. I *love* drunk," Sophie babbles from the edge of my bed. I open my drawer and take out one of my T-shirts. I have no idea where the other half of her outfit is, but the thought of her losing it in the first place makes me want to break shit.

Slowly, I walk over to her sitting on the bed. Her eyes are glassy and somewhat spaced out, but she watches each move I make. I place the shirt over her head, pulling her arms through each hole like a child. Her body is swallowed up by the black fabric that hangs loosely off her small frame. While she looks hot wearing my clothes, she shouldn't have ever lost hers to begin with.

There's no way I want to scare her or yell at her before she has a chance to get to know me, but going off with a guy she's never met and accepting drinks from him was the stupidest thing she could have done tonight. It's one of the reasons I kept my own sister away from this place for as long as I could. At least Cara knows she messed up. No use yelling at her anymore for something she can't fix any easier than I can. All we can do is keep her away from Caleb.

"What's wrong, Cara? You want a drink?" Sophie asks.

"I couldn't find you for over an hour, Sophie. You scared

the shit out of me," Cara tells her as she wipes her eyes with a tissue. "I thought you were in trouble, which you clearly were. Kipton's been pissed at me since we got separated."

"I'm good. It's all good. You want to dance?" Sophie stands up, my T-shirt falling to her knees reminding me how tiny she really is. Being all of a hundred pounds, it obviously wouldn't take much for her to get wasted.

"Your party's over, Sophie," I remind her while I continue to pace back and forth over the plush carpeting in my bedroom. Running my hands through my hair, I try to figure out how to handle my next problem—Caleb. He *will* be set straight at some point tonight. Sophie sits back down on my bed and Cara plucks another tissue out of the box before joining her.

I roll my eyes at her dramatics. Maybe I was a little hard on her, but she needs to stop worrying about guys all the damn time. "Cara, please stop crying. I can't take you upset too."

"Then stop yelling at me! I get it. She's drunk. I lost her. I'm sorry, Kipton."

"Carrraaaa, I'm not lost. I was downstairs drinking, then upstairs drinking, then through the window drinking, then dancing and now I'm sitting here with you two party poopers." She bounces on the bed trying to get Cara to smile. Cara's wired the same way I am though and doesn't give in to Sophie's playful mood.

"Sophie, I was so scared something happened to you. It was my idea to drag you here and then I lost you. Caleb doesn't have the best reputation you know."

Sophie reaches over and hugs Cara. "It's okay. Stop crying and have a drink! Caleb took me, not the boogeyman. He's not even that scary. Did you know he bites?"

"What do you mean, Sophie? Who bites?" At the mention of Caleb's name, I start to lose my cool again. When I walk back over to the bed to get details out of her, I notice a mark on her neck and a shadow on her forehead. After turning on the bedside lamp, I discover the knot near her temple. "What the hell happened to your head, Sophie?"

"Caleb hit my head and dropped me," she says with a

giggle.

"He did what?" Cara and I shout in unison.

"He ran me into the wall, but it didn't hurt. Then I fell off his back and went *boom*." She crashes her hands together for added effect before continuing. "Ya know, I don't feel anything actually. It's *amazing*."

"Kipton, that bump looks bad."

"It is bad, Cara. If she wasn't wasted I'd take her to the emergency room. But she'll get tossed off the team and in a lot of trouble if I do." I crouch in front of Sophie and run my hand over her forehead. She automatically leans into my touch and looks into my eyes. Her skin is as smooth as satin under my rough fingertips. I'm mesmerized by her gorgeous blue eyes as she places her tiny hand around my wrist, holding me in place. The connection is too intense. Quickly, I stand up and lean against the wall to slow down my breathing.

"How much did you drink, Sophie?" Cara asks, oblivious to the mini moment I just shared with her roommate.

"Um. Beer, wiggly shots, regular ones too. Oh, and juice out of the garbage. Can you believe they drink out of the trash around here?" She laughs hysterically, falling over on the bed in the process.

"Shit," I grumble. How the hell could Caleb give someone her size that much alcohol? If he had any intention of screwing her tonight I'll fucking kill him. He's already going to hear about the hickey. As I start to envision bashing his face in, Sophie's expression changes. Her skin becomes pale and her carefree smile disappears. Something tells me she's not loving being drunk anymore.

"Cara, bathroom," Sophie says in a panic while holding her stomach in both of her hands.

She will never make it down the hall in time so I grab the small trashcan next to my bed and rub her back as every ounce of alcohol she consumed reappears. When she starts to dry heave and fights to catch her breath, Cara starts to cry again. "This is all my fault. Sophie, I'm so sorry."

"Cara, did she eat any dinner?"

"I don't know. She went to the gym and then we came

here. She didn't go to the dining hall with me and Drew tonight."

"I'm going to kill, Caleb," I announce through gritted teeth. Sophie's body goes limp next to me. Laying her on her side in case she gets sick again, I tell Cara to find me a cold wash cloth. Sophie's eyes roll back in her head briefly and I start to worry she may have alcohol poisoning.

"Kipton." She moans my name softly.

"Sophie? Can you hear me?" I tap her cheek gently, trying to rouse her from her sleep. She opens her eyes and smiles innocently back at me.

"Yeah. I hear you," she whispers. "You make me stupid."

"You're not stupid." I gently brush her hair out of her eyes. She watches my lips for a few seconds as I speak to her before shifting her gaze to meet mine.

"I want you to kiss me, but I threw up." For the first time, her cheeks don't turn pink while talking to me.

I blow out a breath, not wanting to hurt her fragile drunken feelings. "Sophie, I can't kiss you."

"That's okay. I know I'm too ugly for a guy as hot as you are." She looks sullen as she closes her eyes as if it physically pains her to look at me for another second.

"You're not ugly and that's not why I won't kiss you. I won't because you're drunk."

"Coach says I suck. I miss home. My mom would be so mad at me right now. I'm like *him*." A tear escapes her eye and I gently brush it away before it falls down her flushed cheek.

"You're perfect, Sophie."

"You're the hottest guy I've ever seen," she mumbles.

She's definitely experiencing some hard-core liquid courage right now. Alcohol must be her truth serum. While I'd love to pump as much information out of her as possible while she's lit, I won't. I would rather earn her sober confessions. "I'm nothing special, Sophie." It's the truth.

"I'm sleepy," she says as her eyelashes flutter open and closed.

I tuck her tiny frame under the covers and pull my comforter up to her chin. She snuggles down into my bed and gives up her fight, already breathing soundly. "Rest, Sophie."

When I stand up, Cara is watching me intently from the doorway. "I never thought I'd see the day, but you actually have a thing for her."

"Cara, stop. She's your roommate. Don't make this into more than it is." I quickly change my shirt in case anything got on it while Sophie was getting sick. Cara's still keeping an eye on me, waiting for me to confess, but I won't.

"I call bullshit Kippy, but whatever." Thankfully she drops the subject quickly and lets me off the hook without one of her rounds of twenty questions.

"Stay here with her in case she gets sick; I have to talk to Caleb." He *will* learn to respect the girls that come into this house. Granted some girls do come here specifically looking for a hook-up, but there are girls similar to Sophie who haven't been here before. There's no way I'm risking anyone's safety as long as I live under this roof.

Cara eyes me suspiciously. We're both relieved Sophie's calmed down and resting peacefully, but she has something to say. She always does. "You know it's okay to be into her, Kip. You don't have to pretend with her. She's the real deal."

"I don't know anything about her, Cara, but I get the impression she might be. I'm sorry she got mixed up with the wrong guy tonight." Cara nods her head and sits down on the worn recliner in the corner of my room. She starts messing with her phone, probably texting the library douche who is responsible for making her lose Sophie in the first place.

"I'll be right back."

"Take your time. I'm good and she's okay. I think she got it all out of her system."

Bounding down the stairs, I find Caleb's pathetic ass next to the keg trying to sweet talk two chicks, as usual. The only reason he stands next to it is to get first dibs on all the girls that walk into the house. It's a jackass move and I'm pissed he pulled it with Sophie and my sister.

He finishes filling up the blonde's cup and notices me. "Dude, how was she? I should be pissed at you for getting some before me. Sexy little thing and probably fun to toss around in bed too, am I right?"

It takes two seconds for my fist to connect with his jaw. He recoils from my punch, instantly grabbing his face in pain. "What the hell was that for, you asshole? You should be thanking me for doing your dirty work!"

"Don't you ever fucking treat her like a whore or pull that shit with anyone in this house again. You got me? She's been upstairs barely conscious from all the shit you gave her."

He rubs his jaw and pierces me with his eyes. *Go ahead and try me, Caleb. I'll bring it ten times harder than you can handle.*

"Dude, I didn't force her to drink anything. She willingly drank the shit. I can't help this was her first party. So back the *fuck* off. How do you even know her anyway?"

Her first party? Ever? This is news to me. "She's my sister's roommate. Not that I owe you any explanations."

"Oh, now it makes sense. You've already made a move. She's all yours then dude. There's plenty of pussy to go around. Sloppy seconds ain't my style anyway."

I reach out and grab the collar of his preppy polo, pulling him within inches of my face. There's no way he's going to forget what I have to say again. "Caleb, you'll learn to watch your damn mouth or I'll throw your ass out of this house. Being on the team doesn't mean you run the show. This is your last warning." I let go of his shirt and forcefully push him against the wall. *I'm done with his shit.* He flips me off, but I let it go. His ego has been bruised enough for now.

After a look around, the party appears to be winding down. I tell the two couples making out in the stairwell to take it elsewhere so I can get back upstairs. The house looks trashed, but the freshman will clean it in the morning. Those are days I do not miss.

Inside my room, Sophie's still passed out cold in my bed while Cara's busy fixing her make-up in front of my mirror. "Going somewhere?" I ask quietly so I don't wake Sophie.

"Drew asked me to come back to the dorm to hang out. He's on night shift and has to stay up so I offered to keep him company. That's if you're okay watching Sophie. I'll stay if you want me too."

"No, it's fine. Who is Drew? Your RA?"

"Yeah."

I walk over and lean against my dresser while she finishes messing with her face. "You know he's not allowed to date his residents."

"We aren't dating, we're hanging out. Don't go getting all big brother on me again."

I hang my head in defeat knowing I have to add this guy to my radar along with the rest of her flock. It's only the first week of school and already she has at least two guys on her tail. "Cara, why can't you ever make life easy for me?"

She pops her lips together after putting some sparkly shit on them. "You know you don't have to keep an eye on me. I'm a big girl, now."

"You're my little sister, so I do. I swear between you and Sophie this year might kill me." I glance over at Sophie and notice how innocent she looks tucked into my bed. The thought of Caleb's lips touching her skin has me contemplating punching him again.

Cara clears her throat to get my attention. "You know my roommate isn't allowed to date my brother."

Her rule catches me off guard and surprises me. Her roommates have never been off limits to me in the past. "Cara. I–" sputtering over my response, I can't get my brain to form a complete sentence, so I give up before I say anything she can use against me later.

"That's what I thought. Have a good night big bro. Please return her in the morning." She reaches up and kisses my cheek.

"Cara," I groan. I wipe the sparkles off with the back of my hand. "Do you have a ride? You're not walking back to the dorm alone this late at night."

"Yeah, Drew said the same thing so he's sending his friend to come get me. Don't worry; his friend's an RA too and completely responsible." She punches my arm playfully, "See, you two would get along." I roll my eyes knowing I'd have no time for a life if I befriended every guy she took an interest in. She changes her next conquest about as often as she changes her clothes.

"Behave, Cara," I warn. I've had all the action I can handle for one night.

"I always do, Kippy. See ya tomorrow."

After she leaves, I change into some sweats and take my shirt off, tossing it on top of the dresser. I try to get comfortable in the recliner, but I can't sleep. The chair is too damn uncomfortable and knowing Sophie is in my bed doesn't help either. For the first time, there's actually a chick in my bed for the sole purpose of sleeping. And she's fucking beautiful. Why can't my sister have an ugly roommate again this year? The first chick who watched Star Wars on a continuous loop definitely kept me away. I'd only heard her speak a handful of times the entire time they shared a room and it was in Darth Vader's voice. Creepy chicks are not for me.

Another thirty minutes pass as I sit and watch Sophie sleep. Her eyelashes flutter a few times and she moans, but never fully wakes up.

Still shocked it was her first party, I can't even comprehend the idea of being a junior and never living it up like we do here every single weekend. I thought parties were part of the college experience. But from the small glimpse I've seen of her sober, she isn't like most girls. I may not know why yet, but I will. Especially now that I know she wants me to kiss her.

The thought doesn't help my current situation any because when I close my eyes my mind wanders to the memory of Sophie dancing to top of the table. My dick twitches to life immediately. I won't be worth a damn tomorrow if I don't remove the image of her toned stomach from my brain.

Risking potential bodily harm, I give up on the recliner, instead lying on top of the covers next to Sophie. She starts to stir and I worry she's about to be sick again or kick my ass out of bed. Instead, she nuzzles into my side catching me completely off guard. I've never cuddled with a chick before. If I'm in bed with someone, it's usually to fuck, none of which has anything to do with sweet caresses or affectionate embraces.

"Kipton," she mumbles.

"Sleep, beautiful."

CHAPTER *five*

Sophie

I WAKE UP DISORIENTED AND with an intense case of cotton mouth from a night I don't entirely remember. The sun shining through the curtains is killing my throbbing head and I'd do anything for it to disappear. *Give me water or give me death.*

Surprisingly, the scent of Kipton's cologne is still lingering on my bedding and I cringe at the reminder of being caught indulging in the aroma. But as my body continues to scream in agony with sore muscles and a headache massive enough to cripple me, I now have bigger problems to worry about. Not to mention, I'm so nauseous I could throw up.

Clutching the blankets to my chest, I sit up slowly yet still make myself dizzy. When I realize I'm not in my bed let alone my own bedroom, I panic. My eyes dart around the room, searching for anything familiar. But nothing is my own and Cara's nowhere to be found.

I don't recognize the muscular back and shoulders lying next to me in the bed and I'm scared to find out who they belong to. *I have to get out of here.* My skirt is still on my body, but the fabric of someone else's T-shirt, scrapes my sensitized skin. I have no idea where I left my own shirt and boots. *I have to get out of here.* Throwing the covers off of me, I climb out of the bed, unsure of how I got into it in the first place. How could I be so stupid—so careless with my body? Up until last night, I hadn't been with anyone sexually since things with my ex came crashing down. I stuff those unwanted memories back into the vault and focus on finding my boots and purse.

One sideways glance at the clock on the nightstand assures me I've made a colossal mistake. *This can't be happening.* Tears prick my eyes. Coach Evans is going to kill me if I'm late to practice let alone hung over. Between the dizziness and the shooting pain in my head, I'm having trouble staying upright, but after the speech Coach gave me yesterday, I have to show up regardless of my protesting body.

Turning my head too quickly, I lose my balance as an intense pain rocks my brain. I stifle my sobs with the back of my hand, careful not to wake up the guy in the bed. I search the carpet for the boots Cara let me borrow and see one peeking out from underneath the bed. I get on my hands and knees in search of the other. Swaying slightly to the side, I fight gravity to keep moving forward. But I spot the other boot all the way on the other side of the room by the window. As quietly as possible; I crawl over to fetch it. I stop moving when I hear him clear his throat. "You're up."

Raising my head, the last person I expect to see is Kipton. In shock, I sit back on my heels and stare completely dumbstruck. Kipton's sleepy eyes are staring back at me not giving away an ounce of information about the night. Instead, his look is intense as his gaze shifts to my neck. Whatever he sees makes him cringe. I touch the area of skin he's focused on with my fingertips and discover it's tender.

Standing up, I shuffle to the mirror hanging above his dresser. "What the fuck?" I lean closer to the glass, trying to get a better look at the bruise on my neck. I know what it is and it looks trashy. Another reminder of a portion of the night I don't remember.

Things only get worse when I spot the gigantic lump on my forehead. "What happened to me?" I whisper against the glass of the mirror, fogging it up with my breath. The injury convinces me I've been violated in some way yet the mood around me seems unthreatening. None of it makes sense.

Clutching my head with my right hand and my neck in my left, I capture Kipton's fierce reflection through the mirror. His eyes soften only when they meet mine. He looks different first thing in the morning—sexier if that's even possible. If I thought I was attracted to him before, seeing him naked from the waist up only solidifies it. His chiseled torso taunts me, suddenly making me self-conscious about being intimate with him and not remembering. *What did I let him do to me?*

"I have to go. I'm going to be late for practice." I scramble to put my boots back on and wet my fingertip to try to remove some of the black mascara that's smudged underneath my eyes. Refastening my ponytail is painful with each tug of my hair sending more shooting pains to my forehead. Gingerly, I run my fingertips over the bruise on my head and wince. It's incredibly sore to the touch. "Shit."

Searching for my wristlet; my anger intensifies when I can't find that either. "Where is it?" Tears start to fall again, my frustration mixing with my embarrassment. I hate the way he's watching me.

"Come 'ere a minute, Sophie" Kipton scoots to the edge of the bed, the sheet falling away from his body. I let my gaze fall to the floor so I'm not tempted to stare at him. My body trembles from the shock of the unknown combined with the pain from my throbbing temples.

Complying, I go to Kipton, wiping away my tears with the back of my hand. He reaches out his arm and pulls me closer so I have no choice but to sit down on the edge of the bed next to him. "Sophie, you're shaking."

As he reaches up to inspect my head, I lean away from his touch before he can make contact with my skin. "Don't." He appears stunned by not having permission to touch me.

"Sophie, I'm not going to hurt you."

"It already hurts. I don't know what happened and I'm in so much trouble. I need to get back to the dorm."

"Shh. You're okay." Reaching for me again, he lightly grazes his thumb over the bruise while nestling his fingers in the strands of my hair. The action is intimate and somewhat adoring, both of which I don't understand, especially coming from a guy I barely know. There's no urgency or dominance in his actions. Instead he appears genuinely concerned with his soft touches and careful inspection.

When I can't take the intensity of his touch any longer, I speak. "I'm fine." But my eyes lie as much as my actions. He knows I'm in not fine—at all.

"Sophie, you need to get your head looked at. I couldn't take you last night because you were so drunk."

"No, I know. Thank you. I would have lost my scholarship."

"Yeah. That's why I didn't want to risk it. But I feel like I messed up."

"I promise I'll be okay. I take falls all the time at practice." Kipton blinks several times and I know he's about to call my bluff.

"I can tell you're in pain. You could have a concussion. I've had one. It's no picnic."

"I know. I've been there too, but I'm late. I need to get going." He nods reluctantly and brushes his thumb down my cheek before tucking a stray strand of my hair behind my ear. "Thanks."

"Give me a minute to put a shirt on and I'll drive you."

"Okay. Thank you. Do you happen to know where my shirt is?" I play with my hands nervously, embarrassed that I have to ask him for my own clothing. I couldn't be more disappointed with myself.

He turns his head to face me and pauses, his eyes roaming up and down my body. I glance down at my horrendous outfit. You can't even tell I have a skirt on with the T-shirt hanging all the way down to my knees. "No I don't. I wasn't the one who took it off. Do you remember anything about last night, Sophie?"

"Honestly, not much. I remember coming here and losing Cara in the crowd. Then I met up with Caleb at the keg. He showed me around and gave me some drinks. Everything after that is a blur."

"That's what I thought." He pulls a T-shirt over his head, grabbing his keys as soon as it's in place. I fidget, wishing this wasn't so awkward. "Come on, I'll take you back to the dorm." He opens his top dresser drawer and pulls out my bag. I sigh in relief that it's not lost.

"Thank you."

"You don't have to keep thanking me, Sophie."

I don't argue. Instead, I follow him downstairs. From the looks of it, the rest of the house is still asleep. Guys and girls are passed out on various couches throughout the living room. There definitely won't be any signs of life inside the house for a while.

Kipton uses his remote entry to unlock a black Chevy Camero. The outside of the car screams vintage sexy while the interior is sleek and modern. Of course he would drive a hot car. I roll my eyes at his level of male perfection and manage to make myself laugh despite the circumstances.

"What's so funny?" Instead of hopping in the driver's seat, he walks around to the passenger side and opens the door for me. I stare at him for a moment too long, surprised by the chivalrous gesture. "You getting in?" he asks with a smirk while leaning against the doorframe. It should be illegal to look that good having just rolled out of bed.

"Oh. Yeah. Sorry." I climb inside, immediately noticing the smell of new leather from the upholstery. When he starts the engine, the entire car powerfully purrs to life. The vibrations light a torch inside my body from my ass to my toes.

Despite how much I want to forget about last night, I still can't stop harping on the fact that I may or may not have had sex with Kipton. He glances over at me from the driver's side, his eyes inspecting my head for the millionth time this morning. Once he gets his fill, his gaze drops to my lips. I lick them instinctively and his eyes heat up to an even deeper shade of blue. It's too personal for this early in the morning, so I stare out my window and try to block him out.

"You okay, Sophie?"

No I'm not. "Did you, I mean, did we, well you know. Did we?" I ask shyly, still unable to look at him.

He pulls out of his driveway, heading south onto Main Street. It's only a short half mile drive back to the dorm and he remains silent until we pull into the parking lot at the top of the hill overlooking my dorm. The same hill I've had so much fun trekking up and falling down.

He still hasn't responded once the car comes to a stop and as much as I want to know the truth, I'm too ashamed to stick around for the answer. As I open my door, he reaches over and grabs my free arm, preventing me from leaving. I glance at his large hand holding onto my small wrist. His fingers wrap the entire way around with room to spare. Slowly, my eyes travel from his fingertips back up to his eyes. The expression on his face surprises me and I know I'm getting an answer whether I like it or not.

"No, Sophie. We didn't. I prefer my women conscious."

I nod at his words, realizing my question was more of an insult. "I'm sorry, I assumed with being in your bed and all. I've never had this happen before, sorry."

"You have nothing to apologize for, Sophie. Caleb's the one who should be apologizing, and he will as soon as I remind him what a jackass he is."

"Caleb? Did I—do it with him?" I cringe at the thought of what may have happened to me last night. I'm not even attracted to Caleb.

"No," he says as he shifts uncomfortably in his seat. He stares blankly through the windshield. "But it might have happened if we didn't find you when we did." He sighs and rubs his thumb and index finger over his eyes, appearing frustrated. "Next time, please don't accept drinks from guys you don't know, no matter how safe they seem. Caleb isn't a bad guy, but he's always looking to score. I almost kicked his ass last night. He's lucky I only punched him once."

I turn to face him. "You were in a fight because of me?"

"Yeah, Sophie. I was."

"Were you hurt?" I pray my stupid actions didn't cause him any pain.

"No, he never touched me. He got his warning served to him though."

"Did Caleb do this to me?" I ask as I brush my finger over my aching forehead.

"I didn't see it happen, but you told Cara and I something about him running you into a wall. You also said you fell on the stairs. I'm not sure what all that means exactly, but I don't like it either way."

"Jesus. No more parties." I hang my head, completely ashamed with myself. I knew better than to touch alcohol. Having my father's DNA and watching him self-destruct over the years should have been more than enough to prevent me succumbing to peer pressure. But I failed anyway. Maybe I'm no better than he is.

"Was last night your first?" he asks.

"Yeah. Lame I know. First time I drank too. You see how well that went."

"*Shit.* I had no idea, Sophie. I should have never pressured you into coming. I'm sorry all of this happened to you because of me."

I put my hand back on the door handle. I can't sit here any longer because I don't want him to see me cry again. "I'm okay Kipton—none of what happened last night is your responsibility. It was my own stupid fault for wanting to have a fun night out like the average college girl."

His eyes take on the same searing declaration as earlier. "Nothing about you is average, Sophie, but what do you mean?"

"Nothing. Just rambling. Thanks for the ride. Coach Evans is going to kill me for being late." I shut the car door and yank up my T-shirt dress, tying it in a knot at my waist with the hopes that my walk of shame will appear less shameful. Kipton waits until I'm safely down the hill before pulling away—his tires grinding up some loose gravel.

I walk inside to find Drew and a very flirty Cara sitting at the front desk. There's no way she could have slept considering she's still wearing last night's outfit.

"There she is! Morning, love."

Her perky ass is too much right now. "Here I am," I mumble back.

"Is my brother coming in?" She looks behind me to the glass door, expecting him to follow me inside.

"No. He left." I glance at Drew who looks very interested in hearing about my night. He crosses his arms over his chest and smirks at me. "What?" I say entirely too snippy.

Drew holds in hands up in mock defense. "I'm not saying

a word. Glad to see you let loose a little although you look like hell. Cara told me you puked your guts up but what happened to your head?"

"Thanks, Drew. There will be no more parties or late nights for me. I can't handle this shit. I'm also about to get my ass handed to me from my coach so if I'm not home by dinner, send a search party. As for my head, the hell if I know." Drew busts up laughing at me, but Cara smacks him and warns him not to tease me.

"Don't sweat it, Sophie. We've all had a night or two like that," Drew admits.

"Ugh. I'd rather not experience another." I press the elevator button, but change my mind when the doors don't open. Instead, I take the stairs two by two. After the second flight I have to stop and rest. Suddenly dizzy, I take a minute to get my bearings before continuing back up the flights. Maybe this wasn't the best idea.

I grab my shower caddy and rush to wash the remnants of last night from my body. I can't show up to practice sporting this horrendous street walker makeover. Tilting my head back to wash my hair proves more of a challenge than it should. Gripping the wall so I don't fall over, I do the best I can. It's too painful for even the spray of water to hit my forehead. For once, I'm relieved when my shower is finished, not wanting to linger a second longer than necessary.

Although refreshed, I still look like hell. Grabbing the last granola bar in the box, it'll have to suffice as breakfast. I also chug a Gatorade knowing I'm dehydrated from the combination of alcohol and getting sick.

Just as I'm about to leave, I remember the mark on my neck and hurry to find my foundation. Dotting a few dabs over the mark, I do my best to cover the hideous hickey. As long as the make-up doesn't sweat off me before the end of practice, it should cover the evidence of my out of control behavior. Part of me wishes it was from Kipton so its existence wouldn't be so shameful because the thought of Caleb sucking on my neck taints any thoughts of possible pleasure.

CHAPTER *six*

Sophie

BY THE TIME I GET to the gym, I'm huffing and puffing. My hair, still wet from the shower, is painfully pulled into a ponytail on the top of my head while I fling my bag onto an empty bench inside the locker room. I don't bother wasting the time it would take to stash it safely inside a locker. My body begs me to slow down, but I can't.

Shedding my warm ups, I pile them in a heap on top of the bag before rushing through another set of gym doors. Arriving to practice late and without an excuse is the equivalent of asking to be put on probation. Jeopardizing my spot on the team for a night out is not who I am, at all—ever. Allowing Kipton's pleading coupled with his spectacular muscles to throw me off my game was immature. In fact, my one night of fun wasn't everything it was cracked up to be. My conscious has a tight hold on my behavior for a reason. I need to start listening to it again.

"Nice of you to join us this morning, Sophie. In my office, now," Coach yells from the other side of the gym.

If he cuts me from the team, I'll lose everything. My hands shake as I nervously sit down on the small, white chair in his office. Running through my mind are ten excuses about why I was late, but none of them seem believable considering the lump on my head. *Think, Sophie.* I can't lose my scholarship.

Coach walks in the room and starts his speech before he

even makes it to his desk chair. "So, tell me, Sophie, what was more important than showing up on time this morning? For someone new to the team, you're not making a great first impression. Your teammates have to trust you as much as I do to get the job done. Right now, they're not convinced you should even be in the gym let alone the line-up."

"I can explain, Coach. Last night, I went out to dinner with my roommate and we were in an accident. I had a bad headache so I had trouble falling asleep. I slept right through my alarm this morning by mistake." It's not a total lie. I did go out with Cara, and I did have an accident. It may not have happened in a car, but I still hit something.

I'm an awful person. I hate liars. My dad used to lie to my mom about every single thing he did. She caught him in his own lies more times than I can even count.

"You do have a significant bruise on your head. Did you see a doctor last night?"

"Um. No. It didn't start to bruise right away and I can't afford the cost of the ER. All of my family physicians are back home."

"I wish you would have gone anyway, Sophie. I can't let you practice until you're cleared by a doctor. Since you don't have one of your own, you can see the team physician when you finish up here. I can't let you practice until a head injury is ruled out. You could do more damage if you fall."

"Thank you for understanding, Coach. I'll see the doctor right away. I'm anxious to get back into the gym and work-out. I've been sticking to my amped up conditioning program as you asked." He doesn't need to know I haven't eaten a decent meal in over twenty-four hours all while getting drunk and injured in the process.

"I'm glad to hear that, Sophie. Let me know what the doctor says. Hopefully it's nothing too serious; you can't afford to miss any gym time."

"I will, Coach, thank you. I'll be back to practice as soon as I can."

"Hold onto this." He reaches out his arm and hands me a business card with his information printed on it. "Everyone on the team has one. I know I'm your Coach, but I'm also here as a mentor. You can reach me anytime. Okay?"

Out of the corner of his eye, he inspects my head again. Part of me knows I didn't completely sell him on my excuse. Regardless, I accept the offered card and thank my lucky stars he's letting me off the hook. Maybe my injury is punishment enough for him. "Sure. Thank you, Coach."

I leave his office before he has a chance to change his mind about probation. If any of my teammates were at the party last night, I'll get kicked off the team for lying *and* drinking. I didn't cross paths with any of them, but considering I don't remember a large portion of the night, I can't be sure one way or the other. I have to get my shit together, and fast. My life's complicated enough without all this added bullshit.

THE DOCTOR'S EXPECTING ME WHEN I arrive to his office. I fidget in the waiting room chair praying he buys my line of bullshit about the accident. My palms are sweating from going over the story in my head enough times to keep my facts straight which is tough at the moment. My thoughts keep getting jumbled together in a mix of fiction and reality.

"Sophie. Come on back."

I stand up to follow him, but get a little dizzy. He's watching me intently so I play it off as best I can.

"How long has that been happening?" His brow is furrowed and he looks to be studying my every move. The tap, tap, tap of his pen on my file folder is enough to make it hard to concentrate on his words.

"My bruise?" I question.

"No. The dizziness. You lost your balance when you stood up." He's already writing things down on my chart. That can't be good.

"Oh. Since this morning. I hit my head last night, but I'm fine." I refuse to tell him how much pain I'm in. There's only one place I need to be and it's at practice.

"I'll be the judge of that." Inside exam room number one, he shines a light in my eyes, measures my pupils along with my reflexes all before firing off a few mental exercises. I stumble over my numbers when I'm asked to count backwards from twenty, but I blame it on my nerves. I'm then asked about our presidents and a slew of other random trivia. Other than drawing a blank on the former presidents, I breeze through the questions—or so I think. The physical tests do me in completely. I can't walk in a straight line let alone backwards. My balance is shot to shit no matter how hard I try to concentrate on my movements.

"Sophie, I'll be frank with you. You need to go have a scan. I can't clear you until you have it. Your dizziness and hesitation with the mental exercises has me concerned. I'm ninety percent positive you've received a concussion from your injury. No matter how large or small, it's still the same process for recovery. I'll go over the scan results when I receive them, but for now, I'm pulling you from practice until further notice."

"But I'm okay. Honestly, I'm fine." I protest.

"Have you had a concussion in the past?"

"Yes."

"All the more reason to be extra cautious. Gymnastics is a risky sport as it is, Sophie. I'm not willing to allow permanent damage to your body and you shouldn't either. You'll get back to the gym faster if you listen to what I'm saying and follow my instructions."

"Can I at least do cardio?"

"Walking is fine, everything else can wait. Your body needs to heal. You can't run while you're dizzy, Sophie."

I hang my head knowing that walking won't help me with conditioning at all. I hop off the examination table and accept the order form for the test. While all of this seems ridiculous, I'm wise enough to know it's necessary. Whether I like it or not, I messed up and have to play by their rules now.

"Believe it or not, I do understand your frustrations, but we have to be smart about this. With your prior concussion history, it takes less and less each time to produce a more severe result. Come back and see me in a week, Sophie. It's not up for debate. We'll reevaluate your condition and see what we can add to your workout regimen. If you have any trouble in class, please tell your professors to give me a call. I'll confirm your condition."

"Okay," I whisper, knowing I don't want to accept the words he's telling me. "Can I go now?"

"Yes, take this card. This is where you need to go for your test this evening. It's also on the top of the order form. Please have someone take you. No driving until next week either."

"Okay. I'll find a ride."

Lost in a daze of stupidity and anger, I leave the doctor's office. I spend the entire walk back to my room going over every reason why I deserve to fail. Moving to Alabama has made me doubt ever leaving home. I've made more poor choices in four days than I have since I was a rebellious toddler.

Replaying over and over in my mind, I hear my mom warning me not to let her down. Having been a gymnast herself, she knows how big of an accomplishment it is to be on this team. In fact, she talked about it from the moment the letter of interest arrived until the moment I walked out the door on moving day. It's obvious she's trying to live out her dream through me. Maybe that should bother me, but it doesn't. Because in my crazy mind, it means she sees I'm worth something—that I have value.

Completely defeated, I sigh when I open the door to my room and find Cara curling her hair, as usual. Evening classes begin tonight, with the rest starting in the morning. I remember she has a class, but I can't remember which one. *Damn concussion.* "You have class tonight, right?"

"Yeah, an art elective. This should be interesting. I can't even draw stick people, but how bad can pottery be, right? They made it look sexy and fun in the movie *Ghost*. Plus Drew's in the class. So I'm looking forward to it."

"Maybe they'll let you act out the scene for extra credit if your pottery sucks."

"Girl, I wish!"

I sit down at my desk and fire up my computer. I have to figure out how far and in which direction the imaging center is so I can get on the right bus. My tired brain doesn't want to handle all the logistics, but I don't have a choice. I jot the directions down on a notepad, certain I'll never be able to recall each and every turn if I don't.

Cara sprays her hair and gags a little before walking over to my bed. She sits down and faces me at my desk. "So what happened? No practice?"

"Nope. Off for the week thanks to my *Girls Gone Wild* audition last night. Apparently I have a concussion and he's sending me for a scan tonight. I was hoping you could take me, but I'll figure something else out. I can't drive on top of all the other shitty news."

"Ohmigod! Sit down, put your feet up. I'll get whatever you need."

"Cara, I'm fine." I laugh at her dramatics.

"I'll call Kippy, he can take you." She takes her cell phone off the charger and starts pushing buttons. I spring up from my bed and yank the phone out of her hands. "No!" Grabbing my head in pain, I sit back down until the pressure in my skull subsides.

"Sophie! You're scaring me."

"I got up too fast, I'm okay. Please, I'll take the bus. Don't bother your brother." My head is killing me. I need darkness and a nap.

"You aren't taking the damn bus, Sophie. Kippy won't mind at all. He's here for us, you heard him the other day. He said so."

How do I tell her I don't want to see her brother because I'm insanely attracted to him and he causes me to make poor life decisions that leave me wallowing in a pool of regret? "Cara, I'll take the bus. Please drop it. It was bad enough he had to haul my hungover ass home this morning."

"Fine, but I *don't* agree with your choice. I'll be back in a little bit. I want to see what time Drew plans on leaving for class tonight." With her freshly curled ponytail bouncing behind her, she swiftly leaves our room with her southern attitude in full effect.

Already worn out from the day, I lie down on my bed, instantly comparing the thread count of my sheets to Kipton's luxurious bed. I close my eyes and picture him shirtless, sprawled out with his head on his pillow and the thin sheet draped over his lower half. Only this time, it's not covering him entirely, allowing me to see every solid inch of his manhood. I shiver from the thought.

My mind begins to take things a step farther, as I mentally reach out and scrape my fingernails down the ridges of his abdominal muscles. I take my time inspecting every inch of his skin, placing soft kisses along the way. I dip my tongue in each valley before going up and over each toned group of muscles. Over and over, I continue until I reach the end of his glorious six pack abs right above the real prize.

I pull my blanket up to my chin and start to inch my hand lower to the throbbing between my legs. Pretending my hand is his, I hesitantly touch myself. At first it feels wrong; almost shameful. But the faster I go, the better it feels. Easily working myself into a frenzy with a few quick strokes, I'm close to falling over the edge to the vision of Kipton touching me while kissing me passionately. His lips are all over me, his tongue working magic between my thighs. A few more seconds and my entire body explodes. I moan his name and ride out each and every wave of pleasure. Before I have a chance to catch my breath, my cell phone vibrates next to my head. I grab it, still slightly panting from lust overload. Tapping the talk button, I slowly open my eyes and see it's Kipton on the other end. Panicking, I want to hang up, but can't now that I've answered.

"Hello?"

"Hey."

I suck in a deep breath, his voice igniting my pulse a second time. I focus on calming each inhale and exhale, forcing away my blissful paradise.

"Sophie? What are you doing?"

"I was resting."

"Then why do you sound out of breath?"

"Do I? I'm not. I was laying here taking it easy like the doctor recommended." *I was picturing you naked and you gave me the best orgasm of my life.*

"Is Cara there?"

"No. Cara went to Drew's room. I only got back about twenty minutes ago."

"So, you're all alone?"

"Yeah, I am." Why is he asking so many questions?

"Sophie, what were you really doing? Nobody gets that out of breath from sleeping unless they've woken up from a nightmare."

"Kipton. I'm fine. Everything is fine. What do you need?"

"I need you to tell me the truth."

He's not going to let this go. There's no way in hell I'm admitting I came to the vision of him touching me. And inflating his ego will only potentially add to my troubles. I'll stay silent until he's forced to hang up on me.

"Sophie?" He taps the receiver and pushes a few buttons. Both are too loud for my aching head to stand. I pull the phone away from my ear and curse, "Damn it, Kipton."

"Then just answer me."

I continue to ignore him.

"Okay. If this is how you want to play it, then you can listen. Maybe I'm way off base here, but I don't think I am. Maybe you did lie down with the intention of resting, but the second your pretty little head hit the pillow, you were reminded of being in my bed. When you couldn't get your mind to focus on anything else, you started picturing all the sexy ways I could please you with my body. From there, you started touching yourself and from the sounds of it . . . I just missed the best part. Am I right, Sophie? Were we both naked too?"

Holy shit! How did he do that? Was I that obvious? He's shocked me right out of my silent treatment. "What! No. I was resting. Why don't you believe me?"

"Tell me the truth. Who were you imagining when you touched yourself?" I can picture his sexy grin as he's saying these words and it turns me on even more.

"This conversation is *not* happening. I'm going back to my nap. I'm hanging up now, Kipton."

"Wait! Say yes or no and I'll drop it." *Why does he even care?*

"Yes or no."

"Don't get smart with me, Sophie. Please tell me. I need to hear you say it."

"Jesus. Yes! Okay. YES!" I shout.

"*Fuck.* That's so hot, Sophie. I gotta go. I'll pick you up at four for your appointment." The line goes dead before I have a chance to respond or argue. *Cara.* I'm going to kill Cara. I roll over and bury my face in my pillow. I'd scream but my head is hurting too bad. Everything was fine with my life before I came to this damn school. Now I'm daydreaming about a guy who throws my entire world off its axis simply by looking at me. He's never even touched me intimately and I can't stop wondering about all the earth-shattering ways he could make me lose control. And what is it with this bed! First the pillow, now this.

I close my eyes again, annoyed with both Kipton and Cara. My mind is still reeling from being caught, but I'm woman enough to admit I needed some relief. Kipton and I haven't spent much time together, but it's obvious my body wants him.

I'm only laying down for a few seconds when the phone rings again. "Seriously?" I grumble. So much for getting any rest.

"Aren't you done harassing me yet?" I jokingly say into the receiver.

"Sophie?"

Shit. It's not Kipton. "Yes. This is Sophie. I'm sorry I thought you were someone else."

Laughing, he continues, "That's okay. This is Coach Evans. I was just calling to see how your visit with the doctor went."

"Hi. Um. It went as well as can be expected, I guess. He pulled me from practice and I have to have a scan done later this evening. I'm really sorry I have to miss some time. I'd rather be in the gym."

"It's okay. Just do what they tell you to do so you can get back to your training. And let me know about your test results. I'm sure the doctor will send me reports, but I'd like to hear from you too."

"Sure. I'll let you know. Thank you for calling."

"No problem, Sophie. Get some rest."

"I will. Goodbye."

Maybe Coach isn't as bad as I thought.

Now all I have to figure out is why Kipton wants me to leave so early for my appointment. Then, I can relax. Or at least try to.

CHAPTER *seven*

KIPTON

I WAS COMPLETELY THROWN FOR a loop the moment Sophie picked up the phone. Her surprise when she heard my voice combined with her sexy breathing clued me in. She was definitely up to something—and I hoped it was entirely sexual. Of course it could have been almost anything, but I'm a guy—and my mind defaults to sex with little effort.

At first I was afraid to pry for details in case I was wrong, but I thought it would be fun to mess with her. Considering I was right with my assumption, I'm glad I asked. I only wish I could have watched her fall apart in person.

I have a few hours before I have to pick her up, purposely leaving enough time for the two of us to stop and get some dinner. I'm not thrilled with leaving her all alone until then, but I didn't want to push her too far out of her comfort zone. I wish she would have reached out to me on her own for a ride, but thankfully Cara called me before Sophie put her ass on a damn bus instead. I told her and Cara to call me if they ever needed anything. Apparently, I need to refresh Sophie's memory.

I yawn for the millionth time today. My eyes burn and I know I should take a power nap. Having trouble dozing off last night, I finally had better luck once I stopped staring at Sophie. Waking up to her beautiful blue eyes locked on my naked chest had me instantly aroused. I'd wanted nothing more than to grab her tiny waist and show her exactly what she does to me, but I have to be patient. After today, I want her to see me as a person she can trust and depend on—one that cares about her as more than just a friend. Who knows, we could be as compatible as oil and water, but I won't be satisfied until I taste her lips and find out for myself.

I unlock the screen of my phone to find an incoming text from Sophie. My finger hovers over her name, but I hesitate. If she even tries to cancel, I'll haul ass over to her dorm and show her how serious I am about taking her to her appointment. Cara warned me she can be stubborn. But so can I.

Sophie: You know my appointment isn't until six, right? You don't have to pick me up until 5:30.

Kipton: We're going to dinner first.

Sophie: Why?

Kipton: Because we need to eat. And I want to discuss a few things.

Sophie: What if I'm not hungry and don't want to talk?

Kipton: Then you can sit and listen.

Sophie: Am I in trouble?

Kipton: Not yet.

Sophie: You're being weird.

Kipton: Do you like weird?

Sophie: Not that I know of.

> *Kipton: Then what do you want me to be?*

> *Sophie: Asleep.*

> *Kipton: Why?*

> *Sophie: Because every time we talk or see each other I do something stupid.*

Laughing, I type out a teasing response but delete it before sending. I shouldn't make fun of her when she's already feeling vulnerable. She *has* been caught in some interesting situations though. It's crystal clear how much I affect her and hell if it doesn't turn me on. Instantly I'm hard again from the thought of her sweet voice coming undone in her bed, writhing back and forth from the thought of my touch. The next time she loses control, I want to be responsible for it—in person. Deciding to keep things bland and basic so we can get through her appointment tonight, I type out a standard response, making sure she complies.

> *Kipton: See you at 4.*

> *Sophie: Okay.*

That was almost too easy, but I'm glad she didn't fight me on it.

Although I'd rather catch up on some sleep, I need to shower so I have time to talk to Cara about the interest she seems to have taken in her resident advisor. The last thing I want is for her to get kicked out of the dorm for crossing some stupid rule in the code of conduct. My sister doesn't always have the best judgment when it comes to guys.

As soon as I step under the warm spray of water, I tilt my head back and let it cascade over my face. With my lack of sleep combined with my pent up sexual energy, there's no way I can leave this house before I take the edge off. Otherwise, I can't be held responsible when Sophie ends up in my bed instead of at her appointment.

It's shitty of me to revert to the mental picture of her wasted and dancing practically topless at the party, but it's too perfect not to get me off in a matter of minutes. My orgasm rips through me so powerfully; I have to steady myself against the shower wall. If it's this good just thinking about Sophie, I can't even imagine what it'll be like buried inside of her. When I realize I'm game for round two, I turn the dial all the way to the right, allowing the subarctic temperature of the water to wash over me, hopefully sending my insatiable desire down the drain. I can't walk around with my jeans strangling my dick all night.

WITH METALLICA BLARING FROM THE speakers of my car, I tap my thumbs against the steering wheel and bob my head to each drum beat. I pull up to Sophie's dorm and instinctively glance at her room window. I don't know what I'm expecting to see, but the curtains are drawn as they should be.

Once inside, I sign in at the front desk and wait for permission to go upstairs.

"Room 301?" The guy manning the desk questions as he checks my name on the list.

"Yeah. My sister lives there."

"I'm their RA."

I eye him tentatively and although he looks nice enough, I need to get to know him before I make any decisions one way or the other. "So you're Drew."

He smiles. "I take it Cara mentioned me then?"

"You could say that."

He laughs and looks very okay with being the topic of our conversation. "You two have plans?"

"No. She has class."

He nods his head knowingly. "Ahhh. The roommate."

Hell yes, it's the roommate. Has he not noticed? On second thought, he better never notice. "Dude, it's not like that. Sophie needs a ride and Cara offered my services."

"She looked like hell this morning when she strolled in here. Cara mentioned something about a concussion. Sucks."

"That it does. I better get up there. I'll see you around." I start to walk away, but my brotherly instinct kicks in full force. I turn around and clear my throat which makes him look up from his paperwork. When I have his full attention, I continue, "By the way, if you hurt my sister I'll kill you myself."

He nods his head and smiles. "Noted."

"Have fun tonight," I yell over my shoulder before the elevator doors close behind me. Despite my warning, I'm actually glad Cara has a thing for him and not some other douchebag. At least Drew has his priorities straight and seems responsible. He's making my job easier and he doesn't even know it.

Knocking on the girls' door, I wait for one of them to answer. I purposely came a few minutes early so I'd have to come up and get Sophie. Nobody answers, but I can hear music playing. Twisting the door knob, I slowly peek inside in case one of them is standing close to the door. I snicker when I spot Sophie singing into her brush as she fixes her hair. She's never going to win a Grammy, but it's incredibly amusing.

"Ahem." Quickly shutting the door, I look over my shoulder and see Cara standing with her arms crossed. *Oh here we go.*

"It's creepy to find my brother peeping into my bedroom! What are you doing Kipton?"

"Oh, calm down. Nobody answered when I knocked. I was entering slowly so I didn't scare anyone."

"And it's not scary to find you with one eyeball pressed into the crack of the door? If anyone saw you, I'll just die."

Maybe she has a point. "I'm sorry, Cara."

"If she's even naked or half-dressed I'll get you kicked out of here. I know people, Kipton! She may be the current object of your lust, but she's my roommate and I really like her. So back off!"

I salute her authority which only pisses her off more. She punches me fairly hard for a chick, but not with enough force to make me flinch. Backing away from her door, I let her go inside ahead of me. Sophie jumps as soon as the door fully opens, realizing we may have heard her rocking out. When she sees me smirking, her cheeks flush. I wink at her, making her blush even more. Something tells me we're both thinking about her pleasuring herself right now. If Cara wasn't here, I might even take a chance and kiss her. *Shit, I'd love to kiss her right now.* But I can't.

She tosses a few things in a purse large enough to carry a few groceries before resting the straps on her shoulder.

Jingling my keys back and forth between my hands, I give her all the time she needs to finish up. "You ready, Sophie?"

"Yeah, pretty sure I have everything." There's still plenty of room inside her giant bag, so she very well may find more shit to stuff in it. Instead, she walks over to the door. Expecting me to leave, I wait until she's standing next to me before I open it. Nudging her playfully, she smiles back at me. "What?" she asks.

"You look extra short today."

"Kipton, really? Don't pick on her," Cara adds as usual. Her and her damn rules.

"I'm used to it, Cara. I hear it all the time back home. I'm aware I'm vertically challenged."

Although she was full of life a minute ago, she suddenly looks tired. I also don't miss the dark circles under her eyes. At least she covered up the hickey. Not that I'd mind if people assumed I put it there, although one on her inner thigh would be so much more fun.

"Hey, it's okay. I'm not offended," Sophie says while nudging me as she brushes past me.

I'm left staring at her perky ass. Cara gets in my face, whispering as quietly as she can while still telling me off. "Kipton, I swear if you fuck up my living arrangements, I will kick your ass! Stop it, now. Off limits, remember? And stop checking out her ass!"

I put my hands on her shoulders, forcing her off her tippy toes and out of my face. "Down, girl. I can't make any promises. Gotta run, sis."

I hear her growl in frustration as I jog down the hallway

to catch up with Sophie. "She's extra feisty today." Sophie smiles up at me and I swear it's the most gorgeous smile I've ever been given. If she keeps that shit up I definitely won't be able to hold back much longer.

"You do look nice; I was just joking about being short."

She glances up at me, but only gives me a quick one word response. "Thanks."

We walk side by side, relatively quiet the entire way to my car. She's nervous as usual, but there's definitely something else on her mind tonight. Right now she seems indifferent to everything. Then again she has a head injury so her mind's probably reeling. I open her door for her, watching her slide into the passenger seat. Sophie grabs for her seatbelt right away while I close her door.

I follow suit and when I turn the key in the ignition, my radio is shouting out lyrics on full blast. Quickly grabbing the dial, I lower the volume. "Sorry about that."

"Not a problem." She doesn't even look at me, instead choosing to stare out the window on her side of the car. Checking my rear view mirror, I back out of my parking spot. It's a short fifteen minute drive to her appointment, so I choose to take her to the famous fifties diner located in the plaza across the street from the imaging center. This way, we can sit and talk for as long as possible before the test. I'm also dying for a patty melt.

The car shuts off, but she doesn't move. I tap her shoulder to get her attention. "We're here. You okay?"

She nods her head. "I'm good."

"Where'd you go? You were spaced out."

She unbuckles her seatbelt and opens her door. "Nowhere. I'm good," she says as she climbs out of the car. Of course I stare at her ass again like a dick and then get out of the car myself.

Once inside, I look over the menu deciding quickly on my usual melt and fries. Sophie's sitting across from me in the booth scanning the menu. "Whatcha getting?"

"I'm not overly hungry. Probably a garden salad and some water." She closes her menu and lays it on top of mine. *What?*

"There's no way you can come here and get lettuce, Sophie. This place is famous for milkshakes and burgers."

"Coach would kill me if I ate all that. It's bad enough I can't practice or exercise, I'll never get in shape at the rate I'm going. He's going to cut me, I know it."

So *that's* what's been on her mind. It all makes more sense now. Remembering back to her drunken confession about being too ugly, I suddenly want to have words with her coach. How the hell can he tell someone the size of Sophie she's out of shape? She wouldn't have been given a scholarship if she wasn't talented. But I know what it's like to be your own worst critic. I have to word what I say to her perfectly, or she'll believe what her coach told her. Before I can get a word out, the waitress stops at our table. "What can I get you two?" she asks.

I respond before Sophie has a chance to open her mouth. "We'll take two patty melts, a large fry, and two chocolate shakes."

"Coming right up." Tammy, as her nametag tells me, scoops up the menus and sashays across the checkerboard floor with her order pad and pen.

When I chance a glance at Sophie, she looks stunned. "What?" I question.

"Kipton, I said I need a salad. Why would you do that?"

"You said you need it, but what do you *want*, Sophie?"

She's shaking her head back and forth, visibly pissed off with my selection. "It's not a matter of what I *want*, Kipton. Nothing ever is. I wanted to live a little last night and look what that got me—a concussion with an entire team and coach who don't want me in the gym anymore. I've never screwed up more in my life than I have this week, so stop trying to tell me what I want. All you've done so far is cause trouble with your damn winks and sexy smiles. So stop fucking with me!"

I grin, loving when she gets all fired up. "You think my smile's sexy?" I tap her foot under the table with my boot which only makes her glare daggers at me.

"Out of everything I said that's the only thing you choose to comment on? Seriously?"

"No. I heard it all, but since it's all bullshit, I responded to the only truth you told."

"It's all a fact, Kipton. I've never told a lie until yesterday when I made up an excuse about being in a car accident. My coach told me to get in shape, not eat cheeseburgers and get drunk."

"So you *do* admit I'm sexy then."

She throws her hands in the air, exasperated by the conversation. "Oh for fuck's sake! You know you're hot as hell so stop trying to make me say it."

"I'm glad we had this talk, Sophie."

She rests her head against the back of the red pleather booth and closes her eyes the same time the waitress places our plates in front of us. Sophie opens her eyes and stares at her burger. Not waiting for mine to get cold, I dig in and take a bite. Moaning, the taste of the warm melted cheese mixed with the beef assaults my taste buds in the most spectacular way. I make each bite as dramatic as possible until she decides to give in to my food-gasm. She watches me the entire time I'm chewing. Once I swallow, she picks up her own burger and sinks her teeth into the warm bread.

"So much better than a salad, right?"

"It's good, but I still hate you."

Laughing, I pop a fry in my mouth. "I'll take whatever you give me, Sophie. It takes way more energy to hate than love, so you must really want me." I wiggle my eyebrows up and down and see her trying to hold in her laughter. Failing miserably, she starts eating *and* laughing. It's the most amazing combination. I never want her to believe she's anything less than beautiful.

CHAPTER eight

Sophie

PUSHING MY PLATE AWAY FROM my overly indulgent hands, I realize the mistake I've made. My stomach's bloated and the only thought I can focus on is the grease currently sticking to my ribs. If I were to step onto a scale right this minute, I'm positive the number flashing before my eyes would be one I'm not willing to accept.

"You finished?" Kipton asks from his side of the booth. He's polished off his entire meal without an ounce of guilt or hesitation, even licking his fingers as the last bite of burger passes through his lips.

"Yeah, I couldn't eat another bite. It was delicious." A mistake, but delicious.

"Nothing beats Momma June's recipes that's for damn sure." He sits back and rubs his satisfied stomach.

"Does she own this place?"

"She does. I've been coming here since I was little. She would spoil the shit out of me, sneaking me extra fries or giving me free milkshakes before my mom could say no."

"That's cute."

He stares at the aged white Formica covering the table top, twisting his discarded straw paper around his middle finger. "One of my better memories."

Part of me wants him to elaborate, but when I can't focus

on anything other than the damaging meal I've consumed, I excuse myself to the restroom. Hoping it's bigger than the size of this diner, I'm thankful to see a private handicap stall with a separate entrance. Shutting myself inside the small room, I lean up against the wood door, sweat beading on my forehead from the anticipation of what I'm considering.

It's been months since I've had the urge to purge. Back when my dad would stroll home drunk in the middle of the night shouting at my mom, I would hide inside my closet with my trashcan. Mentally begging my mom to back down before she regretted it, I would work myself up to the point of making myself sick. When it wouldn't happen naturally, I resorted to forcing my body to heave. After the shouting finally stopped, I was left hollower than the time before. But for whatever reason, I was relieved. No more cursing from my father about what a pathetic wife my mom was, no more anger from my mom about what a disappointment my dad was, and no more reminders of the mistake I had always been. All that was left was a shell of a body to be put back to bed—and that was the easy part.

My ritualistic behavior continued until my mom served my dad with the divorce papers. I remember crying because he was moving out. Not because I'd miss him, but because I wasn't sure I could make it through a day without getting sick. Whether I used him as an excuse or he really did set me off, throwing up relaxed me. It made my body have a purpose because they never knew how powerful their words were—how much they tore me up inside. And no matter how many apologies my mom tossed at me, it was never enough. A girl can only be told so many times she's a burden and a mistake before she begins to believe it herself.

But the day dad left for good, I turned a corner I never saw coming. With little effort, I started sleeping peacefully—the years of exhaustion finally catching up with me. Gone were the nights I spent huddled in my tiny closet singing songs to drown out the shouting. In some strange shifting of the universe, the divorce saved me from myself as much as it gave me and my mom our lives back.

But as I shuffle slightly closer to the toilet, I'm reminded of the comfort that comes from a purge. I should reach out to my therapist, but since I've yet to set up an appointment with anyone here at school, I'm on my own. Waging a self-inflict-ed battle with my brain, my hands begin to shake. I pause to clasp them together while staring into the mirror at the dis-gusting vision of my own reflection. Knowing my willpower failed me again tonight, I'm pissed at myself for repeatedly allowing Kipton to put another barrier between me and my dreams. He isn't aware of the years of therapy I've endured to cure whatever screw I have loose in my head. Those are my dad's words, not mine. Little does my dad know he's the one who spent a lifetime cranking it tighter and tighter until I spiraled out of control. I can't let Kipton weave his way in just as my dad did with my mom. She used to have dreams too before he fucked them up.

But I'm not stupid enough to believe this is all about a cheeseburger. It's about control—the control I've worked so hard to maintain inside the gym and the control I've craved at home. Slowly, it's being ripped away from me. Inch by inch, minute by minute, I'm edging closer to the ledge. A ledge I've toppled over enough times to know I'm not strong enough to come out unscathed.

I inhale and exhale repeatedly, trying to convince myself to go back to Kipton. When I know the desire is too strong to back down from it, I refuse to waste another precious second. This is to prove I'm in control—that nobody will ever dictate my happiness again.

Nervous about forcing myself to throw up, it becomes second nature the moment I jam two fingers down my throat. Nothing happens the first two times, but I don't give up. *I can't.* On the third attempt my insides contract painful-ly, expelling the contents of my stomach into the toilet. Each retching second is replaced with a euphoric numbness. And much like the past, I'm relieved. The purge is every bit as soothing as I remember it to be.

I continue until I'm positive there's nothing left inside me, flushing the toilet in satisfaction. The guilt will eventu-ally slam into me, but not until I savor the moment. When I stand up completely, the pressure inside my head becomes unbearable. Reaching out for support, the cool tiles on the wall hold me upright, steadying my swaying body. Desperately needing to get out of the bathroom, I lean against the wall all the way to the sink. I'm one hundred percent confident I made the right decision despite the incessant throbbing in my temples.

Despite what I did, my years of therapy aren't forgotten. If I were to call my therapist right now and admit what just happened, she would ask one thing and one thing only. *Why?* My response would be simple yet complicated. *Because it erases the wrong.* It's the only answer I've ever been able to give to her question and the only way I can justify making *it* better.

After splashing some cool water on my face and rinsing out my mouth, I slowly come back down from my high. I dig around in my purse for a stick of sugar free gum that instantly makes my mouth water from the cool spearmint flavor. Swallowing painfully, I'm certain my throat will be raw for the rest of the night. It's nothing I can't handle though—I'm back in complete control of my universe.

Maybe a part of the old Sophie came back to life tonight, but I don't fear her—not yet. With my head held high, I return to Kipton. Just like Coach Evans said, temptation is all around me. I'll show him I'm strong enough to resist—that I want to win more than anything else.

Kipton looks concerned when I slide into the booth. "You okay, Sophie? You look pale."

"I'm good. A little tired." I take a few sips of the water left sitting on our table even after our plates have been cleared. I'm thankful the waitress thought to leave them behind. The cool temperature of the water helps to soothe my throat. "How much do I owe?"

"Not a cent. You're my date tonight, darlin'.'"

"Thanks for covering the bill, but you didn't have to. I'm fine with paying."

He ignores my offer entirely, being nothing but the gentleman I've known him to be. "I wanted to."

"Okay." I'm too worn out to argue as much as I'd like to pay my own way. I slide my weakened body out of the booth and Kipton follows closely behind me. His fingers graze the small of my back. The gesture, although foreign to me, appears slightly possessive. When I glance over my shoulder, Kipton offers me one of his signature winks. He's aware his touch is affecting me. I only wish I didn't crave it as much as I do. It's wrong to want it, but maybe it doesn't have to be.

"You nervous?"

"Kinda. I don't like anything related to the doctor." Because they make me tell the truth, but I don't share that information with him.

"You'll be fine. It'll be over before you know it and then we can get back to our date." He rests his arm around my shoulder and looks confident about his plans. I'm fine with it as long as he keeps me out of trouble. Or maybe I'm just too weak around him to decipher anything threatening.

THE YOUNG RECEPTIONIST BLUSHES WHEN I step up to the counter. She's glancing between the paperwork and Kipton while rattling off which ones to sign and what she needs from me. He gives her a smile and leans further inside the open window. She looks thrilled he's inching closer, maybe even hoping he asks for her number. "Isn't she beautiful?" he whispers.

My pen slips off the signature line and draws a line onto the counter top. I stare at him like he has two heads. "Kipton!"

The receptionist sputters, trying to figure out an appropriate response to his statement. I almost feel bad for her—almost. But considering he does it to me every time I'm around him, I enjoy it instead.

Kipton backs away from the window with a smirk. "It's not my fault my date's smoking hot." He walks away and finds a seat near the TV. Flipping a few channels, he finds ESPN and gets comfortable. *Make yourself at home.*

Before I have a chance to sit down next to him, the technician calls me back to the dressing area. It's a damn good thing they don't take my vital signs because right about now my heart is nearly thumping out of my chest. Kipton continues to surprise me every time he opens his mouth. So much so that the entire time I'm lying on the table, I'm busy trying to put his words into context. Either he's just a natural born flirt, or he speaks the truth. I'm not sure which it is yet, but I'll figure him out sooner or later.

"You can sit up, you're finished."

"Already? That was fast."

Laughing, the technician says I'm free to go. Other than the discomfort of lying down and being as still as possible, the test only lasted a few short minutes. It took me longer to change into and out of the gown. Not that I'm complaining.

Exiting the dressing area, Kipton's sitting in the far corner of the waiting room paging through a magazine. He moved since I left him. Giggling when I realize he's reading a popular gossip magazine, I stand in front of him, but he doesn't even see me he's so engrossed in the article. "So what's the scoop?"

Kipton's head snaps up and he quickly closes the magazine, returning it to the side table. "It's all they had." He's full of shit.

I bend down and pick up a men's fitness magazine off the top of the stack. "Then what's this?"

"I didn't see that." He stands up from his chair with a smile on his face, not the least bit embarrassed about being caught. "How was your test? You all done?"

"It was easy, thankfully. We can go." I turn around towards the exit, but Kipton puts his hand on my shoulder from behind, halting me in my tracks. His body is flush against mine causing my heart rate to increase from his body heat alone. When I sense him inching closer, I'm positive he's about to kiss my neck. Leaning my head back towards his chest to give him better access, I close my eyes as his lips brush against my ear. He's so close, his warm breath on my skin sends goose bumps down my arms. Eager to hear what he wants from me, I anticipate the sexy suggestion. Leaning even closer, he whispers so nobody else in the room can hear, "Your shirt's on backwards."

Mortified, I look down and realize he's right. The brand logo is on my back instead of across my boobs. I slip inside the bathroom in the waiting room to fix it. The simple task of turning around my top has me winded and suddenly exhausted. *This is ridiculous.*

When I open the door, Kipton's leaning against the wall waiting for me. "That's better, beautiful."

My cheeks redden from his endearment, but I'm not embarrassed. Part of me might even like it. While my body's reaction to Kipton continues to confuse me, I can't convince myself to tell him to stop. Between the touching and the sweet words, he's not making it easy to resist his charm.

After tucking me back into the passenger side of his car, he turns the radio on. I flinch from the intensity of the bass. "Can you turn it down a little," I ask. My head is once again throbbing.

"Sure." He reaches for the dial and turns it so low we can barely hear the words. "Are you okay?" he asks again.

I rub my temples hoping for a little relief. "Damn headache."

"I'm sorry. Do you have anything in your purse you can take? I might have something in the glove box."

"I ran out, but I'm sure Cara has something in the room until I can get to the store."

At the next red light, Kipton glances at me and rubs my knee soothingly. His touch has me squeezing my thighs together tightly. "I hate seeing you in pain, Sophie. Especially when it's my fault."

I turn my head to look at him. The old Sophie would have made him feel the regret of his ways regardless of the truth, but I'm not *that* girl anymore despite my moment of weakness tonight. My purge pushed my reset button. It's as close as I can come to getting a do over because this time I'll get it right—I'm solely responsible. "Kipton, none of this is your fault. If anything, you made it better."

Raising an eyebrow he doesn't comprehend what I'm trying to say. "You helped me at your house when I was sick, let me sleep in your bed, bought me dinner, and drove me to my scan. You're taking care of me better than I've taken care of myself." After the admission springs free, I realize the truth of the statement. Maybe I still am my own worst enemy, but I refuse to go down without a fight this time.

"Then you shouldn't be against running inside here with me." He pulls into the drug store parking lot and jogs over to help me out of the car. Surprised that he would care enough to stop for pain medication, I gladly go inside with him. The more time I spend with him, the more I discover how different he is. Sure he's incredibly hot and probably gets any girl he wants, but there's way more to him than an overprotective big brother or an insatiable college guy with his pick of the crop every night of the week. His nurturing side probably doesn't get showcased very often, but I'm glad I'm the one who gets a glimpse.

"Over here." Kipton nods his head in the direction of the headache meds and I follow like a lost little puppy. It only takes a second to scan the shelves before finding my usual. Grabbing the biggest bottle they have, I already revel in the relief that's about to come my way. At least I hope so anyway considering I've never had a headache this intense before. "Need anything else?"

"No, I'm good." We take our place in the checkout line behind several other customers. Why they only have one person working is beyond me. This is the only store close enough to campus for students to walk to. I worry about holding Kipton up, but he waits patiently beside me before wandering off to check out a sale display.

"Look what they have!" He holds up Honeybuns and beams with excitement.

"You can't possibly still be hungry?"

He shakes his head like I'm in trouble for questioning him. "Have you ever tried one of these? All the sugary goodness mixed with the honey—it's a taste bud explosion. I can already taste it on my tongue."

"No, I haven't." I'm almost embarrassed at how his description is turning me on. Unable to wait a second longer, he rips open the packaging with his teeth. "Kipton, you didn't pay for it yet!"

"So what?" He mumbles around a mouthful.

"You can't eat the merchandise and then leave."

"Does this make you nervous, Sophie. What if I opened another one and took a bite?" He reaches over and pulls another package off the display. Challenging me with his eyes.

"Kipton! Put it back." Instead, he opens the cellophane, moaning while indulging in another sugary pastry right in the middle of the store. "You're acting like a child, you know." I glance over my shoulder expecting to see several annoyed customers. They're all staring at him as I suspected, only they don't look annoyed. Instead their eyes are dancing with amusement waiting to see what he'll do next.

"I like making you squirm," he admits while he continues to chow down his dessert. My eyes widen and he laughs at my response, not even realizing the sexual innuendo until after he said it. "Sophie, if it's this easy with food, imagine what I'd do with my mouth."

I gasp, shocked he said that out loud, let alone in front of other people. None of them seem to care, yet I find myself inching closer to the register, praying the line starts moving. When I reach to take my wallet out of my purse, I realize I left it in the car. Without money to pay, I have to step out of line and do this all over again.

Kipton quickly swallows and coughs, "Hey, where ya going? I'm sorry. I shouldn't have said that."

"No, it was fine. I mean it was out there, but amusing. I guess. If you're into that and all." Flubbing my words, I talk in circles. Why don't I go ahead and announce he can have his wicked way with me while I'm at it? "Can I have your keys, I forgot my purse."

"I've got it covered. No worries."

I sigh, "Kipton."

He taps the top of my nose with his finger. "Sophie."

"Thank you." I lower my gaze to the carpet feeling foolish and in entirely too much pain—constantly.

"Hey." Kipton nudges me with his elbow to get my attention. I don't look up so he nudges me again. "Sophie, look at me."

I respond to his request, but suddenly I'm overcome with emotion. "Kipton." I pause, unsure of how to put my thoughts into words. Right now forming a sentence seems too intense for my battered brain to handle. I pinch the bridge of my nose concentrating on releasing some tension. I'm smart enough to know I made my headache ten times worse when I threw up at the diner.

"Your head?" he questions.

"Yeah. It's killing me." I keep my response vague on purpose. Although I trust him after everything he's done for me, I'm not sure I'll ever trust him with my deepest, darkest secrets. Some things are better left unsaid.

He wraps his arm around my shoulder. "It takes time. You'll be your normal self again soon. I promise." Nodding my head, the only thing I can do is take his word for it. Because I sure as hell don't feel normal right now.

"Here, open up. Honeybuns cure everything." I move to the side, trying to get away from him, but he assumes I'm being playful. "Come on, take a bite, I can't eat both."

"You should have thought about that before you opened them!"

He reaches for my side, tickling me. I appreciate his attempt to make me feel better. Just as I laugh, he tries to stuff the bun in my mouth. I dodge his arm at just the right moment, successfully avoiding him. "Kipton, that wasn't nice. Some icing went up my nose."

He picks up a travel size pack of tissues, also on display at the check-out area, and hands one to me. "Will you stop opening everything!"

Laughing, he tosses our purchases on the counter. He has the clerk scan both of his pastries along with my medicine and now some tissues. I grab the receipt off the counter to see how much I owe him, but he snatches it out of my hand before I get a good look.

My purse is lying on the passenger seat when we get back to his car. I tuck the drug store bag inside and settle into my seat. Thankfully, Kipton doesn't bother turning on the radio this time, instead choosing to drive peacefully back to the dorm. While the silence is welcome, it also plays tricks on my tired mind. Only intending to close my eyes for a brief second, the motion of the car lulls me to sleep.

"Sophie." A warm finger trails back and forth down my cheek, trying to bring me back to the land of the living. Instead I fall into unpleasant memories.

"You want to make me happy right, Sophie?"

I inch closer to his warm embrace. "Of course I do, you're my whole world."

"Then what's stopping you, baby?" He lazily runs his fingertips up and down my arms. While it feels good, I'm scared. Scared that once I say yes, I'll never be able to take it back. I don't have much in this world that's completely mine other than my body. But I won't lose him either — I can't. He's all I have.

"I'm nervous."

Blaine pulls me even closer; his warm breath tickles my ear. "Let me show you how good it feels."

The words are on the tip of my tongue, but I can't quite get them out. He needs me and although I need him too, it doesn't feel right. But I can't expect him to wait around forever, especially if he can get it somewhere else. My dad is proof of that theory. If I don't give Blaine what he wants, I'll lose him. "Blaine."

"Yeah, Baby. Tell me you want me too." His kisses inch down my neck and move across my collarbone. The sensation sets me on fire, yet I can't let go of my nervousness enough to really enjoy it.

"Blaine, I do want you. You know that."

"But?" he questions.

"Will you teach me? I don't know how to make you feel good."

He smiles and suddenly my decision might not be the wrong one. Finally looking pleased with me, he brushes his knuckles down the side of my face. "Baby, you don't have to do anything. I'll handle it."

"Okay," I whisper.

"Yeah?"

"Yes."

One simple word. One giant mistake. A piece of myself I'll never get back.

I lurch forward, opening my eyes to complete darkness. My semi-reclined seat stays in its relaxed position as I sit up. Although dark outside, I can see enough to know my vision is blurry. I blink rapidly trying to get a clear view of the world around me, but it doesn't come into focus. Not even Kipton.

"Kipton?" I reach out for the dashboard in front of me, holding on tightly.

"I'm right here, Sophie. You're okay. You fell asleep on the way back. I didn't want to wake you."

Although I'm safe with him next to me, my clouded vision is freaking me out. Tears threaten to fall as my eyes glass up. "My eyes aren't right. It's fuzzy."

Without missing a beat, Kipton turns the key in the ignition. "We're going to the hospital."

"No! Turn the car off. I want to go to my room and lay down. It's probably a migraine and once I take some of the medicine you bought I'll sleep it off."

"Are you sure? It doesn't seem right, Sophie."

"Positive." I don't have any other choice without insurance to pay for the hospital bill. Plus, I can't have my parents finding out about the party.

Reluctantly, he begins helping me out of the car. "Where's your shirt?" I might not be able to see perfectly, but his smooth chest can't be mistaken.

"I had it under your head so you wouldn't get a stiff neck while you were sleeping."

I peer up at him through my double vision. "You did that for me?" I'm shocked he would go to such trouble let alone sit in a car for an hour, half naked, while I slept.

He kisses my forehead gently. "Sophie, you underestimate me." I'm about to apologize but he knocks the wind out of me when he picks me up, cradling me in his arms like a small child.

"Kipton! Put me down! I'll walk." Kicking my feet and clawing at his arms, I realize it's a waste of time. I'm barely moving despite my efforts.

He laughs at my pathetic attempt to find the ground, making my entire body rub against his warm chest. Resigned to do things his way, I wrap both of my arms around his neck and hold on tight. As I crane my neck to make sure we don't fall down the hill, his stubble tickles my cheek. Instinctively, I nuzzle closer, relishing in the connection far more than I should be. None of the excitement can be good for my already raging headache.

Assuming his efforts were to help me through the dark, I'm surprised when he doesn't bother to set me back on my feet once inside the dorm. Instead, he keeps moving into the waiting elevator. "Hit the button for me, Tink."

"Tink?" I question.

"Yeah, you're all light and tiny. Like Tinkerbell."

I stare at him and then at the round buttons on the elevator wall. But the numbers all blend together and I'm not sure which to push. It's from the concussion, but I'm positive a tiny bit has everything to do with being wrapped up in Kipton's arms. "Hit number three."

I do as I'm told and then rest my cheek against his shoulder all while loving the safety of his strong arms. Kipton may be able to handle my concussion, but *I* can't handle him knowing how fucked up I actually am. Because as much as I don't want to admit it, I have way more than a crush on Kipton.

CHAPTER *nine*

KIPTON

CARRYING SOPHIE INSIDE, I CAN'T stop thinking about the way her legs would feel wrapped around my waist as I held her up against the wall. She has a sweet sexiness about her and she's absolutely clueless about how desirable she is. So much so that I often resort to teasing her like a middle school boy trying to get his first kiss. Hell, I'd probably blow from a first kiss with her at this point. But when we do fuck, and we will, I plan to show her exactly what's been missing from her sex life. *Me.*

While I'd been preoccupied imagining every way I'd love to claim her, she was so exhausted she fell asleep in the passenger seat of my car. I might never get to see her beautiful face resting on my pillow or her tiny body cuddled up in my bed again, but I was willing to risk creeper status to soak up every second of her company tonight.

While we aren't on an official date, I still tried to make the night memorable for her considering it revolved around shitty circumstances. But mark my words, when Sophie does let me take her on a real date, she'll be the first to experience the Kipton romance package. Hopefully, she'll see I'm not interested in a casual hook-up. But until then, I focus on the beautiful girl snuggled up in my arms and wait. I'll wait for her to want us as much as I do because for the first time I'm not in a hurry.

"You can put me down now. I'm okay."

"Your eyes?"

"It's not as bad as when I first woke up."

Squirming in my arms, her big blue eyes look anxious again, as if she's slowly reconstructing her protective barriers. I'd love to know what goes on in that gorgeous head of hers. I agree to put her down, but not on her feet. Instead, I sit her on top of the old metal heating unit outside her room. It doesn't look super sturdy, but she's so tiny it doesn't matter.

Her arms fall from my neck and rest on her thighs. Missing her touch immediately, I cage her in with my body, my palms on either side of her legs. Inching closer to her lips, she leans back, her head softly bumping against the wall. I reach for the back of her head to rub the spot that came in contact with the painted concrete bricks. "Watch your head, beautiful."

"Sorry."

I can tell she's nervous when her voice cracks as she apologizes for bumping her own head. The way she's fixated on my naked chest, blinking lazily while licking her lips, drives me crazy. I place my finger under her chin, lifting her head slowly so she has no choice but to look directly into my eyes. We stare at each other for a few seconds before she musters the courage to speak. "Are you going to kiss me?" she whispers.

"That depends." I *need* to kiss her, but I also don't want her running away from me afterward. Not to mention my sister told me I'm not allowed to touch her. Of course that only makes me want to touch her more, not to spite her, but because it tells me Sophie's worth the chase.

"On what?" Her eyes are darting from my eyes down to my lips and back up again.

Encouraging her, I wet my own lips with my tongue. She surprises me when she lifts her finger to trace my bottom lip with her fingernail. *Holy shit.* The move is seductive, and her simple touch has me craving her even more.

As quickly as she touches me, her hands clasp together in her lap like she got caught with her hand in the cookie jar. Of course that couldn't be farther from the truth. She can do whatever she wants as far as I'm concerned.

"You're allowed to touch me, beautiful." She needs the reassurance as much as I need her to touch me again.

She tilts her head to the side. "Am I?"

"Absolutely."

"Why?" she questions.

Before I can respond, there's a loud thud against her room door followed by something heavy crashing against the floor. "What the fuck was that, Sophie?"

"I have no idea!"

She pulls me closer to her for protection as my free hand reaches for the door knob. I twist it, ready to rush in, but it's locked. "Hand me your key." She wiggles to the edge of the heater and I quickly grab her around her waist placing her feet back on the floor, forgetting how short she is.

"Thank you." She blushes self-consciously and digs the key out of her pocket.

Taking it from her, I shove it into the lock. When I push the door open far enough to take a look around, I see red, orange, and every other color of the rainbow. Mostly I see someone about to get his ass kicked. I shield my eyes the best I can as two naked bodies continue grinding back and forth on each other oblivious to their audience. "Get the fuck off my sister!"

Sophie rushes in the room. She's caught off guard by the commotion in Cara's bed and bumps into my side. She takes one look at the nakedness and scurries back into the hallway. I can't say I blame her. I shield my own eyes and turn around to face the closet. On the floor in front of me, the pole lamp is laying on its side and the light bulb's shattered into pieces from the impact of the fall. A bunch of clothes are piled up on the floor haphazardly and the memo board that usually hangs inside the door is also on the floor with a few thumb tacks strewn around the carpet.

"Kipton! Get the hell out of here. Don't you know how to knock?" Cara shouts.

"Don't you even start with me. I was bringing Sophie back from her appointment, not stopping by to chit chat. This room is destroyed and I swear to God, Drew, if you don't get your ass away from my sister I will throw you out of here butt ass naked. Hurry it up!"

"Kippy, you can't tell us what to do. You're the one who needs to get out of here. NOW!"

"Hell no. Your roommate has a concussion and wants to go to bed. She slept in the damn car for an hour. She needs her bed and some peace and quiet as much as you need to put your damn clothes back on."

"Fine! Then we'll go to his room."

"Thank you. Wait! No you won't. *He* will go back to his room and you'll keep your own ass here."

"Kipton," Sophie whispers from the doorway.

I'm so worked up having walked in on my sister having sex that I forget who's calling my name. Turning my head to the doorway, I yell, "What!" She flinches and immediately I regret my harsh tone. I close the distance between us, but she takes a step back, unsure of my actions. I don't like it because never in a million years would I ever hurt her. "Come here." I pull her into a hug and she wraps her arms around my waist cautiously. After a few seconds, the tension melts away from her touch. "I'm sorry, beautiful."

"It's okay. I know you're upset."

"Oh, so you're allowed to touch Sophie, but I can't come within a mile of Drew. How typical man whore of you."

I turn my head to a fully clothed Cara and Drew watching us. "You better watch what you say," I warn.

"Why? It's the same thing!"

"I gave Sophie a hug, I didn't have her naked in my damn bed."

"But you want to!"

Sophie unwraps herself from my body and leans against the wall. She looks embarrassed and I'd do just about anything for my sister to shut her trap. "Cara, please don't do this right now." I don't want her to fuck up any progress I've made with Sophie tonight. We were having a good time despite the circumstances.

"Well at least you finally admit you want her. Maybe there is hope for you yet, brother."

I look at her like she has three heads. "But you told me

not to–"

"I know what I said, but when have you ever listened to me? Now will you please get out of here so I can say goodbye to Drew? You've clearly ruined my chances of experiencing an orgasm tonight."

"Christ, Cara." Groaning, I shut the door and focus on my date. I'm not done with her yet even though our moment was also ruined by their sexcapades.

"Are you okay?" Sophie asks. Her voice is timid and I realize she's never seen me lose my shit before.

"I'm fine. I'm sorry if I scared you."

"You didn't."

"I raised my voice like an asshole. I'm sorry."

"Don't be, it's over. It's not every day you walk in on your sister having sex. I don't imagine that's too much fun." She's trying not to laugh at the absurdity of the situation.

"It's not and it better never happen again, but thank you." I need to touch her, so I wrap my arms around her snugly this time. She locks her arms around my back, accepting my apology completely. I savor our connection for as long as possible before I have to leave. I hate having to say goodbye while she's not feeling well. "Do you want to come back to my place? You don't have to stay here in this brothel by yourself."

Laughing, she smiles the first genuine smile I've seen since dinner and I melt like ice cream on the fourth of July. Take my man card, universe, it's all yours.

"I'll be okay. Thanks for everything today. I appreciate you rearranging your schedule for me."

"Promise me one thing." I reach for her hand and interlock our pinkies.

"Pinkie swear?" She giggles. "I haven't done that since elementary school."

"Yup. It's that important."

She tilts her head to the side, contemplating what I'm asking of her before I even get the words out. "You have to tell me what it is first?"

"Next time, come to me when you need something." Before I finish my sentence, she's already looking away from me. I lift her chin back up so she's absorbing every word I'm saying. "Anything, Sophie. Okay? Please call me, text me, email, whatever form of technology you prefer. Just don't shut me out, okay?" She hears me, but doesn't respond. "Okay," I question again. I need some kind of confirmation.

Smiling she nods her head and says, "Pinkie swear." *God she's adorable.*

I hug her one more time before placing a kiss on the top of her head. I'd much rather have her lips, but this will have to do for now. I don't want our first kiss to be tainted by the memory of Drew's naked ass every time we look back on it. "Sweet dreams, beautiful." I take a few backwards steps away from her. She stands rooted in the same spot with her hand covering her heart.

"Bye, Kipton."

Turning around, I'm pleased with the progress we made tonight. While I understand her independence is important to her, she needs to realize she can have everything she wants and still be mine. That I'm sure of.

I'm not even halfway to the elevator when I hear Drew yelp like a teenage girl. Laughing to myself, I know the fucker stepped on a tack. *Justice served!*

CHAPTER *ten*

Sophie

IN A DAZE FROM OUR goodbye hug, I smooth out the hair on top of my head where Kipton's lips came in contact with the strands. Tonight was the first time his actions gave off the impression of *more*. He's been flirtatious, but he's never given me physical proof that he wants me. Tonight was more than a friendly gesture yet not enough to cross any lines—unlike Cara and Drew.

Peeking inside our room, I give Cara another minute to say her own goodbyes considering Drew's tongue appears to be shoved down her throat. When I hear her moan Drew's name and fall onto the bed, pulling him along with her, I quietly close the door to give them some privacy. Thanks to my car nap and medicine, I'm no longer entirely exhausted and my vision isn't screwed up anymore. It was scary enough to have me praying it doesn't happen again though.

I'm about to sit on top of the heater and wait, but another moan and slap come from the other side of the door. Not wanting to hear the play by play, I take a walk while they finish getting each other out of their system. Something tells me Cara isn't giving up tonight until she's been thoroughly satisfied.

Passing by several dorm rooms, some girls are watching movies, a handful of guys are playing video games and a few others study quietly amongst the chaos. I could stop and chat, but I settle for some fresh air. It's a nice night with a gentle breeze to dull the humid air. I take full advantage and sit on the ledge of the marble fountain that separates our dorm from the next. I dip my finger into the cool water, hoping there's nothing grotesque or alive below.

I've always been a daydreamer, creating visions of the life I always wished I lived. Now is no exception because all on its own, my mind travels back to a half-naked Kipton carrying me in his strong arms. He took care of me without even being asked. A guy's never done that for me before unless they knew some form of repayment would be headed their way. My ex always expected sexual gratification as his form of payment. But I wouldn't consider anything he ever did even comparable to what Kipton did for me tonight. With Blaine, our interactions always felt forced, like if I messed something up I'd pay for it. So, while I struggle to believe Kipton wants me for me and not simply for the pleasure I can give him, I still need a little convincing as far as that goes.

I jump when my phone starts ringing in my hand. Juggling it back and forth, I'm thankful when it doesn't fall into the fountain, instead landing safely on my lap. "Hello?"

"Are you okay, Sophie? Where are you?"

"Kipton? Yeah, I'm fine. Why?" Hearing his voice has me smiling like a loon. I didn't expect to hear from him for a couple days. I always thought guys have some kind of three day call back rule to make girls want them yet make it known they're the ones calling the shots.

"Cara said she couldn't find you and you weren't answering her text messages. Where are you?"

He's worried about me. "I'm sitting at the fountain. They weren't done yet after you left, so I took a walk."

"Motherfucker. I'm going to kill the both of them. I'll come and get you. You should be in bed resting, not sitting in the dark all by yourself."

"I'm fine. I didn't see her messages, but I'm already on my way back inside." He sighs and I'm pretty sure he's in his bed from the muffled rustling I'm hearing in the background. I find myself wishing I was back in his bed next to him.

"Sophie."

"Yeah?"

The line is silent for a few long seconds before he exhales like he's battling with what he wants to say to me. "Nothing. You're sure you're okay? I'm sorry my sister is such a pain in the ass."

Part of me is disappointed when he doesn't elaborate. It's been nice to feel wanted by a guy—a guy I don't fear. "You don't need to apologize for her. I happen to know she's awesome. Her brother is too." I'm so lame when I flirt.

"So now I'm awesome *and* sexy." I love flirty Kipton. I mean *like*. Sheesh. Turn down the hormones.

I giggle and pretend to be annoyed. "Yes, we've already established you're nice to look at."

"The feelings mutual, you know," he murmurs.

He catches me off guard. "It is?"

"Yeah, Sophie. It is."

I fumble for something to say and when I come up with nothing but air, I decide to end the conversation. I wish I was better at this. "I should go. Thanks for checking on me."

"You don't have to thank me."

Yes, I do. For so many reasons. "Night, Kipton."

"Night, beautiful."

Hanging up, I exit the elevator and round the corner smiling from ear to ear. The door is wide open when I reach our room, but there's no sign of Drew. Cara's sitting on the edge of her bed messing with her phone, her leg bouncing nervously.

"Sophie! There you are."

"Here I am." I change into some pajamas, my mind a million miles away.

"You're mad at me aren't you?" Cara asks.

I turn sideways with a surprised expression on my face. "What? No. Not at all."

"I'm sorry I have no will power when it comes to Drew. It was rude of me not to kick him out when you got back."

Setting down my brush, I close the door to my closet. "Trust me, Cara. It's okay. He looked like an amazing kisser." I laugh at the visual they gave me of him practically sucking her entire face off.

"Ohmigod, Sophie. That's not the only thing he's amazing at. I've never gotten off so many times in one session."

I pull back the blankets on my bed, sliding under the cool sheet. Having no idea what she means, I'm almost afraid to ask. But I do anyway when curiosity gets the best of me. "Session?"

"You know, from start to finish. Foreplay until the deed is done."

I prop my head up on my elbow so I can look at her while we're having this enlightening conversation. "I'll have to take your word for it."

"What do you mean?" She asks as she fixes the disheveled comforter on her own bed before climbing underneath.

"I've never well, you know."

"WHAT!" Cara shrieks.

"What?" Maybe I should have kept that tidbit to myself. There *is* such a thing as oversharing even if Cara has no boundaries. I've never gotten off during sex though. My one and only relationship wasn't the healthiest. It was a lot of trying to please him and not myself. A lot of give with barely any take.

"Sophie please tell me you at least toot your own horn then. Maybe a B.O.B?"

"Who is Bob?"

"*Holy shit.* Bob is a battery operated boyfriend. My God, you're practically Sandy from *Grease,* blond hair and all."

"Too pure to be Pink," I fire back at her. *Grease* happens to be one of my all-time favorite movies so I get what she's saying completely.

Cara sits up on her bed and scoots to the end as close to mine as she can get. "Tell me more, no pun intended," she giggles.

"I've never met Bob or any of his other friends. Sex with my ex was pretty standard. Nothing kinky or off the wall going on. As long as he got off, that's all he cared about and it definitely lacked the passion I saw between you and Drew tonight." That should hold her over for now.

Cara flops on the bed dramatically and squeals. "This is going to be so much fun."

"What is?" I'm afraid to find out what she's busy cooking up in that adventurous mind of hers.

She claps her hands together and her eyes light up with excitement. "Turning you into a seductress."

"What? I don't even have a man, Cara."

"Yes, you do. You just aren't admitting it yet. We can go buy you some sexy lingerie tomorrow and turn you into an irresistible piece of ass."

"No way, Cara. I'm doing fine on my own."

"The hell you are! But whatever. If you don't want my help then I have another suggestion."

This ought to be good. "I'm not sure I want to hear any more ideas out of you."

"But you want my brother? Don't you?"

I lie back down and turn to face the wall. I'm all done with this confession fest.

She must sense my fear because the next time she opens her mouth, her voice is tender. I can tell she's dropped the ploy to sex me up. "It's okay if you do, Sophie. He's a good guy when he wants to be. I was against the idea of you and him dating at first, but only because I was scared he would steal you away from me all the time. Considering you both have a thing for each other, I promise I won't interfere."

He really has a thing for me? "Now you're talking nonsense. He doesn't want me, Cara. While part of me thinks he may have been hinting at more tonight, I think we're only ever going to be friends. He could have kissed me tonight, but he didn't. And we were really close."

"That's where you're wrong. Let me fill you in on a little secret, Sophie. My brother doesn't text girls, check-up on them, take them places, or any of that relationship type stuff."

"Then why is he doing it for me?"

"Because he finally found a girl worthy enough. Something tells me he isn't going to give up until he has you *all* to himself. I happen to agree with him."

I try to contain my smile, but fail miserably. "You saw us hug; it's not a big deal, Cara." The idea of him wanting me blows my mind. I have a hard time looking at him without blushing let alone actually kissing him. If he touched me touched me, like beyond a kiss, I'm not sure I'd even survive.

"Earth to Sophie," Cara says, while chucking a small throw pillow at my bed.

I'm not paying attention and it hits me in the stomach. "Ugh, what was that for?"

"Oh shit! Did I hit you in the head? I forgot!"

"No, I'm fine. What were you saying before you pelted me?" I toss her pillow back onto her bed where it belongs.

"You like him don't you?"

"Goodnight, Cara." I roll over, officially ending our pillow talk.

Laughing, Cara claps her hands. "I freakin knew you two had a thing. Goodnight, Kipton lover."

I snort at her lame comeback, smiling from ear to ear because she's absolutely right. This girl has a big ole crush on her brother. Sleep. I need some sleep.

"HIS NO GOOD, SORRY ASS is leaving. I've had enough of this shit. This is the last time that man plays me for a fool. On our property for christ's sake. In front of all the neighbors. He can have his skanks. I'm done."

I tiptoe into my parents room, where I find my mom pulling every item of clothing my dad owns from his closet. An open suitcase rests on top of the bed. Once everything's off the hangers, she piles it into her arms and stuffs it inside. Pieces are hanging over the sides and it'll never close. Determined, she grabs his cologne from the dresser and tosses that in too. "Mom, what's wrong?"

"Go back to bed, Sophie. This doesn't concern you."

"But Mom, -"

"I said GO, now!"

Obeying her order, I slink back into the hallway out of her line of vision. She slams the suitcase closed to no avail. There's too much fabric blocking the zipper's path. Pounding her fists on top of it, she lets out a blood curdling scream loud enough to wake the dead. Giving up her futile efforts, she falls to her knees and sobs into her hands. Within seconds, she's laying in the fetal position in the middle of her bedroom floor. Shaken, I've never seen her so helpless—so out of control. Desperately wanting to comfort her, I risk her anger and move closer.

The front door slams and there's laughter mixed with obvious drunkenness. Footsteps come stomping up the stairs, so I bolt back inside my bedroom, not wanting to be in the way of my father.

"What the fuck you doing woman?"

Mom sits up and wipes her tears from her eyes. She never lets him see her tears. "Get out of this house. You're a pathetic excuse of a man. How dare you bring one of your tramps into my home. I've put up with a lot of your bullshit over the years Dean, but this is the last straw. I've had it and I deserve better. My daughter deserves better than this pathetic example of a family."

"Don't you dare preach to me. She's your daughter, not mine, Victoria. But I've been here and I've taught her as much as you have over the years."

I should be in my room like mom asked, but I can't watch him destroy her any longer. She's all I have. I need her. "You're right, Dad, you did teach me a lot. You taught me exactly who I don't want to be."

"Sophie, go back to your room. Please," *mom begs.*

Dad walks over to me and gets in my face, the whiskey on his breath almost knocking me over. I hold onto the wall for support. He's never hit me, but I've never pushed him either. I've never been strong enough to say a word—until now. Now, I'm old enough to know this isn't how life was intended to be. My mother shouldn't be on the floor in a heap of numbness. I shouldn't have to hide in my closet.

"Dean, baby. Are you ready to go?"

Standing at the top of the stairs is a woman dressed in a skin tight red dress, her chest spilling over the plunging neckline. Appearing as classy as a two dollar hooker, she smacks her pink bubble gum and twirls a piece of her over processed blond hair.

"You brought her in here?" *I don't know why I'm surprised, nothing he does ever makes sense or is deserving. He's a pathetic excuse of a human being most of the time.*

He has the audacity to laugh at me. "I pay the bills around here, Sophie. What I say and do is none of your damn business. Never* has been and it never will." His smile morphs into an evil grin. "I didn't want you back then darling and I don't want you now either."

"Dean!" Mom yells. "You've done enough damage for one night. Get whatever you need and leave. I'll leave your things on the porch. Pick them up in the morning or they're going to the dump where they belong."

Dad backs down, taking his little whore along with him. I hear her cackle all the way to the front door. "I'm going to bed." I turn and walk to my room. Mom's standing in the doorway of her bedroom just as shell shocked as I am. We should expect this behavior by now, yet it's still a mind fuck each time. I pray mom's strong enough to stand by her word and have this be the last time. Something tells me it's simply another attempt for her to make her husband see her—to make him understand she can be gone from his life permanently. He's never respected her the way a man should respect his wife and she's a fool for putting up with it.

"Sophie, I'm sorry," she cries. She knows her threats were nothing but a bunch of lies.

"Don't be." I shut my bedroom door and my eyes fixate on the trashcan next to my desk. Relying entirely on muscle memory, I end up in the closet, hunched over top of it purging every bit of anger, sorrow and resentment inside of me. It's painful, but so are my emotions. Is it too much to want a family who gives a shit about each other? Too exhausted to move, I fall asleep next to a pair of worn sneakers and my favorite stuffed bear. Teddy's always loved me.

I wake up covered in sweat, searching for the closet door. When I realize it was nothing more than a nightmare, I clutch my pillow wishing I could erase the past from my mind. I've come so far since those days, and I'm worried I'm slowly slipping back into the darkness. Maybe it's because of the changes that go along with moving away or the concussion. It could be my infatuation with Kipton for all I know. But I don't want the pain to come back. Mom may have left him, but he'll never be erased from my memory.

Now that I'm awake, the relief of the purge is gone. But, I crave it all over again. When I feel like I can't hold it in another second, I slip out of the room and find the closest bathroom. It's late, so I have my pick of stalls. Without wasting any more time, I choose the first one and release the hatred living inside of me. As painful as it is, it's the relief I desperately needed—it always takes away the pain.

Twice in twenty four hours, Sophie. You're slipping. I don't even notice Drew standing outside the restroom. I bump into his chest, and stagger backward. "Excuse me," I dazedly mutter.

"You okay, Sophie?"

I give him a thumbs up and keep walking. Only now do I realize the chattering of my teeth. Adrenaline's coursing through my body so rapidly my heart is pounding in my chest.

"Sophie, you all right?" A sleepy Cara asks.

"I'm fine. Just had to go to the bathroom. Go back to bed." *More lies.*

"Okay."

ANOTHER HEADACHE FILLED DAY PASSES and by the time morning comes again, all I want to do is sleep in. But I can't because once I do get back into the gym, I'll only regret it.

Cara's already left for her first class. The dreaded eight in the morning class she wasn't able to avoid like the rest of us. The girl loves her sleep, too, so I feel sorry for anyone who crosses paths with her this morning.

I feel like hell on my way to the dining hall to get my daily granola fix. The café is bustling this time of the morning and although I look as bad as I feel, I don't have to worry considering I only know a handful of people in Alabama. As I sit alone at a corner table, I find myself eyeing each person as they exit the line mentally cataloguing which of their features I want to steal. There's no shortage of good looking people on this campus, that's for sure. So far I've taken the brunettes long legs, the blondes amazing green eyes, and the wardrobe of the red head. All put together, I'd be a dream.

It keeps me busy enough that I almost forget about my test results. They can't be great considering the thumping in my head refuses to go away for more than an hour or two at a time. Taking it easy would be the smart thing to do, but it's killing me not being able to train. Since I can't show up sweaty to see the doctor who put me on restriction, I power walk instead of jogging to his campus office. He said no running, but if my feet never leave the pavement entirely, I'm still technically following the rules. And it's cardio regardless.

The office is just opening and I step aside a few window washers already working hard. I nervously clamber inside, waiting my turn at the front desk.

"Can I help you?" The receptionist asks.

"Yes. I need to see the doctor about my test results. My name's Sophie."

She smiles warmly. "He's expecting you this morning. I have your papers right here."

Before she can buzz his office, I notice him chatting with another student athlete in the small waiting area. As soon as he finishes, he acknowledges me. "Sophie, you can come back."

"Thank you."

He eyes me up and down, making me nervous. "I saw you hustling by my window and figured you were on your way in. You're not pushing it are you? You look tired."

I'll have to be more careful. "No. I've been taking it easy."

"Okay. Have a seat." He opens my file and pulls out the transcribed report from my CT scan. "The test results were as I suspected. No fracture or anything serious to worry about, but you're still consistent with a concussion. I'd like you to remain out of practice for the rest of this week and the next."

"Shit," I mutter. I was expecting this news, but it doesn't make it any easier to hear. There's no way I can afford to miss that much time. Coach won't like it.

"I promise you it's standard. You won't see any of the football players back in action for a few weeks after sustaining the same injury. With your permission, I'll send a leave of absence form to your coach so he has your diagnosis in writing. It won't affect your standing with the university as far as scholarship money is concerned."

"Sure, that's fine. Is there anything I can do in the meantime?"

"Take the rest of the week to rest as I already said. Next week you can resume your workouts, but scale them down."

This isn't the news I was hoping for. "Okay."

"I'll check in with you in a few days. I have your contact info and please come in right away if anything changes or worsens."

"I will. Thanks for seeing me."

"You're welcome, Sophie. That's what I'm here for." We shake hands before parting ways.

As soon as I'm outside, I pull out Coach Evans business card and dial his number. He asked me to call him and as much as I'd rather not, I know I have to face the music. Hoping I get his answering machine, I'm nervous when he actually picks up his phone.

"Hello."

"Hi. It's Sophie. From the team."

"Hi Sophie. What can I do for you today? Are you feeling any better?"

"I was just calling with my test results. The doctor is sending you paperwork, but I wanted to tell you myself like you asked. With my concussion and all, I have to miss this week and next. I'm really sorry."

"Don't be sorry. Accidents happen. Did he find anything else on the scan? I assume it was negative?"

"Yes. It was. It's just a waiting game now until I can come back."

"We look forward to having you back."

"Thank you."

"Call me anytime to check-in. Okay?"

"Sure, I will. Thank you."

"Talk to you soon, Sophie. Take care."

"You too. Bye."

Although that once again went better than expected, I'm still totally bummed I'll be missing more time than I'd wanted. Tempted to give my body a test, I want to show Coach

Evans I'm a hard worker despite the warning from the doctor. I'm sure he's being overly cautious considering the danger of gymnastics.

Once the doctor's office is out of view, I start to jog slowly. When the coast is completely clear, I concentrate on each stride, digging deeper the farther I go. With the wind in my hair, I live for the exercise I've missed out on.

Considering my condition, I make good time for the first half mile of my run, but I stop moving altogether when the pounding in my skull is back in full force. I rest in the grass under a shade tree and wish I had thought to bring some water with me. I'm a long way from the dorm, so I know I need to start walking back or I'll miss my next class. I'm wobbly when I get back on my feet and reach out for the tree trunk to steady myself. "This was stupid," I say to nobody but myself.

After walking for a solid five minutes, I look around and realize I'm not sure which direction I came from. The store fronts on each corner are identically designed creating further confusion. Having only been in this town for a short time with little time to explore, I have to go with my gut and take the street to my right. I walk for a few more blocks and things start to look vaguely familiar. This has to be the way I came. Two more blocks and I stop directly in front of the wrestling house where Kipton lives. That explains why the street looked familiar. From what I remember, if I take two rights and a left, I should run right into my building. Or would it be two lefts and a right? Stomping my foot in frustration, I decide to go right.

"Are you here to see me or dance on the sidewalk?"

I jump, startled by the company I wasn't aware I had. Kipton's leaning over the railing of his porch watching me with an amused expression on his face. This day just keeps getting better. "Which way is my dorm?"

"You're lost?" he questions.

"Yeah. I went to the doctor's office for my test results."

"Sophie, the doctor's office is on the other side of campus. How did you end up over here?" He looks concerned and walks down the porch steps to meet me on the sidewalk.

I shrug my shoulders, afraid to state the obvious. "I went for a run."

"Did he clear you?"

I kick around a stone on the ground with my sneaker so I don't have to see his less than amused expression when I tell him the truth. "Not exactly."

"What *did* he tell you?" His voice hardens ever so slightly and I know he won't like the truth.

Refusing to lie to Kipton, I fess up and admit my wrong. "To take the rest of the week off and next week I can start working out in the weight room."

He crosses his arms and forces me to look at him with his body language alone. He's angry. "So, you didn't care for his news and did your own thing instead."

I hate how childish he makes my decision sound. "Something like that."

He nods his head knowingly, aware that I didn't follow instructions. "I can't tell you what to do, Sophie, but you need to listen to him. I don't want to worry about you roaming the streets all because you got mad."

My natural reaction is to get defensive. I've always had to fight my way through conversation at home. "I'm trying, Kipton."

"Are you?" he challenges.

"Yes!"

"You sure about that? You look really tired."

"I didn't sleep well, not that it matters."

"Of course it matters, Sophie."

I want to ask him *why*. But I don't. "I have a class to get to." I start walking in the direction I'm facing, not caring if it's the right way or not. I'll find the dorm one way or another.

"Sophie."

I wave him off, not bothering to stop and turn around. The last thing I need is another lecture about screwing up. At the end of the street I turn left, praying it will bring me another block closer to the dorm. Just as I become more confident about my navigation skills and increase my pace, a loud horn stops me in my tracks. "Jesus." I clutch my chest from the shock.

"Hop in."

Hesitantly, I lean on the side of the car, peering into the open window. *Damn.* Kipton looks delicious with his aviators on. "You scared the shit out of me."

"Well, you wouldn't stop long enough to get into my car. So here I am." *No shit.*

"If I get in, are you going to yell at me?"

"Nope. I'm only taking your pretty little behind back where it belongs." Every ounce of anger inside of me dissipates from the sight of his smile alone.

"You sure do know how to charm a lady, Kipton." I open the door to his car and slide inside.

"Where to my lady?" he jokes.

I laugh even though I don't want to. "Very funny."

"Well you seem to know the lay of the land around here so well." I punch him in the arm for mocking me. "Ouch!" He pulls a U-turn and purposely makes a big show about going in the *correct* direction back to my room. *Point made, Kipton.*

"Thanks for the lift." And I *am* thankful I don't have to worry about missing class. I'll even have enough time to take a quick shower before I leave.

"You want to get some lunch?" He glances at me before driving through the next intersection.

"Na. I'm good. I had some granola before my run."

"That's it?"

"It was plenty."

"Chicks," he says shaking his head. "Well, I could eat a house so I'm going to get something before class. You have any plans tonight?"

"Nothing other than my usual school work."

"Tonight's the monthly under the stars on the football field. They play a movie on the big screen in the end zone. You want to go with me?"

"Like on a date?" I blurt out.

"Yeah, a date. Would that be okay with you?" He reaches over and squeezes my thigh.

I push my body into the seat, digging my feet into the

floor mat to get a grip on reality. *A date with Kipton.* Maybe Cara wasn't talking complete nonsense last night. "I'll go with you."

"I'll pick you up at eight then." He stops the car next to the sidewalk and leaves it running. Swallowing the lump in my throat, I chance a peek at him before I leave. "Okay. Thanks for the ride." I climb out of the bucket seat and he coughs suddenly but regains his composure when I look at him wearily. Plastering a panty-melting smile on his handsome face, he's as cool as can be. "Anytime, beautiful."

CHAPTER *eleven*

KIPTON

I CHOKE ON MY OWN spit as Sophie gets out of the car. Her ass looks so damn hot in her skin tight spandex pants. I think their called yoga pants or some shit. I wait until she's inside the building before I pull away so I can enjoy each retreating step she takes. It's going to take every ounce of willpower in my reserves to keep my hands from smothering her body the second I'm with her tonight. She's agreed to a date and I'm not about to screw it up.

After stopping in to see Momma June at the diner, I return to the house with a take-out bag filled with enough food to feed half the house. Thankfully, a few of my roommates are back from morning classes and grab the bag out of my hands before I'm entirely through the front door. As I sink my teeth into my own burger, my phone rings. "Talk to me," I say around a mouth full.

"Hey, Kipton?"

"Yeah, who's this?"

"It's Drew, from Johnson Hall."

"I know who you are and I know where to find you." How could I forget about walking in on his naked ass? I drop my burger onto the paper wrapper, shuddering at the memory. Not much turns my stomach, but naked male ass cracks having sex with my sister are definitely on the list.

"I didn't think you'd forget. I got your number from

Cara's paperwork, I hope that's okay. Anyway, I was hoping you could stop by the next time you come to see your sister. You know, so we could talk. Things got a little awkward the other night." I give him props. He doesn't sound the least bit nervous about approaching me even after I found him on top of my sister.

I'm curious about what he wants to discuss, so I take the bait. "Tonight should work. I'm picking up Sophie at eight. Does seven thirty work for you?"

"Yeah, man. It does."

"See you then." I'll hear him out, but I'll never be comfortable with the idea of him screwing my sister if that's what he's looking for. He's lucky I'm a patient man.

After finishing my lunch I debate texting Sophie, but I don't want to come on too strong too fast. Instead, I busy myself on the Internet, looking up the hours of The Perfect Petal flower shop. I have no idea if she's a flower girl, but usually chicks appreciate the sentiment. Somehow I end up on an edible fruit arrangement page, but toss that idea out the window. With my next class looming, I decide to think about my options during class. Considering it has nothing to do with my major, I'm sure I'll be bored out of my mind. I needed one more second level science requirement to graduate. Since I'm not into dissecting any creatures in biology or worrying about elements on the periodic table in chemistry that left me with the stars. *How bad can astronomy be?*

Looking around for an empty seat at one of the tables in the back of the room, I spot a blonde in the right corner, texting on her phone. Upon closer inspection, I discover this is by far the best class I've ever taken. The seat next to her has my name written all over it.

Sneaking up behind her, I cover her eyes with my hand. "Guess who?" I whisper.

Clawing at my hands, she spins around with fear written all over her face. She softens once she realizes it's only me. "What are you doing in here?" she questions. Her eyes dart around the room as the other students stare at us. *Let 'em look.*

I toss my book bag onto the table and sit down. "I'm here for class. Same as you."

"*You're* taking astronomy?"

"Yeah, why's that so hard to believe?" I pull out my notebook and await her answer. This should be good.

"It isn't, I guess. But I didn't peg you for a star gazer."

I lean closer to her. "We do have a date tonight you know. Under the stars." She blushes and nervously looks down at the table. She leans over and digs into her book bag, for what I'm not sure. Her face is on fire and she doesn't want me to see.

I wrap my fingers around her arm and pull her into an upright positon while using my foot to scoot her chair closer to mine. "Look at me, Sophie."

She stares down at my foot controlling her movement. Although cautious, she finally looks at me without shying away.

"Don't be nervous around me, okay? Be Sophie. Say whatever you want whenever you want. Can you do that?"

"I can try," she responds while chewing on the end of her pen. I reach up to her nose and tap the end because I love the way she scrunches up her face each time I do it. If she wasn't already adorable enough, this assures it.

We don't get to discuss anything else with the professor taking his place in front of the whiteboard to begin class. The first thing he covers are lab partners. Luckily, it's the person seated next to us. That worked out perfectly if I do say so myself.

The first hour of class passes quickly with little nudges and scribbled notes to Sophie on pieces of paper. A few times she had to cover her mouth with her hand to keep from laughing at the ridiculous conversation.

As a special treat, we're moved to the planetarium to finish class. As we file into the seating area, Professor Bell describes what will be our world for the next semester. He rambles on saying something about being able to map out the entire sky by the end of the course. It sounds boring as hell, but I'll do whatever he wants if it gets me sitting in the dark next to Sophie twice a week. Sign me up for extra credit too.

I'm entirely too comfortable in my reclined seat and could doze listening to the monotone voice from the recording going on and on about the Milky Way galaxy. From the corner of my eye, I notice Sophie pulling her knees to her chest while hugging her legs with her arms. She's so tiny the seat could fit two of her. Folding into a tight ball of blond gorgeousness, I lean over so she can hear me. "Are you cold?" I make the mistake of looking down after asking and can almost see her ass cheek with the way her shorts are riding up. *Jesus.*

"It's freezing in here!" She whispers back while running her hands over her arms to generate some warmth. Personally, the temperature is comfortable, but she's not exactly carrying around any extra pounds to insulate her either.

I hate knowing she's cold so I do the only thing I can to help her and take off my top T-shirt. I wore a plain white one underneath so I'm not naked in class or anything. Her eyes watch me the entire time, curious as to what I'm up to. When I lean over and drape the shirt across her legs, she gasps in surprise. "You can't undress in the middle of the planetarium!"

"Are you still cold?"

She starts to speak but pauses before answering. "Well, no. Not anymore."

"You're welcome."

"Thank you, Kipton. I wasn't being ungrateful. I'm sorry."

"Sophie, you don't have an ungrateful bone in your sassy little body. Now make a wish."

She tucks her hands under my shirt and gets comfortable again. "Why do I have to make a wish?"

"If you were paying attention you would see the shooting stars on the ceiling, beautiful girl."

Giggling, she leans her head back to rest against her seat. She squeezes her eyes shut tight while making her wish. I can hope it has something to do with me because I only intend to step up my game. I'm drawn to her and I need to find out more. This class combined with our date tonight will hopefully work in my favor.

"Did you make a wish?" I whisper.

She nods her head. "Yep."

"A good one?"

"I hope so."

I lean in close to her ear. "I know so." And I do. Because if it had anything to do with the two of us, it was a perfect wish. She cuddles under my shirt and blushes.

Class ends and we're dismissed, but neither of us move to get up. Instead, we stay rooted in our seats watching the rest of the class file out of the room. "What are you thinking about over there?" I ask.

"My wish," she responds quietly. Her body stays facing forward but her head turns so her eyes are staring into my own. We sit in silence, simply looking at each other's features for a few seconds before the anticipation strangles me, forcing me to make a split second decision. I lean closer to her, praying she wants this too. When she doesn't move away, I know I've been given the okay. "Kiss me, Kipton." Her words are small, barely above a miniscule whisper, but I hear them loud and clear.

Leaning overtop the armrest, it digs into my stomach but the only sensation I'm aware of is the softness of her lips as we meet each other for the first time. The kiss starts off slow as we're testing each other out. When I realize the only part of our bodies actually touching are our lips, I place my hand on the nape of her neck pulling her even closer to me. I run my tongue over the seam of her lips, seeking entrance. Never hesitating, she opens for me and the kiss is kicked up another notch. The moment is sexy as hell. She moans softly into my mouth assuring me she's enjoying this as much as I am.

Not wanting to break our connection but knowing we need a better position, I pull back far enough to wrap my arms around her slim waist, hauling her onto my lap. Instinctively, she straddles my hips as her hair forms a sensual curtain around our faces. "You're so fucking beautiful, Sophie." I dive back into her lips, this time more aggressive than the last. She kisses back, matching my intensity.

My hands slide under the hem of her shirt where I come in contact with her baby soft skin beneath the fabric. Desperately wanting to strip her bare, I know we can't take it that far inside the planetarium. Instead, I remove my hands from underneath her shirt and squeeze the soft globes of her ass, bringing her as close to my body as physically possibly. The frayed denim strands of her shorts tickle my fingers as I caress her thighs. Caught up in the moment, she grinds against me.

"Kipton," she moans again when I move my mouth to the side of her neck, gently sucking and leaving small kisses. I want my lips to be the ones she remembers touching her, erasing any memory of Caleb's hickey.

"Sophie, you smell so good." She slides her chilled fingers underneath my shirt and scratches her nails softly down my abs. The sensation has me hard as steel behind the zipper of my shorts. Each move she makes gets a little bolder. When I'm positive I can't wait another minute to get her naked, the lights come on, illuminating the front of the room. "Shit."

I don't spot him right away, but find Professor Bell near the side entrance preparing for his next class. I stay still, but Sophie gasps and stands up quickly. Her foot gets caught in the seat and she quickly loses her balance. I steady her with my hands and pick up our bags, tossing them both over my shoulder. By the time I exit the row of seats, she's halfway to the door already. With embarrassment written all over her face, I chuckle. She's a sexy little thing when she's all worked up and I fully intend to explore her more tonight.

With her head down, she passes by Professor Bell who finally notices the two of us scrambling out of the room. I'm on cloud nine and not ashamed in the least bit about getting caught considering that was the best first kiss I've ever experienced. "See you next week, Professor." He smiles and shakes his head. Even he has to realize how perfect the planetarium is for an impromptu make out session. I jog to the exit, hoping Sophie didn't already leave. Remembering I still have her bag, I relax as the sunshine blinds me when I step outside the building. I spot Sophie standing at the bottom of the staircase waiting apprehensively. Her blond hair is sparkling from the light of the sun which only makes her look even more angelic.

"In a hurry, beautiful?" She blushes as usual. It appears shy Sophie has returned. Only now, I know better. The little vixen that came out to play a few minutes ago has the potential to blow my mind. Sexy Sophie is going to be so much fun to get to know. "Hey."

"I have to drop this class. There's no way I can go back in there and see Professor Bell. He has to think I'm such a slut."

Her expression makes me laugh even though I try not to. "You worry too much. He was our age once you know. In fact, he was smiling when I walked by him."

"He was?"

She's looking hopeful that this might not be as serious as she expected. I'm going to do everything I can to make sure she doesn't shut down completely. "Yeah. He didn't say a word about it. It's not like he saw anything anyway."

"God, I hope he didn't. I'm so embarrassed."

I hand her bag back to her even though I don't mind carrying it. "Even if he did, it's not like college has detention. Don't sweat it, okay?" She shakes her head in agreement, but I'm not convinced she's over it.

"I better get back to the dorm before Cara wonders where I am."

"Come on, I'll drive you back." I turn toward the parking lot but she doesn't follow.

"No, that's okay. The walk will be good for me."

"Sophie." She's already clamming up on me.

"I appreciate the offer, but I have to stop being so lazy."

"You're not lazy and you're supposed to be taking it easy. We're still on for tonight right?" I'm not leaving until I'm positive she hasn't changed her mind.

"Yeah. Why? "

"Just making sure. You seem nervous."

"I'm fine."

"Do you regret our kiss?"

"No."

She's not giving me an inch with any of these answers. "Did you at least enjoy it?"

Finally she smiles. "Yeah."

"Come 'ere." Sophie walks into my open arms and I cuddle her. She doesn't move right away, so I soak up the feeling of her against me. Rubbing my hands up and down her back,

I never thought I'd be so down with cuddling. But there's so much more I want to do with her. "That was only the beginning, Sophie." She shivers despite the warm temperatures. "I'll pick you up at eight tonight."

"I'll be ready." She releases me and when she does I realize how much I don't want her to leave. She turns to walk away, but I reach out my arm, pulling her back to me before she's out of reach. Not saying a word, I kiss her one more time knowing it's going to have to hold me over until tonight. I take my time exploring her mouth all over again. She's as eager as she was the first time. But when she sucks on my tongue, I almost blow.

CHAPTER *twelve*

Sophie

I'M NOT ONE FOR PUBLIC displays of affection in the middle of the quad, but Kipton's kisses are my favorite addiction. It's been awhile since I've made out with anyone, so I'm probably rusty, but I have no problem practicing on his lips. My body was on fire inside the planetarium the second he touched me and I'm still coming down from lust overload. If he's capable of those skills outside of the bedroom, I'm scared of what he's capable of doing to my body beneath the sheets.

I've spent the entire fifteen minute walk to Johnson Hall replaying our first and second kisses in my mind, not even paying attention to anyone I've passed or bothering to look both ways before I crossed the street. Magically, I've floated back to my dorm still in one piece of romantic mush. I touch my fingers to my lips and smile. Part of me wants to continue to get lost in the moment, but I've felt this way before about a guy and lived to regret it.

"Earth to Sophie," Cara says from the comfort of her bed. Must be nice to have the entire afternoon off even if she did have to suffer through an eight o'clock class.

"Hey Cara." I open the fridge and grab a bottle of water.

"So how was it?"

"We went to the planetarium." I can't even say the word without smirking. It's my new favorite place on campus.

Even though it feels slightly forbidden now.

"*We?*" Cara asks with knowing smirk.

"Your brother's in my astronomy class. Can you believe that?"

"Yeah. He told me when he called."

"He called? What for?"

Cara sits up and crosses her legs Indian style, hugging her pillow to her chest. "To see if you were home safely."

It's oddly comforting having him call to check on me. Maybe he's as affected by the kiss as I am. "Does he want me to text him or something?" I have to play it cool or Cara will be all over me for details.

She smiles. "I'm sure he'd love that. But it can wait until you fill me in."

Shit. "Okay, what do you want to know?"

"About the kiss for starters." Shocked by her request, I spit some of my water out of my mouth wetting the floor in front of me.

"He told you!" I ask in shock. I didn't realize he swapped stories with his sister so freely. Especially with how pissed he was catching her doing the deed.

"No, but you just did. I knew something was up when he called to check on you. Then you waltz in here like a fairy princess practically petting your freshly kissed lips."

"Cara, I was not." *I totally was petting them.*

"You were. So, as much as it pains me to ask about my brother's skills, how was it?"

I smile at the memory of him pulling my body on top of his, unexpectedly removing me from my chair. "It was good." *It was fucking fantastic!*

"That's it? Good?" She looks at me knowingly, waiting for more.

"Are you sure this isn't too weird for you."

"Oh, it's creepy as all get out but I love you both and need to know regardless."

I dive onto my mattress and giggle. "It was freaking amazing, Cara. I've never been kissed so passionately in my life. Your brother has amazing lips."

Cara flops back on her bed and quickly covers hear ears

with the sides of her pillow, creating thick earmuffs surrounding her entire head. Groaning, she rolls around like she's in pain. I, of course, can't stop laughing at her reaction. I knew she wouldn't be able to handle it.

Drew strolls in our room and looks back and forth between Cara and I wondering what's going on. Cara's oblivious to him even being in the room. "What's her deal," he asks.

"Ask her, I'm sure she'd love to tell you all about it."

He sits down on the edge of Cara's bed and sneaks his hand under the blanket. I'm pretty sure I know where he's headed so I look the other way even though I can't see anything. When I hear Cara's high pitched squeal, I assumed correctly.

"Shit, Drew. I thought you were Sophie!" Drew's dying of a laughter fit which earns him a love tap to the gut.

"Sorry, babe. When's dinner? I'm starving."

"You're always hungry." She rolls her eyes and sits back up, rearranging her shorts in the process.

"Mostly for you." He leans in and kisses her on the mouth. They're entirely too cute and it makes me wish Kipton lived in the dorm too. "Since I can't have you right now, let's get pizza for dinner."

"You can have me later. Little Italy works for me. They even have the crushed ice in the soda fountain." Cara moans and licks her lips. The girl has an ice addiction.

"You're an easy woman to please, you know that Cara?" Drew declares.

She smiles adoringly at him and holds his hand, interlocking their fingers as she fiddles with the ring on her thumb. "You always please me." She looks up at him through thick lashes and I can tell she's about to jump him from the looks of it.

"Guys, cut it out! I don't need to hear about your sexual shenanigans."

Cara's quick with her comeback. "Says the girl who was sucking face with my brother all afternoon."

Drew raises his eyebrows in surprise. "Bout time. Oh, and speaking of Kipton. I forgot to tell you he's stopping by to talk to me tonight before his date with Sophie."

Cara's freak out coming in 3, 2, 1. . . ."What! Why would he do that? I'll kick his ass." Drew and I both crack up at her exuberant reaction.

"Calm down, killer. It was my idea. I called him and asked," Drew assures her.

Cara huffs and crosses her arms defensively as she looks back and forth between Drew and I. "You two are making me nuts. First I hear about Kipton's lips, now my, well whatever you are is calling him to chat." She waves her hands back and forth between her and Drew in exasperation.

"What do you mean whatever I am?" Drew questions.

"Well, I don't know. We never discussed anything." Her cheeks heat and for the first time, I get a glimpse of shy Cara. I wasn't sure she existed.

"Then let's make it official."

Cara's eyes widen in surprise. "You're sure?"

"Yes. We're having sex aren't we?" Drew leans in to Cara and claims her lips in a sweet, chaste kiss. It's very PG for the two of them.

"We are, but that doesn't mean anything."

Drew looks like she just slapped him. "It means something to me. You're mine."

"I didn't mean it the way it came out, Drew. Just that it doesn't *have* to mean something if you don't want it to."

He caresses her cheek in his hand and places a few more soft kisses on her lips. "Well, I want it to."

"You're sure?" Cara asks again for clarification she knowingly doesn't need.

Drew jumps on top of her in the bed and pins her arms above her head. "Ask me again, I dare you," he challenges. Cara starts laughing as Drew tickles her senseless. I'm worried clothes are going to start flying so I chime in before either of them forget I'm sitting here.

"Okay kids, playtime's over. As romantic as that whole moment was, I need to get a little work done before my own hot date tonight."

Drew climbs off Cara and huffs. "Fine. I'll let you two ladies do your thing. I'll be back for pizza in an hour though."

Cara sits up, resting on her elbows while she watches him leave our room. I don't miss the blissful look in her eyes as she realizes she has officially landed herself a boyfriend. I'm happy for her, although slightly jealous of their effortless connection. Maybe someday I'll be able to dive head first into a relationship without carrying a bunch of heavy baggage along with me.

I take out my astronomy notebook and page through my chapter notes. Doodling in the margin, I draw a few hearts and stars haphazardly around the paper. My mind becomes lost in thoughts of Kipton simply from opening the textbook for the class. Deciding this might not be the best time to tackle my astronomy homework, I find my phone and fire off a text to Kipton.

Sophie: Thanks for checking on me.

Kipton: Always.

He replies within seconds, making me smile at the words on the screen. *Always.* I've never had an always anything. I almost don't know what to do with the letters, but I welcome them.

"Hey, Sophie."

"Yeah, Cara?" I turn around in my desk chair and am surprised to see Cara looking incredibly defeated.

"What's wrong?"

"I dunno. I'm happy, but really *really* nervous," she admits.

I get up from my chair knowing my work will have to wait. "About what exactly?"

"I don't want to screw it up with Drew."

I have no idea where she's going with this. "Okay. Why would you screw it up?"

"I don't have the best track record when it comes to dating guys. I've been looking for a guy like Drew forever. I finally found him, but what if he's too good to be true?"

"There's no magic eight ball that can predict the future. But you guys are adorable together. Honestly, I think he's just as lucky to have you. Enjoy spending time with him and don't hold yourself back because you're scared. But if things do get more serious than they already are, you should have this conversation with him. Let him know where you stand. And maybe the other guys didn't work out because they weren't who you were supposed to be with."

"I can do that. Are you going to take your own advice?" She cuddles back down under the covers of her bed.

"Well played, Cara. But probably not. I haven't had the best history either." Of course I'd love nothing more than to kiss Kipton repeatedly, but as soon as I'm healed, I'll be in the gym on a full time basis. There won't be time for movies under the stars, dinner dates and cuddle sessions. That's what worries me.

"So you're never going to make out with my brother again? Even after how happy it made you?"

"I never said that." I take another sip of my water and clear my throat. It still hurts from making myself sick. "Gymnastics, Cara, it always gets in the way, but that's what's most important to me. Guys come and go, but the sport is my one constant." I refocus on my phone, hoping she takes the hint that I don't like talking about this.

"Were you burned in the past?"

Okay, definitely not getting any work done. I get up and move to my own bed, placing some distance in between the two of us so I can express what I need to say. I'm not about to sit around the campfire singing Kumbaya while hashing out my past, but I owe her an answer.

"Maybe. But there hasn't been a guy worth my time either. I opened up my heart once and all I got out of that was used and tossed aside like yesterday's trash. So, maybe I am jaded, but I've never been around a relationship that stood the test of time either. My dad was a fuck up; my first boyfriend took what he wanted and moved on. I have nothing to go on. It's easier to focus on what's important and put my heart into my gymnastics dream instead of someone else's hands—nobody's ever taken care of it. I have to build my own life, for me. If someone ends up joining me for the ride, awesome. But if it doesn't happen, I'm okay with that too. I don't need a man to make me happy. I have my own goals and ambitions."

Cara blinks her eyes, seeming somewhat surprised by my honest answer. "I'm sorry, Sophie. I had no idea."

"Don't be, I'm not. It is what it is."

"Can I ask you about your dream?"

"I guess." There's honestly not much to tell. It's a pretty cut and dry plan I've mapped out for myself. "What do you want to know?"

"Tell me about it." She rolls over onto her stomach and rests her chin in her hands taking great interest in any details I'm about to tell her.

"All I want is to be the best gymnast I can be, to get good grades and land my dream job. That's it. I've never imagined a husband or kids in my future. I know what I want and what I have to do to get it. That doesn't mean I won't have a little fun along the way."

"You honestly don't want a family?"

"I have my Mom now that my Dad's gone. That's good enough for me."

She stares at me, probably wondering what to say without telling me I'm a selfish bitch. "You deserve so much more than that, Sophie. You're amazing and I'm not saying you're gonna marry the first guy you decide to date, but Kipton cares about you. I've seen the look in his eyes when he's around you. The night you were sick and passed out in his bed, I've never seen him like that."

"Maybe so, but it still doesn't change what I want out of life. History's been known to repeat itself and I don't ever want to live in hell again. People change over time, Cara. In fact, times usually not on our side at all. It does crazy things to our minds and makes us hurt the people we're supposed to love. So, no. I don't really want to be with someone who has the potential to hurt me."

"It doesn't have to be like that, Sophie. It doesn't have to be only gymnastics and work. You deserve to be loved because I know you have the potential to be someone's forever. I promise you there's a way to still be independent without being alone." She walks over and hugs me. I return it, sensing she needs the comfort more than I do. Without knowing my history, she'll never understand where I'm coming from. And that's okay—it's bad enough I have to relive it in my dreams.

"Will you tell me what happened with your first boy-friend?"

I scoot over on my bed so she can sit down with me. "There's not much to tell. He was a year older than I was and moved into the same development that I've lived in all my life. He had a similar situation as I did, with his parents going through a divorce. Neither of us wanted to be in our houses most of the time because of all the fighting, so we would go for runs. Thankfully, I was at gymnastics during most of my free time—maybe that's why I'm so attached to it. It was my saving grace when I had nothing else to turn to. Anyway, as I was running by his house one day, he joined me. At first I was nervous about this random guy being in my personal space, but he was easy to talk to."

Cara's listening intently, hanging on my every word.

"For a while, I felt like he was all I had. So, of course, I wanted to please him. I couldn't make my parents happy or love each other, but I could control the way he felt about me. It's lame, I know that now. But when you're seventeen and desperate for affection and attention, you do stupid things."

I fiddle with the tag on the pillow I'm clutching in my lap. Cara reaches over and holds my hand. "You don't have to tell me more if it's too hard?"

I nod my head that I do. "Each night, he would sneak into my bedroom after my mom was asleep. Most nights, my dad would take off only to return sometime in the morning to get ready for work. But I always made sure Blaine was gone before the bar closed, just in case my dad came home drunk off his ass and looking for drama. Eventually, my dad stopped coming home altogether and I didn't have to wor-ry about Blaine being there. Things moved faster once that happened."

"I'm sorry," Cara says.

"Don't be. All you can control is yourself. I'm still learn-ing that."

"You don't have to continue if it's too much."

"It's okay. I've never told anyone all of this, but I trust you." Cara squeezes my hand again and sadly smiles given the circumstances. "One night, Blaine came over and the usual kissing progressed to more. I was scared, but he had this way of making it seem like I owed him things. Of course it wasn't the case, but he knew how desperate I was for affection. Not physical either, just in the general sense of the word. I would have been fine with a casual friendship, but it wasn't enough for Blaine. Little by little, he took things farther assuring me he loved me. It had been so long since I heard those words from anyone; I wasn't sure how to process them. The only way I knew how to show him I loved him was to let him have all of me. I wanted him to feel how much I loved him in return—for him to know I was *his*. Of course he said all the right things at the right times and I figured my uneasiness was coming from inexperience and not his feelings for me.

Assuming we were officially together considering we had sex and all, I was shocked when I saw him at school kissing another girl at her locker. The very next day, Cara. He didn't even pretend to hide it either. He came to my window every night for a week begging for me to let him inside. Eventually, I let him convince me his weak moment was a mistake and that it would never happen again. He had a way with words.

Our relationship continued in my room each night, but over time, it was more about sex than anything. Now that he had me, he didn't say sweet things to me anymore. There was never cuddling, long talks about our future, or plans together. It was purely physical. And when he had his fill, he would leave me alone to fall asleep in a puddle of tears. I tried to bring back the affectionate Blaine I fell for, but it only made him angry. Really angry."

"Did he hurt you, Sophie?"

One blink is all it takes to bring the tears back. "Yes." I wipe my tears and continue—my voice shaky from the emotion of retelling the story. "There was no way I could love him or trust him anymore, Cara. He was exactly like my Dad. A liar, a cheat, and a fake."

"Did your Dad hit you too, Sophie?"

"No. Only Blaine. My Dad was all verbal abuse, years and years of it. Not that it makes it any better."

Cara leans over and hugs me tightly. "Sophie, I'm so sorry. You're worth so much more than the way they treated you. You have to believe that."

"I'd like to believe I'm worthy of someone's love, Cara. But the two guys I've looked up to both let me down. My Dad never loved me and made it very clear he didn't want me. Blaine was only pretending to be in love with me in order to get what he wanted physically. And once he did, he turned into a monster. I never saw it coming either, so it hurt even more. Especially after he knew what I was dealing with at home."

"He's an ass, Sophie. I hate him. Why would he do that to you?"

"I have no idea, but maybe that's why he picked me. He knew how fucked up I already was."

"How did it end?"

I manically laugh. "Gymnastics of all places. It's saved my life on so many levels. My coach noticed bruises on my arms and legs. There's not much you can hide in a leotard. But all it took was one call to the authorities and it was over. *One* call, Cara, that I didn't have the nerve to make myself."

"None of it is your fault, Sophie. Please believe that. You're a survivor, a fighter."

"Pizza time, ladies!" Drew announces before he's even fully into the room. "Oh, did I interrupt?"

Cara releases me from her embrace, winking at me while doing so. She's up to something.

"You did, but we're willing to let you in on it if you shut the door," she playfully tells him. His eyes gleam with excitement. He leans against the door, shutting it with his body instead of his hands. His eyes haven't strayed from Cara's once. "Good boy."

Drew shakes his head yes and waits for his next command. "Kiss me, Drew." Without a second thought, he walks over to her and picks her up. She straddles his waist with her legs and spins around to pin her up against the closet door. As much as I'm wondering how long she's going to let this charade play out, I clear my throat to remind them I'm still sitting here. Cara giggles and lets her legs fall from his waist to the floor. "I'm sorry, Sophie. How could we leave you out? Drew, I want you to kiss Sophie now."

Frozen in place, he hesitates to move. Briefly, he looks at me before turning his attention back to Cara. It takes all I have not to bust out laughing. Cara cuddles up to his side and runs her hands under his shirt. "Don't you want to make us both happy, Drew?"

"Um. Uh. But doesn't she have Kipton? I mean I don't want to get my ass kicked. He already found me with you, Cara. What if he shows up and sees the three of us?"

"So you don't want to play?" Cara whines like a spoiled child who isn't about to get her way. She's a fabulous actress. I'll give her that.

"I was just hoping for pizza, but I'm down with whatever will make you happy."

Cara can't hold a straight face any longer and snorts. "Good answer." She jumps into his arms again and kisses him senseless. He responds with a deep moan to which I ignore and grab my purse.

I clutch the straps in my hand and smack it against Drew's back to hurry them along. "Let's get some pizza, guys. You can have your tryst afterwards."

Drew looks somewhat disappointed although relieved. "You two are evil. But if you can promise I won't get my ass beat, I'm still game."

"We'll keep that in mind for a rainy day," I assure him.

"Hell yeah!" It doesn't take much to excite him.

"Go grab an elevator, babe. We'll catch up, okay?" Cara kisses him one last time and sends him on his way while I lock up. She waits until I'm finished before speaking. "I want you to know you're not fucked up, Sophie. You're the most beautiful, selfless person I've ever met. I know we've only known each other a short time, but I mean it. You were dealt a shitty hand so far, but it can only get better. Give my brother a real shot. Let love in, Sophie. I promise you won't regret it this time."

I give her a hug, appreciative of her heartfelt words. "I'll try my best, Cara. Thanks for listening. I didn't mean to drown you with all the heavy stuff today."

"You drown me any day of the week. I'm here. Always."

"Thanks, Cara."

I'd love to believe Kipton is different because I'm not sure I can handle it if he's not. Casual with him will work. It's the serious I'm afraid of because I won't survive another failure. My heart can only be broken so many times before it turns to dust.

CHAPTER *thirteen*

KIPTON

I ARRIVE AT JOHNSON HALL early, hoping the talk with Drew is quick so I don't have to waste any more time before seeing Sophie. Not even bothering to wait the few seconds for the elevator, I take the stairs to the third floor. As I exit the stairwell, I catch a glimpse of Sophie walking toward her room. Cara and Drew playfully punch each other as they walk in the opposite direction toward his room. Hopefully they'll be fully clothed by the time I get there. After the walk by sexing, I don't think I can handle much more.

Before I can catch up to Sophie, she stops in the bathroom. Knowing I won't be able to concentrate on a word Drew says if I don't see her first, I anxiously wait for her in the hallway. I take out my phone, going through some texts but only bothering to respond to the important ones. A few more minutes pass before I hear the sound of someone gagging painfully. Worried it's Sophie, I sneak inside to check on her. Knocking on the door softly so I don't scare her, I wait for her to speak. But she doesn't. "Sophie, are you okay?"

There's no response other than another round of gagging and vomiting. "Sophie? Can you answer me so I know you're okay."

Through labored breaths, she finally responds to me. "Leave me alone. I'm okay"

Her tone is harsher than normal, but there's still no way

I'm leaving her. "Open the door, beautiful."

"Can you go wait for me in my room, please? Here." Without bothering to wait for my response, her keys sail over the top of the stall door landing on the tile floor instead of in my hand. When I bend down to pick them up, I spot her crouched in the corner by the toilet. Her right hand's dangling by her side, trembling ever so slightly. The left is cradling her forehead.

"Are you sure you're okay?" Something's wrong and I don't like it.

I hear her sniffle and I can't fucking take it. Placing my hand on top of the metal stall door, I yank it open in one swift motion, dislodging the small silver lock from its anchor. In shock, Sophie screams and covers her head with her hands. "Kipton! I said I'm fine. You can't be in here!"

I crouch down to her level. "You don't look fine, Sophie. You're shaking."

"It's just my stomach. I promise it's not a big deal."

"Did you eat dinner?" I rub my thumb back and forth over the top of her hand.

She nods her head, yes. "We went for pizza."

"Come on, I'll walk you to your room. Unless you want me to take you to see a doctor." I stand up, reaching out my hand for her to take, but she doesn't move from her crouched position.

"I'm fine. Please go. I don't want you to see me like this. Don't you have a meeting with Drew?"

"Sophie, I don't want to leave you by yourself. Drew can wait." She flushes the toilet and brushes past me. As she's washing her hands, I walk up behind her pushing her silky hair away from the back of her neck. I lean down to place a small kiss behind her ear, but she tenses up and shrugs away from my touch. "Sophie. Don't do this."

"Do what? Wash my hands?" She reaches over and tears a paper towel from the roll. Drying her hands quickly, she tosses the paper in the trash before walking out on me.

I stand rooted in the middle of the girl's bathroom staring blankly at the paper towel dispenser. *What was that all about?* Earlier today she was on my lap kissing me like her life depended on it and now she's acting like I repulse her. I'd like to give her the benefit of the doubt, but I hate that she's acting so distant. As the shock of the last few minutes wears off, I exit the bathroom just in time to catch a glimpse of her door slamming shut.

Cara comes running around the corner, most likely on her way to find me. "Kippy! Drew's in his room waiting for you. Hurry up." She's tugging on my arm, but I'm not in the mood to deal with her or Drew anymore.

"Can you tell him we need to reschedule. My plans changed. I have to go."

She creases her brow, looking confused. "Why? Where's Sophie?"

"In your room. I want to go talk to her, but I don't think she wants me to. Here. She's gonna need her keys back." Numbly, I press the button on the elevator.

Cara puts her hand on my arm and squeezes lightly. "What happened? You're acting weird." Drew comes bounding around the corner in similar fashion, but pauses after seeing my defeated expression.

"I have no fucking clue. Things were fine when we left class this afternoon, but I saw her a minute ago and she acted like I have the damn plague. I mean she did throw up and all, but she wouldn't even let me comfort her."

"What do you mean?" Both Drew and Cara ask in unison.

"She wasn't feeling good and she wouldn't even let me touch her. Did she say anything about me at dinner?" The elevator door opens, but I let it pass and wait for the next one.

"Shit." Cara says.

"What is it? Do you know something?"

"It's not my place to say, Kippy. I'm sorry."

"Cara, please. What's going on? I'm not leaving until you tell me something."

"Fine. Basically she mentioned something about focusing on gymnastics and how she doesn't have time to date. From what she told me this afternoon, she has a shitty past and has no faith in the male species whatsoever. Her ex was a douche and her Dad wasn't any better. Our talk must have gotten to her because she barely touched her dinner and was in her own little world during the conversation. I feel bad for asking her so many questions earlier. It's obviously a sore subject for her. I mean, she doesn't even want a husband or kids. Can you believe that?"

"Fuck. I had no idea. Can you go check on her for me? She didn't mention whether we're still going to the movie tonight, but I don't want to push her if she's not up to it."

Cara reaches up and gives me a hug. For the first time, I'm thankful my sister is here to help me out. If anyone can get Sophie talking again, it's her. "Don't take it personal. She's working though some pretty tough emotions from the sound of it. I hope one day she'll have the courage to tell you what she told me. But until then, I'll go talk to her and have her call you. Was her head hurting? Is that why she got sick?"

"Your guess is as good as mine. I tried to help her, but she wouldn't let me. She didn't even let me touch her." Cara closes her eyes and exhales. When she opens them, she looks pained. There's more to this story and I'm pissed she knows something I most likely should.

"Maybe she needs a moment to get her shit together. Throwing up in front a guy you like isn't exactly a magical moment, Kippy."

"I guess not." Hanging my head, I press the elevator button again instead of checking on Sophie. I'll let my sister handle it because I'm not willing to completely ruin whatever I started with Sophie this afternoon. Hopefully she just needs a little girl talk to feel better.

"Don't sweat it dude, chicks are fucking crazy." Laughing at Drew, I nod my head in agreement as the elevator doors close. I've yet to meet one who doesn't make my head spin. There's no way I was imagining the kiss we shared earlier today. She wanted me as much as I wanted her. I felt it.

Once outside, I sit on the wooden bench by the basketball courts and watch a game of four on four. Thankfully it's shaded so I'm not sweating my ass off in the sun. I catch myself glancing at my phone every five seconds, waiting for it to chime with positive news from Cara. Maybe no news is good news right now.

When I look up at their window, the blinds are pulled

back on the right side. Sophie's peeking around them staring directly at me. Unsure if she sees me looking back, I shield my squinted eyes from the sun. Before I can get a better look, she's gone.

Agitated, I can't sit still. Shifting around on the uncomfortable bench, I fail miserably at any attempt to relax. The game ends half an hour later, but I don't even know who won. My mind's been solely focused on Sophie. Finally, my phone vibrates with an incoming text.

Cara: She was upset. Calmed her down.

Kipton: I need to see her.

Cara: I'm not sure that's a good idea. She's embarrassed for being rude to you.

Kipton: I'm coming up.

Cara: I figured you would.

Racing inside the building, I take the stairs two at a time before Sophie realizes I'm on my way up to see her. By the third flight, I'm thankful she doesn't live any higher up in the building. My lungs are fighting for some much needed oxygen. Winded but determined to get to their room as fast as I can, I muscle through the last flight.

I knock softly on the door, careful not to startle Sophie if her head's hurting. Cara lets me in. The lights are off and there's music playing from her laptop. She stands on her tip toes to whisper in my ear, "I'll be in Drew's room. Come over if you need anything."

"I will." I'm solely focused on Sophie lying in her bed. She's facing the wall and can't see me yet, but when she inches up the blankets, I know she senses my presence. Afraid to say the wrong thing, I don't say anything until my knee cracks loudly when I crouch down next to her. She flinches but doesn't turn to look at me. "Sophie, can we talk?"

Without moving, she responds, "About what?"

Needing to touch her in some way, I run my fingers up and down the arm that's clenching her blanket tightly to her chest. I'm thankful when she doesn't object. "About us." I probably sound like a fucking woman asking to discuss my feelings and shit. This is all new to me and although it's been a struggle so far, I don't want to give up.

"What about us, Kipton?" Her voice is laced with emotion and I get the impression she's trying not to cry right now. I knew she felt something earlier and now she confirmed it whether she realizes it or not.

"For starters I need to know what happened to the girl I was kissing this afternoon. The one that's always on my mind." She sighs and all I want is for her to roll over and look me in the eye.

"Kipton, I told you there's no time for a relationship in my life—I don't do them. What we did was fun and I enjoyed it. But it doesn't change anything. In a few days, I'll be back in the gym full-time. That's my real life. Not *this*."

"What if I need whatever *this* is?"

"I don't know, Kipton."

"You're really choosing gymnastics?" It's meant as more of a statement than a question. She has a passion that I'm not about to come between, but she could make time for both if she wanted to.

"I have to," she responds quickly.

"But you don't want to?"

Finally rolling over, the tears in her eyes can't be mistaken. Gone is her hard demeanor, instead replaced with the sweet Sophie I've been unable to get out of my mind. "I'm no good for you, Kipton."

That's where she's wrong. "You're perfect, Sophie. I've never craved anyone the way I crave you." She has the same look in her eye my sister did out in the hallway. But I don't know why.

"I don't want to be anyone's toy. I've lived that life and I can't go back."

"Tell me what that means, beautiful."

"It doesn't matter what it means."

"Sophie, it does because nothing you tell me will scare me away. I want you in whatever way you need me to. I'm too far gone to stop."

She turns her head and stares blankly at the wall, shutting me out. "You should go, Kipton."

"I thought we had a date?" I'll do anything to spend a few more minutes with her. Even if I have to beg because I get the impression if I walk out now, she and I will be nothing more than a distant memory.

She shakes her head no. "I want to rest."

"Do you want to watch a movie here instead? We don't have to go to the one on the field." *Please say yes.*

She pauses for a few seconds, her eyes scanning my entire face. "Why me?" Her sparkling blue eyes look like they're a moment away from releasing whatever pain she's holding hostage inside of her.

"Why *not* you?" I question.

"Pfft. I can give you a million reasons."

I decide to challenge her. "Name one."

Rolling her eyes, she huffs and shifts in the bed. "We wouldn't work. I don't have any spare time when I'm in the gym and you're too big of a distraction, Kipton. If you haven't noticed I make shitty decisions when I'm around you."

I shake my head back and forth. "I don't buy it for a second, beautiful. That's a lame ass excuse and you know it."

"Fine, then you come up with a reason why we *would* work since you have all the answers."

My response is automatic. "Because it would kill me to see you with someone else, Sophie."

Seeming shocked by my answer, it takes her a minute to even blink. When she finally does, a stray tear falls down her cheek as soon as her eyelashes meet. Watching its descent, I lean over and catch the droplet with my tongue. My taste buds soak up the salty mixture of sadness. Her hands rise to rest on my shoulders for a brief second before she digs her nails into my skin as she fights for control of her emotions. There's no pain because her tiny fingertips send a shock wave though the fabric of my T-shirt, resuscitating my hopeful heart. *I know she wants this too.*

Without another word spoken, her lips tangle with mine in the most innocent way before our tongues eventually meet. She's challenging my body to either stay in control or break free. When her hands move from my shoulders and glide down my back, I make a split second decision and gently move over top of her, wedging my leg between hers. She keeps her lips locked with mine while exploring with her hands. "Off," she mumbles against my mouth while tugging on my shirt. Reaching behind my neck, I pull it over my head eager to see what she plans to do next. She claws at the blankets between us, trying to get rid of the barrier.

Helping her, I pull the comforter down so I can touch her body. Sliding my hands under her shirt and over her stomach, she sucks in her toned abs when I move to kiss the soft skin around her belly button. Moaning softly, she gives me the confidence I need to continue.

"Kipton," she whispers.

I raise my head to look at her, but her eyes are closed. "Is this okay, Sophie?" She nods her head but I need her words. "I need to hear you, beautiful."

"Yes, don't stop."

"Put your arms above your head." She follows my direction and I easily pull her shirt off. Left in her pink lace bra, I pull the straps off her shoulders. Without removing it entirely, I inch the lace away from her chest. Her back arches as she anticipates my next move. Flicking her pebbled nipples with my tongue, she responds instantly.

"Please, don't' make me wait. I need you, Kipton. Make me feel something else—something good."

"I'm right here, Sophie. You have me." I don't understand her request entirely, but I give her what she wants anyway. We can discuss her second request later. I reach my hand inside her yoga pants and slip under the lace of her panties, touching her wetness. "Sophie, shit."

"Yes, Kipton. More." She grinds against my hand and while I'm content getting her off like this, she sits up. I try to remove my hand from her pants but she stops me, instead reaching for the button on my shorts. Fumbling to release it, she pulls down the zipper before I have to break contact to finish removing my shorts along with my boxer briefs. Her eyes are fixated on my dick and it twitches from the desire in her eyes. Before I take my place on the bed, she removes the remainder of her own clothing and waits for me.

We kiss slowly at first, my hands discovering every inch of her skin I haven't yet touched. She reaches her arms around my waist to pull my body on top of hers. The skin to skin connection is intense, but she's so tiny I'm afraid I'm hurting her, so I use my knees to take some of the pressure off her body. I want nothing more than to be inside her, but I have to be sure this is what she wants. "You're sure, Sophie? We can stop whenever you want."

"I need this. Don't make me wait."

"Beautiful, I don't have a condom with me." My damn wallet is in my fucking car. Figures the one time I'm not prepared, I'm given the perfect opportunity to claim my girl. I expect her to end this once I tell her the truth, but instead, she grabs my face in both of her hands. Sucking on my bottom lip, I groan from the sexiness. In between kisses, she surprises me again. "It's okay, just pull out."

I'm hesitant at first, wanting to do things the right way with her, but when she tightens her legs around me and I brush against her wetness, that's all the confirmation I need to slide inside her. Her heat blows my mind and while I want to take it slow for her, I have to move. Her soft moans mixed with little grunts of pleasure encourage me even more. Wanting her to experience the same sweet ache of pleasure I am, I reach down between her legs to help her find her release. She jumps the second I touch her. "Kipton, ohmigod."

Like two greedy lovers in need of a fix, we both savor each push and pull. A thin sheen of sweat breaks out over my body as I use every ounce of restraint inside of me to make sure she's thoroughly satisfied before pulling out and coming on her stomach. It's intense and she watches the entire time. I've never had a connection with someone the way we do.

My arms begin to shake from holding myself up, so I grab a tissue from the box next to the bed and clean her off before flopping down next to her—completely exhausted. Carefully,

I roll onto my side so we both comfortably fit on her small twin bed. Pulling her close, she willingly melts into my chest for a brief moment before scooting away and sitting up.

She pulls the sheet off the bed and wraps it around her body. Standing up, she carefully puts her shirt on without ever dropping the sheet an inch. I've seen her entire body naked, yet she's suddenly self-conscious. She does the same with her pants, leaving her bra and panties lying on the bed.

"You're body's amazing, Sophie, you don't have to hide it from me." She finally glances in my direction, but it feels more like she's looking through me than at me. Her sudden detachment doesn't make sense. She was present every second our bodies were joined.

"You should go, Kipton. I don't want you to, but you need to."

Sitting up, I look at her like she's lost her damn mind. There's no way in hell she's kicking me out after we had sex. At least not until she explains herself. "Excuse me?" I question, when all other words fail me.

"You should go," she replies softly.

"Are you fucking kidding me right now?" I raise my voice louder than I should, but this time, I don't apologize for it. I'm pissed and she needs to know I won't play games. Either she's in or she's out because tonight wasn't just a casual fuck by any means.

"I told you before you climbed into my bed that I can't do relationships."

"So you're going to ignore everything that happened?" I'm standing in the middle of her room naked as the day I was born arguing with a girl about kicking me out. *Karma is a bitch.*

She shakes her head. "No, it was good."

"Good? It was more than that, Sophie, and you know it."

"Kipton, nothing's changed. I wanted that as much as you did, but I can't have *this*." She gestures between the two of us alluding to our connection. "I'm sorry."

I pick up my discarded clothing as quickly as I can, stumbling a few times while trying to put my shorts back on. She wants me to believe this was purely physical, but the way her body responded to mine, it was so much more than that.

I may be angry about the stunt she pulled, but I don't want to argue with her. This goes far beyond gymnastics and I need to know why she's so damn hesitant. I try like hell to keep my damn mouth shut, but I can't. It has a mind of its own. "I know you crave me too, Sophie. You can go on pretending you don't, but we both know the truth." I walk closer to her and she turns her head. "You want me as much as I fucking want you."

She doesn't look at me. Instead she stands by the door with her arms folded protectively across her chest. As mad as I am at her for not taking what's hers, I still can't deny the way I'm drawn to her. I should be humiliated, I'm being kicked out, but instead, I feel sorry for her. Cara warned me she has a wicked past, but if she's not willing to open up to me about it, I'm not sure I'll ever be able to fix the way she feels. So if all she wants right now is a quick fuck, then I have no choice but to give it to her.

"I don't know why you want to deny it, Sophie, but you know I want you. And not for what we just did. I want you because for the first time in my life, I needed a girl. My past isn't all rainbows and butterflies either, but I care about you enough to work through my own bullshit to change. I'm sure Cara's told you a bunch of shit, but whatever she's told you is in the past. I've changed for *you,* Sophie. I'm not that guy anymore. So if that's what is holding you back, don't let it."

"This isn't about you, Kipton. Not at all."

"Then what, Sophie? Please help me understand."

"I can't."

"Can you honestly look me in the eye and deny you want me?" I pause, waiting for her to change her mind and run into my arms, but when she doesn't move, I know we're done. Silence fills the room. "I guess this was a mistake." This time it's me brushing past her, leaving her alone with her thoughts.

She closes the door as soon as I'm completely through, not even bothering to watch me leave. Standing in the hall-way with one hand on the knob, I lean my head against the wood. When a strangled cry leaves her, it takes all I have to keep from going back inside. But this is what she wanted and as wrong as it is, I'll walk away.

CHAPTER
fourteen

Sophie

"I GUESS THIS WAS A mistake."

Sobbing, I slide down the closed door into a heap on the floor. He could have said anything to me and I would have been okay. Anything—except that. Like a knife slicing my skin open, his words gut me. Kipton's words are just like *his*.

But he's not.

I'm too scared to want him, yet terrified that if I walk away; I'll never feel the way I feel when I'm with him. "We aren't a mistake, Kipton." I cry into my hands. My body shakes from the pain of his words. He doesn't know what I've lived through. He doesn't know the emptiness inside me and I don't know how to let him in.

What have I done?

Maybe *I'm* the one who made the mistake.

I kicked him out.

Crouching tightly into the corner of my room next to the door, I hyperventilate. *Nobody understands.* Love has always been my number one enemy and now that I met Kipton, I don't know how to find acceptance. I've spent so many years hating, I'm not sure how to do anything else. Because I do—care about him. Yet I'm petrified of the backlash love has shown me over the years—of being let down and dismissed time and time again.

I take deep cleansing breaths through my nose and out my mouth. My chest isn't quite as tight—my fingers only slightly tingling. Replaying Kipton's gentle touches in my mind over and over, my heart rate decreases, the sweating stops, and finally my anxiety levels out. I rest my head against the wall and the tears return without any provoking. But I'm not spiraling with anger this time. No, this time, I'm simply sad. *It's over.*

The door opens and I'm shifted farther to the side. Cara slips in quietly. I should move, but I don't have the strength.

"Sophie, what's going on? Where's my brother?"

"He's gone," I whisper.

She sits down on the floor next to me. "What happened? Why are you crying?"

Unsure of what to tell her, and not willing to have another panic attack, I have to get out of the room. Standing up, I grab my bra from the bed. Replacing it, I put on my running shorts and a tank top. The only thing that will take my mind off the past hour is exercise. Kipton's gone and that's not going to change.

"Sophie, answer me. What's going on?"

"I'm going for a run."

"Are you allowed to do that?" She questions.

"Does it matter?"

"Sophie. Of course it matters."

Grabbing a sports drink from the small fridge, I chug it before I leave. I'll need it to get my body through the workout. "I'll be back later. I need some fresh air."

"Okay," She responds quietly. I pass Drew on my way out and am thankful Cara has him. If either of us deserves happiness, it's her.

Once outside, I pause to look around, deciding which route to take. Still not entirely familiar with the town, I do my best to remember which way will avoid the wrestling house while still getting me to the gym. Out of the corner of my eye, I do a double take when I spot Kipton hugging a girl. He reaches his hand up to touch her hair and Déjà vu hits me hard. Thoughts of catching Blaine making out with *her* at his locker resurface, but I push them away before they have a chance to consume me. *He will not ruin me—step. He will not hurt me—step.*

The gym's deserted by the time I get there. I skip the weight room and go right for the balance beam—my favorite. I'm thankful for the peace and quiet; although I'm not sure being left alone with my own thoughts is safe right now. Running my fingertips through the leftover chalk on the beam, I hoist myself up to sit on it. Straddling my legs around each side, I propel myself upward into a handstand. The sensation of being upside down makes me slightly dizzy, but I do it anyway. Inhaling deeply, I know without a doubt this is where I belong. I've been missing the rush of adrenaline—the accomplishment of learning something new. The only other thing I can compare it to is being intimate with Kipton. He sends me to heights similar to the thrill of competition.

But I don't deserve him and I never will.

CHAPTER *fifteen*

KIPTON

LEAVING SOPHIE'S ROOM WAS ONE of the hardest things I've ever had to do. The emotion on the other side of the door leaves me confused and angry. If she's so upset about telling me to leave, then why is she pushing me away? Her actions conflict with her words and I'm more determined than ever to figure out what's going on inside her head.

Deep in thought, I'm oblivious to the meeting I walk in on in the rec room. I excuse myself though with an apology for the interruption. Once outside, the fresh night air relaxes me slightly, but not enough. Tonight I'll need a few drinks to take the edge off.

"Kipton! Wait up."

Turning around, I notice a cute brunette hurrying after me. Looking vaguely familiar, I figure I know her from one of the parties at the house. Praying I haven't slept with her and don't remember, I wait for her to speak first. I've been known to suffer from foot in mouth syndrome.

"I thought that was you. At least I was hoping so I wouldn't look like an idiot," she says.

Upon closer inspection, I have no clue who this chick is. "Hey, what's up?" I adjust the brim on my hat and stuff my hands in my pockets jingling the loose change inside. Hopefully she says something to clue me in.

"How've you been? It's been awhile."

"Pretty good. How are you?" Okay, so I knew her a while ago. That doesn't help.

"You have no idea who I am do you?"

Laughing, I put my hand on the back of my neck while looking down at the crack in the pavement. "Honestly, I'm not one hundred percent positive. You look familiar, but this campus is huge. I'm sorry."

"That's okay, I've changed. We had freshman English together."

"Wait, Emily. Right?"

Playfully punching my arm, she smiles bigger this time, "You *do* remember."

Hell yes I remember. I had the biggest crush on her, but she was dating some asshole on the football team already. She's a local. "We wrote that god awful short story about ghosts and battle fields for our final project. It's been a few years, come here." I pull her into a friendly hug and she laughs.

"That was awful! I'm impressed you remember."

I touch the strands of her hair, flipping up the ends. "I was thrown with the hair color change and well, you um, grew up." She used to be a blonde and is now sporting a huge rack.

Throwing her head back in laughter, I'm instantly taken back in time to a place when things were fresh and easy. College was beginning and I had my entire four year academic career to look forward to. Being a senior, the pressure of the real world constantly breathing down my neck is a mind fuck. "You've grown up too, ya know." She takes an appraising view of my body and under normal circumstances, I'd invite her into my bed without a second thought. Considering I only left Sophie's a few minutes ago, that's not about to happen. Instead, I smile at the compliment. "I have to get back to this sorority meeting with some of the freshmen pledges, but we should hang out sometime. That's if you're available and all."

I like her style. A chick who isn't afraid to take what she wants, unlike someone else I know. Sophie's face flashes into my thoughts, but I push her away. The same way she pushed me out the door.

"You and the quarterback didn't work out?"

"God, no. He's a certifiable asshole."

"Let me get your number." She hands me her phone and I text myself from it, then text her back. "There, numbers are exchanged." I'm not interested in her sexually, but Emily's a cool chick and we used to have fun in class. "Maybe we can meet up for lunch sometime for old time's sake."

Giggling, she looks at her phone like it's been encased in diamonds. "Sounds good." She stops laughing and leans in to hug me again. "You should text me tonight."

"I just might." The night's still young for college life, but my head's not in the right place to entertain her. Not to mention, I still haven't given up on Sophie. Not entirely, anyway. Winking at her, I turn and walk away.

"Bye, Kipton."

I'm not more than a hundred yards away from the dorm when I sense Sophie's presence. I don't know what it is or why, but I turn around and see her jogging away from the dorm. She's not supposed to be running or exercising until next week.

My gut reaction is to go after her, even if only to make sure she doesn't hurt herself. The anger and fresh defeat encourage me to do the exact opposite, but remembering the way she moaned my name a short time ago, my decision is made for me.

I'll never catch up to her, but she stays within my sight the entire way. I'm relieved when she slows down before stopping in front of the gym. I hang back a ways, hoping to blend in as I hide under the darkness of the sky. After she goes inside, I wait a few seconds before I follow her.

Dumbstruck, I watch her flip around on the balance beam. Delicate yet powerful, she does each trick with ease and for the first time I see how talented she is. In no rush, she leaps from end to end; her beautiful body making her movements appear effortless. Making sure I stay in the shadows, I'm in complete awe. When she's finished, she flips off the end. Landing hard, she reaches up and holds her head. Instinctively, I bolt from my hiding place to make sure she's okay.

Sophie's leaning against the side of the beam still clutching her temples. I forget she has no idea I'm behind her and when I rest my hand on her waist, her scream echoes off the rafters. Flailing her fist into my face, she lands a solid punch to my left eye. "Holy hell, Sophie. It's me!"

"Shit! I'm sorry. How was I supposed to know you were in here?"

"Well now you know." I rub my eye and can already sense a headache brewing. "You have a solid right hook for as small as you are."

She hops up onto the beam and sits down, bringing her closer to my eye level. I move in and place my hands on either side of her. Her small body is easily encased by mine. "Why are you following me?" she questions.

"Because I saw you running and was worried you'd hurt yourself."

Releasing her messy pony tail, she blows a few strands of hair out of her eyes. "You didn't look too worried about me while you were chatting it up with that girl. Got her number and everything."

She's jealous and I happen to enjoy every second of it. It reaffirms everything I already knew. "You saw that?"

"I did."

"It wasn't what you think, Sophie."

She uses her pants to wipe some leftover chalk off her hands. "You sure about that? Did you make plans?"

"No."

"No you aren't sure, or no you didn't make plans?"

I love that she needs to ask me for specifics. "No, Sophie. We didn't make plans. In case you forgot in the half hour since I was inside of you, I want *you*."

She sucks in a deep breath, but keeps the questions flowing. "You hugged her."

She's so stubborn. "I told you it wasn't what it looked like."

She cocks her head to the side trying to play tough. "I'm supposed to believe that?"

I know it's wrong before I even say it, but I say it anyway. "Like I'm supposed to believe you don't want me? Or do you only fuck and run? "

She turns her head away, refusing to acknowledge me standing right in front of her. Tossing my words back at me, she says, "it wasn't what it looked like."

I reach up and make her look at me so she comprehends every word I'm saying. "Then don't judge me and I won't judge you." I inch closer to her, wrapping my arms around her waist. She has no place to look, but into my eyes until I hug her and rest my head against her stomach. Brushing her fingers through my hair, I'm hopeful she's ready to acknowledge what's going on between the two of us. But much like a moment is, it's over before it has a chance to multiply.

"Kipton, I have to get going."

Damn it. "Why do you keep running, beautiful?"

She shrugs. "For exercise."

"You know what I mean. Why do you keep running from *me.*"

I search her face for any clue about what to do next. Her resolve slowly crumbles right before my eyes, but as fast as it disappears, she's fighting to regain control again. Before she can come up with any other ideas, I kiss her. It's not slow, innocent or forgiving. It's a claiming kiss as my lips tangle with hers so roughly our teeth clash a few times. *Sophie has to be mine.* Placing my hands under her ass, I'm ready to hoist her off the beam and around my waist until she freezes and pushes me back.

"I can't do this, Kipton. I'm sorry."

"Sophie. Don't run. Stay with me. Be *mine.*"

She softly whispers, "It's the only thing I know how to do right now."

I need to know why. "Let me teach you how to stay."

She looks pained when she says, "Please, Kipton. Forget about *us.* It's easier that way."

"And if I don't want to?"

"Then I'll make you." I recoil like she punched me again, this time in the stomach. She spins around to the other side of the beam and hops down. Grabbing her shoes, she runs out of the gym as fast as her legs will carry her. But I don't try to follow her this time.

I may not have taken her seriously when she kicked me out of her room, but I know now it's a done deal. Anything I have left to say will fall on deaf ears.

She wins. And I hate to fucking lose.

THE NEXT COUPLE WEEKS PASS by without having spoken to Sophie. Cara's asked me to come by her room a couple times, but we always settle for meeting at the coffee shop instead. I can't risk running into Sophie outside of class after the way things ended. I've been trying to erase her from my memory, even going as far as to make out with a few random chicks at last week's party. It didn't work. None of their mouths felt as incredible as hers. It's effortless with Sophie when she decides to let go.

For the first two weeks after our sexual explosion, I was checking in with Cara on a daily basis about Sophie's progress. Unfortunately, she was benched another week after admitting her dizziness hadn't entirely subsided. Knowing how upset she must have been, I desperately wanted to contact her on my own. I tossed that thought aside the day she switched partners in astronomy. She wasn't kidding when she said she would make me forget her. Little does she know her actions have the exact opposite effect on me, the distance only making me want her *more.*

Cara assures me Sophie's been throwing all of her extra time into running and going to the gym, much like I have. She sees her in passing, but they haven't spent much time together the past three weeks. Of course that earned me an *I told you so* of epic proportions and a reminder of why Cara had wanted me to keep my distance in the first place. Briefly I regret messing up their relationship, but not enough to take back the desire I still have for her. Because let's face it, if Sophie came to her senses, I'd still want her.

There's a party at the house tonight that I'm not sure I'm up for, but know I need to attend. If there's one way to forget Sophie, it's to get drunk and make a new memory with someone else. Although it's the same damn thing every week, drink, get drunk, and wake up with a raging hangover, it beats staying up all night thinking of *her.* Not wanting to drink on an empty stomach, I decide to see if my sister wants to go to dinner beforehand. I'm also man enough to admit I'd like to find out what Sophie's doing tonight.

The number committed to memory, I dial without scrolling through my contact list. "Hello?" *It's a dude.*

"Drew?" I question

"No, man. This is Tyler. Who you looking for?"

"My sister, Cara. Is she there?"

"No, she's at dinner with Drew. They left about twenty minutes ago. Want me to tell her you called?"

"No. I'll call her tomorrow." I should end it and hang up here, but I'm a glutton for punishment apparently. "Is Sophie there?"

"She is, but she can't come to the phone right now."

"Why not?"

"She's in the shower. Can you call back a little later?"

I know what she looks like in that pink towel, and it pisses me the fuck off to know he will too. I don't know who Tyler is, but I don't like it. At all. "No thanks. I'll pass." Without another word, I hang up. Tonight's party is looking better and better by the second. In fact, I know the perfect solution to my problems. Not bothering to waste another second, I dial Emily's number. I need to have some fun because this whole not giving a shit thing isn't working out.

"Hello."

"Hey Emily. It's Kipton."

"Well it took you long enough. I assumed you weren't interested." I hear the teasing tone in her voice and can sense her smiling on the other end of the line.

"Exactly the opposite. In fact, I'm very interested in seeing you tonight."

"You are? Well, I'm very interested in seeing you too," she confesses.

Unfortunately, she knows she's a hot piece and can get what she wants with little effort. I'll play her game for now. "I'm glad to hear that. There's a party at my place in a couple hours."

"Okay. Do I need to bring someone with me or am I yours for the night?" She's still direct and easy. Exactly as I planned.

"That's up to you, but you may be occupied for a little while. Your friend's free to join us if she's into it."

"I like the sound of that, Kipton."

Holy shit. I was joking but hey, the more the merrier, right? I play it cool even though the only chick I really want in my bed is Sophie. But I'm a guy regardless and my dick is in full agreement that a threesome would be hot as hell. I'm human, not a saint.

You only live once, right?

CHAPTER
sixteen

Sophie

I'VE BEEN DOING A DECENT job of avoiding Kipton. Astronomy is the hardest because he spends most of the class staring at me. I don't even have to look at him to know he's doing it. He wasn't happy when I made up another lie to convince my professor to switch lab partners as well as my seat. Blaming it on a conflict of interest, I was able to build a case of how it was causing strain in my relationship with my roommate. As it turns out, getting caught making out in the planetarium actually worked in my favor. While it won't be nearly as fun to map the sky with Oliver, the brainiac from England, at least I won't be tempted to make out with him.

Along with angering Kipton, I also let down Coach Evans. My body finally passed inspection with the team doctor, but it only took one routine on the uneven bars to send my equilibrium into shock all over again, sidelining me for another week. Frustrated with my uncooperative balance, running has been my saving grace and the only thing my body seems to tolerate without an all out war. I still get headaches off and on, but nothing intense like the first week after my concussion.

Tyler, the captain of the men's gymnastics team, has been sidelined with a nagging ankle injury. We've been training together in the weight room while everyone else is in the gym working on their routines. Understanding how important it is to get back to training, he's been helping me come up with an awesome conditioning program that will impress Coach once I'm at full strength. I've already toned up more than I thought possible and have built a friendship in the process. Finally my body is beginning to work with me instead of against.

Tyler's girlfriend goes to school about an hour from here, so they don't get to see each other as often as they'd like. From the second I heard he was attached, I knew he was safe. Under normal circumstances, I'd be hesitant to open up to another guy, especially after the way things escalated with Kipton. But Tyler is more like the brother I've always wanted. In fact, he walked back to the dorm with me tonight after our workout to borrow my psychology notes. He's lucky I'm the queen of note taking and have almost every word the professor spoke written down in my notebook. He's busy scanning through each page, picking out the most important topics, while I shower.

With it being Thirsty Thursday on campus, Cara's been trying to get me to go to a party with her all week. I told her I'd consider it. The last thing I want to do is risk running into Kipton, but I can't keep pushing her away. Eventually, I'll have to see him again in a social setting. While a month of not speaking has been helpful to keep my training on track and my anxiety low, it's been pure torture at the same time. A part of me is excited to catch a glimpse of Kipton.

Since we had sex, I've fallen asleep to memories of our connection almost every night. By replaying him kissing me over and over, I'm able to fall asleep in a blissful state of hyperawareness. On nights I get lucky enough, we meet up in my dreams and get even more comfortable with one another. I never push him away when I'm asleep. If only I could be the same girl during the daytime.

Finishing up my shower, I change in the bathroom so I'm not naked in front of Tyler when I return to my room. It would be disrespectful to his girlfriend, not to mention he and I don't operate that way around each other. It's refreshing.

I open my door quietly, so I don't interrupt his studying.

"How's it going?"

"I'm finishing up. I don't know how you manage to write everything down, but I'm thankful you do. This will make catching up so much easier. Although next time, I'm using a copy machine." He shakes out his writing hand and I laugh.

"You're welcome. I'm glad they're useful to someone because I like taking notes way more than studying them."

"I don't like it either. Oh, before I forget. Kipton called."

Freezing in place, my face heats. Tyler doesn't know everything about our history, yet I'm embarrassed at the mention of his name. So much that my hands are shaking causing me to drop my towel twice while trying to hang it up on the hook in the closet. I take a deep breath before responding, making sure my voice is even and nonchalant. "Was he looking for Cara?"

"Yeah. He asked for her, but he asked for you too after I told him she left with Drew."

I spin around on my heel in surprise. "He did?"

Smiling, Tyler packs up his notebook and places mine on my desk. "I assume you two are well acquainted."

"Somewhat. He's Cara's brother." I start applying my makeup so I have to look into the mirror and away from Tyler's knowing eyes. Even though he suspects something, I'm grateful he answered the call. I have no idea what I would have done if I'd been the one to hear Kipton on the other end of the line. Knowing my typical response to his voice, I probably would have panicked and hung up on him.

"And?" he questions.

"What do you mean?" I play dumb hoping he drops the subject.

"Nothing. Nevermind." *Thank the lord.*

I finish my makeup and quickly dry my hair before tossing it up in a ponytail. I'll add some curls to give it some life before I go out tonight. "You ready for dinner?"

"I'm starving. What do you say we have a cheat meal and get some Tex-Mex? There's a great place right off Main Street."

Shit. That's close to Kipton's house. "Sure. Sounds delicious. I could go for a taco." In reality I'm not sure how my stomach will hold up. Since ending contact with Kipton, my nightmares have come back in full force. Almost every night I've been rushing to the bathroom in the middle of the night, replacing horrible memories with the calmness of a purge. The after effects have been making eating difficult with my stomach often protesting what I put inside it.

The walk is quiet at first before Tyler breaks the silence. "You okay, Soph?"

"I think so."

"It was the phone call wasn't it?"

I nod my head. "He's a hard guy to forget."

"Why do you have to forget him?"

"I have my reasons. It's complicated, I guess."

"It usually is when it's right."

"Seriously? I thought it was supposed to be easy when you're with the right person."

"Nope. I'm with the right girl and never get to see her. If that's not complicated I don't know what is."

Here I am worrying about avoiding Kipton and Tyler would do anything for a chance to see his girlfriend on a daily basis. "I'm sorry. That would really suck. You must miss her a lot."

"I do." For a brief moment his own protective shield falls, but he doesn't let it stay that way for long. "But enough of the serious shit. Let's eat ourselves into a food coma."

"I'm game."

It turns out I couldn't stop at one taco—or two. Inhaling my entire main dish along with corn bread, beans, and rice, I'm stuffed by the time we leave the restaurant. The flavors were outrageous although harsh on my scratchy throat. It's nice to taste something other than the bland dining hall food though.

"You want to stop for frozen yogurt while we're at it?" Tyler asks.

"I can't eat another bite, but if you want some, we can." Silently I pray he doesn't want to stop. My stomach can't handle it.

"I guess you're right. We did enough damage with the tacos." He rubs his distended stomach and I laugh.

"I'll race you back." Taking off, I turn this into a game when in reality, I'm only running because I'm close to throwing up.

"Sophie!" He yells after me. Not one to pass up a challenge, he takes the dare and sprints alongside me with ease. "Can we stop now? I'm going to throw up if I keep this pace."

"You wimp. Are you going to let a girl beat you?"

"Hell no!" He kicks it up a notch and zips past me. His body inches further and further away from me. Spotting the dorm in the distance, I keep it in my sights knowing that's the end goal. No match for his longer legs or speed, we meet up again by the fountain. "So what do I get for winning?" he questions triumphantly.

"The honor of knowing you can kick my ass any day of the week." I clap for him and continue walking. "In running that is. I'd wipe the floor with you on the beam." It's my best event and he knows it.

"Considering guys don't even compete on the beam, Sophie. I'd say you're right about that."

He walks me to the front door and gives me a hug. "Thanks for the notes."

"Thank you for dinner."

"You're welcome. See you tomorrow." We part ways and I run inside the rec room, finding the first available bathroom. After some trial and error, I've discovered it's the least used bathroom in the dorm. As expected, the stalls are all empty and I waste no time sticking my fingers down my throat, helping my body find relief. It doesn't take much of my own effort before I gag repeatedly, the heat of the spices from the tacos burning my throat and nose. I try to slow down, to ease the stinging pain, but it doesn't help. Combined with the acidity of my stomach, I've created a volcanic eruption of molten lava. I knew it was a bad idea to eat that much considering I've been struggling with soup.

I've gotten better at gauging when I've completely purged. There's no specific evidence, but rather a notion from within. Satisfied, I wipe the tears from my watery eyes, the exertion causing every muscle to tighten up. I reach for the flusher and pause. Gasping, there's blood in the toilet and on the back of my hand. It's happened before, but never this much. With my throat comparable to the grit of sandpaper, I know I have to give myself a rest from vomiting. This isn't healthy. But I feel ten times better now that I've gotten it out of my system. It's not the same high that comes with a real purge though; this is done out of necessity rather than to right a wrong.

"Was that you in there? Jesus, Sophie," Cara says.

I hate being caught. It makes me feel even more shameful than I already do. "My Mexican fiesta didn't agree with me at all."

She eyes me warily, but says no more about the subject. "Are we still going out tonight?"

"Yeah. I'm fine. That's if you still want to go."

"You're not sick?" She questions.

"Not anymore. I'm doing better actually." I'll be one hundred percent as soon as I chug a Gatorade and brush my teeth.

She claps, her excitement spilling over to me. "Okay. I'm so excited to hang out again. Let's leave in an hour. I have to stop by Drew's quickly, but I'll only be a minute."

I flick my ponytail. "Sure. I'll start working on this mop of hair."

My mind still reeling from seeing blood in the toilet, I turn my attention to my hair and work on making myself look presentable. If I do run into Kipton tonight, I don't want to look like shit. Maybe someday there will be a chance for the two of us to reconnect. Until then, I'll continue to visit him safely in my dreams where I don't have to worry about if he'll leave me, or grow to hate me.

"Do you want to borrow something to wear?" Cara asks as soon as she returns to our room.

"I know you won't approve of anything I have."

She laughs and shakes her head in agreement. "Here, wear this jean skirt you wore last time and try this tank top with it. You can wear the same boots too."

I hold up the top, taking in the sparkly sequins lining the front. Is she trying to make me look like a disco ball? "The same skirt and boots? Won't people notice?"

"I hate to break it to you, Sophie, but your clothes didn't stay on long enough for anyone to notice other than asshat Caleb. Please try to keep your distance from him tonight. You have a better shot of staying clothed that way."

Rolling my eyes, I know she's right. "I can't argue with you there. There will be no excessive drinking or nakedness tonight, Cara. I promise."

Laughing she snorts. "You said that last time and look what happened."

Man she's going for the jugular tonight. "You made your point, Cara," I remind her.

"Sorry. Kipton won't let anyone else touch you anyway."

"He won't be keeping tabs on me all night." *Will he?*

"You are so clueless, Sophie. My brother still has it *bad* for you."

"Not anymore." I made sure of that.

"You do realize that avoiding him won't work forever and eventually you're going to give in and have wild monkey sex again."

"Cara!" I clutch the top to my chest as my mouth hangs open in shock. "What do you mean *again?*"

"Oh come on, I know you two did it. Now you're both avoiding each other and it's because of me. So tonight I vow to change that. I'm reuniting you both, making it clear that I don't have a problem with you two dating. I thought I had already made that clear, but apparently not. You two are a pain in the ass when you're tiptoeing around one another. Make out already! You're sad. I see it in your eyes. I don't want you to be."

Feeling the blood drain from my face, I sit down on the edge of my bed. "Maybe I'll stay in tonight. You go without me." I don't want her to play matchmaker. This has nothing to do with her opinion of the two of us together. It's about my choices—how I need things to be for my own sanity.

She pulls me by the arm off the bed. "Oh no you don't. Now let's go see Kipton and get you laid." Shoving me to the closet, she picks up the skirt and sticks it in my hand. "Change."

"Cara! He's your brother! You can't say those things."

"I told you I don't care. I'd rather he picks you over some blond bimbo with fake knockers and a nonexistent IQ. Think about it, whoever he marries I'll have to be around all the time. I refuse to set myself up for torture if I can help it. Now move it, woman."

"You know I'm a blonde right?"

She shoves me forward again. "Yes, I do. But you're not a moron and your boobs are small. Keep it moving."

Looking down at my chest, I sigh. Well she's right about that. I slide on the jean skirt and am surprised when it hangs off my hips. This can't be the same skirt as last time. "Cara, are you sure this is the same skirt?"

"Yes, why?"

"Just checking." I grab a belt from my wardrobe and fasten it around my waist. I'd like to credit the weight loss to my conditioning, but I'm not stupid enough to believe it doesn't have something to do with getting sick all the time either. I'll have to start doing a better job of resisting.

I THOUGHT WE'D BE ONE of the early arrivals at the party, but the house is already full. Without question, Caleb is manning the keg, dishing out pick-up lines as fast as the cups fill with beer. Cara stops me near the keg. "Sophie, can you grab my beer. If I don't pee right now I'm going to explode."

"Sure. I'll wait for you by the stairs."

"Thank you!"

She dashes off and I laugh at her urgency. "Hey, Good Lookin'. You back for more?"

"Nope. Not tonight. I'm getting Cara a beer." Caleb eyes me appreciatively and slowly fills Cara's Solo Cup.

"You're looking extra hot tonight. You sure you don't want a drink?" he questions.

I shake my head. "Nope. I'm good." I don't need any motivation to act like a fool again. This is my second party; surely I'm wiser this time around.

"That's a shame. You'd have more fun if you drank."

He hands me back the cup, overflowing slightly with sticky white foam. "Sorry about the head."

I narrow my eyes at him. "The what?"

"Head. The foam."

That's a new one for me. "Oh. It's fine."

"I forgot you're new to this party thing. Lick your finger, then stick it in and swirl it around. It'll make it all better."

I stare at the cup watching the bubbles slowly pop. I'm not molesting the beer. Cara can do whatever she wants with her cup. "Thanks for the tip." I roll my eyes and walk away.

"Hey, Sophie."

Looking back at Caleb over my shoulder, he nods his head signaling me to come back over. "Yeah?"

"You're overdressed. Let me know when the show starts."

Scoffing in disgust, I smack him in the chest and walk away. He laughs at my reaction and keeps pouring beer. Nobody is getting a repeat performance out of me.

Waiting for Cara, I lean against the stairwell and sway back and forth to the music. As I scan the room, waiting for her, I notice commotion over by the Tiki bar. As a few bodies part, leaving a small area to peer through the crowd, I'm reminded of the power of alcohol. Lying on the bar is a gorgeous girl with her shirt pulled up, exposing her flat stomach. Taking a body shot out of her belly button, Kipton looks like he's having the time of his life. Behind him, there's another girl running her hands up his back underneath his shirt. I wanted to see him tonight, but I never imagined he would be doing *that*.

I sink into the corner of the room, wanting to disappear into the ancient wallpaper. If I could wash my eyes out with soap to remove the racy image I would. Gone is the reminder of his lips touching mine, of him inside me, kissing around *my* belly button. As crushed as I am, I know it's my own fault for pushing him away. Did I really expect someone like him to fight for me? *No.*

"I'm back. The line was forever long. What'd I miss?" Cara asks.

"Eh. Not too much. Caleb told me to get naked and your brother's doing body shots off some hooker over there while another gropes him from behind."

Cara stands on her tippy toes and peeks around a few dancing bodies. "What is he doing! Who are those girls?"

When Kipton helps body shot goddess off the top of the bar, I see it's *her*. The girl he was talking to outside of my dorm. The one he touched. The one he said he didn't make plans with. I should have known better than to believe him. I can't compete with all of that even if I wanted to. She looks straight off a runway with her chic wardrobe and perfect body. Instantly, my mood shifts from jealousy to annoyance. It's time to get even.

Looking around the room, I don't see anyone I know besides Caleb. As much as I don't want to lead him on, he's my only option. The fact that Kipton isn't his biggest fan makes me all the more eager to get to him. "I want to dance, Cara."

"I thought you don't like to dance?" she questions.

I smile and shake my ass. "Tonight, I love it."

"Oh hell. What are you up to, Sophie?"

"Nothing I can't handle." Sashaying over to the keg, I tap Caleb's arm. He finishes filling the cup in his hand and bends down to hear me speak. "Do you have to pour beer all night?"

Looking confused, yet hopeful, he shakes his head. "No. Why?"

"Will you dance with me?"

Smiling from ear to ear, he drops the tap and turns to face me. Towering over my small body, he beams, "I thought you'd never ask." I take his hand and he leads us into the throng of sweaty bodies grinding on the dance floor. I search for Kipton and see him kissing both girls at the same time—a triple kiss. Gasping, I cover my mouth in shock. Tongues and lips are all over each other. It's filthy and everything a guy would dream of—it's everything I'm not.

The more I tell myself not to care, to forget him, the more I find myself drawn to him. I thought giving my body to Kipton would help me move on. But now that I know what it feels like to have him inside me, I realize one time with him will never be enough. He made me feel—he made me come alive.

Caleb pulls me close, our bodies touching at every possible connecting point. There aren't any sparks and definitely no fireworks booming in the sky. The only way I can make dancing with him believable is to pretend he's Kipton. And the second I replace his blond hair with Kipton's dark brown color, I close my eyes and get lost in the memory of his touch. Working myself up to the point of needing release, Caleb's own arousal is stiff against my back. His hands roam to my chest and down to the waistband of my skirt where he slides the tips of his fingers beneath my belt to graze my lower belly. Everything about his touch is wrong, but since I'm envisioning Kipton in my mind, it's incredible. Moaning, I lean my head onto Caleb's shoulder. He spins me around so I'm facing him. "Jump up and wrap your legs around me, Sophie."

I do as he says and once we're at eye level, he kisses me hard on the mouth. But as hard as I try, I'm reminded it's not Kipton's tongue asking for permission to enter. When I open my eyes to stop him, it's like a cold bucket of water was poured directly over my head. Caleb's eyes are lust filled, ready to take our connection to the next level. All I can focus on is Kipton watching me from the stool at the Tiki bar—his date suddenly absent.

"Caleb, put me down. I need a breather." I'm mortified I let things get so out of control with a guy I can't even stand most of the time. He sets me on my feet, not releasing me from his grasp entirely.

"Let's go up to my room, baby." He pulls up the hem of my tank top to touch more of my stomach. I look into his eyes and blink slowly as I comprehend his invitation. We get pushed farther into the crowd right as one of Kipton's girls return to his side. He pulls her in between his legs and kisses her on the lips with enough force to almost knock her over. She reaches out and braces herself against his shoulders. His fingers are splayed across her lower back and the sight of the two of them makes my stomach churn.

Remembering Caleb's offer, I answer easily. "Yeah. Okay. Let's go." Without a word, Caleb leads me through the mass of bodies to the staircase. Each step takes me further and further away from the guy I truly want. The one who sets my body on fire from one simple look. I'm not paying attention and bump into Cara halfway up the stairs. She pulls me aside, letting Caleb continue to the top.

"What are you doing, Sophie?"

"Hanging out with Caleb."

"Don't do this. You'll regret it," she warns.

"It's not like I have any other options tonight." I'm letting my anger win.

Cara huffs and rolls her eyes. "That's bullshit and you know it, Sophie. I don't get this cat and mouse game you and Kipton are playing, but it needs to stop. Now!"

"Come on, babe." Caleb reaches for my hand and pulls me up the last few steps before leading me down the hallway.

"Don't you even fucking try it, Sophie."

Frozen in place, I drop Caleb's hand. When I turn around, I'm met with a smiling Cara and a fuming Kipton. "Come on, Caleb. Let's go have a drink." Cara pushes Caleb back downstairs before he can cause a scene. He's obviously had a few drinks already because he goes willingly, looking at Cara like she's his new conquest. Cara won't put up with any of his bullshit and will have him safely parked next to the keg in no time.

Wearily, I chance a peek at Kipton. "Where are your dates? One girl not enough for you these days?"

Showing little emotion he replies, "Emily's downstairs with her friend."

I nod my head. *Emily.* I hate that name. "That's nice. Shouldn't you be using her as your personal shot glass?"

"Jealous?" he questions.

Damn right I'm jealous. You're mine! "Nope." I pop the p for added effect.

"You sure about that, beautiful?"

"Don't call me that."

"Why not? It's the truth."

His admission makes me want him even more. "Because you had your mouth all over Emily's."

He takes a step closer, pinning me against the wall. "You know damn well whose mouth I want, Sophie." I look away, suddenly needing more air than he's allowing me to breathe.

"Whatever." I try to squeeze out from his intense hold, but he moves right along with me. Each time I try to escape, he matches my every move. Walking backwards, I realize I'm out of room to run. The only place left for me to go is in his bedroom. Sliding around the door jam, I find myself in a familiar situation. Only this time, I'm sober. We stand rooted in the middle of his room in a standoff of sorts. The sexual energy is charged and ready to detonate at any moment.

"Are you done running yet, Sophie?"

"Who said I'm running?" He takes a step closer, and I counter with a step back. We keep this up until I'm trapped against his closet door.

He runs his knuckle down my cheek. "You're always running. Please stop fighting us, Sophie." Picking me up around my waist, he deposits me on his bed—never breaking eye contact. "I want you so fucking bad. I can't get you out of my head."

"What about Emily?"

"She's not you, Sophie. You're the one I want. I never should have kissed her and I'm sorry I did, especially in front of you. You didn't deserve to see that no matter how mad I was."

Yes. I want him too. We're grasping at each other's shirts, lost in the moment. His kisses taste like shots of whiskey mixed with the cinnamon from his gum. It's all man. Reluctantly, I pull my mouth away from his. "I'm sorry, too, Kipton. I kissed him."

"I'll break his lips later, just kiss *me,* beautiful." His name tumbles out of my mouth over and over as I moan against his lips. He sucks on my neck sending shockwaves pulsating throughout my body. His shirt is off before I have time to even ask him to remove it. Running my needy hands over his naked back, there's a knock on the door.

"Kipton, are you in there?" It's Emil*y.*

Quickly, I pull my shirt down to cover my boobs and adjust my skirt. I use the ponytail holder around my wrist to fix my sexed up hair. It's knotted up from Kipton's fingers mixed with the sweat from dancing. "I should go."

"No. Stay. I'll tell her to leave."

"I got carried away, I'm sorry." I catch my breath and move towards the door.

"Let me guess, this was a mistake."

Not again. Spinning around, I shout at him with every ounce of anger built up inside me. "Will you stop fucking saying that," I cry. "I'm not a mistake," tumbles from my lips barely above a whisper.

"I know you're not, Sophie."

Needing air, I pull open the door and come face-to-face with Emily. If looks could kill, I'd be dead. "Why are you in here? Where is he?" she asks.

I don't bother acknowledging her presence as I step around her and into the hallway.

"Did you just sleep with that girl?" Emily questions.

"Not tonight, but I have. And her name's Sophie."

She glances at me before kicking the door shut in my face. I flinch as it slams before sinking to the hardwood floor. Resting my head in my hands, I blew it—again. The thought of him being alone with her makes me queasy. Desperately, I want to run back into his room, begging him not to touch her. Instead I envision him naked, thrusting inside her. It sends me over the edge.

Hurrying into the bathroom, I splash cold water on my face. Still lightheaded, it's not enough to erase the pain. And although I haven't eaten anything since the last time, I make myself throw up. Desperately needing to right a wrong—both of our wrongs, I gag painfully. With nothing to expel, all that's in the toilet is some bile mixed with blood. *More blood.*

Sobbing, I cry for not being strong enough to fight for the guy I want, and for being stupid enough to believe I was capable of having a real relationship. I warned him I was too fucked up—too broken by my past. But he wouldn't listen. Instead, he kept pushing for more even after I assured him I wasn't capable of anything even close. He made me need him and now that I do, it's too late.

My phone vibrates with an incoming text.

Cara: You okay?

Sophie: No. In the bathroom upstairs.

Cara: On my way.

Knowing I need to get my shit together before Cara sees me, I rummage through the cabinets until I locate some mouth wash. Gargling, I spit it out as the burn of the alcohol on my already angry mouth stings terribly. The room tilts sideways before it spins. I sit down on the small rug in front of the shower to get my bearings. I hear Cara knock on the door, but I can't get up to let her in.

It's not locked so she opens it herself and rushes to my side. "Sophie, are you okay?"

"Dizzy. I'm okay."

"Let me help you up." She takes my hand and pulls me to a standing position. I'm weary, swaying back and forth slightly.

"I want to go home, Cara."

"Okay. Can you walk?"

"I'm not sure." There's no way I can walk the entire way back to the dorm.

"Hang on. I'll get Kipton's keys. I only had half a beer. I'm fine to drive."

"No! Don't bother him. He's probably busy."

Laughing at me, she says, "he has it coming." She doesn't bother knocking, instead she tries the knob. When she finds it locked, she kicks the door repeatedly with her boot until Kipton answers the obnoxious banging. It doesn't do any favors for my already throbbing head.

"What the hell are you doing, Cara?"

Peeking through the space between the bathroom door and the door frame, I'm able to see Kipton. Although his shirt's still off, his pants are on. Sighing in relief and holding onto a sliver of hope, I duck my head, tears leaking from my eyes. I did this to myself. I pushed him to her.

Cara scoffs at him and gets right to the point. "Give me your keys; I need to drive Sophie home. And put your shirt back on."

"What? Why?"

"Because you're not a man whore." She spins on her heel, but he grabs her shoulder before she gets away.

"No. Why do you need my keys?"

"She's not feeling well."

"Again? Where is she?" he questions.

"Give me your damn keys, please."

Kipton's about to hand them over to her, but pauses. "Are you okay to drive? Were you drinking?"

"I'm fine. Only had half a beer," she assures him. She grabs the keys from his hand and rushes back to me. "Okay, Sophie. We can go. Let me help you back up."

My heart is racing, but it's not from the site of Kipton. "Cara, my chest." Before I hear her response, I'm reaching out to grab the sink. I can see Kipton's silhouette in the doorway, watching me closely. "It's tight and pounding."

"Sophie, what's wrong?" he asks.

"I need to go home." My chest is so tight. I clutch at my throat, rubbing my skin.

"Kipton, baby. Come back to bed," Emily purrs. She's wearing his shirt and nothing else. The site alone makes me want to gag all over again. She looks exactly like one of my dad's trashy sluts.

Kipton does a double take of her and looks livid. "Where are your clothes, Emily? It's time for you to leave."

I stare in horror between the two of them. Kipton stands in front of me, forcing me to look at him. "This isn't at all what it looks like, beautiful. I didn't—I wouldn't."

I need to get away from Emily before I scratch her eyes out. Bracing myself against the wall, I use it for support as I walk down the hallway. With Cara's help, I'm able to make it to the kitchen. But before I can get outside to the car, Kipton's by my side.

"You know me, Sophie. I'm not that guy anymore. You're what I want. Not Emily or anyone else."

I swallow around the lump in my throat. It would be so easy to believe him. But the truth is, I'm not sure I do. "Goodnight," I whisper. With my heart in pieces, I walk to the car where Cara's waiting to take me home.

"You okay?" Cara asks on the drive to the dorm.

That's a loaded question. "I will be."

Back in the dorm, Cara makes sure I'm safely tucked in my bed before she excuses herself to see Drew. "I'll be right back. I just want to make sure he knows what's up in case Emily or Kipton come back here. I doubt she would have the guts to, but you never know with my brother."

"Take your time, I'm okay." I toss around to get comfortable, hoping to fall asleep so Cara doesn't feel obligated to babysit me, but my phone rings.

"Hello."

"Are you okay?" *Kipton.*

"I'm fine. I'm going to bed." Pulling the phone away from my ear, I'm about to hang up when I hear his desperate plea.

"Sophie, wait."

I'm too tired to play games, but I answer him anyway because part of me is thrilled he bothered to call me in the first place. "What?"

"I didn't sleep with her."

Am I supposed to believe that? They were both practically naked. "I don't care either way, Kipton."

"I know you care because I felt the same way when I saw you with Caleb." He sighs into the receiver. "Jesus, Sophie. What are we doing?"

"I dunno? You tell me."

"I swear I didn't have sex with her."

"You were in there with the door shut and she came out wearing your clothes, Kipton. How do you explain that?"

He sighs and continues his explanation. "We sat on my bed and I told her all about you. She's jealous, Sophie. Really fucking jealous. That's why she came out in my T-shirt. She took her own clothes off and took that shirt out of the wash basket. I didn't touch her, I swear to you."

I know all about jealousy. It's what caused me to seek revenge in the first place. "I believe you."

"You do?" He sounds surprised he didn't have to fight harder to convince me. We were both acting like such jackasses tonight.

"Yeah. I do."

He sighs again. "Are you in bed, beautiful?"

"Yes."

"God, I want to be with you right now. Please say yes, Sophie."

He has no idea how much I want him to hold me in his arms right now. "I want to. More than you know."

"Then say the words and end this."

"I think we did enough damage for one night. Maybe we can start fresh tomorrow."

"Yeah. Maybe."

"Cara's back. I should go. Good night, Kipton."

"Night, beautiful," he whispers.

I pray sleep takes me to my dreams quickly because I need Kipton.

CHAPTER
seventeen

KIPTON

MAYBE I'M A FOOL, BUT I'm willing to wait Sophie out and give her the time she needs. Space is a different issue entirely. I can't promise not to keep trying. I'm a persistent man when I know what I want and I want Sophie. From the tone of her voice on the phone, I thought she was about to break down and give up her fight.

Desperately wanting to help her, I have no idea where to begin. Maybe I could if I knew what was holding her back in the first place. She's obviously scared, I get that. I just need to know why. Everyone has a past and I'd never hold hers against her, or run from it.

The minutes continue to tick by on the clock, as her words continue to eat away at me. I'm about to get up to find a bottle of Jack when my phone pings with an incoming text. Calls this time of night usually aren't good, so I'm praying Cara's safe. Unless it's Emily. I doubt I've heard the last from her. When Sophie's name appears, I'm not sure if I should rejoice or worry.

Sophie: Kipton.

Kipton: Hey beautiful.

Sophie: I'm sorry.

Kipton: For what?

Sophie: Everything.

I have to see her regardless of the direction this conversation takes, so I climb out of bed and find a pair of clean sweats and a shirt. When I go to grab my keys off the key hook, it hits me my car is at the dorm. *Shit.* Not wanting to lose her while she's willing to talk, I text Sophie back while I figure out what to do. Unsure of exactly the right words to say, I decide to go for the truth. I could very well scare her off, but it's a chance I'm willing to take. Her apologizing is a big deal and I'm hopeful we're making progress despite everything that went down.

Kipton: I miss you.

Sophie: I miss you too. I messed up.

Fuck it. I'll run the entire way to her dorm if I have to. I jam my feet into my sneakers, not even bothering to undo the laces. Those precious seconds I need to save. Bounding down the stairs, I'm ready to get my girl. But when I open the front door, I freeze.

"Hey."

"Sophie. How did you get here? What are you doing here?" I shut the door behind me and move closer to her, still keeping enough distance between us so she doesn't run.

"I drove your car. I probably should have gotten your permission first, or told Cara I was taking it, but I needed to see you. Please don't be mad."

"Beautiful, I could give two shits about my damn car right now. All I care about is that you're here." Before I can say anything else, she breaks down and sobs into her hands. Her shoulders shake under the exertion of her emotions. "Come here, baby." Without any coaxing, she willingly runs into my open arms holding on to me for dear life. Her small fists are filled with the fabric of my shirt, stretching it tightly across my back. I hold onto her, afraid she might change her mind at any second. I have no idea what made her come here, but I'm thankful she ran *to* me this time instead of away.

I let her cry for as long as she needs—until she's able to talk. When she shivers from the cooler night air, I risk speaking. "Sophie, will you come inside with me?"

"Yes." She sniffles and wipes her tears with her sleeve, but doesn't let go of me entirely. I'm more than okay with that. "Were you asleep?" She softly asks.

"No. I was staring at the ceiling thinking about you."

"You were?" Her surprise is shining in her big blue eyes.

"Pathetic, huh?" She shakes her head no and I smile. "Is it okay if we go to my room? It's still a mess down here from the party."

"That's fine." She holds onto my arm until we get to the stairs. She lets go of me reluctantly, but I keep my hands on her the entire way up.

Inside my room the mood shifts the second I close the door. Before I can even contemplate what to say first, she's on me. Assuming she needs me as much as I have missed her, I don't waste a second getting her undressed. She's tugging on my shirt, unable to lift it over my head by herself thanks to our significant height difference. After I toss my shirt onto the floor, I finish undressing her and kick off my sneakers. Picking her up, I place her in the center of my bed where she looks beautiful with her blond hair cascading over my black sheets—a few strands covering her chest. "Hurry, I need you, Kipton."

Removing my pants and boxers, I quickly slide on a condom. Resting on top of her, I can't go any farther until I make sure this isn't about sex. "Look at me, beautiful." She turns her head and stares into my eyes so intensely I feel the energy between us. *I need her.* "I'll give you what you want, but you have to promise me you won't run afterward. Can you do that?" I pray she says yes because I want her too damn much to stop.

Slowly she blinks as I wait for her answer. "I'm done running, Kipton."

Her words are music to my ears. I should make sure she's ready for me, but I'm greedy. Slamming into her, she cries out in what I hope is ecstasy and not pain. "Did I hurt you?"

"No. Don't stop."

"You're *mine*, Sophie. Do you hear me? *Mine.*"

She moans softly and closes her eyes as her head tips back in pleasure. While I love watching her come undone beneath me, I need her to look at me. "Baby, eyes." They open and as her gaze meets mine again, I see the emotion as much as I feel it in our connection.

"Kipton," she moans. "Harder. I need you."

I pump into her harder, wanting her to feel as incredible as I do. "You have me beautiful. I'm not going anywhere. I promise."

She nods her head and grabs onto my shoulders as we create a steady rhythm. Back and forth, in and out, each minute better than the last. Before long her nails dig into my arm as she shutters and cries out. Watching her come is the most erotic moment I've ever experienced. Whether it's because it's her, or because I need her so damn much; I'm positive I don't want to be without her. It only takes me another few seconds before I lose control, pushing into her one last time.

Once we're both completely sated and satisfied, I roll onto my back, taking her with me. I'm not ready to break our connection, so I hold her close to me, staying inside her for as long as she'll let me.

Neither of us speaks a word as we float back down to earth. At first it's peaceful bliss, but soon the silence becomes stifling. As tired as I am, she needs to tell me what brought her here in the first place. An hour ago she needed more time. I need to know what changed since then.

With her lying on top of me, I cover the two of us with the sheet so she doesn't get cold. Running my fingers up and down her back, she nuzzles her cheek into my chest. Her hair smells like her flowery shampoo and it's quickly become my favorite scent. "What's going on, beautiful?"

She trembles, but answers, "I needed to see you. I tried to sleep after we talked, but I couldn't."

"I'm glad you came here."

She smiles against my skin. "I bet you are."

She jerks her hips and contracts around me causing me to groan from the sensation. I'm ready for another round, but we need to talk this out first. Focusing on the conversation instead of her body, I respond. "No, Sophie. It's more than sex for me and you know it."

She nods in understanding. "I know it is. I had a fight with your sister."

"About what?" I'm not sure I want to know the details of their girlie drama, but if it was enough for her to run to me, then I want her to open up. Her body tenses and stiffens up before I realize she's crying again. Her tears slowly splash onto my chest and slide down my arms. She's been through so much shit the past few weeks, I desperately want to take away her pain—but I have no idea where to begin.

"I can't tell you. I'm not crazy though. I swear."

"Beautiful, I already know you're not crazy. Please talk to me." I wait for her to lead into conversation, but she's still hesitant. Hugging her even tighter, she's so fragile in my arms, but she's the same Sophie I've fallen for over and over again.

"I can't stop, Kipton. It started again at the diner, but then it was just like all those years. Over and over, I did it again and again. I let my family and my insecurities win again. Everything about it is wrong and I've worked so hard to move past it, but I fell right back into the same pattern. Now Cara hates me. She screamed at me, Kipton."

"Stop what, Sophie? Why is Cara upset?"

My phone rings on top of my nightstand. I want to ignore it, but considering it's Cara, I have no choice. Reluctantly, I ease out of Sophie as she clings to me. I hold her hand and as I'm about to place a kiss on her wrist I notice some dried blood. Before I let my mind wander to where it came from, I lean over and answer my phone. "She's gone. I've looked everywhere for her; scoured every inch of the dorm before I noticed she took your car. We need to find her!"

"Cara, slow down. Sophie's here. I have no idea what's going on yet, but someone needs to fill me in. You're both freaking me out."

"Hang up! Please, Kipton." Sophie's hoarse voice begs me. I keep my arm around her so she can't get away from me. She swats the phone out of my hand and I struggle back and forth with her to calm down.

"Relax. It's okay. We'll figure this out." Her body relents and she hugs my pillow, still shaking. Cautiously, I pick my phone up off the bed. "Cara? You still there?"

"Yes! Don't listen to her, Kipton. She needs help. I knew something was up with her. I fucking knew it."

"Cara slow down. Take a breath and tell me what you mean."

Beside me I hear Sophie softly crying. "Now you'll hate me too," she whispers.

I brush the hair away from her gorgeous eyes. "Sophie, I could never hate you." It breaks my heart to see her like this. I try to rub her back for comfort, but she curls into an even smaller ball of brokenness.

"Kipton, listen to me. I didn't want to get involved, but I don't think I have a choice anymore. Not after tonight. She's been making herself throw up. I found her earlier in the rec room bathroom after she went to dinner with Tyler. It was so damn bad I heard her from outside the bathroom. Of course that was blamed on bad food from the restaurant. Basically she doesn't eat and when she does, she throws it up." Cara takes a breath after talking a mile a minute. I'm about to speak, but she continues. "But there's more to it than that because she did it at your house tonight too and she didn't eat anything. It doesn't make any sense, but Kipton she's going to kill herself if she doesn't stop."

I remember back to the night I was supposed to meet with Drew and saw her getting sick. The night she kicked me out. "I'm hanging up, Cara." I turn on my side, staring at the back of Sophie's head as she cries. I'm afraid to touch her and I don't ask any questions. Why would she do this to herself?

Sophie turns her head to look at me and is utterly devastated. Her gorgeous blue eyes are red rimmed, glassy and lacking their usual vibrant color. "Cara told you, didn't she?"

"Yes, she told me. Why Sophie?" I'm having trouble comprehending why she would physically harm herself. And to learn she did it when she was with me at the diner—I had no idea. How could I be oblivious to the whole thing?

"Because it helps me cope. Everytime I do it, I'm erasing a part of me I can't deal with."

"What do you have to erase? What can't you deal with?"

"My past. My life. Everything, Kipton. I'm so tired of being knocked down. I'm never good enough—not for my Dad or Blaine and now Coach Evans. Someone is always trying to change me—to make me something I'm not. And when they stop trying to change me, they just wish I didn't exist at all."

"I *need* you, Sophie. I *want* you. You have me and you have Cara."

"I've tried to change. Years of therapy helped, but I don't think I'll ever escape the demons in my head. They're too powerful and visit me even when I'm asleep."

"How did this start?" I question.

"Years of emotional abuse from my Dad. And then both kinds from Blaine." Her answer crumbles around a choked sob.

"Baby, no." I shake my head in disbelief as rage fills me. "Who is Blaine?"

She nods her head letting me know it's the painful truth. "Blaine's my ex. He would beat the shit out of me and mind fucked me so many times I believed I deserved it," she cries.

"Beautiful. You would never deserve that. I'll fucking kill him, Sophie. I swear I'll find him and beat his face in for what he did to you."

"No. It won't do any good. This is who I am, Kipton. That's why I've tried so hard to push you away. Because it's bad enough I live this life. I don't ever want to drag anyone else down with me."

Rage mixes with the most intense sadness I've ever felt. I knew it was bad, but it's so much worse than I imagined. "It'll get better. We can make this better—together." Making promise after promise, I pray I can make them come true.

"There are no second chances for me, Kipton. Coming here was a chance at a fresh start—this *is* my second chance. And I'm fucking it up."

"Then you'll get a third because I'm not giving up on you,

Sophie. Not now and not ever."

She hangs her head. "After I hung up with you earlier, I felt so lonely. Eventually I fell asleep, but you didn't visit me in my dreams like you have the past few nights. Instead, it was my Dad reminding me how worthless I was. I don't want to listen to him anymore." She sniffles and brushes tears from her cheeks. "I fought to wake up, but Blaine was behind him. He was just about to hit me like he has so many times—with the back of his hand across my cheek. It stings so bad, Kipton." She clutches her face in her trembling hand.

"But you woke up, beautiful. It was just a bad dream. You have me now. I won't let him hurt you ever again."

"Then why didn't you come see me? That's the only time I don't have nightmares—when I dream about you. "

"I'm sorry, baby. Please don't cry. You know I'd be there if it was up to me."

"I know. It's not your fault. I'm sorry."

"You have nothing to be sorry for, Sophie. Can you tell me what happened after that?"

"Cara was downstairs with Drew, but came back to check on me. There I was hovered over the trashcan for her to see. I was so ashamed, but I was even angrier because I wasn't finished. Kipton, I swear I don't want to do it. I know it's not actually making anything better in my life. I've just been going through a really hard time and old habits came back the second I started spiraling out of control. You have to believe me."

I rub my hands over my face as I try to process the play-by-play she's giving me. Scared shitless for her, I'm worried everything from her past is coming back with a vengeance. But she's smart; she would never do this unless she felt she had no other choice. "I do believe you, Sophie. What happened next?"

"Cara screamed at me. The words that came out of her mouth killed me. I know I'm a fuck up; she doesn't have to remind me. Then she was crying and shouting that I needed to get help. Something about killing myself and I couldn't take any more. I grabbed keys off the TV stand and ran. When I noticed they weren't mine, I remembered we drove your car home from the party. At first I wanted to drive as far away from this town as it would take me. I wanted to go back home of all places, but I ended up driving to your house instead."

"This town is your home now, Sophie. You can't keep running. And Cara's right, you do need to talk with someone about this. I'll help you as much as I can—I promise." She looks unsure—not yet convinced. Something tells me she's never had anyone help her through it before. It's probably been a lonely journey with nothing waiting for her on the other side. "What's the blood from on your arm?"

She flips her arm around, searching her skin. "There's no blood."

Holding up her wrist I point it out to her. "Right here."

"I don't know." Her eyes dart around the room, nervous-ly. She's lying.

"I'm only going to say this once Sophie. I need you to tell me the truth, right now. No secrets. We're done with secrets. No more running either. If we're going to do this, you have to be all in, no matter what."

She wipes her tears and shakes her head in disbelief. "I can't believe you still *want* me?"

"Why the hell wouldn't I? I've been trying to tell you that, Sophie, and now that I know more about why you were pushing me away, it's making more sense. I know you want me too. I'm not wrong about that, am I?"

"No, Kipton. You've never been wrong about that." She lies back on the bed, slightly more relaxed in comparison to her earlier melt down.

I need her to look at me while we have this conversation. Reaching over, I wrap my arms around her and pick her up so she's on top of me again. This time she's straddling my hips. She uses her hands to cover her chest and stomach, but I shake my head at her. "Don't hide from me. You're perfect." She drops her arms shyly. I can sense her nerves and with little warning, I blurt out what I've wanted to tell her for so long. "It didn't take much to do me in, Sophie, but I've fallen for you. Hard. But either you have to be *all* mine or nothing. This back and forth is killing me. We still have a lot to discuss and work through, but I need you to know where my head's at as far as you and I are concerned."

It takes her several excruciating long seconds to do anything other than stare. She blinks repeatedly. At first, I'm worried she's having another dizzy spell. "Sophie?"

"Kipton, I–" She turns her head and looks toward the window, words failing her. "I don't know what to say."

"You may not want to hear all of this right now, but it's the truth. I'm putting myself out there, like I'm asking you to do. It's scary as fuck, but I know what I want. What do *you* want?" Holding her hand in mine, I rub my thumb back and forth over the palm of her hand. "You don't have to say anything if you're not ready. But I needed you to know where I stand."

She watches her hand in mine before exhaling deeply. "How can you possibly want me? I'm an absolute mess."

I raise her chin with my finger, forcing her to make eye contact. "You had me so intrigued from the moment we met, but I won't lie, Sophie. What you're doing scares the shit out of me. I want you to get better. I need you to."

Her tears start to fall. And for the first time since she arrived, the real Sophie's cracking through the surface. "I'm scared too." She tries to shield her face from me, but I won't let her.

"I know you are, beautiful. Come here." She slides off my chest and curls up under my arm.

"Nobody's ever told me those words before, Kipton."

"What words? That I want you?"

"Yes. It's always been a lie or hate."

I kiss the top of her head with the realization that it doesn't matter what her answer is. I'm all in regardless. "I'll never hate you."

It's only when my arm starts to fall asleep that I realize she never answered either of my questions. "Please tell me what the blood is from."

Without skipping a beat, she responds honestly. "From throwing up."

I figured as much, but my heart aches for her. As I pull her even closer, her phone rings. Searching the bed for her pants, she pulls it out of the back pocket of her jeans. "It's Cara," she says.

"Are you going to answer?"

She shakes her head and lets it ring. Turning her phone off entirely, she tosses it on the bedside table and pulls the comforter over her naked body. "Is it okay if I stay until morning? I'm not ready to go back yet."

"Of course it is. I want you here with me."

"Thank you for not judging me and for not yelling."

"I'd never yell at you or judge you, Sophie. Get some sleep. It's been a long ass day." I lean over to kiss her lips. My intentions are innocent until she grabs the back of my head and deepens the kiss, surprising me again.

"Thank you." When she releases me, I place one last peck on her lips, mouth and neck before lying back down on my side of the bed. I want nothing more than to hold her all night, especially if it keeps her safe in her dreams, but I wait for her to make the move. At first she stays where she's at after shifting around several times. We've never shared a bed together unless I count the night she was unconscious.

Before long, her breathing evens out and though my eyes are closed, I'm aware of her movements. Slowly, her tiny arm reaches across my chest, using it as an anchor. Her head nestles into the crook of my arm and one of her legs rests over-top of mine. I squeeze her ass in the palm of my hand and kiss the top of her head. Strands of her hair are tickling my nose so I blow gently to rearrange them.

Appreciating each second I get to hold her in my arms, silently I say a few prayers for healing while begging God to help us through tomorrow and each day after. I assume she's asleep until her lips softly peck my chest with a tiny kiss. "I've fallen for you too," she says barely above a faint whisper. Although she may not have wanted me to hear, I know we have a shot after her honest confession.

I won't let her lose the fight.

CHAPTER
eighteen

Sophie

WAKING UP IN KIPTON'S BED isn't nearly as scary when you can remember the events of the previous night. Unfortunately, they still weren't pleasant. I almost wish I couldn't remember my night, but then I wouldn't have the memory of Kipton telling me I was *his*.

I roll over in the bed expecting to find his handsome face, but his side is empty. Before I have a chance to worry where he went, the door opens. Slipping back inside the room, Kipton greets me with a warm smile. "Morning, beautiful."

I try not to, but I can't control it. Blushing from his endearment, I manage to squeak out a good morning of my own.

"Breakfast is served." He sets a tray of food on the end of the bed and leans down to place a gentle kiss on my lips. I could get used to waking up like this every day.

"What's all that?"

Smiling broadly, he waves his hand in front of the tray like he's Vanna White. "I made you breakfast in bed."

I'm impressed. I don't know many college guys capable of cooking anything besides toast or slapping some meat between two slices of bread. "You know how to cook?"

He scoffs playfully. "Of course I do. I took Home Economics in high school."

Laughing, I cuddle up under the warm blankets. "So you can make grilled cheese, french toast, a smoothie, and macaroni and cheese?"

"Technically yes, but my mom also taught me a bunch of other things. It's our thing—cooking together. Cara can't cook for shit though." That doesn't surprise me at all. He slides underneath his side of the covers and pulls the tray on top of his lap. Bacon, pancakes, scrambled eggs, granola, and strawberries fill up every inch of the tray. "I didn't know what you like, so I made a little of everything."

I smile at his thoughtfulness and take a bite of the fruit. The berries are fresh, sweet, and delicious. Reaching over, I offer him a bite which he takes. I pull my hand away from his mouth, but he sucks my finger inside with the strawberry. Gently sucking, he flicks the tip with his tongue. After a few more seconds of teasing, he releases me from his mouth and swallows.

"Do you have class today?"

"What?" How he can go from sucking on my finger to regular conversation without skipping a beat is beyond me. My finger is still tingling from his tongue and he's already moved on to something else.

Smirking, he knows how much his touch affects me. "Class. Do you have any today?"

"Oh. No. I have Friday's off this semester. You?"

"I'm off too."

I pick up another berry and take a bite. It's cold on my sensitive teeth. "Can I have the granola?"

"Of course you can." He hands me the bowl with milk already in it. We eat in silence for a few minutes, but it's not awkward. I'm wondering when he's planning on addressing the drama from last night. I know we still have a lot to talk about despite any progress we made—I'm going to get an earful at some point.

I almost spill my cereal when a bang strong enough to rattle the windows has someone cursing downstairs. Kipton laughs. "Don't worry, the guys are downstairs cleaning up the mess. They usually have very colorful language to go along with their hangovers."

"And you sit up here and listen to them suffer?"

"Hell yeah, I do. I was in their shoes a few years ago. I've earned my freedom."

I finish the last few bites of my granola and place the bowl back on the tray. "It must be interesting living here." I look around for something to put on, but I don't see my clothes. "Where are my things?"

"I hid them."

"Why would you hide them?" I try to pull the sheet off the bed, but he has it tucked in at the bottom so tightly it won't budge. I'm not comfortable enough to get up fully naked to look for them.

He places the tray on the floor and rests against the headboard. "So I can keep you in my bed all day." He rubs his hands together deviously like he's cooking up a plan.

I giggle from his excitement. "As much as I would love that, I have to go to the bathroom first. Can I borrow a shirt or something if you're not going to give me my clothes back?" I wait for him to move, but instead he sits staring at me. Playful Kipton is gone. I punch his arm, hoping to bring him back. "I'll only be a minute. What's wrong?"

He leans over the side of the bed and grabs one of his clean T-shirt's from the wash basket. "Nothing. Here." Instead of handing it to me, he pops my head through the shirt. I stick my arms in the sleeves and pull it down to cover most of my body. The shirt smells like him and I might have to keep it.

"Thank you. Be right back." I scoot off the bed and hurry to the bathroom at the end of the hall with a very angry bladder hurrying me along. I shut the door and rush over to the toilet. In my haste, I forget to check the seat before sitting down and fall in. Yelping in surprise, I grasp onto the corner of the sink and the toilet paper holder to hold myself up. Gagging, my feet find the floor and I can stand to put the seat down. Men!

I didn't ask if I can take a shower, but I hop in anyway, turning the water on as hot as I can tolerate it. There's no way I'm climbing back into Kipton's bed with all those germs on my body.

Soaking up the warm spray of water, I'm instantly revived and refreshed. Three bottles of body wash line the shower wall and after sniffing each one, I easily know which belongs to Kipton. I pour a little into my hand and lather up, replacing the germs with his irresistible scent.

I'm forced to wrap Kipton's t-shirt around me instead of a towel when I finish. My butt is barely covered and the fabric is soaking up the water from my body quickly. I open the bathroom door and check for his roommates. When the coast is clear, I run back to Kipton's room. Slipping on the hard wood floor, I end up shutting the door with too much gusto, slamming it loudly. "Sorry. Do you have any extra towels in here?" When I turn to face the bed, Kipton's crouched over with his head in his hands, grasping onto his messy morning hair. "Are you okay?"

He lifts his head and glares at me. "Are you?"

"I'm fine, now."

"Sophie, please don't do it in my house."

Completely confused by his mood swing, I don't know what to say to him. I'm freezing from the shower and desperately want my clothing back. "I didn't *do* anything. Can I have my clothes?"

"No."

Is he for real right now? "Why not?"

"Because you need to listen to what I have to say first."

"What's up your ass all of a sudden?"

"Help me understand why, Sophie?"

I have no idea what he's asking me. "What did I do? Why are you acting so weird?"

"You threw up your breakfast didn't you?" He stands up and starts pacing.

Understanding why he's being so cold, but not willing to put up with it, I defend myself. "Not that I need to justify myself to you or anyone else, but I went to the bathroom. To pee!"

"So, you eat, run to the bathroom as soon as you finish, and come back showered?"

"Yes. I want my clothes, Kipton. Tell me where you put them."

"You can't have them until you answer me," he shouts.

Tears leak from the corners of my eyes. I'm so angry I start to shake. *He doesn't believe me.* I raise my voice another octave, "Give them to me. You're being an ass and have no idea what you're talking about. Maybe you should get your facts straight before you go accusing people of shit they didn't do."

"I'm an ass because I don't want the girl I care about shoving her head in the toilet every time she puts food in her mouth?"

"Stop it! You don't know what you're talking about, Kipton. And you have it all wrong."

"Sophie you can't keep this up. You'll kill yourself. Do you even realize that?" He throws a pillow at the wall and when that doesn't give him the satisfaction he needs, he launches his cell phone instead. It doesn't shatter into pieces, instead falling on top of a pile of clothing.

The bedroom door opens and Caleb's standing in the doorway looking back and forth between Kipton and me. "What's going on, guys? Kipton, I could hear you yelling through my bedroom wall."

"None of your fucking business." Kipton snaps back.

I jump from the unexpected roar of his voice. While I usually avoid Caleb, I couldn't be more thankful he walked in when he did. He reaches his hand out cautiously, unsure if I'll accept it or not. When I do, he walks me out of the room. "Are you hurt, Sophie?"

"No. Not physically." Inside his room he hands me a pair of his shorts and a T-shirt to put on. Kipton's drenched shirt is barely clinging to my body. "Thank you." I wipe away my frustrated tears, remembering the words my mom always told me as she bitched about my dad. *Never let them see your tears, Sophie, it's a sign of weakness. Save your tears for your pillow.*

Caleb watches me, but doesn't try to interfere. For once he knows when to shut his mouth. "Come on, I'll take you home."

"Thank you, Caleb." As the words leave my mouth, I hear tires peel out of the driveway. This time, Kipton's running.

With him gone, I take a minute to wrap my head around our argument. At least I know he has very little faith in me. I thought he understood why my life is the way it is, but obviously he didn't hear everything I was saying to him last night. Or maybe, I wasn't conveying things the way I needed to for him to understand. Either way, I don't deserve his anger or judgment—especially without him knowing all the facts.

"You ready?" Caleb asks.

"Yeah."

By the time I get back to my dorm, Cara's waiting for me outside on the bench next to the entrance. "Sophie, I—"

"Save it Cara, I'm not in the mood." I was upset at the house, but now I'm angry. How dare Kipton judge me the way he did. I stomp up the stairs, grinding his assumptions into the cement. Screw. You. Asshole.

"Sophie, my brother didn't mean it. He's worried about you. He would never be able to live with himself if something happened to you. Especially at his house."

I stop walking up the last flight of stairs. Facing her, I tell her the truth. "Well he no longer has to worry about me. I won't be at his house or in his damn bed. And I know he's your brother, but I'm done, Cara. Done. So if you have a problem continuing to live with me, tell me now. I'll pack my shit and get out."

"No, Sophie. You don't mean any of that. Of course I don't want you to move. You and Kipton care about each other. Don't give up on him. He's an idiot sometimes, but he wants you in his life. That's why he got so mad. He can't lose you."

Under normal circumstances I might take her words into consideration, but not today. "He's making me fucking crazy." I stalk down the hall, not even caring about the clothes I'm holding onto so I don't walk right out of them. Heads are popping out of rooms, left and right, trying to get a look at the drama unfolding. Normally I'd be embarrassed, but right now it's the least of my worries.

"Sophie, wait," Cara stops my hand from turning the door knob. "Before you go in there, you have to calm down."

Oh hell no. "He's in there isn't he?"

"Sophie, please. Calm down. You two need to talk."

I don't listen to her and when I open the door, I find Kipton sitting on my bed much like the way I found him after my shower. Only this time, he looks remorseful instead of angry. "What do you want, Kipton?"

He looks directly into my eyes. "I'm sorry, beautiful. I lost my shit, and I never should have accused you. I needed to cool off, but as soon as I got in my car I realized what an ass I was. Arguing won't help you, I know that and I'm sorry."

Does he deserve my forgiveness—probably. Does it mean he's going to get it—not right now. "But you did anyway. And you know what, your words hurt. Especially after you told me we were in this together. But you lied—it's *always* lies. Nobody can handle the truth."

He takes a couple steps closer to me. I hold out my hands to stop him, but he continues anyway. "I'm not going anywhere until we talk, Sophie."

"Then I'll leave." Stalking over to my closet, I pull out sweats and a tank top to replace Caleb's borrowed clothing. I stuff them into my purse and grab my sneakers. I toss the boots back in Cara's closet and continue packing what I'll need for the rest of the day. I'll find a hotel room where I can be alone.

Kipton watches me pack, but doesn't give up. "I brought your clothes back. They're in the bag on your desk."

"Thanks," I reply coldly as I continue packing my bag.

"Sophie, you can't leave. We need to talk. Last night some pretty heavy shit was dished out, but we never addressed it the way we should have. Yes, I treated you like shit and jumped to conclusions. But I did that because I don't know your triggers, or anything about what it is you do. So let's sit down like two rational adults and talk this through."

I hear the words he's spewing, but I'm in flight or fight mode—and flight is winning. "I don't do well with liars, Kipton. I'm tired of false promises."

"Give me a chance to make it right. Please."

I shift my purse on my shoulder and almost give in. But I'm tougher than he thinks. Misguided, maybe. Off track, yes. But for whatever reason, his accusations hurt more than any other argument we've ever had. I gave him a glimpse inside the darkness and he threw it in my face. "Please move."

"I can't do that Sophie."

I turn around and pick up the room phone. Dialing Drew's number, I wait for him to pick up.

"Guys what's going on? I'm getting complaints about an argument."

I hang up now that Drew's standing in the doorway. "I was dialing your number. Can you please escort Kipton out of the building? I'd like him to leave and he's refusing." Kipton glares at me. *Oh well.*

Drew looks back and forth between the two of us and sighs. "Everyone have a seat for a minute." He closes the door so it's just the four of us and shifts into resident advisor mode. This ought to be fun. "Cara, do you mind waiting in my room?"

"She can stay," I tell Drew. "I want her to hear every single word so I don't get accused of anything else today." I glare back at Kipton, but he's no longer looking like he wants to throw things. Instead, his eyes have softened and he's watching me cautiously. The longer our gazes are locked, the more my defenses start to crumble. I fight hard to put them back in place, but I'm not sure I succeed. I snap out of it when Cara slithers her way behind Drew and takes a seat on her bed.

Drew stands in the middle of the room, directing his conversation my way. "Sophie, I'll start with you. I won't pretend like I don't know what's been going on because I owe you more than that. Cara's been up front with me and explained her concerns and what she's witnessed. As your advisor, it's in your best interest to meet up with a campus counselor. Obviously, I can't force you to do anything, but I will have to write up an incident report today because of the complaints."

"You're serious right now? All because Cara can't keep her damn mouth shut."

Cara's face pales and she shifts around nervously on the bed. "Sophie, I've been so worried about you. I needed someone to talk to. Drew's my boyfriend."

I laugh at her reasoning. "So much for not mixing business

with pleasure, huh? You know I can report you, Drew? For dating your residents. From what I hear, that's frowned upon."

Cara gasps. "Sophie, please don't get him in trouble because of me. I was only looking out for your best interest."

"I know I'm being a royal bitch right now, but none of you get it. At all. None of you have spent a day in my shoes. You've lived privileged lives with country clubs and fancy cars while I've been fucking dying inside. So whatever I'm going through right now, I'll deal with on my own. Only I can make it better—not you."

Drew bravely speaks first. "Sophie, we can't force you to do anything, you're right about that. But you're speaking out of frustration."

He doesn't know me. "No, I'm pissed off everyone's acting like I'm fucking crazy. I just want to get out of here."

"You're great at running, Sophie." Kipton's been quiet up until this point, sitting at my desk waiting for the right time to throw his two cents in.

"Kipton, protecting yourself isn't running. There's a difference."

He screeches the wood chair legs against the tiles on the floor and stands up. He looks pained or maybe slightly stunned. "Why do you have to protect yourself from *me?* I'd never hurt you."

I glance at the watch dangling loosely around my wrist. "You've been breaking my heart for the past thirty five minutes." I try to keep my emotions in check. To show them all how strong I am. Truthfully, I'm about to break.

After pausing for a few moments to collect his thoughts, Kipton crouches down in front of me. He places his hands on my thighs and while I don't want him touching me, I don't make him move. "I know I was out of line and I'm sorry I jumped to conclusions. But you need help—like it or not. I wouldn't have had any reason to accuse you today if it wasn't an issue."

I fight hard to stay strong. "I know that." His words are the most painful to hear because they matter the most to me. Last night I told him I fell for him, and I meant it.

"You're lucky you've had friends around to pick you up when you got yourself into some scary situations. But you're so much better than all this. Because the girl I'm looking at right this second, I love her like fucking crazy. You make it so hard to keep my head on straight, but you're worth every ounce of frustration. Do you hear me, Sophie? You're worth it. Whatever is locked up inside of you, we're gonna get it out."

My eyes are about to spill over and the second I blink, I'll be forced to let go of my pride.

Kipton continues his confessions as I sit here silently. My throats too clogged with emotion to speak. "I want all of you, Sophie. I told you last night I was in this for the long haul and I meant it. But just like we promised, no more lies. No more running. Let's tackle the demons *together*."

I'll do anything to get Kipton up off the floor because if he says one more thing to me, I'll break down entirely. "Okay." I whisper.

"Yeah? We're okay?"

I nod my head, yes. "It's my fault for not getting in contact with the therapist when I arrived on campus. I should have known I'll never be strong enough to be normal. Her card is in my wallet. I'll call her today."

"We don't think you're nuts, Sophie," Drew adds. Cara's now in his arms, softly crying against his chest. Clearly she's as overwhelmed as I am.

"Maybe I am. I'd like to be alone if that's okay." They need to hurry. I can't hold my tears in much longer.

"Sure." Cara and Drew leave without question, but Kipton hasn't budged. As much as I want to find peace in his arms, I can't forget how he hurt me today. His accusations felt like a dagger to the heart and our tempers did nothing but add to the drama. His temper scared me; it reminded me of my dad going off on my mom. But mine wasn't much better and I can't fault someone for giving a shit. Nobody's ever noticed let alone cared about what I was doing to myself.

But he *loves me*. I don't know what to do with his words and it makes me feel even more out of control than I already am.

Kipton reaches for my chin, forcing me to look at him whether I want to or not. His blue eyes are sparkling with unshed tears of his own. "I meant every word, Sophie. I do love you."

It's too much. His words are suffocating me and I need air. "Kipton, no." I shake my head back and forth. The only person I've ever heard those words from is my mom. I've always understood hatred better than love. At least I knew what it physically felt like. I could even see it. But love is so much more mysterious. It's not always tangible. That confuses me—to have to rely on trust in order to believe it.

"I'm not going to deny it anymore."

"I forgive you, Kipton. I wish I could forget. But it all stays inside me no matter how hard I try to forget about it."

"I'm not asking you to forget anything, but I want you to know you have me to lean on. I'm not going anywhere, Sophie. No matter how much you push when you're in doubt, I'll push back harder."

"Kipton, I don't know what to do with all of this. My head feels so jumbled up every minute of the day." I suck in a breath, unable to get rid of the tightening in my chest as I teeter over the edge of a panic attack. "I can't figure you out." Without further warning, the dam breaks. I reach out for him as my tears soak my cheeks. I'm not supposed to cry, but it's no longer up to me.

"Come here, beautiful." I cling to his warmth as I continue to sob. I've never experienced anger out of love. It's such a foreign concept. But if it's possible, then maybe he's my safety from myself. "Please don't cry. You have me now."

I choke on a sob, but let out every ounce of anger, pain, grief, and sadness that's strangling my sanity. Kipton wants me and I need him. Because when I'm in his arms, I feel stronger. Strong enough to fight another day.

"Let me love you, Sophie," he whispers in my ear.

"How, Kipton?"

"I'll show you—everyday."

CHAPTER
nineteen

Sophie

KIPTON'S HELD TRUE TO HIS word which is another thing I've had to get used to—someone making a promise and actually keeping it. My dad used to promise my mom he would change, or tell her he would work on his laundry list of flaws, but he never did. Over time, he only became bitter and resentful of the woman who was trying to change him instead of accepting him for the man that he was. I use the term man lightly, because my father loved alcohol more than his own family. Whether he was at the bar until early morning, or getting caught in the back seat of his car with some bar whore, my mom always knew. She didn't have to see it first hand to know the rumors swirling around town were true.

One night when the arguing became too much to bare, I sat outside on the roof next to my bedroom window and made a pact with myself to never settle in love. I'd rather be alone than in a loveless relationship like theirs. I remember leaning my head against the siding of the house, as I searched the sky for the star that sparkled the most. I begged that star to grant me my one wish—to give me the power to be strong enough to survive this life on my own and without regret. From that night onward, I let the happiness my ex stole from me and the pain of my parents arguing dissolve—instead becoming peacefully numb. I stopped making myself physically sick, but mentally, I wasn't any better. Who knows, maybe I was never truly living, rather only existing in my day-to-day life. Either way, it was much easier to look forward to tomorrow when it wasn't already lacking hope before the sun ever rose.

My plan worked for a while with the numbness never wavering. That was until Kipton came into my life, but it wasn't just him that sent me spiraling. It was all the changes and the pressure of living up to expectations I wasn't sure I deserved. My mind was constantly at war with my body, warning me what would happen if I ever messed up—and did I ever. Between the concussion and giving myself to Kipton, I was afraid to get emotionally attached. And as expected, when love was thrown into the mix, I started to drown.

But Kipton's shown me over the past three weeks just how hard he can love. Whether it's his text messages or in every kiss, he's been incredible. I try to stay in the present, but living in the moment isn't easy. Connecting with my emotions brings painful memories to the surface—ones I've worked hard to deny ever existed. But Kipton's reminded me the benefits of an optimistic attitude. Without dwelling on the negative, I'm no longer waiting for the fear to chase away my happiness.

As I sit here in astronomy lab revived and happy, it's tough to stay focused on my assignment. My mind easily tempts me with a vivid play-by-play of my planetarium tryst with Kipton. Squirming around on my chair, I can't dull the ache inside of me.

As I continue to estimate star locations in the sky, a piece of paper lands on my notebook. Quickly snatching it before the professor notices, I smile as soon as I read the words. Apparently, we're on the same wavelength.

Wanna go make a new memory in the planetarium?

Giggling, I look up and find Kipton gazing over his shoulder. He winks and my stomach flutters in response with hyper butterflies ready to take flight. Mouthing the words, *behave,* I jump when I realize Oliver is taking in our entire exchange. "Boyfriend amusing you?" He asks, with his glasses balancing on the tip of his nose. I have the urge to push them back up on his face so they don't fall off, but he eventually stops staring at me long enough to adjust them on his own.

"Um, yeah. Sorry."

"That's a shame."

As I erase a mistake on my paper, I whisper, "Why's that a shame?"

"Because I have a lot to offer a lady, too. When you requested to be my partner I figured you were hot for me. I've noticed you sneaking glances at me during class."

Snorting, I stifle my laughter with a couple of coughs. Kipton turns around to make sure I'm okay. I give him the thumbs up and he shakes his head before going back to work. His lab partner spends most of the class popping bubbles and twirling her hair. Kipton says she smells like a mixture of cotton candy and cat urine. The thought of him animatedly describing her to me has me laughing all over again. I rest my head on the table as my shoulders shake. We're dismissed during my laughter fit, but I can't stop laughing. "What are you doing, beautiful?"

I lift my head to see everyone filing out of the classroom. "Sorry. I'm good."

"Don't apologize, I could watch you laugh all day. But Oliver ran out of here like the place was on fire."

"He thinks I want him."

Kipton chuckles and tucks my notebook inside my bag for me. "Poor guy."

He and I walk hand in hand back to my dorm. I tighten my sweater around my middle, the fall weather's been intensifying the closer we get to the holiday break. He pulls me close to his body to shield me from the wind while my hair whips around my face like I'm stuck in a tornado. I insisted we walk to class today, but I'm wishing we could hop into Kipton's warm car instead. I also don't miss the fact that he hasn't said a word to me since we left class. "You're quiet Kipton, what's up?" I don't like quiet, it makes me anxious.

At first he doesn't answer, but then changes his mind. "I didn't want to pry, but how have your sessions been going? You haven't said a word about them since you started."

"They're okay. Michelle is nice. She's easier to talk to than my therapist back home."

As promised, I've been seeing a counselor on campus. Being diagnosed as a depressive bulimic was hard the first time, but hearing it from Michelle put a whole new spin on how out of touch I've been with reality and my body. I may have thought I was recovered before I came to Alabama, but it never really goes away—I'll always have the compulsions inside of me.

It's helped to sort through my past, turning every tiny detail into a valid observation of what led me down this path in the first place. Eventually we started relating it to my present by working through the years I've been depressed. It was clear to see how anxiety driven I really am. There are very few things I *don't* fear. Between the mental mind fucks and the physical abuse, I've used purging as a crutch to simply survive.

Despite the progress I've made, I still have the desire to purge when I'm stressed out, or hit with a nightmare in the middle of the night. But each time I'm tempted, I'm supposed to grab my journal and write out my thought process. And not an overview, she wants every single detail.

At first I was hesitant because my words were all over the place. When I'm having an anxiety attack or refraining from a purge, I don't operate in complete sentences. My thoughts are incredibly negative, self-depreciating, and dark. They hurt to write as much as they tear me up to read after the fact.

I wouldn't ever read them if I wasn't forced to at the beginning of each session. There's no small talk in therapy. Instead, Michelle makes me read each new journal entry aloud. Painstakingly, I go over each line and figure out why I felt that way and how I can process it as a lesson instead of beating myself up about it. At first I was frustrated because despite reading and taking feedback from the entries, I was still repeating some of the same thoughts and mistakes over and over. It became impossible to believe I'd ever be able to break the addiction. And that's exactly what it is. The highs and lows that go along with a purge are hard to stop craving.

Convinced the therapy exercise wasn't working for me, I was ready to give up. But patterns aren't easy to break and neither is addiction. So while I'd love to be able to say I've refrained from purging, I can't. It's still as much a part of me as before, even if the frequency has lessened. With Michelle's help, I'm more aware of my negative thought process and maybe even a few of the triggers. I definitely won't be cured overnight and have a lot of deep rooted issues in regards to my childhood to sort through. I was never given a chance to fully grow into the adult I am now. But with time and a lot more patience, it can only get better. *I think.*

Kipton squeezes my hand. "I'm proud of you, Sophie. It takes strength to face your demons the way you are." He pulls our joined hands to his lips and kisses the back of my hand. "I don't expect you to be perfect though. I know you're still struggling."

"Thank you for saying that. I'm trying to be what you need." We increase our pace slightly, both anxious to get out of the cold.

"You already are what I need, Sophie. That will never change."

I don't know how I got so lucky to find Kipton, but it's moments like these I thank my lucky stars for him being able to see beyond my imperfections enough to really love me—the way I always dreamed but never knew existed.

Usually we take a short nap after class, but today Cara's extra chatty while she waits for Drew. "So what's the plan for Thanksgiving break? The dorms close Tuesday and we don't have to be back for almost a week."

Considering I have very little to go home to other than a lame pizza tradition, I don't jump to answer her question. My mom and I usually order take-out and watch movies on the couch. I haven't had a turkey dinner with all the fixings since I was ten. I'm looking forward to seeing her, but I know it won't be good for me to be back in the house. There's so many painful memories lurking in that house.

"Hey." Kipton nudges me with his arm.

"Sorry, what were you saying?"

"I asked what your plans are. If you can get away, I'd love for you to come meet my family for a couple days."

"Meet your family?" I've never met the family before.

"You don't have to, but I'd like you to come stay with me

after you spend some time with your mom. I can show you where I grew up and went to high school. You might have to sit through a little boring conversation, but I promise I'll make it worth your while."

The thought of meeting his parents scares the ever loving shit out of me. I'm not sure I can do it considering I'm not like the cookie cutter blondes from the country club they're used to seeing. "It's only a week, Kipton. The break might be nice."

"You need a break already?" Cara asks. She finds this amusing and claps for her brother. "Nice job, Kippy. It only took you three weeks of official dating to drive the poor girl insane."

I laugh at her, but Kipton's not the least bit entertained. "Cara, can you give us a minute alone?"

"Uh oh. Sorry, Sophie. I'm out." She stands up and takes off running without having to be asked a second time. Maybe I should run too. I don't want to be away from Kipton for the entire break, but I'll also be missing my therapy sessions. I don't want to take two steps backwards while we're away.

Kipton's facing me on my pillow, holding my hands in his. "You don't want to come?"

"Yes and no." This whole honesty thing is exhausting, but Michelle told me one of the best ways to avoid my negativity, is to address it the moment I feel it.

"Why not?"

"They don't know about my issues. Unless one of you said something. I know you're a close family." I duck my head, feeling ashamed that my screwed up self has to put a damper on his plans for the two of us. I'm not sure if his family will accept me, or label me too broken to repair.

"No, they don't know. And they won't unless you want them to. I've never brought a girl home, Sophie. I'm just as nervous as you are."

This surprises me. I was sure someone made it home, even if it was just a high school girlfriend. "Never?"

"Never. Come on, beautiful. Don't deprive me of showing you off to my friends and making them jealous. I've waited a long time for this."

I appreciate him trying to make light of the situation and make it about his needs instead of my weaknesses. "I have to see my mom on Thanksgiving Day, or she'll be all alone."

"That's okay. I want you to see her and have fun. That will give you a couple days with her and then I'd get you for the rest. We eat at the club on Thanksgiving Day, but the day after my mom insists on cooking to make up for it. Will that work? I want to spend Thanksgiving with my girl. Christmas too. So we can make plans for that whenever you're ready."

This must really be how it is when you're in a real relationship. The compromise and joint celebrations I've only seen in movies. Although I'm slightly overwhelmed at the way Kipton is pushing me to do all these things as a couple, I'm nervous. For once in my life I think I'm strong enough to get it right and experience normalcy. "I'll come. It's been awhile since I've had a real sit down dinner. And if your parents will accept me, then I'd love to meet them. Will Cara be there too? I think it would help having her there."

"Of course she will. Probably Drew too at some point. So you won't be all alone in the spotlight."

I smile. He gets it. "Okay. I'm in."

"Thank you, Sophie, for being brave enough to try. They're gonna love you as much as I do." He snuggles me closer, my head now resting on his chest. His steady breathing is slowly lulling me to sleep.

"Kipton," I whisper.

"Hmm." His voice is deeper than normal, lighting me up inside.

"Thank you for inviting me."

"You're welcome."

I lay in his arms for several more minutes soaking up the warmth of his body and safety of his arms. My eyelashes flick against his skin before I'm too content to fight off sleep another minute. For once I'm looking forward to the future.

"Please let me be strong enough."

CHAPTER *twenty*

Sophie

THE LAST FEW DAYS BEFORE break fly by and before I know it, it's the night before I'm headed home. Everyone's buzzing around campus packing bags and gearing up for one last night of partying before we all go our separate ways in the morning. As of today, I've completed my necessary counseling hours in order to rejoin the gymnastics team at the end of the break. It wasn't mandatory that I leave, but considering the shape I was in, a leave of absence was the smart thing for me to do.

Although I've lost weeks of training, Coach Evans has been surprisingly supportive of time away. At first the thought of telling him the truth almost was too much to bare, but Kipton insisted on joining me for the meeting. Maybe it was his presence that dulled Coach's wrath, but he was reasonable of all things. Assuring me I can still be ready for the start of the season if I work hard enough, I didn't find myself hunched over the trashcan that night. Instead, I was with Kipton, enjoying a normal night out with my boyfriend.

"You almost ready, Sophie?" Cara asks while curling the same strand of hair three times in a row until it bounces perfectly.

"Whenever you're done, we can go. Are we waiting for Drew?"

"No. He's meeting us there after his shift."

"Okay." I hear my cell ringing from inside my purse. It's Kipton. "Hello."

"How long until you get here?" He shouts, over the background noise.

I pull the phone away from my ear and rub my aching eardrum. "Cara said she's ready so we should be leaving in about fifteen minutes, maybe twenty." Cara throws her brush at me and I duck to miss it. "You almost hit me, Cara!"

"Fight nice, girls." He laughs. "There's no rush. I just wanted to make sure I was outside when you got here to walk you inside."

"That's sweet, but I think you just want to keep me away from Caleb."

"I have my reasons, beautiful. He may be one of them. Text me when you get here if you don't see me, okay."

"Okay. See you soon."

"Bye, babe."

I sigh louder than necessary and toss my phone on my bed. Giving myself one last look in the mirror, I decide this is as good as it's going to get.

"What's wrong? You seem blah tonight, Sophie." Cara asks.

"I think—nevermind." I flop down onto my mattress and watch Cara put the finishing touches on her make-up.

"No. We aren't leaving until you spill it. Something's nagging you. I can feel it. What's going on?"

I'm hesitant, but I open up to Cara anyway. She can't help she's related to my boyfriend. "I don't think I'm sexy enough for your brother." I'm ready for her to flip out on me, but instead, she laughs. A full out, cracking up, hysterical laugh. I glare at her, wishing she would stop making a joke out of this. "Forget I said anything."

I stand up and cross the room to find my purse, rooting around inside for my keys and ID.

"Wait. You're serious?"

"I was. But never mind."

"I'm sorry, Sophie. I shouldn't have laughed at you, but why would you think that? My brother is crazy about you.

Anyone can see it."

I shrug my shoulders, unsure if this is the kind of conversation I can have with her considering the circumstances. But she is my best friend on campus.

"Come on, tell me," She begs, with a puppy dog face.

"I'll tell you, but can you be my friend and not his sister for a few minutes?"

Looking worried, she scoots close to me on my bed, ready to listen. "Sure, go ahead. Hit me with it."

Cautiously optimistic this won't freak her out, I let my words flow carefully out of my mouth. "I'm worried I'm not sexy enough for him. Or that maybe he's not attracted to me in all the ways he should be. Remember the night at the party, when those two girls were on him. They were smoking hot. Even I admit that and I'm a girl."

Cara pauses, tries to speak, and then stops again. Finally, she continues, "Have you discussed this with your counselor? She's way more qualified to help you with this than I am. I'm afraid if I say the wrong thing I'll trigger you."

Her hesitation is exactly why it's so hard to be open with others. They think I'll run to throw up if I don't like their advice. "No, I promise you won't. It's not about throwing up or anything like that. It's the only thing I can come up with when I try to figure out why he doesn't want to be intimate with me anymore."

"Since when does my brother not want sex? Let me rephrase that. Since when wouldn't a hypothetical guy resembling my brother who is not my brother not want sex."

Although this is a serious conversation, I laugh at her attempt to separate her genes from Kipton's like I asked her to. I knew I was asking her to do the impossible. "It's okay. You can call him your brother. But that's what I've been trying to figure out. It's embarrassing, but it's been a couple weeks now. Not once has he made a move other than kisses, or a few sensual touches. It never progresses to anything more. Don't get me wrong, I'm happy with him, but I'm worried I don't do it for him."

Cara stands up and shakes her head no. "I highly doubt that's the case." She paces back and forth just like he does when he's stewing over something important. I smile at their noticeable similarities. "He would never cheat on you, Sophie. Sure, he's had his fair share of chicks, but he wouldn't do that to you."

"Well I hadn't even considered that, but now you're freaking me out."

"No. He's not. He would never do that to you. I'm just thinking out loud. It doesn't make sense, but maybe he's just taking things slow. Do you want me to talk to him? I'll ask him what's up."

"Oh. God, no! This stays between the two of us. I'm begging you, Cara."

"Okay, calm down. But if you don't get some tonight and break out of this funk, I may have to say something. It's just not right. A girl has needs too."

Yes, I *need* my boyfriend to want me. "I'm fine, I promise."

"If you're sure." I shake my head that I'm good. "Let's get going. I need a few shots after that."

I reach over and snatch my cell off the bed. The screen lights up and the call from earlier is still connected. Stabbing at the red x on the screen, I die a thousand deaths.

Cara turns around when she realizes I didn't follow her into the hallway. "Now what?" She huffs.

I stand staring at my cell in shock. "Cara, the call. Your brother's call. It never disconnected."

"So?"

"So! I think he heard our entire conversation just now."

She rolls her eyes and stomps back into the room. "You don't know that for sure. Kipton has ADD most of the day. He probably hung up a long time ago. "But the timer was still running. If he hung up, it would've stopped."

Cara takes the phone out of my hand and inspects it. She checks the call log and notices the extended time on the previous call. "I doubt he could hear even if he was trying to eavesdrop."

"I think I'll stay home."

Cara grabs my arm and hauls my ass into the hallway, kicking the door closed in the process. "No. We're going and we will have fun. Stop dwelling on things you can't change. It's one of our goals on the board remember?"

After I started therapy, Cara and I hashed out our differences. We even went as far as making a roommate agreement. I thought it was silly, but she insisted it would bring us that much closer. Although she just mentioned one of my goals, we both try to work on all of them together. That way it's easier to keep each other on the right path.

Regardless of my embarrassment, I suck it up and drive the two of us to the party. It's time to face the music. When I pull into the gravel lot next to the house, I cut the engine and stare blankly ahead. The warmth of the heater is quickly being replaced by the chill in the night air. "Are you coming inside, Sophie?"

Before I can answer, Kipton's opening her door. "Cara, a few of your friends are inside playing beer pong. Can you give us a minute please? I need to talk to Sophie alone."

"Sure, Kippy. Go easy on her though." She pats his shoulder and hurries inside the house.

Kipton takes Cara's place in the passenger seat of my car. The way he's looking at me can only be described as feral. I swallow the lump of apprehension in my throat just as my chest begins to rise and fall rapidly. I'm afraid to speak first, but the tension is too palpable to continue in silence.

"Kipton?" I say his name in the form of a question, hoping he will explain why we're hanging out in the car and not going inside to the party.

"Sophie."

I twist my fingers in my lap, nervously. "Um. Do you need me to drive you somewhere?"

"No."

These one word answers are killing me. "What's wrong?" I need him to ease my fears.

"Do you see the treehouse atop the tree in the backyard?" I turn my head to the right. "No, the other side of the yard."

I crane my neck to look in the other direction and spot it in the distance. It looks like it's in the neighbor's yard though. "Yes."

"I want you to go wait for me inside."

Is he serious? "I can't climb a tree!"

"There's slats nailed into the tree trunk to climb up. It's safe."

My heart is thumping in my chest. "Why aren't you coming? What's going on?"

"I need you to climb up and get completely naked for me. Then, lay down on the blankets. Can you do that for me?"

Holy shit. I clench my legs together, his directions adding to the anticipation of what's to come. "I think so. But why can't we go to your room? Where it's warm."

"Because I'm going to make you scream so loud, we need to be outside for the air to soak up your cries. After I finish, we can go inside and do it all over again if you want." He leans close to my lips like he's going to kiss me, but pauses. "But you'll have to be quiet inside."

"Quiet. Okay." Right now I'll do anything he asks. "Why though?" I'm positive I already know the answer, but I ask him anyway to torture myself.

He cups my chin in the palm of his hand. "Because I love you. And every inch of this gorgeous body. It's mine and I don't want you to ever doubt how much I want you, again."

I try to duck my head, but he doesn't let me. Instead, he forces me to look into his eyes. "You heard, didn't you?"

"I heard every word and I'm glad I did, Sophie."

"Oh."

"And I'm so mad at myself for not giving you what you need—for making you doubt yourself."

"Kipton, it's okay. It's nothing. I was making it a bigger deal than it is."

"It's everything. I need you, beautiful. There isn't a moment of my day that I don't spend wanting you. I'm sorry it's been so long since I've made love to you. I was worried you weren't ready after everything that's happened. But now I know I was the one overthinking everything. I'm relieved I heard your conversation even if I should have hung up."

"I always need you, Kipton. Please don't ever think you're too much for me to handle. You ground me. I feel my best when we're together."

He squeezes my hand in his. "I'll always be your rock,

baby." He reaches over and unbuckles my seatbelt. After placing a tender kiss to my lips, the heat returns to his eyes. "You have five minutes to get ready for me."

I don't know if it's the thrill of the moment, or the promise of what's to come, but I can't get out of the car fast enough. After stumbling over some loose gravel, I trek through the piles of leaves littering the yard. My nerves are already revved up, but the tree seems to grow in size as I inch closer and closer. I slow down and glance back toward my car. Kipton's still sitting inside, but I'm too far away to make out what he's doing. Is he really going to make me climb this damn tree?

I reach out and test a few of the wooden boards nailed to the trunk of the tree. When they seem secure enough to hold my weight, I begin to climb. Halfway up, I make the mistake of looking down. For a moment I debate reversing back down to the ground, but when I remember Kipton's promises, I keep moving higher.

Once inside the treehouse, I flex my hands a few times to restore circulation. After grasping each rung so tightly, I wince when I touch the palm of my right hand. Certain I have a splinter; I try to search for it but can't find anything. Expecting bare floor boards, cob webs, and a family of ants, I gasp when I take a look around. This was no spur of the moment decision.

CHAPTER
twenty-one

KIPTON

AFTER OVERHEARING SOPHIE'S CONVERSATION WITH my sister, I realized that by giving her space in the bedroom, I wasn't helping her recovery. Instead, I made her feel unwanted and insignificant—two things that couldn't be farther from the truth. Instead of being upset with her for not coming to me with her worries about our relationship, I was proud of her for talking it through instead of letting it eat her alive.

But the moment Sophie ended the call, I went to the basement and rounded up some of my camping gear. It took a lot of energy to haul it all up into a tree, but I owed her romance and several weeks' worth of sexual attention.

After blowing up the air mattress, unfolding two sleeping bags, and replacing the batteries in the lantern, the space was looking a lot cozier. I even hung a few of the gaudy campsite bulbs around the ceiling and plugged them into the lantern jack. In all of twenty minutes, I transformed the space into our very own love shack.

As I sit here in her car watching nervously as she climbs up the side of the old oak tree, I'm only able to relax once she's safely inside. I told her five minutes, but I wait almost fifteen before jogging to meet my girl.

The climb is easier the second time around, especially

with both hands free. I expect Sophie to be waiting for me under the warmth of the sleeping bags, but as I lift my body onto the platform, I get the opposite. My beautiful Sophie is completely naked, lying on her side with her silky blond curls draped over her shoulder. All of this was supposed to be for her, but she's the one giving me the gift.

"Shit, baby. You look incredible." I stand gawking, ready to blow my load before I even touch her. She crooks her index finger, inviting me closer. Afraid to blink for fear she'll disappear, I shuffle over to the mattress.

"You're overdressed, Kipton."

This confident side of her is so damn hot. "Beautiful, this was all for you. I'm supposed to be seducing you tonight."

I have to touch her, so I bend down on my knees to taste her lips. She holds the back of my head in her hand, determined to set the pace. Her kisses taste like cherries, most likely from one of her Jolly Ranchers she's always sucking on. I'd be satisfied kissing her like this all night, but I'm eager to give her more.

Hurriedly, I strip my clothes off, tossing them on the floor in a heap. I climb on all fours next to her before sliding under the sleeping bag, covering the both of us. Sophie cuddles close before climbing on top of me, her body so soft against my skin. Before I touch her anywhere else, I have to kiss her again. Greedy for her lips, I nibble and bite my way through the seam of her lips—our tongues mingling the moment they touch. I'm hungry for more as I knead her naked ass in my hands. She lets out a sultry moan, tipping her head back in pleasure. *Damn, she looks amazing.*

Placing soft kisses on my chest, then my stomach, she's inching lower with each peck. I don't want her to stop. Her mouth feels too good and when she uses her tongue to trace over the hard ridges of my abs, I fight to regain control. "Sophie, wait."

Her head pops up and her cheeks redden. *Shit,* I wasn't trying to discourage her.

"I'm sorry." She rolls back onto the air mattress and clutches the sleeping bag. I miss the warmth of her soft curves already.

"No, I didn't want you to stop." I have to start thinking with the right head. Sophie tilts her head to the side and creases her forehead in confusion. I'm not making any damn sense.

"What's going on, Kipton? Isn't this what you asked for? You said in the car–."

"No, beautiful. I know what I said in the car, but tonight is supposed to be all about *you*. You don't have to do anything, or say anything. It doesn't matter what you think I want. I did this for *you*—let me make you feel good." She still looks uncertain. "What's wrong?"

She swallows and licks her cherry stained lips. "Nobody's ever done anything like this for me, especially without expecting something in return."

"It's all you, Sophie. Now are you ready to be wow'd?"

She giggles and her eyes light up. Finally she says, "Wow me, Kipton."

I end up doing just that, several times, until we're both so exhausted it's too much effort to move inside the house. Instead, we cuddle up under the moonlight in our own little world away from the chaos of college life. We're safe, satisfied, and complete.

"Thank you."

"Baby, you don't have to thank me for loving you. And you'll never have to question how attracted I am to you again. I won't let you forget this time."

It's never been this intense after sex. As long as I got off, I was happy. In fact, before Sophie, I'd be dressed and on my second drink by now. What she and I share is different, insanely different. But I crave it.

She holds tight to my hand, her body slightly trembling. Assuming it's from the mixture of sweat and the chill of the night air, I pull her closer to my body. "I love you, Kipton," she whispers against my chest.

For a minute I think I imagined it, but after her body tenses up, waiting for my response, I know it was real. "God, beautiful. I love you too." If possible, I squeeze her even tighter. She has no idea how her words just lassoed my entire heart, pulling tight with no intention of easing up. She's it for me. She's fucking *it*.

"DO YOU TWO LOVE BIRDS have any idea how long it took me to find your asses?"

What the? I wipe the sleep from my eyes and turn my head. Cara's standing at the end of the mattress tapping the toe of her boot against the wood. "Shhh. You'll wake Sophie. Why are you even up here?"

"I should ask you two the same thing. I broke two nails climbing up here to make sure you were still alive. Two, Kipton!" She holds out her mangled nails like it's my fault she's incapable of climbing a damn tree.

"How did you know we were up here?" Sophie questions. I didn't realize she was awake. Leaning over, I place a kiss on her forehead. She wraps her arms around my neck and finds my lips.

"Excuse me, can you stop making out and answer me?" We don't stop. "Guys, come on. That's gross." We still don't stop. Sophie smiles against my mouth and our laughter mingles with our kisses. She's enjoying this. Finally, Cara kicks the air mattress and jolts us hard enough that we break apart. "Are you done, sucking face?"

"No," I respond honestly. "Not so fun is it?"

"Ugh. Well I'm ready to go back to the dorm. Let's move people. And, I apologized about you catching me with Drew." She claps her hands like Mary Poppins and shushes us.

"Trust me, we hear you." I'm almost afraid to ask, but I torture myself anyway. "Where did you sleep last night?"

"In your bed with Drew."

"Oh hell," I groan. "Did you at least change the sheets?"

"We slept, Kipton. There was no sex. But now I regret that. Especially since you two were in a damn tree all night leaving me stranded. I looked everywhere for you two."

She's going to love this. "Can you climb back down without killing yourself so we can get dressed?"

Her eyes widen and her mouth pops open. "You mean.

You're both naked right now? Under there?" She gestures toward the sleeping bag. The only barrier between us.

"Yes." Sophie rolls on her side and can't help but laugh at her roommate.

"Oh for the love of god, you two, that's disgusting. Someone's gonna get a damn tick. Put some clothes on and hurry up!" She sits back down on the wood floor and eases her way onto the ladder. I don't hear any noise, so I assume she makes it safely to the bottom. It's confirmed when I hear the pile of leaves under the tree rustle with each retreating footstep.

We do have to get moving, but I want one last moment alone. She's going home today for a week and I'm not used to being in separate beds let alone different towns. "Good morning, babe." I roll on top of her, covering her body entirely with mine.

She peers up at me and smiles. "Morning."

"Sleep okay?" She nods her head and rubs her fingers over the back of my head. It tickles, but I don't make her stop. "I'm bummed I have to let you out of here."

"Can we do this again sometime?" She looks so hopeful I'll say yes.

"It's not too rustic?" Most girls wouldn't last an hour up here.

"No, I like it up here. It feels a million miles away from the rest of the world. Just me and you in our own cocoon."

I smile. My girl is awesome. "Anytime you want." I lean over and grab her clothes from the side of the mattress. She sits up and lets me help her dress. The clothes are chilled from the cool morning air and she grabs the blanket for warmth while I get myself dressed.

"Hurry up! I'm cold!" Cara shouts from the ground below us.

"We better hurry, Kipton." Sophie inches closer to the ladder, inspecting the ground below. "Whoa. It looks higher in the daylight."

"Oh no you don't." I reach out to pull her back toward me wrapping my arms around her middle from behind. "You sure you have to go home today?"

She doesn't respond. I wait another few seconds, but she

doesn't move either. "Hey." I spin her around to face me. "What's wrong?"

She shrugs her shoulders and stares at the wall of the treehouse. "Nervous about going home." I don't want her to struggle the entire time she's away, or to revisit old habits. It would be easy for me to convince her to stay with me, but I know she needs to figure it out on her own. "I'll be okay."

I'm not sure if she's trying to convince me, or herself. "Do you want me to go with you?"

"No. You need time with your family. I'll be fine. I'm making it a bigger deal than it is. You ready?" She finally takes a breath and scoots over to the ladder. I don't stop her this time.

"Go slow, okay." She nods. "Wait. Let me go first so I can help you down."

We switch places and I keep one hand on her ass the entire way down. For safety of course.

Reluctantly, I walk her to her car. Cara's thrilled when Sophie unlocks the doors. "About damn time." She's being a tough ass, but we both know she loves seeing me with Sophie.

"Why didn't you just get a ride back with Drew this morning?" I question.

"Because he had to be at the desk at six in the morning and I thought I should find my roommate first."

"Thanks, Cara," Sophie says.

I open Sophie's car door and before she gets inside, I tuck a stray piece of her hair behind her ear. She ducks her head and tries to smooth it out. "I must look awful."

"You look sexy. I like your freshly fucked look."

Hitting me in the chest, she can't help but laugh. "Be good this week."

"You have nothing to worry about and I'll call you every day. I'll probably text you all day too." *I'm so whipped.* "And Saturday will be here before you know it. Then, I'll have you in my bed for a whole week."

She digs her keys out of her purse and pauses. "I don't think so."

"Why not?"

"I can't sleep in your bed with your parents in the house!"

"You can and you will. It's not up for discussion." I pat her butt and urge her inside the car. She goes reluctantly, but wants to argue about it more. "Drive safely; let me know when you leave."

"Okay."

I signal for her to roll her window down. She does and as soon as there's enough room to stick my head inside, I plant one last scorching kiss on her lips. "I love you, beautiful."

"Love you, too."

I pray she comes back to me in one piece.

CHAPTER
twenty-two

Sophie

THE PAST HOUR I'VE PACKED and repacked enough times to know I'm procrastinating leaving the dorm. If it wasn't closing, I'd probably stay another night and drag it out even longer. Cara's packed and sitting on her suitcase watching me finish up.

"I'm gonna miss you. Home will suck without our nightly chats," Cara whines.

I give her a hug, wishing I could skip going to my house entirely. But seeing my mom again will

be nice. "It's just a couple days and then you can show me around your place." I'm trying to convince myself as much as her. *I can do this.*

She rests her chin in her hands and pouts some more. "Doubt it. Kipton's gonna hog you the whole time."

"I promise you and I can have girl time. I'm sure he has other things on his schedule too."

"Doubt it," She repeats solemnly.

"Oh will you stop." I pick up my suitcase and am thankful I can roll it out of here without breaking my back. "Give me a hug. I have to get on the road." Cara stands and wraps me up exactly like she did on move in day.

"Bye, hooch."

Laughing, I return the sentiment. "See ya, slut."

It's only after I leave the dorm that I get blasted with more emotion than I know what to do with. This place, this town, finally feels like home. And I have to leave.

In a daze, lost in my own thoughts, I don't spot the flower on my windshield until I'm next to it. Tucked under one of the wipers is a gorgeous red rose. I bring it to my nose, inhaling its aroma. I lay it next to me on the passenger seat before stuffing my bags into the trunk. While I warm up the car, I type a note to Kipton. I'd call, but I'll probably cry if I do.

Sophie: Thank you for the flower.

Kipton: You're welcome. Leaving?

Sophie: Yeah.

Kipton: Be careful. Take breaks. I don't like you driving so far all alone.

Sophie: I promise I'll stop when I need to.

Kipton: Okay. Call me when you can.

Sophie: I will. Love you.

Kipton: That's never going to get old. Love you too, beautiful.

After a quick stop for gas and another for lunch, the five hour drive back home takes closer to six. I'd gladly drive another couple hours if it meant I could put off going inside a little while longer. But as I pull up outside the brick two story home that's still over-flowing with memories I'd like to forget ever existed, I know it's now or never.

I can still see the crack in the pane of my bedroom window that was never fixed. If I move the dresser a few inches to the right, I'll also find a hole in the wall from a thrown

lighter

textbook. If only it was that easy to camouflage the emotional cracks and holes I've collected within my mind the last twenty years.

Mom's still at work, so I head inside, unsure of how I'll feel once I'm on the other side of the front door.

It's open which surprises me. I slowly enter, nervous about what I may find considering mom's car isn't here.

"W-what are you doing here?"

"I should ask you the same thing. I'll be discussing it with your mom. She's meeting me for dinner tonight."

"Oh. You still have a key?" I don't like that my mom hasn't changed the locks after he moved out. That's the first thing she should have done.

He has the audacity to laugh at me, but I'm supposed to be in here, not him. "Of course I have a key. She might have wanted to divorce me, but she never stopped loving me."

"She *did* divorce you." I step forward and move toward the kitchen.

"That's what she wanted you to believe at the time. But she never showed up in court; couldn't convince herself to sign away our marriage once and for all. I can't say I blame her." He opens the fridge and helps himself to a beer. *That hasn't changed.*

I brace myself against the kitchen table for support. He has to be bluffing. "No, she wouldn't do that."

"She did. I'm still as much her husband as I am your father. At least according to the records."

"That can't be. She wouldn't lie to me. She's all I have." My arms start to shake under my weight. I stand up tall, not letting him see my fear.

"Don't go getting all dramatic. Did you really expect her to sit in this empty house all alone once you were gone? The day you drove away was the day she got her life back." He walks over to the drawer and pulls out a pack of cigarettes.

"I never expected her to stay single, but I also never wanted her to end up with you again either." *Why would she go back to him?*

"Don't you see, Sophie. It was *you* all along. You were the problem. You *are* the problem. Now, I have her back and if

233

you don't like it, you can stay elsewhere. In fact, that might be a better idea regardless. Who knows what bullshit you'll try to fill her head with this time."

I shake my head back and forth. He's talking nonsense. He has to be. This is my *mom* we're talking about. The only parent who has ever shown me an ounce of love.

"Do you live here again too?" I question. I don't know why I ask. Each response just upsets me more than the last.

"Not officially, no. But I'm here enough."

I shouldn't say it, but I risk it anyway. That's how much I hate this man. "Do you still cheat on her too?"

He sets his beer on the edge of the counter and rests his right leg over his left. Crossing his arms, he narrows his eyes at me. I blink once, but not a second time. "That's none of your damn business. She gives me the attention I need now that you're not sucking the life out of her. She's the woman she was before you were born."

There's no way I can stay here if he is. I walk by him, dragging my suitcase along with me. I don't trust leaving it in his presence. Thumping up each stair, I'm thankful my room looks untouched. Mom still has the things I moved from the apartment arranged like they've been here all along. Tracing my finger over some of the dust left sitting on the desk top, the air feels filthy with him being here.

Digging around in my closet, I pull out anything that has meaning or value. Filling up a few more duffle bags, I lay them next to my luggage. Everything else they can keep.

One last trip into my closet is all I can handle before the memories threaten to eat me alive. Just looking at the darkness inside has me wanting to throw up. I spent so much of my childhood hiding inside, I'm not sure I've ever fully escaped. Before I can give in to the temptation, my mom comes home.

Spying, I lean over the railing in the hallway, trying to hear the bullshit their spewing to one another. "Dean. No. I told you to stay away this week. It's just one week. Then, she's back at school."

He mumbles something, but I can't make out the words.

"I miss her, and I want this week to reconnect. I've barely

spoken to her since August. I even took off from work." I hear a bottle being tossed into the recycling bin. That's a sound I used to fall asleep to night after night.

"Dean, please. I love you. I love you both. Please don't make me chose you over my daughter."

She loves him?

I can finally hear him speak. "I already know you'd pick her. You always do," he shouts.

After all he's done to the both of us, she actually *loves* him? It's too much. This is all too fucking twisted.

I load up my right arm with the duffle bags and pull my heavy suitcase with the left. It fights me down each step, twisting from side to side. When the strain on my wrist becomes too much, I let it tumble to the bottom ahead of me.

"Sophie, where are you going?" Mom rushes over, inspecting me.

"I can't stay here. Not with him and not with you. How could you lie to me Mom? How?" I shout.

"I'm so sorry, Sophie. I wish I was stronger. I do. But I've been so lonely. I'm sorry." She cries into her hands, aware of how her decisions have destroyed our relationship.

"Let her go, Victoria."

"Dean, I need her," Mom begs. "She's my only daughter."

"You two can have each other." I turn to leave, but my pride gets the best of me. Another question I've always wanted to know the answer to, yet never had the courage to ask comes flying out of my mouth with little warning. "Why do you hate me so much?" I ask him.

"It's not a matter of hate. I just never believed you were mine. Eventually I found out the truth. You may think I was the only one who cheated, Sophie. But your Mother wasn't faithful either. You're the proof."

"Dean!" Mom cries. "Why would you tell her that?"

"Don't yell at me, woman. Tell Sophie how she got that scholarship. Enlighten her. Maybe then she'll stop only hating me."

"Mom?" I question. "What's he talking about?"

She sobs harder. "Sophie. You weren't ever supposed to find out. Dean, how could you!"

"Tell me!" I shout. She flinches from the bite of my words and falls onto the floor.

"Coach, Coach Evans is your Father, Sophie. I couldn't risk my marriage so I begged him to stay away. But it failed anyway. I failed."

"My Father?" I question in disbelief. *Coach Evans is my father.*

She can't get her words out and nods her head instead. I have to sit down. Instead of pulling out a chair at the table, I sit on the floor where I'm standing. My thoughts are running a mile a minute and I remember the scholarship he just brought up.

"H-How did I end up with the scholarship, Mom? Did you bribe him?"

"No, honey. No. You earned it. He's wanted you since you were a freshman, but I wouldn't let him take you from me. I was so scared it was about more than just the team, Sophie." She hiccups and struggles to get her words out. Reality crashing down hard on her, but even harder on me. "Gymnastics was my dream once, too. Just like Adam—Coach Evans. We were working together at the gym here in town and made a mistake one night after we closed up. It was just that one time, but I got pregnant. He wanted more from me, but I was already married to Dean.

Regardless of the facts, Sophie, I never regretted you. I didn't. But Dean was already suspicious of the two of us. Once I quit my job and didn't see Adam every day, I thought it would get better with Dean, but it didn't. He always knew without me having to say a word. Everything was confirmed when Adam came to see you and I wouldn't let him. Things got so ugly between the three of us, and you didn't deserve a life like that. I'm so sorry, honey."

"You did this. All these years I've hated myself because of him, Mom. You could have stopped him and you never did. You let me live a life I hated."

"I was wrong. I'm sorry, baby. I'm sorry," she pleads. But her apologizes are too late. The damage has been done.

"I hate you so much." There's so much more I want to say to her—things she deserves to hear from me, but I can't.

236

Instead, I storm out of the house, tears streaming down my cheeks. Unsure of what to do or where to go, I drive. I make it just outside of town before my emotions strangle me and I have to pull over. Climbing over the passenger seat, I stumble to the ground. My knee is bloody from the fall, but I don't have time to pay attention to it. Without any coaxing, I throw up along the side of the busy roadway. Not giving a damn who sees me as I painfully gasp for air. Each breath I take hurts, but I welcome it. I understand it. Something I'll never be able to say about my mom's confessions.

Propped up against my dirty car tire, my ass on the asphalt, I sob. Unable to get up, I let the blood dry on my skin where some loose gravel has imbedded itself underneath my skin. I should clean it up, but I don't even feel the pain.

Numb. Completely numb.

I've never loved my dad, yet I mourn the loss of the only father figure I've ever known. He may have treated me like shit all my life, but after learning the reasons why he hated me, it makes me appreciate having never known the truth. Maybe he didn't hate *me* as much as he hated the reminder of what I represented—a wife who strayed, who cheated. "He should have fucking left us," I yell into the open air. There's nobody around to hear me, yet it feels like the right thing to do. I beg someone to hear me—to understand the pain inside of me.

Coach Evans is my dad. No matter how many times I remind myself, it doesn't make it any easier to comprehend. I've spent over three months both fearing and trying to impress my own father. Every decent part of the miserable life I've lived has been a lie. I fucking hate my mom and what she did to me. And I fucking hate gymnastics. It's dead to me. The both of them.

I'm not sure how long I sit on the filthy ground before I drag my tired body back inside the car.

I can barely see out my swollen eyes, but I drive toward school, unsure of what to do next. I can't get into my dorm over break and I have no money. The little bit I have won't feed me let alone be enough to afford a place to stay.

There's absolutely no way I want my mom's money, but

I stop at the next bank anyway to use the ATM. Withdrawing enough money to stay at a hotel for a few days, I don't even feel guilty. It's the least she can do after the bomb they dropped on me. I'll consider it a parting gift. *An I wish I was never your daughter gift.*

As I finish tucking the cash into my pocket, my phone chimes again. I'm surprised I have five waiting texts from Kipton and only *one* from my mom. Her's doesn't beg me to return—instead encouraging me to be safe wherever I end up. *Like she gives a shit.* I finish reading her text as another comes through. One last attempt to convince me how sorry she is. *So am I, mom. I'm sorry I was ever born.*

I respond quickly to Kipton, never letting him know I'm in the middle of a crisis. Instead, I tell him I made it safely and plan on spending the rest of the night with my mom. Refusing to ruin his time off with my shitty home life, it's the only way I can justify the lie. *He deserves so much better than me.*

The first hotel I find is too expensive, but I eventually come across one about an hour away from school that fits my budget. I wanted to drive further south before having to stop, but I'm too tired. It's dark and I've already spent most of the day on the road.

Once I check in, the first thing I do is raid the vending machine. I only have enough quarters and ones to buy some water, two packs of crackers, and a pack of candy. It'll have to hold me awhile, not that I have much of an appetite anyway.

Going through the motions of a shower, I rest under the hot spray of water. Each drop that hits me washes away a little of the hope I've been gathering the past few weeks. Hope that my life was finally headed in the right direction, to a place that would bring me happiness in a world I didn't fear at every turn.

I'm cold when I pull the shower curtain open and stare at my pale skin in the mirror. From the outside I look like every other girl on campus—normal. But inside, that's where the hatred resides. Glancing at the toilet, I want to give in again, but there's nothing left to give.

Caged in by my thoughts, I turn on the TV, the noise

helping the silence from being too overwhelming. The pajamas I dig out are wrinkled and thin, the blankets are scratchy, and the bed a little lumpy. But at least I have a bed to sleep in and a roof over my head.

I try to rest, but their confessions replay over and over in my mind. The weight of the truth is more powerful than any lie they've told me over the years. Not wanting to spiral completely out of control, I rifle through my suitcase for my journal. As fast as the words come to me, I jot them down.

I'm nothing. Lies. All lies. He never loved me. I'm not his. She lied. Cheaters. Lies. I'm a mistake. They never wanted me. Lies. He's not my father. They didn't want me. They don't want me. They never wanted me. He knows I'm his. He doesn't want me.

Tears begin mixing with the black ink leaving blotches on the pages. After writing the same variations of words over and over, I don't feel any better. Instead of continuing, I launch the pen at the wall, followed shortly after by the journal. I curse my therapist for her worthless advice. It's the first time my emotions have been too strong to finish an entry and it scares me.

Frantically chewing on my thumbnail, the world closes in around me. Experiencing a full blown panic attack, my tunnel vision competes with my rapidly beating heart. I try counting out loud to keep from passing out, even smacking my cheeks to stay present. Nothing works. Instead, I lie in the center of my bed, face down until my body stops shaking. It could be minutes, although it seems more like hours until I settle down. Teeth still chattering, I stretch my arms and legs, releasing the locked muscles. My body as equally exhausted as my mind, I fall into a restless sleep, waking often. Each time I open my eyes I pray I'm in Kipton's bed, safe and sound. But I'm disappointed when the grungy hotel walls taunt me instead.

I'll survive today, but I don't want to do this again tomorrow.

Alone.

CHAPTER
twenty-three

Sophie

DAY TWO WAS MUCH LIKE the first with an overwhelming sense of loss for a family I've never had continually gnawing at my heart. My anxiety is at an all-time high, my mind in a constant state of confusion. It's enough of a struggle to stay present in the moment let alone imagine a life without the only parent I've ever loved.

Instead of driving further south, I stayed in bed with the curtains drawn. There's no money left for a decent meal and my stomach has stopped begging to be fed.

Kipton's tried to call, but I always respond by text knowing I won't be strong enough to hide the truth from him otherwise. He doesn't need to be drawn into my pathetic existence. Not until I get things figured out and have a solid plan.

Since I can't afford to spend a third day in this hotel, I have to check out before they kick me out. Finally showered, I don't bother drying my hair. Instead, I toss it into a messy bun, change into clean clothing, and turn my key in to the front desk.

Stuffing my bag back into the trunk of my car, I realize it's the only home I have—the only thing that belongs to me besides the clothing in my bags.

The cars only running for a few minutes before the gas gauge lights up. "No." Banging my palm against the steering wheel, I say goodbye to the little money I have left. My stomach is silent yet desperate for food. My thirst dying to be quenched. The vending machine snacks have run out and I'd do anything for one more Cheeto.

Desperate enough to try mom's ATM card before leaving the gas station, I'm expecting it to willingly spit out a twenty. I'm shocked when the account has been closed. *Him, he did this.* I'm so angry I leave the card sticking out of the machine, hoping someone can make it work and drain the account. *Asshole.*

Slamming my car door, I kick up the dirt in the parking lot when I pull out. A cloud of dust that's eerily similar to my mood follows me as I speed down the road. Each turn and mile blend into the next—my drive completed by muscle memory.

An hour later, I make it back to campus with nowhere to go. It's only Wednesday and I'm not due at Kipton's until Friday. He would want me to run to him, but I'm hesitant. As much as my wounded heart needs him, my pride is too ashamed to go to him. He has it all, and I have nothing. Eventually, I worry he'll get tired of loving someone who's unfixable; someone that holds him back from the happiness he deserves.

But as I sit here wondering where to go, I know Kipton and Cara are my only answers. Against my better judgment, I reluctantly dial Kipton's number when I can't come up with any other solution. Without money, my options are limited.

"Hey, beautiful."

Hearing his voice fills me with relief. "Hi, Kipton."

"What's up? I've missed you. You've been so busy." I hear another guy's voice in the background giving him shit about me. Kipton covers the phone with his hand and tells him to shut his trap.

"I miss you too." *So much.*

"Hang on, I'm having trouble hearing you over the TV and Eric." A door closes and it's much quieter. "I'm back. You sound sad, babe. Are you okay?"

I pause before answering, preparing a more cheerful tone of voice for my response. "Of course I am. But do you think I can come see you earlier?" *Please say yes.*

"Is it going that bad with your Mom?"

"It's fine. I just miss you and Cara. It's weird not seeing her crazy ass every day."

He laughs and the sound alone is enough to know he's where I need to be. "I'd tell you to come now, but I'm going to a game with my buddy Eric in a little while. I'll be all kinds of jealous if I know you're here and I'm not. How about first thing tomorrow morning? That soon enough?"

"Yeah. That works." I lose my forced chipper voice as the reality sets in that I'm spending the night in my car. In the cold. Alone. *It's not his fault*

"You're sure you're okay?"

"Yeah." *Where am I going to go?*

"Sophie, I'd cancel if I could, but it's his birthday. You know I'd rather be with you."

I want him to have fun with his friend, so I lie. "I'm not mad at all. Have fun with your friend and I'll see you in the morning. Okay?"

"Okay, beautiful. Can't wait to see you. Call me if you have trouble finding the house tomorrow."

"I will."

"Love you."

"You too." I hang up as the sadness makes it hard to speak. All I want is to be in his warm arms tonight. To lay my head on his chest and know I'm safe.

There's a secluded parking lot behind the back entrance of the gym that I drive to. I'm able to stay out of view from the public until I come up with a better plan. Not wanting to waste any gas, I turn the car off and sit in silence. A couple hours of rustling leaves and everlasting silence. Every second feels like a minute, every minute an hour.

When a campus security guard comes to patrol the lot, I take off. But instead of searching for another lot to hide in, I drive to the wrestling house for the simple fact that it reminds me of Kipton's warmth. Sitting outside his house makes me feel closer to him—closer to someone who loves me. Maybe the only one who has ever loved me.

It's here I'm reminded of the crazy parties, the alcohol,

and the night we spent together in the treehouse. My chilled body has me tempted to check the house for an open window, but I decide against trying to break in. The last thing I need is to be found trespassing. It's bad enough I'm on the property at all.

Each time a car passes, I watch to make sure it keeps going. No one can see me sitting here, yet I feel like I'm on display for the whole world. In my rear view mirror I spot the treehouse and know that's where I need to go for sleep.

Expecting it to be empty, I sigh in relief when I find a sleeping bag rolled up in the corner. I waste no time shaking it out and climbing inside. I'm not sure why it didn't make it down with the rest of the things Kipton brought up, but I'm thankful regardless.

As the sun sets, I lose the light inch by inch. No longer illuminated, I huddle into the corner desperate for warmth. It doesn't help. Too weak from not eating anything today, I struggle to stay awake. Dozing on and off, too afraid to let my body relax entirely, I focus on happier times—when I wasn't scared of my own shadow.

I don't remember falling asleep, but I'm startled awake and fight to wake my foggy brain. My eyes struggle to separate the shadow from the night's darkness. A hand touches mine and I scream. Wrapped inside the sleeping bag, I can't escape. "Please don't hurt me. Please," I beg.

"It's me, Sophie. I'm here."

How did he know? "Kipton?"

"Yes, baby. It's me."

"Kipton," I cry.

Clutching onto him, I fall into his lap, my legs still stuck inside the sleeping bag. But I don't care because he holds me tightly, whispering words of comfort in my ear. "It's okay. I'm here. I'm here, beautiful."

I struggle to find my voice. It's thick with emotion and clogs my throat. "How? How did you find me?"

He reaches his hand out to push a few messy pieces of hair out of my eyes. "Caleb called me. He saw your car sitting in the lot, but couldn't find you. God, Sophie. I panicked and drove straight here. What's going on? Why are you in the treehouse?"

"I got home and it all went to hell. Dean was there. He's not my Dad, Kipton. He never was and that's why he's always hated me. But my mom didn't divorce him like she said either. It's all been one big lie. My entire life has been a sham. And now my Mom loves Dean more than she loves me."

"That's not true. She's your Mom. She loves you."

"No, Kipton. I don't think she does. Not the way I thought anyway. I've held her back from her dreams; took away her happy marriage when I was born. She had an affair while married to Dean. Coach Evans, Kipton. He's my *Father*." I sob.

Kipton holds me in his arms, comforting my shaking body. Admitting it makes it that much more real. Hearing the words aloud rather than stuffed inside my tired brain, make it the spoken truth. "I'm so sorry, Sophie. I'm sorry you were alone."

"He's destroyed me all these years because I'm the proof she cheated. A constant reminder. I'd hate me too."
"No, Sophie. You don't deserve anyone's hate." I wish his words were true. "I knew something wasn't right when you called me earlier." He shakes his head and sighs. "Have you been here since you called me?"

"It all happened Monday. I was only at my house for a half hour before I left."

Kipton pulls me away from his embrace, holding me in his outstretched arms. His eyes look angry, but he doesn't raise his voice or show me any other emotion besides compassion. "Monday? But you were busy. With your Mom. You said-."

"I lied." I hang my head not wanting to see the anger morph into pity. "I was ashamed and embarrassed. I'm sorry I lied to you."

He hugs me tight, kissing the top of my head over and over. "Where have you been?"

"In a hotel. But I ran out of money. I didn't know where to go so I drove here. I'm sorry I didn't tell you the truth."

"I'm the one who's sorry, Sophie. I can't believe you've been all alone. Have you eaten? Are you hungry?"

I nod my head yes. "I had snacks on Monday night and Tuesday morning."

"Sophie, it's almost Thursday."

"I know. I ate a few things from the vending machine, but Dean closed the bank account. I didn't have a way to get more money out."

"That asshole," he grumbles. "Come on. Let's go eat and then I'll get you settled in my room."

"But your family."

"We can go back in the morning. Tonight, we're staying here. They know why I left. Don't worry about them."

"Okay." As long as I have him. I just want him.

"Come on, beautiful. I'll help you down. Go slow, just like last time." I let him pull me up and out of the sleeping bag. Before we go down, I roll it back up.

"Sophie, you don't have to do that. Leave it."

"You have no idea how glad I was you left it up here. Almost like you could predict the future. You always give me what I need—even when you're not with me."

"If I could predict the future, I would have never let you go home."

"As much as it hurts, I'm glad I did. I found out the truth. I finally got the answers I've always been searching for."

He nods his head. "True. But that doesn't mean it makes it any easier."

I hang my head. "The truth really hurts, Kipton." I don't want him to watch me cry, but a few tears leak from my eyes and fall onto the bare floor boards. The thirsty wood absorbs them before the wetness has a chance to spread.

"You have me, Sophie. I'll be your family."

CHAPTER
twenty-four

KIPTON

SOPHIE CLUTCHES MY HAND THE entire ride. I use my left hand to turn and shift, not even caring about the inconvenience. She needs me, and I won't let her down. My heart fucking broke when I found her inside the treehouse. That was after I put it through the most uncertain half hour of my life. Not knowing where she was scared the ever loving shit out of me. But I found her, and although worn down and starving, she's in my arms again. Exactly where she belongs.

"Where are we going, Kipton?"

"The diner. Is that okay?"

"Yes, but I'm a mess. Maybe I should wait in the car."

"You'll still be the most beautiful girl in the place." She tries to let go of my hand, embarrassed by my comment, but I grab it back before she moves it too far away from me. "I was scared tonight, Sophie."

"You were?"

"Yeah. I was. I still am." I need her to realize how much she means to me; to know that I'd be devastated if she gave up on herself or on us.

"Why?"

I find a place to park and turn the car off. This particular conversation will have to wait until I get some food inside her stomach. That's my top priority right now. "Eat. And then we'll talk."

She follows me out of the car before I can make it around to open her door for her. I hate when she does that, but I don't try to correct her.

We settle into a booth in the back of the restaurant—the one we had our first date in. "Do you know what you want?"

"You can order for me again. You did well last time we were here."

I smile, happy she's willing to trust me with something as silly as ordering food. After ordering breakfast for two, I put the straw in my orange juice and do the same for her.

"Thank you," she whispers. Her voice is as tiny as her body—frail and fragile.

"About what I said in the car. About being scared." She stops drinking, staring at me in confusion. This might make me sound like a punk, but she needs to be honest with me, and I need to always be honest with her. That's the only way what we have will work. She has lived a life of secrets and I don't want that for us.

"Why are you scared? You have everything, Kipton."

"I have been very fortunate. But none of it means shit unless you're with me, Sophie." There's too much distance between us, and I don't want her to feel bombarded, so I get up and slide next to her on her side of the booth. She scoots over next to the window and angles her body to face me. *Here's goes nothing.*

"I'm scared because I don't want you to give up. You've made so much progress and are working hard to beat your depression. I couldn't be more proud of you. But I'm selfish, Sophie. I need you in my life and I can't lose you. Please don't stop fighting. I don't ever want you to hurt yourself because you feel alone. I'm here. I will *always* be here. You make my life better."

I notice the slight trembling of her hands and wait patiently for her to work through her anxiety. Her foot nervously taps the floor underneath the table. I only know because she's making the bench bounce ever so slightly. Working up the courage one nervous second at a time, she confesses. "I'm scared too, Kipton." *Thank fuck.* I'd be even more worried if she wasn't.

She meets me in the middle, her head finding my shoulder. I wrap my arm around her and rub her arm softly. "What scares you the most?"

"I don't want to be that girl anymore, but I hurt so bad inside, Kipton. It kills me over and over—every time I'm reminded that I was a mistake. Even the woman who gave birth to me finally had enough of me. How do I stop loving her after all these years?"

"You don't have to. Not if you don't want to."

"It's so frustrating because as much as I want to hate her, I can't. And that pisses me off so bad. I want her to feel as shitty as I do."

She takes a sip of her juice as our food arrives. Staring at the table, she doesn't touch anything. I wait patiently before handing her a fork. She accepts, but I'm careful not to push her. I can tell she's struggling with her thoughts. "Sophie."

She takes a bite of her egg white omelet. "This is good."

I'm not hungry, but I eat my omelet anyway so she doesn't have to eat alone. A few more bites go into her mouth before her fork falls from her fingers and clatters against her plate. "Sorry." Picking it back up, she continues to eat.

"Your Mom deserves to feel your anger. They both do. They can't expect you to be anything other than devastated. But remember that family doesn't have to be blood. I'll be your family. My family will be your family. I've told my Mom all about you. She can't wait to meet you. Cara hasn't stopped talking about you either. That's why she flipped out on you so bad, because she loves you."

"I love her too."

"You came into our lives for a reason, beautiful, and we're not letting you go."

"I love you both, Kipton. It scares me how intense my feelings are for you though. I didn't even know I was capable of loving someone the way I love you. That's why I ran from it so many times. I didn't want the past to repeat itself and I didn't want to fail you."

"It's real. I promise. Everything we feel for each other is how it's supposed to be."

She nods her head and although broken, she's still the girl I need. And I'll fight to bring her back entirely. While I have her talking, I decide to take it a step further. "How do you feel about Coach Evans?"

"I'm done with gymnastics. It's tainted like everything else in my past. All these years I've wanted to be the best so my Mom would be proud of me. I needed a purpose for her love because I wasn't sure I deserved it. And Coach Evans told me gymnastics was in my blood- that I was born to be a gymnast. He only said that because he knew who I was."

"Maybe, but it doesn't mean you're any less talented."

"I hate him and I barely even know him. He never fought for me."

"I'm sure he had his reasons. Not that it makes them right."

"My Mom was an amazing gymnast too. When I started out as a little girl and wasn't half bad, she was thrilled. But I think it ended up being an easy way to keep me out of the house for longer periods of time—so she could try to keep Dean happy. As I got older, I didn't even care I was hardly home because it kept me away from the arguing. All this time I've spent thinking gymnastics was my saving grace and it's really been nothing but a bunch of bullshit."

"I'll support any decision you make."

"If I quit, I have to quit school too. There's no place for me in Ashland anymore, but anywhere has to be better. Maybe I can work here until I find something permanent."

She's not quitting school or leaving. I'll figure something out. She can live with me and I'll apply for every student loan I can find for her. "My Dad's in finance. He'll help you with some student loans. You'll lose your scholarship, but not your education. I promise."

"How do you always have all the answers, Kipton?"

"I definitely don't have all the answers—not by a long shot. I'm just trying to help you because without you, I won't be happy. That sounds selfish, but it's the truth. I need you too, beautiful."

"I'm thankful you're willing to help. You always make things seem so easy." She tucks her messy hair behind her

lighter

ear, still nervously bouncing her leg.

"Then I'm doing my job."

"What job is that?"

"To love you and protect you. No matter what."

"Your specialty." She smiles for the first time and I feel it—every face splitting inch of it.

She picks up her fork and works it between her fingers. "Are you going to eat some more? Or are you full?"

She stares at her plate and looks determined. It doesn't have anything to do with the eggs I don't think. "I'm going to finish this and then I want you to take me to bed."

"You must be so tired."

She shakes her head yes. "I am. But I want to love you first."

She can do whatever she wants to me if it makes her happy. "I'll love you all night long, beautiful." She rests her head back on my shoulder and takes a few more bites of her eggs.

"You saved me again, Kipton."

"And I'll never stop."

CHAPTER
twenty-five

Sophie

"SLEEP WELL?"

I turn my head to the soothing sound of Kipton's voice. Staring into his crystal blue eyes, I'm thankful to be with him again. He leans over and kisses my lips. The movement causes a draft under the blanket and I shiver. "Com'ere." I slide over and he spoons me from behind. Instantly, I'm ten degrees warmer. He even covers my feet with his own. "What were you thinking just now?"

"It would probably scare you."

He squeezes me tighter. "Now you have to tell me."

"Just how thankful I am for you. I don't know where I'd be right now if you hadn't found me."

"I feel the same way, beautiful."

He kisses the top of my head and snuggles me closer. "You're always so warm. What time do we have to leave?"

"There's no rush. Whenever you're ready."

"Okay. I need to take a shower first."

"Nope." He pops the p right in my ear and I flinch in surprise.

He's messing with me, but I'm sure he has an excellent reason. He usually does. "Why not?"

"You can shower, but it has to be with me."

"Why?"

"It's my turn to pay the water bill this month. I'm trying to conserve."

"With you?" *I've never done that before.* It feels so personal; so intimate.

"Yup." He pops the p again.

I swat at him. My efforts are wasted since he's behind me and out of reach. "Will you stop that!" I'm laughing and he digs his fingers in my side making me laugh even harder. "Stop! I have to pee!"

"Come on, let's shower and then I'll make you some breakfast."

It sounds like a good deal, but does he expect me to walk naked all the way down the hallway?

He releases me and hops out of bed. Holding out his hand, he waits for me to drop the blanket and expose myself.

"Um. I just need my shirt or one of yours."

He takes both of my hands in one of his and pulls down the blanket. "Nope. Don't be nervous around me. I've seen you naked in bed. Every gorgeous inch. This is no different."

"It's usually darker," I mumble. He hears me and chuckles.

"Don't fear the light. Just go with it."

"If you say so." *Here goes nothing.* I scurry down the hallway quickly. He laughs at my urgency.

"After you." He gestures for me to go into the bathroom ahead of him. I shimmy past, linking my hands behind my back to hide my ass from his view. He swats at me and I yelp in surprise. "Put both of your hands on your head."

"What? Why?" I'm hesitant, but eventually do it. "Now what?"

Kipton leans against the wall, taking me in from head to toe. I hope he's enjoying himself because I'm not. A mischievous smile covers his face. "Put your hands on your shoulders."

I roll my eyes, but listen.

"Now your knees."

I follow his directions.

"Now on your toes."

Again, I comply.

"Faster and repeat after me, head, shoulders, knees, and toes."

"Kipton! You asshole." He ducks when I toss a loofah at his head. Not that it would do any damage even if it hit him. Seeking justice, I punch him hard on the arm.

"Ouch, no hitting! I was only trying to loosen you up. Now, hop in."

"You're bossy today, ya know."

"Always."

Once under the warm spray of water, I wait for him to make this experience sexual—for him to touch me. But he does nothing more than shower. I'm okay with it, yet disappointed at the same time. He takes his time washing his body while I work the shampoo through my hair. I follow with conditioner and body wash. He watches, but never touches.

"See, you lived." He wraps me up in a fluffy blue towel large enough to fit two of me. "Not as hot as the pink towel, but it will do."

I look down at it and wonder what the difference is. A towel is a towel to me. "Why's the pink one better?"

"Because the second I saw you wrapped up in it, I knew I had to make you mine. And hell if I didn't want to see what was underneath it so damn bad." His eyes drop to my lips, before closing the remaining distance and kissing me softly—once and then again.

"How did you know? We were strangers."

"Because you carry your emotions in your eyes, Sophie. I could tell you wanted me too."

"I was scared of you," I admit.

"Why?" He rubs a towel over his hair, making it stick up in a disheveled mess. He looks hot. Seriously hot. "Sophie?"

"Sorry. Um. What was I saying? "I've never felt something instantly just from looking at a guy. Of course I didn't love you or anything that deep, but the way you looked at me I can't describe. It made me feel wanted. I've never had that happen before."

"I'll always want you, beautiful. Now enough of this serious shit. If you don't stop we'll never get on the road."

"Me?"

"Yes, you. When you say those things to me, it makes me want to get you naked."

He does realize we're in the bathroom, fresh out of the shower? "I already am."

"We should put some clothes on."

He leaves the bathroom in a rush and I hurry to catch up to him. I'm not done with him yet. He's reaching inside his closet, but I put my hand on his bicep, dragging my nails down his skin. "I don't want clothes yet, Kipton."

He groans. "Oh yeah? What *do* you want?"

I free his towel and drop my own. He wants me to be more comfortable, so I'll show him exactly what I want. "Touch me he-"

There's a hand on my knee, shaking me slightly. "Hmm?" I murmur. I'm just getting to the good part.

"Wake up, sleepy head. We're almost here."

Blinking slowly, I look around. The houses are huge, all with perfectly manicured lawns. Even the bushes are fancy. "It was just getting good."

"What was?" He asks, while keeping his eyes on the road.

"My dream."

"Tell me about it. You were making some adorable noises."

I cover my mouth in surprise. "No, I wasn't!"

"You were. What was happening?"

"Well, we showered together."

He smiles. "I like this dream already."

"And we were just about to do things in your room."

"What kind of things?" Interested in the details, he turns the radio off.

"Sexual."

"I would hope. Tell me one."

"Well, we were naked in your room and I was begging you to touch me."

"I'd never make you beg, unless you wanted to. But where did you want me to touch you?"

"You know where." My cheeks flush with unspoken sexual desire.

"Where, Sophie?" He inches his hand between my thighs,

forcing me to part my legs ever so slightly. "Here?" He moves a few more inches. "Or maybe here?"

"Yeah, there," I practically pant. His fingers move back and forth a few times and I clutch his wrist to hold him tightly against my body. Just as things begin to heat up, he removes his hand and places it back on the steering wheel leaving me needy and impatient.

"We should act out this dream of yours tonight. I want to make sure your fantasies come true."

Only he would find it acceptable to get me hot and bothered before meeting his parents. "Funny."

"What's funny? I'm serious. It's happening." He pulls into a long driveway lined with tall trees. It screams southern money. The house is the most elegantly, beautiful place I've ever been. It's easily three times the size of the house I grew up in. "Wow."

"It's just a house, Sophie."

"A huge one."

"It's the people inside that matter. Not the size. Remember that okay?"

"Okay."

I barely have two feet planted on the driveway before Cara is running toward me. "Sophie!"

She almost knocks me over with her enthusiastic welcome. "Oof. I missed you too, Cara."

"Come inside, come."

"One sec, Cara. Come here a minute, Sophie."

I walk over to Kipton as he asked. "What's wrong?"

He pulls me behind the trunk, out of view from the front of the house. "Nothing. Just don't forget about tonight." He runs his hand up my thigh and between my legs again. Repeating his early ministrations. He rubs back and forth over my sensitive nerve endings before cupping me in his palm.

"I won't forget."

He drops his hand to his side, leaving me in a daze. I glance around, making sure no one can see us. Thankfully, the closest neighbor is on the other side of the trees. Swallowing hard at his reminder, I walk back to the front door to meet Cara. I glance over my shoulder at Kipton. Hoping he's

GIA RILEY

right behind me, I'm nervous when he winks and takes his time gathering my bags. This game he's playing is killing me.

"Mom! Sophie's here." Instantly, I'm wrapped in to a warm hug from a woman I assume to be Kipton's mom.

"She's beautiful. My goodness, you're just adorable. Come, let's talk. I've been so excited to put a face to the name."

"I've been looking forward to meeting you too, Mrs.–"

She interrupts before I can give her a formal greeting. "Call me Lynn."

"Okay. It's nice to meet you, Lynn." We walk down a hall-way and into an office. She pats the sofa next to her and I take my place nervously. Cara closes the doors and leaves the two of us alone.

"I needed time with you right away, Sophie. Both of my children are very open and honest with me. It's the way I've always wanted it. I know we're practically strangers, but I'll never be anything other than honest with you too."

Where is she going with all of this?

"Kipton shared a few things with me before he ran out last night. I'd never pretend not to know. It's not how I op-erate."

I hang my head, twisting my fingers in my lap. I want to get up and run. Kipton promised she wouldn't judge me. Standing, I take one step before Lynn's hand reaches for mine.

"Please, Sophie. Hear me out. And don't be angry with Kipton. He has your best interest at heart."

I can't sit back down, so I stand on shaky legs next to the window. Being able to see the outside makes the conversa-tion less constrictive.

"Kipton also called me last night after you fell asleep. With the way he ran out of here last night, I was worried you were in trouble."

"I was." Admitting you're in trouble is the first step, right?

"I agree with that, Sophie. That's why you're here with me. Both Cara and Kipton already know what I'm going to ask of you."

"You want me to leave, don't you? To stop wasting your

son's time. I'm well aware he deserves better."

"No, Sophie. I want you to stay."

Confused, I look to her for an explanation. She isn't making sense.

"I want this to be your home. When you're on break, over the summer, after you finish, this will be your home."

Is she nuts? "But we don't even know each other. You may not even like me."

She shakes her head repeatedly. "That will never be the case because both of my children love you. I trust their judgment."

My eyes fill with unshed tears. "What if Kipton and I break up?"

"The status of your relationship doesn't depend on your place in this home. It's yours for as long as you want it. You'll have a room of your own."

The tears fall. I sink to the floor unable to believe an entire family actually wants to take me in. "I need to let it all sink in, Lynn. I haven't had many opportunities in my life to love someone, but I know I love your son—more than anything. And Cara's my best friend. I've never known what it's like to have a family."

"You will after today. And I apologize for yanking you in here right away, but I couldn't sit through dinner or wait another minute. You've been through enough. " Lynn closes her eyes and breathes deeply. When she opens them again, a few tears of her own trickle down her cheeks. "You remind me a lot of myself, Sophie. I grew up in a volatile home myself so when I say I understand your pain, I mean it. But it does get better and it will get easier over time."

"It's so hard to give up on my Mom. And I tried to make Dean love me, but couldn't. As far as Coach goes, I haven't even processed the idea of him yet. I've been too busy mourning everything I lost."

Lynn sits next to me on the carpet. "Doug and I don't want to overwhelm you. We won't pretend to be anything other than what you're willing to accept. But this is a safe place. You're not alone anymore, Sophie. It's all here for you if you want it."

"Thank you."

"So you'll stay?" She's hesitant with her request, but in need of an answer nonetheless.

"It's a strange concept with dating Kipton and all. I mean I'm an adult. But if you'll have me." My shaky voice gives away how overwhelmed I am. I've just been given my greatest wish. *Acceptance.*

"We'll get all of your info changed as soon as possible. I never want you to live in a hotel or sleep in a damn tree again." She laughs through a sob of her own and wipes the tears from my face. It's a motherly gesture.

"Thank you, Lynn. The words hardly seem like enough."

"They're plenty." She stands up from the floor and brushes the wrinkles out of the fabric of her pants. "You take all the time you need. I've walloped you with a lot just now. Come out and meet my husband when you're ready. I'm sure Cara would like to show you your room too."

I stay seated on the floor, processing our conversation. Despite the ache in my heart, I've been given a second chance. Praying that I'm strong enough to live up to their standards, I need to discuss all of this with Kipton before I get too comfortable.

Sophie: Can you come in here.

The text barely finishes sending before the office door opens. "I was in the hallway. Are you okay?"

"Hey." He's tiptoeing around the elephant in the room, so I put him out of his misery and address it. "Are you on board with this crazy plan?"

He kneels in front of me, taking my hands. "Of course I am. You're my home, Sophie. Wherever you are is where I want to be. You said yes, right? I'm sorry you walked into that blind, but I was afraid if I said something, you would panic or get upset."

I can tell he's nervous about my decision. "I'm not mad. I'm too grateful to be upset. But I *am* old enough to do it on my own. I'm over eighteen and a legal adult."

He sighs. I'm not trying to be difficult. I'm simply stating the obvious.

"But you shouldn't have to. Yes, we're both adults, but until we graduate and get on our feet financially, you need a place to call home. Hell, I'm a year older than you and I still need it. So don't get caught up in a numbers game. I don't want you to quit school and settle for a dead end job for the rest of your life."

"I don't want to quit school, or live a miserable life either. It would be a repeat of *their* lives."

"You're already more than they've ever been, beautiful."

"Thank you, Kipton."

"For what?"

"*Everything.*"

Before we can discuss anything else, Cara's rattling the door knob. "Sophie? Kipton, it's my turn. Give her back."

I snort, laughing at the way she's turned me into a prized possession. Kipton rolls his eyes as a brother would. "She always was a pain in the ass." He helps me up off the floor and walks me to the office doors. "Love you."

I stand on my tiptoes to kiss him but he easily lifts me off my feet. I lock my legs around his waist and deepen his kiss. "Give. Her. Back!"

Kipton reluctantly sets me back on my feet. Slowly opening the door, Cara reaches inside like a caged animal that's been set free. "Bout time, come on. Let's go see your room. It's connected to mine!"

"Wonderful," Kipton murmurs. He mouths the words *later* to me. Like I'd ever be able to forget his promise.

I'm seriously living in a fairytale right now. From tree houses to mansions—I feel like Cinderella.

CHAPTER
twenty-six

Sophie

THE WEEK WITH KIPTON WAS amazing. The days were uneventful, yet absolutely perfect. We stayed up late watching movies, played board games around the kitchen table, and laughed. Laughter can easily be taken for granted, but never again will I wonder what it's like to laugh so hard you give yourself the hiccups.

I thought it might be awkward pretending to belong to a family that doesn't share any of my DNA. Much to my surprise, it's fairly easy. Worried Kipton would end up feeling suffocated having me around nonstop, he never once said or did anything to lead me to believe he regretted the decision. Sucking up every second of happiness, I had a restless night last night as our vacation came to an end. If it was up to me, I'd put off going back to school for another week. But I have to face the facts and bow out of gymnastics. I dread the conversation with Coach Evans, but I can't stay on the team knowing what I now know. I've had plenty of time to self-reflect on my decision. After lining up the positives against the negatives—the negatives took the top prize without a shadow of a doubt. *It was time I left.*

"You okay, babe?"

"Nervous, but I'm good. I really love your family, Kipton."

He rubs his hand back and forth on my thigh. "You're exactly what we were missing. I've never seen Mom happier."

"It didn't seem like you were ever missing anything."

"Things seem complete now. Like you were meant to find your way to me."

Complete.

Resting my head against the back of the seat, I decide to rip the Band-Aid off before I change my mind. "Can you drop me off at the gym. I'm sure Coach is in his office."

Kipton hesistates. "Now? Don't you want to get settled in your room first?" His dad was on the phone with the school the second campus reopened. He managed to get all the paperwork straightened out with financial aid for my loans to kick in at the start of the new semester. For now, I'd be given a grace period considering the special circumstances of forfeiting my scholarship. I'll be able to stay in the dorm with Cara and life can go on as planned.

"Now's as good a time as any. I'm dreading it, but it has to be done. All the paperwork with the Bursar's Office is in the works."

"Do you want me to go inside with you?"

"No." I have to face him on my own. Just the two of us. Father and daughter.

Kipton forcefully exhales and squeezes the bridge of his nose. The same thing he does every time I stress him out. "Sophie, this is about more than just leaving the team. He's your blood."

"I know he is."

"Are you sure you don't want me to come with you? Just in case."

"What do you think is going to happen? He can't hurt me anymore than he already has."

"I don't want him hurting you any *more* either."

I can't go into his office upset so I don't bother responding. Instead I wait for the car to come to a stop in front of the gym. "I'll text you when I'm done, but I'd like to walk back if you don't mind."

"Sophie." He definitely minds.

"Please, Kipton. I'll meet you back at the dorm. I need to

do this my way."

"Fine. Call me if you need me and I'll pick you up."

"Thank you." I close the car door with shaky hands. My legs carry me inside, but my mind is busy going over the speech I've been rehearsing for the past week. It's all in there; I just hope I can get it all out without him stopping me.

The gym seems bigger after not having been inside for so long. The same smells of the chalk and sweat mix in the air. While they once comforted me, they now make me want to run.

Although most of the office doors are closed, the light radiating from Coach Evans' office seeps into the hallway. Each step toward it brings me closer to the truth of my existence.

One, two, three knocks on the open door until I get the okay to enter. "Coach."

"Sophie." He stands up and points to the couch by the window. "Have a seat. I think we have a few things to discuss."

Shuffling over to the sofa, we waste no time getting down to business. Though asked to sit, I stay standing while holding onto the arm of the sofa for support. "I'm leaving the team, which you probably already know. The office told me you had the official release papers here in your office. I'd like to sign them and be on my way." Now that I've said the words, they carry so much more weight. I'm really giving it all up.

"Just like that? You're quitting after all the years of hard work you dedicated to the sport. You're so talented, Sophie. You have to know this is a mistake. One you will likely regret."

"Gymnastics doesn't make me happy anymore. Not since my eyes were opened to the truth. I have a lot more to dedicate my life to. Things that will give back to me and support me the way they're supposed to without being asked." It's a roundabout dig at his lack of parenting, although unintentional.

"I understand your frustration. But you have the fire inside you, Sophie, to make something great out of this. You can be a winner; make the team stronger. There's a place for you and I'd like you to stay."

"You want me to stay? Or you want to win? Because the way I see it, you had twenty years to ask me to stay and you never did. From my point of view, this has everything to do with *your* success as a coach and nothing to do with me." Now that I've spoken the words rattling around inside my mind, I'm feeling overwhelmed. I claim the edge of the couch cushion, not wanting to be any closer than necessary to him.

Coach stands up and inches closer. Kneeling down in front of me, he removes his glasses and pinches his thumb and middle finger in the corners of his eyes. *Eyes that match my own.* "Sophie, I made a lot of bad decisions in my life—I take credit for them all. But I did what your mother begged me to do. I had no choice."

"Everyone has a choice." *Even me.*

"That's true, and hiding the fact that you were my daughter went against my better judgment, but it's the way she wanted it. I had to do what she wanted."

"That's bullshit. You could have told her to go fuck herself. Who cares what she wanted. What about what I *needed?*"

"Sophie, I'm sorry I kept the truth from you when you came here. It was wrong of me. But I can't do anything about it now any more than I could then. It was complicated. It's always been that way with your Mother."

His words aren't good enough. Standing up from the couch, I pick up the crystal award resting on his desk. An award he took the time to earn. An award he *had* the time to earn. Yet he had no time for his own daughter. After reading the boasting inscription, I chuck it at the wall. "Sophie!" He yells in surprise.

"Do you have any idea the fucking hell I've lived in all these years? A hell you claim to not have a say in. You could have fought for me. Instead, I was stuck with a Mother I had to be perfect to please and a father who refused to give two shits about me. He drank himself into a stupor every night of the week, his hookers and secretaries littering the living room or the back seat of his car. A real shining example of a parent, Coach. Anything you could have offered me would have been better—anything! But you didn't once try to see me, speak to me, or come around. And I would have known because I was always holed up in my damn closet searching for an ounce of clarity about why I was even brought into this world in the first place. Everyone hated me—couldn't stand to look at me." Tears flow freely out of my eyes. For once I'm not worried about showing my weakness. "You ruined my life and you don't even care! It's all about what I can bring to the team—not what I can bring as your daughter. You only want me here because you want to win."

His expression changes from surprise into shock. "Sophie, that's not true."

"You know, I applied here as a freshman because I wanted to work with the Coach I worshipped at the school of my dreams. Yet somehow, I was given a rejection letter—my own *Father* turned me away because life was easier for you as long as you did what she said. I get it now."

He rests his elbow on his knee and rubs his fingertips back and forth over the creases in his forehead. He stares absentmindedly at the carpet, like it will provide him with all the answers he's missing. Finally, he raises his head and the regret shines in his eyes—tears of his own battling with his pride. "I let you down, Sophie. I know I did. But I've always loved you and I've always cared how you were doing. Your Mother wouldn't let me near you. I wasn't even allowed to send mail once you were old enough to know how to read. She was too afraid you'd get your hands on something and start asking questions. She had more to lose than I did. I've never married nor had anyone to hide from. But Dean—he threatened the both of us.

Your mom would bring you to see me at the gym when you were a baby. It was the only way I could see you. Once a month, she risked him finding out so I could see your beautiful face. But he has a lot of power Sophie. And when he discovered what she was doing, he put a stop to it. It killed me to give up our visits, but I was worried about her safety because I knew he drank. She told me pushing to see you would only cause her more trouble. The day you turned one was the last day I held you in my arms. That night was the night the letters started. I couldn't cry enough, yell enough, be pissed off enough, so I wrote you instead. It's the only thing that made me feel close to you."

"Why did you leave *me* with him if you knew what he was capable of?"

"Because I was scared. Scared you wouldn't love *me,* or accept *me.* The same way you were scared I never loved you."

"I don't believe it. I don't," I sob. "You're a grown ass man. One with a career that thrives on molding young minds. Yet you can't figure out how to approach your own child?"

"I was scared of him too, I guess. He had the power to destroy my career—to expose my affair with your Mother. I couldn't lose you *and* gymnastics, Sophie. I needed it to survive—to keep me sane. I failed at being your Father and I'll never be able to get back the time we lost, or make up for it. But I'll pay for it in another life, I'm sure of it." He opens the bottom drawer of the filing cabinet. "These are yours." He hands me a box.

"What is it?"

"Inside you'll find the letters I wrote on your birthday each year since you were born. I couldn't physically give them to you, but I celebrated the day you were born every year. I tried giving your mom money every month, but she said Dean would find it or ask questions. Sophie, I may have failed you, but I *never* forgot you. You're always on my mind. I'm proud of the young woman you've become. You're strong willed and filled with determination. You're everything I've always wanted my little girl to be."

With shaky fingers, I rifle through all twenty letters. Each in colored envelopes with my name scrolled across the front in messy cursive. I wipe away a few tears with the back of my hand. My damp fingers leave prints on the top envelope. "I can keep these?" I don't know why I want to torture myself by reading them, but I know it's something I have to do for closure. It's the only way I'll know if he's telling the truth.

"They've always belonged to you."

"Then I'd like to sign the papers and leave."

Reluctantly, he opens a folder on his desk and rifles through a few papers, signing them by the designated marks before handing them over to me. "I wish you'd reconsider.

We could do this *together*."

My mind's been made up. I'm ready to move on and be done with this chapter of my life. It's time to focus on school and my future outside of a gym. It's controlled me for too long.

I sign my name next to his and can't help but notice the different last names. I should be Sophie Evans—but I was never given a choice. Never given the opportunity to love my father.

Laying the pen on the document, I turn around with my box and leave the office without so much as a goodbye.

Pushing through the doors leading outside as fast as I can, I gulp up the fresh air. I thought it would be a relief to get everything off my chest and out in the open. But now that I have, I realize it will take more than some long overdue words to put me back together.

Holding my box tightly, I'm trying to process his words yet still find it hard to believe he had no say when it came to me. Why would my mom keep him from me? Especially when Dean hated me so much. And why would she choose Dean over him?

The next bench I find, I sit and open the box.

The first letter looks the most worn—like it's been read over and over. I'm not sure what I'll find inside the envelopes, or whether it's all for show—something to make himself feel better about his shitty decisions. But I read the first letter anyway.

My Beauty,

A year ago today was the greatest day of my life, the day you came into the world. Although I'm not with you, I carry you in my heart. No matter the distance between us, I'll always be your guiding light—a protector from afar.

When you're scared, think of me. When you're sad, let me help you. And when you're lost, I'll help you find your way. I may never be your hero, precious, but you'll always be daddy's little girl. I love you to the moon and back.

Love, Daddy

I stuff the letter back into the delicate pink envelope, my favorite color. When I stand up, I notice others staring at me, but I don't care. Let them look. Fumbling the box in my shaky hands, I almost drop it before regaining my composure. I have to get back to Kipton before he worries.

Daddy's little girl. What does that even mean?

"Hi, Sophie." I pass Drew in the hallway of my dorm, but I'm wound too tightly to acknowledge him with more than a small wave.

My door is open, Kipton resting on my bed and Cara watching TV. He sits up and rushes to me when he sees me.

"Sophie."

I give him a pathetic half smile, the words from the letter rattling me.

"How was it?" He asks cautiously.

"I'm not sure. Would you both mind giving me some time alone? There are a few things I need to do." They cautiously look back and forth between each other and then back at me. "I'm fine. But I'd like to be alone."

Kipton's sitting on the edge of the bed, eyeing me cautiously. I'm sure he's waiting for me to break down. He pulls me in between his legs, searching my eyes for clues. He's always able to read me without a word being spoken. "I have no idea what went on, but don't let him destroy you. You've come too far."

"He wrote me, every year. For my birthday. That's what's in the box."

"Can I see?"

"I want to read them first. You can see the one I've already read." These are mine. I need to go through them and process each one separately. I don't think I can handle all twenty of them right now, but I'm too curious not to read another. I'm almost hoping his words changed over the years—became less loving and more resentful. Because after reading the first, it's harder to hate him. And I *need* to hate him.

"Only if you want me too." I set the box down on the bed and hand him the pink envelope. He watches me as he opens it but shifts his eyes to the paper once it's unfolded. It only takes him a second to see the words. They haven't weaved into his soul and wrapped around his heart like they have mine. "Sophie, I don't know what to say."

I take the letter back, nestling it inside the box with its lid. "You don't have to say anything." I place the box on my desk. "I need to say something, Sophie. That's some serious shit."

"Maybe that's all it is—shit."

"I don't think you believe that and neither do I."

I almost wish I never saw the words. "I should get my school work done."

"You did that over break." Kipton reminds me.

"I'm sure I forgot something."

"Sophie, you don't have to look for excuses. If you want me to leave just tell me, but don't push me away."

"I don't want you to go—but I need to cry."

He holds his arms open wide. "Then come let me hold you and cry it out."

I willingly walk into his arms. "Thank you."

"You don't always have to be strong, beautiful. I won't love you less if you cry."

I may never stop worrying about losing his acceptance or his love, but right now, I'm holding on to it as tightly as possible. He's taught me love doesn't need a motive or an excuse. It can simply exist. His is the most patient kind of love there is.

Since I've met him he's caught every one of my tears. Today is no different as we lay in silence while he strokes my back and gives me the strength and warmth of his arms. His love runs deep and I'm blessed to have it.

CHAPTER
twenty-seven

KIPTON

SOPHIE'S BEEN DISTRACTED THE PAST couple weeks, paying more attention to the box on her desk than her school work. Not sleeping well, it shows in her mood. She's saying and doing all the right things as far has her therapy goes, but she's off. She's spent so many years hating Dean, she's having trouble with her mom and her real father added into the mix. Her anger was always specifically driven toward Dean whereas now it's all over the place. She may never be able to forgive all of their faults, but my girl has a big heart and will come to terms when she's ready.

Sophie and I are in a good place, but she hasn't been staying at my place as much as I've wanted her to. Cara tells me she stays up until all hours of the night looking through her letters. I've talked to my parents about it and they assure me it's all part of the healing process. Her emotions are scattered, all playing tricks on her sense of security. If it has to work itself out naturally, I pray it does it soon. Seeing her spirit suffer kills me inside.

It's a little early for dinner, but rather than driving the whole way back home, I walked to the dorms after my workout. I'm careful to knock on the girls' dorm room door, making sure I wait for the go ahead to enter so Cara doesn't go ape shit on me again. When I don't hear a response, I knock again and wait. I'm met with silence for the second time. I try to jiggle the door knob, but it's locked. Pulling out my cell, I try calling Sophie. It rings and rings without a response, finally going to voicemail.

"Hey, gorgeous. I'm standing outside your room. Call me when you get this. I thought we had plans for dinner." I hang up and sit down on the heater at the end of the hallway, deciding to call my sister. Maybe she'll know where to find Sophie.

She picks up on the first ring. "Hi Kippy. What's up?"

"Is Sophie with you?"

"No. She said she had dinner plans with you, so I'm going with Drew. Did you piss her off?"

"Not that I know of, but she isn't answering the door or her phone." I knock again, harder this time, in case she was asleep and didn't hear me before. There's still no response.

"She answer?" Cara asks.

"No. Nothing. You have no idea where she could be?"

"Calm down. I'm sure she ran a quick errand or got held up at the library. I shouldn't tell you this, but there's a spare key hidden underneath the heater in the hallway, the one you're probably sitting on top of."

I get down on my hands and knees and reach under the old metal heater. It takes a minute, but I find it. Thankfully it's hidden well and nobody would ever spot it unless they knew it was there. It's still not the safest thing for two girls to be doing though. "I got it. We'll discuss the key after I find Sophie."

"See, this is why I don't tell you things. You get all worked up. It's better than being locked out of your room in your damn towel and flip flops because you left your key inside your room."

"Yeah, I get it, but we can come up with something safer I'm sure." I stick the key in the lock and push the door open. My heart plummets to the floor. "Sophie!" I run over to her body, lying awkwardly on the shaggy rug in front of her closet door. "Baby, no. Wake up, Sophie!" I yell louder. I hang up on Cara and dial 911. Holding Sophie's lifeless body in my arms, I rock back and forth on the floor as all signs of life appear lost on my beautiful girl.

With the direction of the dispatcher, I'm able to detect a faint pulse on her neck and I pray I'm not imagining it.

I turn around and the hallway is crowded with shocked expressions and tears. Everyone's staring but nobody is helping. "Someone fucking get some help. Please!"

As I finish screaming, Cara and Drew come barreling in the room. Cara's immediately on her knees next to Sophie, tears streaming down her cheeks. Drew's on his phone with campus security rattling off instructions and information. I'm glad he's here.

"What happened to her, Kippy?" Cara's shaking, obviously in shock from the sight of her unconscious best friend.

"I don't know Cara. I don't fucking know." I continue to hold her close to my body, keeping her warm. Cara grabs a blanket from her bed and lays it across the both of us. My hands are shaking as I brush my knuckle across her cheek. Shaking her I start to freak out when she still hasn't woken up. "Sophie, please. Open your eyes. I need to see your beautiful eyes." There's no response from her.

After several excruciatingly long minutes, the paramedics arrive. They take her out of my arms, immediately hooking her up to machines and poking her with an IV. In what seems like seconds, they have her on the gurney with her neck and back stabilized. Moving down the hall, I follow after them, leaving the door to their room hanging wide open. "Where are you taking her?" When nobody answers me, I lose my cool and grab the arm of one of the medics. "Where are you fucking taking her?"

"Son, I'm going to have to ask you to calm down."

"That's my goddamn *everything* you have laying there. I'm not calming down until you tell me what's going on. Why isn't she awake?"

"Kipton, it's okay man. Let them do their job," Drew says as he puts his body in between me and the medic. "We can follow the ambulance to the hospital."

"I want to go with her."

He puts his hand on my shoulder, the other on my chest to hold me back. "They're not gonna let you in the ambulance while you're losing your shit."

Realizing he's right, I apologize to the medic I was harassing and follow them outside. Other students have filled the perimeter of the dorm to gawk at Sophie like she's on display. I'm relieved they don't have to take her all the way up the hill. Instead, they've already driven the ambulance around to the delivery entrance.

"You're good?" Drew asks. "We'll follow you in my car to the hospital, okay?"

"Yeah. Make sure my sister's okay, Drew."

"I will, man. She's my number one."

Climbing in the back of the ambulance, I can't handle the site of Sophie lying helpless and unconscious. Praying to God my girl will wake up, the doors slam and I sit in silence, horrified that I wasn't there to help her sooner.

"Kipton is it?" The medic asks.

"Yes, my name's Kipton."

"I'm going to need whatever information you can give me about her, okay?"

"Sure, yeah. Okay." We hit a few bumps and I'm tossed around. Holding onto the side wall of the ambulance, I steady myself.

"Has she ever passed out before? Any previous conditions that could have caused this?"

"I don't think she's passed out before. She gets lightheaded sometimes." He jots down my comments on the clipboard.

"Do you know any of her medical history? Anything we should know?"

"Shit, she had a concussion a few months back. She hit her head pretty bad. I know she's been having migraines and getting dizzy still. But she said it was getting better each week. Could that be what caused this?"

"It could have, I can't rule that out. But let's let the doctors examine her before we jump to any conclusions. The important thing is that although she's unconscious, her vitals are stable. That's a great sign."

Thank God for that.

"Is there anything else I should put on her paperwork, Kipton?"

"No. I don't think so. She doesn't take medicine for any-thing. But I'm not sure of her allergies. Shit, I should know that." I run my hands through my hair, frustrated that I don't know everything about the girl I love. I rest my head against the wall of the ambulance and close my eyes. I open them when I remember more. "She's in therapy, too, because she throws up. Between the concussion and her past, she's been having a hell of a time." I ramble. He adds my comments to her list and scans my face wearily making me even more nervous than I already am.

I can't see out the window and each turn seems to be tak-ing forever. "Are we soon there?"

"Yes, it won't be more than a minute. You did well, Kip-ton. Thank you."

"She's not crazy," I blurt out.

"I didn't say she was. But the doctors will make sure she has everything she needs once she's inside. After that, it's up to her."

I glance at Sophie, silently pleading with her to wake up; to open her eyes and show me she's okay. But she doesn't. *Fight, beautiful.*

Arriving outside the emergency room, I hop out of the ambulance the second the doors open. They pull Sophie alongside me and rush inside. I'm stopped before I make it to her room. "Young man, you'll need to wait in the waiting area. The doctors will address you after they tend to her."

"I don't want to leave her," I protest.

"I promise she will be okay. Have a seat and I'll update you the second they give word about her condition."

I'm pushed out and left staring at the rustling curtain di-vider. A nurse escorts me into the sterile waiting room. "Kip-py, is she okay?" Cara rushes to my side and hangs on my arm. I wrap it around her needing the comfort as much as she does.

"I don't know. She never woke up." We sit in a couple uncomfortable chairs next to the vending machines. Drew sits Cara on his lap and holds her. The sight of them together makes me want Sophie.

"She'll wake up, guys. She's tough. Just give her a little

time," Drew adds.

"I called Mom, Kipton. She's on her way."

I'm surprised, but I shouldn't be. My mom took to Sophie immediately. They have some kind of unspoken connection I don't understand. "Thanks."

The seconds and minutes multiply and I become restless. Pacing back and forth, I notice it's dark outside—a much starker contrast from the sunshine of our arrival. It shouldn't be taking this long. If she was okay, they would have come out by now.

"Kipton, honey." I turn to the sound of my mom's voice, thankful she's here so I don't have to hold the weight of the world on my shoulders all alone.

"Mom." I kiss her cheek and get lost in her hug like a lost little boy.

"Any word?"

I'm about to tell her no when we're interrupted by a nurse. "Are you Sophie's family?"

"Yes," we reply in unison. The nurse gives us a warm smile.

"I'm Maura, from social work." *Social work? Where's the damn nurse?* I was called to Sophie's case based on some information the medics were given on her way over. About her history. I was wondering if I could speak to you about those things in a more private area. Would that be okay?"

My mom speaks up. "We aren't her blood relatives, I understand there are some privacy rules and regulations we wouldn't want to cross."

"Of course. She's told me about her biological family and the circumstances. I've been given the okay to proceed speaking with you all. As long as you agree."

Of course we agree. I'll do anything to help her. "She's awake? She's okay?" I ask with hope.

"She's doing better and awake. We've spent some time talking. But she was concerned about seeing you all."

I don't get it. "Why?"

"Sophie's gone through several traumatic experiences in a very short amount of time. Her body and mind gave up earlier today. She was overwhelmed and exhausted. The combination of not sleeping, and not properly eating caused her to pass out. Her blood sugar plummeted. That in itself was serious but combined with her recent concussion; the fall she took as she lost consciousness was also a concern. She's a brave young woman with one complicated past."

"Will she be okay? There's no permanent damage?" Mom asks.

"Nothing permanent physically, no. But mentally, she's struggling. Her therapist has been effective, but I don't think it's enough, especially with all the outside distractions."

I let mom handle the questions. My mind's spinning. "What do you recommend for her?"

"I think she'd benefit from inpatient therapy in our Behavioral Health Center. Peer group counseling as well as individual. I'd also like her to meet with her biological family to work through her anger. She has your love and support as I can see, but she needs more."

I stand up, not agreeing with the recommendation. "She's not crazy. Do you have any idea the hell her family has put her through? I'm sorry, but she's not going anywhere. She can move in with me."

"Kipton," Mom urges.

"No, Mom. They aren't sticking her in a padded room like a prisoner. I'll take her to therapy every day. To the woman she sees now."

"Honey, she can't live a full life if she's not well enough to enjoy it—to fully experience it. Let's help her find her joy again. She can't keep holding onto the burden she's carrying. Nobody can survive forever like that. You heard Maura, her body gave out on her today."

"She's been depressed and withdrawn, but she's trying to sort out the letters from her Father and make sense of everything"

"Exactly Kipton. She needs help making sense of her world."

It's selfish, but what if she starts thinking I'm wrong for her too. *It's not about me.* "Can I see her?"

Maura smiles warmly at me. "Of course you can. She's being observed overnight in this department. If all is well tomorrow, they will discharge her to our care. While her therapy isn't mandatory—meaning we can't hold her against her will, we will recommend she remain for the duration. Having your support would make this transition easier for her to accept."

I'm almost afraid to ask, but I do it anyway. "Does she know she's going? Have you told her?"

She nods her head. "She knows." I sigh in relief.

Sophie can be stubborn, but if she says she wants the help they're offering, I'll support her. "Can I see her now?"

"You can all follow me, but just one at a time in the room. She's resting and I don't want to overwhelm her." We follow Maura without question. "Second door on the left."

"Thank you."

"I'll be at the front desk processing her paperwork. If you need anything push the call button in her room."

"Okay." Each step I take toward her, my heart rate kicks up another notch. I don't understand my nervousness. She's my Sophie.

The door to her room is halfway open so I nudge it with my forearm. I'm not prepared for what I see.

CHAPTER
twenty-eight

Sophie

"WAKE UP, SOPHIE. I'M HERE."

I hear Kipton's voice and struggle to get to it. My body fights to pull me back into darkness, locking me inside my dream, but I fight back to open my eyes. The first thing I see are Kipton's baby blues staring nervously into my own. *I scared him.*

My eyes were only closed for a short time, but the words from my sixteenth birthday letter are embedded into the backs of my eyelids. No matter how hard I try, each time I fall asleep, I see his words staring back at me. I've read each letter enough times to have memorized each endearment, each phrase of promise, and each signature.

"I'm sorry."

"Shh. You're okay, beautiful. Everything is going to be okay now."

I glance around the room. Picking at the tape on my arm covering the IV, I flinch when I press too hard. The coolness from the medication seeps into my veins slowly, lessening my headache but not curing my pain. "This hurts."

"It will help you feel better. You fell again."

There are patches stuck to my chest with wires coming out of them. They itch and I disconnect one as I scratch at it. A machine goes wild, beeping erratically, just like my heart. I stare at it, unsure of its purpose, but afraid to move.

A nurse rushes into the room, silencing the beeping and reconnecting me to the wire. Kipton moves out of her way, but stays close to my bedside. "Can we go home now, Kipton?"

"You agreed to stay for a little while. Do you remember passing out?"

He's right. I did agree after speaking to the social worker, but I know they won't let him stay once I'm moved. I wrap my arms around myself, scooting under the crappy bed sheet. All that's wrapped around me is a thin gown and I'm freezing. "Dizzy. I got so dizzy. I tried to make it to the phone, but I don't think I did. That's all I remember. I still feel weak, and my head is fuzzy."

"It'll take some time to get your blood sugar back up. All that matters is you're okay. God, beautiful, I was so scared when I found you." He tucks a piece of hair behind my ear and I lean into his touch. It's comforting.

"You found me?" I question. There's no memory of ever leaving my dorm room.

"Yeah. You were passed out on the floor. I panicked and was yelling for help and trying to wake you back up." He runs his head through his hair and exhales loudly at the reminder.

"I'm sorry I scared you."

He takes my hand and rubs it soothingly. "It's not your fault. We're gonna get you fixed up and you'll be back in your room in no time."

"You really think I should stay?"

He nods his head and no words are needed. He needs me to stay as much as I know I should. "I know I said I would, but I'm scared to stay here without you. Every time I try to sleep, he comes. He won't stop and it's driving me crazy."

"Who won't stop?" I wait for the nurse to leave before I continue. "Sophie, look at me. Tell me what you mean."

"Coach Evans and his letters. They follow me everywhere I go."

There's a knock on the door and Lynn peeks her head inside the room. She glances over her shoulder before scurrying inside to join the two of us. "There's only one person allowed at a time, but I had to see you with my own eyes," she whispers.

"Hi, Lynn. I'm just getting my things together so Kipton can take me home." I hate her seeing me like this. Her house is the only place my dreams haven't followed. I'd do anything to go back there for a while instead of staying here all alone.

Lynn reaches out for my arm and takes my hand in hers. "Sophie, I think you should give it a few days. Stay and let them help you. You've been through so much stress."

I glance between her and her son and make the connection. "You both think I'm crazy, don't you?"

Lynn tightens her grasp on my hand and shakes her head adamantly. "No, Sophie. We don't think that at all."

Kipton takes my other hand and his answer is written all over his face. *He's worried.* "Beautiful, I was so scared when I found you. I can't see you like that ever again. They can help you get back on track."

"Please, Kipton. I just need you. Then I'll be okay." But I can tell by his expression that he doesn't believe my line of bullshit any more than I do. He's always rescued me, but this time he's not enough. This time, I have to do it on my own.

CHAPTER
twenty-nine

Sophie

WAKING GROGGILY, I'M CONFUSED ABOUT where I am. No longer surrounded by machines, this room is empty yet warmer—less sterile. It feels more like my dorm and less like a hospital.

The bruise on my arm remains, but the IV is gone. *Where is everyone?* Cautiously, I get out of bed to explore my surroundings. The hallways are carpeted with warm lights lining the walls. In between each light are wall hangings covered in inspirational quotes.

Passing by a few open doors, everyone looks occupied in some way yet without a care in the world. It can only be described as peaceful ignorance. That is until I reach the end of the hall and see a young girl being walked down a hallway with her hands cuffed behind her back. She doesn't stay in one of the rooms like mine; instead she's taken through a different set of doors. Doors that I don't ever want to walk through.

"Sophie, nice to see you're awake."

I struggle to match the familiar face with a name. *Maura.* "Thank you. It's been awhile hasn't it?"

"Yes, the medication we gave you to help you sleep is very effective. Hopefully you're feeling a little better now that you've gotten some rest."

"I do." I look around for a waiting area, but don't see anything. "My family, I mean my boyfriend's family, have they all gone home?"

"They have. You'll be able to have some time to speak to them if you follow your therapy plan and attend your group sessions. It's important for you to focus on your recovery while you're here. Without outside distractions."

"I understand." Kipton's definitely a distraction. But one I miss.

"I was on my way to your room for your first session. Would you like to grab a drink from the machine and meet me in the first room on the right? Just press the button for what you want. No money needed."

They don't waste any time diving in. "Sure." I press the button for a bottle of water and wait for it to fall. I find the meeting room around the corner and sit down next to Maura. "This is awkward. I don't know what I'm supposed to say or do." My hands are freezing and the temperature of the cold bottle is making me shiver.

"Treat it like any other counseling session. Say what you want or what you need to with the reassurance that I'm not here to judge you. I'm only here to help you work through your thoughts. I want you to begin to process them in a healthy way. Can you do that?"

"I can try."

Maura smiles warmly. "Then you'll do fine."

We spend the next hour talking about my childhood. The few times I have to talk about the closet, I get anxious. So anxious I have to get up and walk over to one of the windows in order to find another breath. Maura watches me and if she's waiting for me to break, she may get her wish.

But instead of dwelling on the topic, she shifts to easier questions about college and Kipton. I'm thankful she isn't pushing too hard too fast. But I'm on to her. She's mixing in things I love with the things I hate. So as much as I dread it, there *will* be more questions about the past.

"Kipton's everything to me. He's the reason I want to get better."

"The only reason?" She questions.

"Right now he's my motivation, but I'm hoping that's not the case forever." I want to do this for him, but I already know I have to want it for myself or none of this will work.

"Do you love him?"

It's the easiest question she's asked me so far. "Of course I do. He's saved me more than once. I'm not sure I'd be sitting here right now if he hadn't found me when he did."

"Why wouldn't you be sitting here?" she cautiously questions.

"I had no place to go. If there had been no Kipton, I would have been in my car for days until the dorms opened back up. And then, I would have quit the team or maybe even stayed just to be able to stay in school. But I wouldn't have been happy. I'd still be living in a lie with a family I can't stand."

"So you rely on him to keep you on solid ground?"

"No. I can do it myself, I always have. Although it wouldn't have been nearly as easy. He found me and took me home. His family accepted me right away, without even having to try to make them like me."

"Why would you have to make them like you? How would you do that?"

"I've always had to work for love. For attention. It was never willingly given. And when it was, it usually came with a motive—one that benefited them and was an inconvenience for me. So for his whole family to open their door to me, to give me a place to stay, it blew me away. Part of me still wants to be perfect so they don't have a reason to see my weaknesses. But I know they already have. The moment his mom walked into the room and saw me, I felt like the air cracked around her as I waited for her to yell at me or to tell me what a failure I am. It's the reaction my Dad and Blaine would have given me."

She takes notes after everything I say, jotting down so much my file is bound to be a hundred pages by the end of this session. "Do you believe you're a failure, Sophie?"

"Sometimes I do. Other times it's easier to blame someone else instead."

We discuss a few more things before she drops a bomb

on me. I didn't see it coming and I'm not sure I would have wanted to. "Sophie, I'm not trying to break you down or push, but I'd like to make you aware of your treatment plan. It includes bringing your biological Father in for a few sessions."

"With me? Like in the same room at the same time?"

"Yes. Before you get upset, hear me out. I'm not asking you to have a relationship with your Mom, Dean, or your Father. What I am asking is that you speak your peace to at least one of them. I think here would be a great place to begin. From the reports I reviewed, you were doing very well until you found out the truth of your paternity and were given the letters. Do you agree with that generalization?

"Yes. I felt really good until I went home for Thanksgiving break. Then it all came crashing down once I found out the truth about Coach. It spiraled even more after I read his letters."

"That's a fair assessment. Would this be something you would consider?"

I stand up and pace. Chewing on my thumbnail, I can't imagine sitting down with Coach Evans and discussing his words. Of course I have so many questions for him. I must have thought of fifty or more after I left his office. "I'm angry with him."

"What makes you angry?"

"That I don't hate him. I hate that I *don't* hate him. I'm supposed to. I should."

Maura nods her head and takes more notes. I'm going to take her pen soon. It's making me nervous. "I can see why you would feel that way. It makes logical sense."

"Do you ever have an opinion, Maura? Or aren't you allowed to tell me what you really think?"

She smiles and laughs to herself, as she takes more notes. "I have all kinds of opinions, Sophie. But they aren't what you need. What you need is help processing your own opinions. Not mine."

"Well a little insight wouldn't hurt. I wouldn't mind." She smiles again, but I'd much rather her talk to me like I'd talk to Cara. A normal conversation with give and take—not all take.

She sets down her pen and removes her glasses. "Off the record. I like you, Sophie. You're going to do well in this program because even if you think you're only doing it for Kipton, I know you're not. You want to succeed. It's how you operate. You've grown up in a sport that's filled with the idea of perfection. But you can't live your life the same way. You are bound to make mistakes—it's part of living. So every time you veer from your path of perfection, we have to keep you moving forward while not getting hung up in what could have been. Throw that ideal out the window because reality doesn't have a set plan. As daunting as it may sound, it's a fact of life. But you don't have to carry the entire burden anymore. I'll be with you every step of the way to help you work through your fears. Sound good?"

"Sounds good to me. But I've never been perfect. I wish I was, so they would have loved me, but I'm not."

"I'm not perfect either, Sophie, and this would be a boring world if we were."

"You wouldn't have a job." I cover my mouth with my hand wishing I could take my comment back. But it's too late.

"You have a great sense of humor," she laughs. "You don't have to bite your tongue around me either, okay? Give me the real Sophie. Not the girl you think I want to see."

Her words remind me of the time Kipton told me not to be so shy around him. "Okay. And I'll meet with Coach Evans. But if it's too much, I'd like him to leave without having to beg."

"You'll never have to beg, Sophie. You're here on your own free will. It doesn't do any good for either of us if I push you too far. It may be hard to see right now, but you hold all the power. You can walk out of here anytime you want. That's the scariest part of my job."

"Me leaving?"

"Yes."

"I'm not following."

"It's simple, Sophie. I want to help you and I can't do that if you're not here. Your success is my end goal."

I roll my eyes, frustrated that even *she* wants something out of me. "That sounds like something Coach would say."

"You're success isn't for me, Sophie. It's for *you*. I want to put hope back into your life. A life that isn't built around what you *have* to give. Instead, only what you *offer*. A lot of people have taken from you, but that's not the way life has to continue for you.

Hope. One simple word with so many possibilities. I like the sound of it.

THE NEXT EIGHT DAYS ARE spent journaling, in group, and meeting privately with Maura. Not being able to speak to Kipton is killing me. I fall asleep each night thinking of him and wondering if he's missing me as much as I'm missing him. Thankfully, I trust he will be waiting for me on the other side of the door once I'm discharged. A much healthier, safer Sophie will be leaving this place, but not before I'm ready. There's several obstacles still standing in my way—two of which are still drowning me.

Today, I tackle the first one—meeting with Coach Evans. As my final step before I leave, it's my greatest obstacle and the one I'd love to fix the most. I've never had a father figure in my life before, and I'm anxious to find out if I ever will. Although I've rehearsed what I want to say to him since I found out the truth, I'm still not sure it's everything I have bottled up inside me. There's only one shot for me to get it right.

Each step I take to the lounge is cautious. Part of me wants to rush to get it over with. The other part of me wants to savor each spoken word as it could be the last I ever hear from him. Unsure of how I'll react when I see his face again, I slowly duck around the corner and slither into the room. I raise my eyes from the floor to meet his and although it's old news, it hits me like a freight train. *He's my father.*

"Hi," I practically whisper.

"Sophie." He stands up from his spot on the couch and waits for me to fully enter the room. I stand near him awkwardly, unsure of the proper greeting given the circumstances. He decides for me and reaches out a hand to shake. I accept. It feels formal and stuffy. Not at all how I want this meeting to go.

I sit down on the opposite end of the couch leaving distance between the two of us. Maura starts the meeting off with some general comments about my therapy. She talks with pride about my progress and I appreciate it. Coach Evans takes in every word, genuinely interested in what she has to say.

After that, Maura takes a moment to check in with each of us. Staying present is something I can struggle with. I tend to revert to the past while thinking of all that could go wrong instead of focusing on all that could go right.

When it's my turn, I'm honest. I tell him about my hurt, my anger, and my frustration. He listens attentively, never once interrupting me. I get out everything I've rehearsed saying, yet I don't gain anything. At least I don't think so. Worried I was overly prepared, I blurt out the only thing left inside my jumbled brain. "I don't hate you."

His head jerks in my direction, a shocked expression covering his features. Maura even looks taken aback. I've expressed something similar to her several times, but as far as she knew, I was still debating one way or the other.

She speaks next. "Sophie, would you like to elaborate on that, or would you like him to respond?"

"Um. I'm not sure. I guess I needed him to know that I don't hate him. I'm sure I did when my mom first told me the truth, but it wasn't for the right reasons. I've spent a lot of time thinking about it. Over and over it never changes. As much as I want to be mad, resent you even, I can't."

"Why do you think that is?" She questions.

"The letters."

"What about the letters?"

"He wouldn't have taken the time to write if he didn't care. At least that's the way I see it. I still wish he would have fought harder for me, but he didn't. The letters don't make up for all the wrongs, but they opened my eyes to a lot of truths. Each one is consistent. They're all about me and how much he loves me."

"I've always loved you, Sophie. Just because you didn't see me, doesn't mean I didn't know what was going on in your life."

"You didn't know how sick I was."

"No. I didn't. But your Mom would send me your school picture every year. And I've seen almost every gymnastics meet. A few I snuck into without her seeing me, and the others, she sent pictures of you with your medal around your neck. The guilt I've lived with consumes me at times. There's no excuse for the way your Mother and I handled things, but I've missed out on so much. It's been a lifetime of punishments, but I do love you, beauty."

Beauty. Dropping my head into my hands, I let him see me cry for the second time. Only this time, the tears aren't angry. Instead, they're forgiving. He *has* made an effort.

And I'm finally ready to forgive this man. Maybe it's too soon or maybe it's taken too long, but I can't put a timeframe on what feels right inside of me.

"Sophie, stay with us. Tell me what you're thinking," Maura moves in front of me and places her hand on mine. It's the reassurance I need to continue. This doesn't have to take me to a dark place. It very well may, but I won't know unless I try.

"I-I forgive him."

She looks into my eyes and instructs me. "Look at him, Sophie. Tell him what you told me. Let him hear you."

Turning my head slowly, the wall seems to rush by faster than my movement. My eyelids flutter open and closed in slow motion—the image of his face going in and out of focus. We sit staring eye to eye until I get the nerve to speak again. "I forgive you, Coach."

Tears of his own trickle down his face, catching on the stubble of his beard before dropping to his jeans. He swallows noticeably and absorbs my words. "If you can, maybe it's too much too soon. You can call me by my first name, or if Coach is all you can handle that's okay too. But I want you to know how happy I am to hear you say those words. I love you, Sophie. I always have and I'll never stop."

"Can I call you Dad?" I whisper.

He shakes his head and wipes his eyes. "I'd love nothing more."

Glancing at Maura, I wait for her direction. But for the first time, she seems content on letting this play out on its own. "I don't know the rules or anything, but maybe you can meet Kipton too. And his family. They've been really good to me. I'd like you to meet them."

Maura interjects quickly. "There are no rules Sophie. What you want is up to you. The sky's the limit now. Once you made the decision to forgive, which you did beautifully, you opened up a world of possibilities."

"I like that. It sounds like the hope you told me about."

My dad smiles fondly as we sit and absorb our newfound peace.

Hope.

One simple word. One endless possibility.

CHAPTER *thirty*

Sophie

Two weeks later

KIPTON STRETCHES, HIS SHIRT RIDING up giving me a glimpse of his sexy body. "You look hungry." He smirks and it's very clear I'm not talking about food.

"Always." He cuddles me in his strong arms where I feel entirely at home.

"I'm sorry I took you to hell and back. Thank you for sticking by me."

"You don't have to be sorry. I just want you to find your happiness and realize your future is where you'll find your joy—not locked up in the past. You won't ever be able to change the decisions your parents made for you, no matter how much you wish you could. Put the letters, the anger, and the hate into something else. Something that makes you happy."

"Change a negative into a positive." I smile up at him. "I like that."

"I like you." He taps my scrunched up nose and kisses my lips softly. "Correction, I love you."

"That's better." I snuggle closer to him.

Kipton reaches for my hand, tracing an infinity symbol on my palm. "You have no idea how happy I am to see your smile. You deserve so much more than you've been given.

You'll always have me, but I want you to have it *all*."

"I do have it all. I have you and a real family—and my Dad."

"Do I get to officially meet him?"

"Of course you do. I already set it up."

He reaches over to his jacket and pulls a little black box out of the pocket. I gasp in surprise.

"Don't panic, this isn't what you think."

"Okay."

"It will be, when we're both ready. For now, I want you to have my promise wrapped around your finger. My promise to always love you and always be yours. I knew a long time ago you were it for me, Sophie. I want to be your world—forever."

Slowly the small box opens and inside is a simple silver band with the infinity symbol etched into it. When I look closer, there's an S and a K on each side. "Look inside the band," he whispers.

"My beautiful." I smile when I make the connection. "My Dad calls me beauty in all his letters."

"Smart man." He slides it on my right ring finger. "You're mine, Sophie."

"This feels like an engagement. Even though it's not."

"This ring doesn't have any diamonds. And you deserve diamonds."

I hold out my hand, admiring my new jewelry. It looks delicate and fits perfectly. "It doesn't need diamonds. It's the meaning that's important to me, not the bling."

"That's part of the reason I love you. It's never about things with you. But after we finish school, have a place of our own and jobs, we can have all the things that matter."

I smile and look into his eyes. "Thank you for this. For loving me when I had trouble loving myself."

"Our worlds collided for a reason, Sophie."

"So you could save me," I whisper. A lone tear sliding down my face. "I feel a million times lighter, Kipton. Every tear, every ounce of sadness—it gave me you."

He kisses my lips, taking his time before pulling away. "Happy Birthday."

"But my birthday's—"

"Today." He finishes.

I look at the bedside clock and at a minute after midnight, it *is* my birthday. "I've been so busy catching up with school assignments, I totally forgot."

"Are you ready for me to give you the rest of your present?"

"There's more?"

"This is only the beginning, beautiful."

acknowledgements

FIRST AND FOREMOST, I WANT to thank my husband for his support. Writing is a crazy journey from start to finish and without his encouragement, I'm not sure my stories would ever be complete. So, thank you for putting up with my neurotic need to type away until I get every single one of my words just right. Life has thrown us a lot of curveballs— thank you for catching each and every one.

To my parents—thank you for getting me hooked on books before I even knew how to ride a bike. And when I wanted to go to the book store to grab a new R.L. Stine book, you always took me and encouraged me to pick out whatever I wanted. I spent so many hours tucked under Nana's blanket getting lost in a world of words. Some things never change—and I'm thankful for that.

To my beta readers, Jena from I Bookin Love to Read, Kylie from Kylie's Fiction Addiction, M.C. Decker, and Stephanie Rose—thank you for taking the time to read Lighter. I've enjoyed your arguments over who gets to keep Kipton. Your suggestions, advice, and encouragement were more than I could have asked for. Because of you, Lighter is STRONG.

Stephanie, you supported this story when it was simply an idea in my head—encouraging me not to give up my dream. Kylie, you're a tough sell and for you to be so excited made my entire year. Megan, you claimed Kipton first—just sayin. Jena, I was the most nervous about you reading Lighter. While you were my toughest critic, you gave solid advice that made my manuscript stronger. Thank you for your attention to detail and passion for plots!

To my proofing queen, Megan Decker—thank you for picking your way through my manuscript. You live in a world of words, and do it well. You're the real life Brooke, and I'm honored to call you my friend. Thank you for keeping me sane in a world of craziness. Love ya, chick.

To the creative forces behind Lighter—Sommer Stein of Perfect Pear Creative Covers, thank you for creating the cover of my dreams. It's everything I envisioned. Christine Borgford of Perfectly Publishable, thank you for turning my words into such a beautifully designed book. It's now a work of art. Giselle from Xpresso Tours, thank you for spreading the word about Lighter. Your organization and prompt responses kept my schedule on track for a seamless reveal and release. Thank you so much!

To my readers—thank you for taking a chance on a girl from the country with a dream to write. Your continued support and love of my characters gives me the biggest rush of excitement I could ever imagine. Many of you have joined Gia Riley's Books on Facebook, and I've enjoyed getting to know you. I hope I've made you proud with this story.

To every blogger who has supported me—thank you for taking the time to post my work. Whether you've promoted or reviewed, each post is noticed and appreciated. With you spreading the word, it allows my dreams to come true. I know you get a lot of requests each day. When you answer my inquiries, it makes my day.

To my friends–ever since I released my first novel, I've met some amazing ladies who keep me in stitches. Whether we chat, toss ideas back and forth, or just gripe about our day, you're there for me.

Nelly from Romance Bytes, thank you for understanding what it means to be a warrior mom. This crazy world we found ourselves in is a little less scary with you by my side. "Different, not less."

Tina Bell, whether I need advice or an ear to listen, you're always there. You get "it" and I'm appreciative of your friendship. Books brought us together, but our friendship is so much more than that.

Kylie Frankel, I'm convinced you're my sister from another lifetime. It doesn't matter if we're discussing your love of Brandon Walsh or the latest from the world of reality television, you keep me in stitches. My world was very bland without you. Mother Goose says, *"Friends Forever."*

Stephanie Rose, you have been on this ride with me from the start. Now it's your turn to make your dreams come true. I couldn't be more proud of you. #AlwaysYou

To my Sweet & Spicy Writer Chicks—Caleigh Hernandez, Mandi Beck, M.C. Decker, Ryleigh Andrews, and S.E. Dean, thank you for giving me my daily dose of laughter. Most importantly, thank you for teaching me about all the proper tools of life. You know what I mean. Whether it's QK, or simply having each other's backs, the book world is so much more fun with all of you. You're all crazy talented, and I love you to pieces. Cali, Creeper, KittyHo, Rexy, Sauce, and Woody for life!

To the ladies of #FYW—your support has been wonderful. Whether you're sharing advice or simply chatting, I've enjoyed getting to know you. There's a ton of talent in this group, and I get excited each time I get lost in your books. #Indiechicksrock

about the author

GIA RILEY LIVES IN DELAWARE with her husband and son. When she isn't busy writing her next novel, you can find her roaming the isles of Kirkland's or up to her elbows in Play-doh.

A firm believer that everyone deserves their happily ever after, she loves creating emotional stories about life and love. Although her nose if often stuck in a book, she loves hearing from readers and connecting with others.

Here's where you can find her:

Website
www.giariley.weebly.com

Email
giarileybooks@gmail.com

Facebook, Twitter and Spotify

Thank you for purchasing Lighter. Please consider leaving an honest review. It's the best gift an author can receive.

books by gia riley

THE REFLECTION SERIES

Between the Pain (The Reflection Series Book 1)

After the Pain (The Reflection Series Book 2)

Made in the USA
Middletown, DE
12 March 2017